SAFETY BREACH

DELORES FOSSEN

UNDERCOVER ACCOMPLICE

CAROL ERICSON

MILLS & BOON

First Published in Great Britain 2019
by Mills & Boon, an imprint of HarperCollins*Publishers*
1 London Bridge Street, London, SE1 9GF

Safety Breach © 2019 Delores Fossen
Undercover Accomplice © 2019 Carol Ericson

ISBN: 978-0-263-27450-9

1219

MIX
Paper from
responsible sources

FSC
www.fsc.org

FSC™ C007454

This book is produced from independently certified FSC™ paper to ensure responsible forest management.

For more information visit: www.harpercollins.co.uk/green

Printed and bound in Spain
by CPI, Barcelona

SAFETY BREACH

DELORES FOSSEN

Chapter One

The moment that Gemma Hanson opened her front door, she heard something she didn't want to hear.

Silence.

There were no pulsing beeps from the security system. No flare of the bead of red light on the panel, warning her that she had ten seconds to disarm it or the alarms would sound. That meant someone had tampered with it.

The killer had found her.

The fear came, cold and sharp like a gleaming razor slicing through her, and it brought the memories right along with it. Nothing though, not even the fear, was as scalpel sharp as those images that tore into her mind.

She dropped the bag of groceries and the gob of keys she'd been holding, and Gemma grabbed the snub-nosed .38 from her purse. Just holding the weapon created a different kind of panic inside her because in the back of her mind, she knew that it wouldn't be enough to stop *him*.

No.

This time the killer would get to her. This time, he would finish what he'd started a year ago and make sure that the ragged breaths she was dragging in and out were the last ones she would ever take.

She forced herself to go as still as she could. Tried to steady her heartbeat, too, so she could listen for any sound of him in the small house. It wouldn't do any good to run. She'd learned that the hard way the last time he'd come after her—because running had been exactly what he'd expected her to do.

Maybe even what he'd *wanted* her to do.

It had been a game to him, and he'd been ready. Good at it, too. That's how he'd been able to fire three bullets into her before she'd barely taken a step.

"Where are you?" Gemma asked, still standing in the doorway. A whisper was all she could manage with her throat clamped tight, but the sound still carried through the quiet house. Too quiet. As silent as the grave.

He didn't answer, no one did, so Gemma tried again. This time, though, she used his name.

"Eric?"

She got out more than a whisper with that try. Her voice actually sounded a whole lot stronger than she felt, but any strength, fake or otherwise, wouldn't scare him off. If Eric Lang had any fears, Gemma had never been able to figure them out, and uncovering that sort of thing was her specialty.

Had been her specialty, she mentally corrected.

These days, she didn't teach criminal justice classes and didn't assist the FBI with creating criminal profiles for serial killers like Eric. Instead, she input data for a research group, a low-level computer job that the marshals had arranged for her. The only talent she had now was getting easily spooked and having nightmares.

And speaking of being spooked, every nerve inside her went on full alert when she heard the sound of the engine. Gemma automatically brought up the gun as she'd been trained to do. She forced herself not to pull the trigger though. Good thing, too, because it wasn't Eric. However, it was someone who shouldn't be here.

Sheriff Kellan Slater.

Gemma instantly recognized him even from this distance and behind the windshield of the unfamiliar blue truck. Of course, it would have been hard not to notice Kellan. The cowboy cop was tall, lanky…unforgettable. Gemma knew because she'd had zero success in forgetting him.

Kellan got out of his truck, but he stopped when he spotted her .38, and he pulled out his gun in a slick, fluid motion. "Is Eric Lang here?" he called out.

That didn't ease her thudding heartbeat. Even though she hadn't seen Kellan in the year since her attack, Gemma hoped this was his version of a social visit. Not that they had any reason to be social, now that the hurt and blame was between them. However, if he hadn't come here to find out how she was, then perhaps he'd tell her that she was imagining things. That her WITSEC identity hadn't been compromised, that no one had actually tampered with her security system and that she was safe.

But Kellan wasn't giving her much of a reassuring look.

With his gaze firing all around them, he hurried onto the porch, automatically catching on to her arm and pushing her behind him. Protecting her. Which only confirmed to her that she needed to be protected.

"Is Eric here?" Kellan repeated.

Gemma knew this was going to make her sound crazy. "I haven't actually seen him since the night he attacked me, but someone turned off my security system." She swallowed hard before she added the rest. "I sensed he was here. And I think he's been watching me. He found me."

Those last three words had not been easy to say, and they'd had to make their way through the muscles in her throat that felt as if they were strangling her.

Even though Kellan hadn't given her much reassurance before, she waited for some now. But he didn't give her any. "Are you sure you just didn't forget to set the alarm when you went out?"

Gemma wanted to laugh, but it definitely wouldn't be from humor. "I'm positive."

Even though she was living her fake life with a fake name that the marshals had given her, all the steps didn't mean she was safe. Gemma knew that, and it was why she was obsessive about taking precautions. Not just with arming the security system but carrying the .38.

"Do you know for sure if anyone's actually inside the house?" Kellan pressed.

Gemma shook her head, and she was about to explain that she'd stopped in the doorway. No explanation was necessary though. Because that's when Kellan glanced down at the floor where she'd dropped her groceries and keys. It was the kind of sweeping glance that cops made, and while Kellan didn't exactly look like most cops, he was a blue blood to the core. A third-generation sheriff of Longview Ridge, Texas—their hometown.

Of course, he'd only gotten that sheriff's badge after

his own father had been murdered, and she knew Kellan would have gladly given it up to have his father back.

"Stay right next to me," Kellan insisted, and he stepped into the small entry. The moment they were both inside, he motioned for her to shut the door.

Gemma did, and while she kept a firm grip on her gun, they stood there, listening. With her body sandwiched between Kellan and the door. The back of him pressed against the front of her.

It stirred different kinds of memories.

Of the heat that had once simmered between them. Of the long, lingering looks that he'd once given her with gunmetal eyes. Of the way his rough hands had skimmed over her body. Years ago, they'd been lovers but had drifted apart when she'd left for college. They'd found their way back to each other and likely would have landed in bed again if Eric hadn't struck first. After that, well, Kellan no longer wanted her that way.

Because he blamed her for his father's death.

Of course, he blamed himself, too, which had put an even bigger wedge between them. Kellan would never be able to forgive himself for what'd happened, and Gemma wasn't sure she could forgive him for not being able to stop it.

All that lack of forgiveness was why she knew something was horribly wrong. This was the last place Kellan would have wanted to come, and she was the last person he'd want to try to protect.

"Wait here while I have a look around," Kellan insisted. "And lock the door. If you hear anything, and I mean anything, get down on the floor." He glanced back over his shoulder at her, and she saw that his jaw had tightened even more than it had been when he'd first arrived. "Understand?" he added.

There was a lot of anger and old baggage in that *understand*. The last time she hadn't listened to a sheriff, she'd nearly been killed and two people had been murdered. Maybe three since one of the possible victims, Caroline Moser, was still missing and presumed dead. She would definitely listen this time.

Kellan stepped away from her, heading first to the kitchen, where he checked the pantry. Since the living room, dining room and kitchen were all open, she had no trouble seeing him, but that changed when he went into the bedrooms. First hers and then the guest room. Gemma just stood there, waiting and praying. If Eric was indeed inside, she didn't want him claiming another victim.

Especially a victim who was trying to protect her.

That's what Kellan's father, Buck, had been doing the night Eric had gunned down him and his deputy. Then Eric had escaped and hadn't been seen in the past year. But unlike the people he'd murdered that night, Eric was very much alive. Gemma could feel that all the way down to her breath and bones.

It seemed to take an eternity or two, but Kellan finally came out from the bedrooms, and he shook his head. "He's not here, but your bedroom window was open. I'm guessing you didn't leave it that way?"

The air stalled in her throat, and it took her a moment to answer. "No. I've never opened that window." Heck, the only times she'd ever opened the curtains was to make sure the window was closed and locked.

He nodded, and the grunt he made let her know that it was the answer he'd expected. "So, someone's been here. Maybe Eric." He went to the keypad for the alarm, brushing against her arm as he walked by her. It was barely a touch, but she noticed.

So did Kellan.

Their gazes connected for a split second before he mumbled some profanity and looked away. He sounded disgusted with himself. Maybe because he didn't want to feel that quick punch of attraction. Gemma didn't want to feel it, either. It was a distraction, and something like that could get them both killed.

Kellan took out his phone and texted someone. Perhaps one of his brothers who were all in law enforcement. Gemma took out her phone, too, ready to call her handler, Marshal Amanda Hardin, but Kellan shook his head.

"Don't involve your handler yet," he said. "There's been a leak, and I haven't discovered the source."

Gemma lost what little breath she'd managed to regain, and because she had no choice, she leaned against the wall for support. Kellan helped, too. Well, he did after he muttered more of that profanity. He took hold of her arm, marched her to the sofa and had her sit before he went to the window. Keeping watch.

"What happened?" she asked. "Tell me about the leak."

He glanced back at her, his tight jaw letting her know she should brace herself, that what he was about to say would be bad news. "There's been another murder."

Gemma was glad she was sitting down, but she had to shake her head. Kellan was a sheriff, and while Longview Ridge wasn't exactly a hotbed of crime, murders did happen there. That was something that

Kellan and she both had too much experience with. However, Gemma couldn't figure out why a murder there would have brought Kellan here to her WITSEC house in Austin, a good ninety miles from Longview Ridge. Unless…

"Did Eric kill someone else?" she managed to say.

Kellan's hesitation confirmed that that was indeed what had happened. "We found the body about two hours ago."

Two hours. That meant Kellan had left the crime scene and come straight to her. "Who was killed?" she snapped.

Judging from the way his forehead bunched up, he didn't want to tell her. But then she knew it was connected to her, or Kellan wouldn't be here. "Iris Kirby," he finally answered.

That felt like the slam of another bullet into her. Oh, God. Iris. Gemma knew her, of course. She knew almost everyone in Longview Ridge. Iris had been her favorite teacher in high school.

Gemma wasn't sure she could stomach hearing the answer to this, but it was a question she had to ask. "You're sure she was murdered? And how do you know it was Eric?"

Without taking his attention from the window, he pulled up a photo on his phone and handed it to her. "That was left at the crime scene. And as for how we know it's murder, Iris died from three gunshot wounds to the torso."

The slams and punches just kept coming, and each of them brought one more wave of the nightmarish images. That's because Eric had shot both Gemma and Kellan's father three times. She supposed Eric considered that his signature. One of them anyway. Leaving notes at the crime scenes was the other. And the picture on Kellan's phone was that of a note.

"'Too late again, Sheriff Slater,'" she read aloud. "'Tell Gemma that Iris didn't suffer. I made it fast as a favor to her. And then tell Gemma that she's next. I know where to find her. Three-twenty-three East Lane, Austin. Our girl didn't go too far, did she?'"

As hard as it was to read those words, Gemma tamped down the rising fear and tried to view this as a profiler. The note was meant to taunt Kellan and her.

And it had.

Along with twisting her insides into knots. Judging from the tight muscles in Kellan's body, it had done the same to him. However, this wasn't proof there had been a breach in WITSEC.

"How would Eric have gotten access to WITSEC files?" she mumbled.

Gemma waved it off though before Kellan could even speculate. Eric was smart, and he was a whiz with computers. He'd even joked once that he would have made a fairly decent hacker, and then had added to the joke that Caroline and she would have made even better ones. Eric wouldn't have needed help from anyone in WITSEC to get into the files because he could have done it himself.

"So, Eric knows where I am," she concluded. "He killed Iris to…what? Send me into a panic? A rage, maybe? To hurt me by murdering someone I knew? Because panicked, angry people don't always think straight, and they make mistakes."

Kellan huffed. "Best to save your criminal analysis

for Eric. When the FBI was looking for him, he was right under your nose, and you didn't even know it."

Because Kellan glanced at her again when he said that, she saw the glare in his eyes. She saw it soften, too, when he regretted giving her that jab.

But in this case, it was true, and she deserved any jab he might send her way. That's because Eric had been her student in a criminal justice class before she'd made him her intern. He'd worked side by side with her, case by case, and until the night he'd tried to murder her, she hadn't known he was a serial killer.

That was the ultimate taunting.

"I believe Eric was here," Kellan continued a moment later. "He killed Iris last night so he had plenty of time to get from Longview Ridge to Austin. Plenty of time to watch you and wait for you to leave so he could break into your house."

Yes, but why hadn't Eric just stayed and waited for her? Had he found out Kellan was coming, and Eric hadn't wanted to deal with a lawman? Especially one who wanted him dead.

Still, that didn't feel right.

Of course, she'd learned the hard way that it was a mistake to trust her feelings when it came to Eric.

"There's Owen," Kellan said, his voice shattering the silence.

Owen, as in his brother Deputy Owen Slater. And he was yet someone else who would want to face down Eric.

"Owen's been working with Austin PD to set up spotters on the road," Kellan added. "Don't worry, Owen didn't tell the local cops who you really are. He said you're a witness in an upcoming trial and that we need to get you back to Longview Ridge."

Her legs suddenly felt like glass, but she forced herself to stand. Gemma also glanced out the window. Owen was indeed out there, sitting behind the wheel of a black car.

"Are you really taking me to Longview Ridge?" she asked.

"Best not to say where we're going in case Eric bugged the place."

Oh, mercy. She hadn't even thought of that. But she should have. Eric had succeeded in rattling her, and he had likely figured that was the first step in getting to her.

"Don't bring anything with you," Kellan instructed when she reached for her purse.

Yes, because Eric could have planted tracking devices on clothes or anything else in the house. She'd had her purse with her when she'd gotten groceries, but maybe Eric had managed to put a tracker on it before that quick shopping trip. Or even while she was at the store. She couldn't take her phone either because he could use it to pinpoint her location. Then, he could follow wherever Kellan was taking her.

Kellan motioned toward his brother, and Owen got out of the car. Like Kellan, he already had his weapon drawn, which meant any of her neighbors could see that and become alarmed. Maybe alarmed enough to come outside and try to figure out what was going on. No one had shown much interest in her in the nine months she'd been there, and now wouldn't be a good time to start.

"Move fast," Kellan said, and that was the only

warning she got before he took hold of her, position-
ing her right next to him. He opened the door and got
them moving.

"Aww, don't be that way," someone said.

Eric.

The voice came from behind them, from inside the
house, and Kellan must have recognized it, too, because he dragged her to the ground next to the con-
crete steps.

"Don't leave before we have time to play," Eric
joked.

And the killer laughed just as the shot blasted
through the air.

Chapter Two

Hell. Kellan wanted to kick himself for not getting to Gemma sooner so this wouldn't happen.

But he hadn't been sure who he could trust, hadn't known how the info about Gemma's location had been breached. His brother Jack was a marshal and would have been his normal contact for something like this, but Jack was in Arizona escorting a prisoner. That's why Kellan had tried to handle this himself.

Now none of that mattered because they could both be gunned down by a serial killer.

Kellan scrambled over Gemma, pushing her all the way to the ground so he could cover her with his body. It wasn't an ideal position, nothing about this was. They were literally out in the open with only the steps for cover. That wouldn't do squat to protect them if Eric came around the side of the house and through a back door. Of course, if he did that, then Owen would see him.

"Were either of you hit?" Owen called out.

Kellan shook his head and hoped that was true. Beneath him, Gemma was trembling. No doubt reliving a boatload of memories, too. But he couldn't tell if she'd been injured, and Kellan didn't want to risk moving off her to find out.

While Owen made a call, no doubt to get them backup, his brother had taken up cover behind the door of the unmarked cruiser. It was bullet resistant, which meant if Kellan could get Gemma to it, she'd be a whole lot safer than she was here. But there was a good twenty feet of space between them and Owen. That was twenty feet that Eric could use to gun them down.

Well, maybe.

When Kellan had searched Gemma's house, Eric hadn't been inside. And Kellan had shut and relocked the open window along with checking to make sure no other locks had been tampered with. So, how had Eric gotten in?

Or had he?

There was something else off about this. The angle of the shot seemed to have been all wrong. It was hard to tell, but instead of coming from inside the house, the bullet had been fired more to the left side of it. If that's indeed where the shooter was, then he and Gemma wouldn't have been able to see him. Neither would Owen—which could be the exact reason the shot had been fired from there.

And that led him to something else that didn't fit.

Eric himself.

There was no reason for Eric to put himself in the middle of what could turn out to be a gunfight. Way too risky. No, he was more the lay-in-wait type, and if he'd truly wanted Gemma dead, he would have just waited inside and shot her when she'd opened the door. That would have given him a minute or two to flee before Kellan had even arrived.

So, who'd fired the shot? And where the hell was Eric?

"I think the voice we heard could have been a recording," Kellan whispered to Gemma.

She went still, obviously giving that some thought, then nodding. A recorder wouldn't have been that hard to hide if Eric had indeed managed to come in earlier through the window. Also, it would give Eric an advantage if they thought he was inside the house. That's where they would be pinpointing their focus when the real danger could be at the side of the house. Or even across the street from them.

That sent Kellan snapping in that direction. "Get down!" he yelled to Owen. Kellan hadn't actually seen anything, but a year of chasing Eric had told him to expect the unexpected when dealing with the snake.

Owen did drop down, putting his body behind the door. Just as another shot came. And just as Kellan had thought, this one came from a house directly across the street. This time, he got a glimpse of the shooter who'd fired out the second-story window. A bulky guy dressed all in black, and he was using a rifle with a scope. If Owen hadn't ducked when he had, he'd be dead.

Which might have been Eric's intent all along.

In addition to being a snake, Eric also liked to torment his victims, and killing Owen would have definitely accomplished that. Along with adding another huge layer of guilt and grief they were already feeling because of his father's murder.

"Hold your position," Kellan instructed Owen. "How long before the local cops get here?"

"About five minutes," Owen answered. "I've texted them to let them know about the gunfire."

That meant Austin PD wouldn't come in with guns blazing. They'd stay back, evaluating the situation while trying to figure how to get Gemma safely out of there. Kellan and Owen would be doing the same thing. Because Kellan didn't want anyone dying today. Eric had already claimed enough lives.

Another shot came—again from the second floor of the neighbor's house. The bullet blasted into the stone steps just inches from where he and Gemma were. Owen pivoted and returned fire. It worked because the gunman ducked out of sight. That didn't mean he was leaving, but the guy might think twice before appearing in the window again.

"I need to stop this," Gemma whispered, and she mumbled something else he didn't catch. "One of my neighbors could be hurt."

That could have already happened. The shooter could have harmed or killed anyone else who happened to be in that house just so he could use the window to launch the attack. However, it was also possible that her neighbor was working for Eric. Or maybe Eric had simply hired some thug to break into the house and fire the shots. Either way, Kellan wasn't seeing how Gemma would be able to do anything to put an end to this.

However, Gemma must have thought she could do something because she moved, levering herself up on her arms and lifting her head. "I'll try to bargain with Eric. It's me he wants."

Kellan put her right back down on the ground. "You don't know that. Don't get Owen and me killed because we're trying to protect you."

Yeah, it was harsh, but it worked because Gemma

stayed put. Besides, it was partly true. He didn't wear a badge for decoration, and that meant he'd do whatever it took to keep her safe.

Even though Kellan seriously doubted that it was possible to negotiate with Eric, he took out his phone. He was about to shout out for Eric to call him, but before he could do that, his cell rang, and he saw Unknown Caller pop up on the screen. He hit the answer button and put it on Speaker so he could keep his hands free in case he had to return fire.

"Want to talk, do you, Sheriff?" Eric asked.

Just hearing the sound of the killer's voice caused the anger to roar through Kellan. He hated this man for what he'd done, and Kellan wished he could reach through the phone line and end this piece of slime once and for all.

"Call off your hired thug," Kellan warned him.

"I will…in about four minutes, give or take some seconds. That's about when the city cops will get there."

Kellan wasn't sure if Eric had heard Owen say that, but it was just as possible the shooter across the street had relayed that info to him. Not just that info, either, but every move they were making. It was highly likely that Eric wasn't anywhere near Gemma's house.

"Why are you doing this? Why now?" Kellan demanded while he continued to keep watch around them.

That included keeping watch of Gemma.

Her breathing was way too fast now, and it was possible she was about to have a panic attack. God knew what kind of psychological damage had been done to her because of what had happened a year ago. Of course, she was hearing the voice of the man who'd nearly killed her, so Kellan doubted she was going to have much luck reining in her fear.

"Why now?" Eric repeated. "Well, duh. Because it's nearly the anniversary of your daddy's death. Which I'm sure you remember in nth detail. I'll bet Gemma remembers it, too."

They did. It was impossible to forget that in only three days, it would be a year since their lives had been turned upside down. And apparently Eric was going to make sure they recalled it by giving them a new set of grisly memories to go along with it.

Kellan tried to fight off the images from that night, but they came anyway. The storm with lightning slicing through the sky. Ironic that it was the lightning that had given him glimpses of what was going on. Just flashes of the horror that had started before Kellan had even gotten on the scene.

When Gemma had figured out too late that Eric was a serial killer the FBI had been after for years, she'd called the sheriff, Kellan's father, Buck, and he'd told Gemma to wait, not to confront Eric until he got there. Instead, she'd attempted to stop Eric when he tried to leave. Eric had then taken Gemma and her best friend/research assistant, Caroline Moser, hostage. Kellan's father, Buck, and another deputy, Dusty Walters, had gone in pursuit, only minutes ahead of Kellan who'd gotten the call after them.

His dad and Dusty had come upon Eric's vehicle that had skidded off the road because of the storm. The accident had happened in front of an abandoned hotel with the mocking name of Serenity Inn. A crumbling Victorian mansion with acres of overgrown gardens and dark windows that had looked like darkened eye sockets. Eric had forced the women at gunpoint onto the grounds, and Dusty and his father had followed.

That's when Kellan had arrived.

Just in time to hear the crack of the gunfire, and then seconds later, he'd seen his father lying, bleeding—dying—on the weed-choked, muddy ground.

Kellan had ordered Dusty to call for an ambulance and stay with Buck while he went in pursuit of Eric who had slipped into the house with the women. Because of more of those flashes of lightning, Kellan had seen Eric shoot Gemma in the shell of what had once been the grand foyer. He'd seen her collapse, and while he was saving her life by stopping the blood flow, Eric had escaped with Caroline in the dark maze of rooms, halls and stairs. Kellan hadn't even managed to get off a shot for fear of hitting Caroline.

For all the good that'd done.

While Kellan had been saving Gemma, Eric had shot through one of the windows at Dusty, killing the deputy instantly. Kellan hadn't known it then, but his father was already dead.

Later, they'd found Caroline's blood in one of the rooms. No body though. No Eric, either. Just a dead sheriff and deputy who'd been doing their jobs and an injured profiler who hadn't done her job nearly well enough.

"You screwed up the investigation," Eric went on. "You didn't get things right when it came to solving your father's murder."

"What the hell are you talking about? You killed him. I got that right." Kellan snapped. Then, he reminded himself, again, that Eric liked playing the tormenter, and what better way to do that than by im-

plying that Kellan had botched something as important as the investigation that followed the murder and
Gemma's attack?

"You need to take a second look at the details of
your father's case. The devil is in those details," Eric
went on. "That's what this warning is all about."

"Warning?" Kellan questioned. "You had someone
shoot at us. That's more than a warning."

"My man didn't hit you, did he?" Eric said, his voice
dripping with sarcasm.

In the distance, Kellan heard a welcome sound. Sirens from the responding police officers. Now, he had
to hope that the cops' arrival didn't cause the gunman
to open fire again.

"Time's running out," Eric added, which meant he'd
likely heard the sirens, too. "Gotta go."

Of course, he wasn't staying around for this. And his
hired gun must have felt the same way because Kellan
saw him run from the window.

Getting away.

That was better than trying to gun them down
again, but Kellan hated that the shooter would escape.
Kellan wanted to chase down the idiot and make him
pay for what he'd done. But that would mean leaving
Gemma—and she'd then be an easy target for Eric.

"One more thing," Eric said. "My advice would be
for you to run because things are about to get very...
loud."

Eric ended the call, and it didn't take Kellan long,
just a couple of seconds, for him to realize what was
about to happen.

"Cover us," Kellan shouted to his brother.

He hooked his arm around Gemma's waist, dragging her to her feet, and with her in tow, Kellan started running toward the unmarked cruiser. Good thing, too.

Because behind them, Gemma's house exploded into a fireball.

Chapter Three

Gemma clutched her hands into fists to try and stop herself from shaking. It didn't help, but maybe it made it less noticeable to Kellan who kept glancing at her while he carried on his phone conversations.

She hated feeling like this—with the nerves and fear all tangled in her stomach. But what she hated even more was that Eric and his hired gun had gotten away. She had no doubts, none, that they'd be back.

And this time, they might actually kill them.

"You need to put some distance between us," she told Kellan.

It wasn't the first time she'd said it, either. She'd repeated variations their entire time at the Austin Police Department. However, Kellan was doing the opposite of distancing himself, because he and Owen were taking her to Longview Ridge. Something she'd been opposed to the moment Kellan had told the Austin cops what he had planned for her.

Gemma agreed with him about her needing protective custody while the Justice Department figured out how her WITSEC identity had been breached, but going "home" had enormous risks. Still, here they were on the interstate, heading to the very place Eric would expect them to go.

Owen was behind the wheel of the unmarked cruiser, and Kellan was next to her on the back seat. Both were keeping watch while they got updates on the investigation. There was also an Austin patrol car with two cops behind them just in case things turned ugly. Eric likely wouldn't be able to set explosives along this route, but he could perhaps cause a car accident.

"Eric will keep coming after me," Gemma repeated when Kellan finished his latest call.

Just saying that caused the sound of the blast to echo through her head. And she could feel the effects of it, too, since the debris flying off the explosion had given Kellan and her plenty of nicks and cuts. None serious, but they stung, giving her a fresh memory of how close they'd come to dying.

Everything she owned was gone, of course. Not that she'd had anything of value. The place had felt, well, sterile. A lot like her life had for the past year. The only real loss of her personal things was her purse and phone. Now she had no cash or credit cards—which meant she had to rely on Kellan to help her. At least for a little while. But once the marshals were cleared of having any part in the WITSEC leak, Gemma needed to call Amanda to see about arranging a safe place she could go.

If there was such a place, that is.

Since Kellan didn't even react to her reminder about Eric not stopping, she gave him another one. "You could get caught in crossfire, or worse, the way you did at my house."

That got a reaction. He gave her a look that could

have frozen El Paso in August, and he tapped the badge he had clipped to his belt.

"That badge didn't save your father," she snapped, but she instantly regretted the mini outburst. There were enough bad memories floating around them without her adding that one. "I'm sorry."

He was back in no-reaction mode and turned his lawman's gaze to keep watch out the window. Gemma watched, too. Not out the window but at Kellan.

Mercy, that face. It still got to her. Still tugged and pulled at her in all the wrong places. Sculptured with so many angles and tinted with just a hint of amber from his long-ago Comanche bloodline. Those bloodlines had blessed him with that thick black hair that he'd probably never had to comb. It just fell into a rumpled mane that he hid beneath his cowboy hat.

There was nothing rumpled about his body. It was toned from the endless work he put in on his family's ranch and the rodeo competitions he still did. Once, she'd seen him take down an angry bull that he'd roped. All those muscles—both the bull's and Kellan's—locked in a fierce battle. Dust flying. Hooves and feet digging and chopping into the ground. The snorts from the bull, the grunts of exertion from Kellan.

Kellan had won.

He had literally taken the bull by the horns, brought it down and then calmly walked away. Gemma thought that was the way he handled lots of things in his life. Not women, of course. He did take what he wanted from them. But never forced or even coerced. He took simply because it was offered to him.

Gemma knew plenty about that because once she'd offered herself to him. And he'd taken.

He glanced at her again, maybe sensing that she was playing with memory lane, and she got a flash of those incredible eyes. That had been the first thing she'd ever noticed about him. Sizzling blue or stormy gray, depending on his mood. Right now, his mood was dark and so were his eyes, but she'd seen them heat up not from anger but from the need that came with arousal.

Arousal that she had caused.

It hadn't been one-sided back when they'd been eighteen, and she'd willingly surrendered her virginity to him on the seat of his pickup truck. She had no idea who'd been on the receiving end of his virginity, but she'd been thankful for whomever had given him enough practice to make that night incredible for her. One that had become her benchmark. She was still looking for someone who could live up to him.

His eyebrow came up, and for one humming moment, they stared at each other until his mouth tightened. It was as if he'd gotten ESP issued with that badge, and he was giving her a silent warning to knock off the sex thoughts. He was right, too, as he usually was. But it had been much easier to slip into those memories than the things she needed to face.

Things she needed to piece together.

Like why Eric had waited a year to come after her? But that could be as Kellan had suggested—because it had taken him that long to find her. However, there were the other things that Eric had said.

You need to take a second look at the details of your father's case. The devil is in those details. That's what this warning is all about.

"Do you believe you could have missed something in

your father's murder investigation?" she asked, knowing it could earn her another of those frosty glares.

It didn't though. Instead, Kellan took a deep breath. "Maybe."

There was doubt, but that could have nothing to do with the way Kellan had handled the case. It could be the guilt over not being able to save his father.

"Eric's never said anything like that before," she went on.

Kellan shifted his position, their gazes colliding. "You've had other contact with him over the past year?"

"No." And she was thankful she hadn't, either. Not just because she hadn't wanted to deal with Eric, but also because she was betting Kellan would have been riled to the core if her answer had been yes. He would have wanted to know why he hadn't been told everything that pertained to Eric since he was looking for the killer.

"Eric left messages for me when I was still in the hospital, remember?" she continued. Gemma hadn't actually spoken to him since she'd been first in surgery and then recovering from her injuries. But the hospital staff had recorded the calls and turned them over to Kellan.

"Yeah, I remember." The muscles in his jaw went tight again. "He threatened you."

She nodded, hoping that he didn't repeat the actual words. Gemma didn't need to hear them again to recall that Eric had been enraged that she'd lived and could therefore testify that he'd been the one to shoot her.

Except she couldn't.

Gemma had some memories of that horrible night, but because of the storm and the darkness, she hadn't seen much. About the only thing she could say for sure was that Eric had taken Caroline and her from Gemma's house in Longview Ridge, and that later there'd been a gunfight.

"I'll take another look at the investigation," Kellan assured her, though it wasn't necessary for him to say that. From the moment she'd heard Eric toss that out there, she'd known that Kellan would dig back into the files despite the fact that he likely knew every single detail in them.

"The Austin cops weren't able to trace the call Eric made to you, and there's been no sign of the shooter," Owen relayed to them when he got off the phone.

Neither piece of information was a surprise. Eric had no doubt used a burner or disposable phone. And as for the shooter, the guy hadn't been in the house when Austin PD had searched it. The home owners hadn't been there when the shooter had broken in, so they hadn't seen him, either.

Now the hope was that there was some kind of trace evidence or prints that the CSIs could use to ID him. Gemma doubted though that he'd been that careless, and if the shooter had slipped up, then Eric would just kill him rather than allow him to be captured and interrogated. Heck, the man could already be dead. Eric didn't like leaving loose ends. It was the whole reason he was so angry with her. So, why had he issued just a warning and not finished her off? Maybe he wanted to torment her first. An easy kill might not be as much fun for him.

"What about my neighbors?" Gemma asked. "Were any of them hurt?"

Owen shook his head and made eye contact with

his brother in the rearview mirror. "Were you able to get any details on the bomb?"

"They haven't been able to find the detonator and until they do, they won't be able to start figuring out who built it. Eric doesn't have bomb-making experience. Or at least he didn't a year ago, so he likely hired someone or spent some research time on the internet."

Gemma had heard Kellan talking with the bomb squad, but she'd only heard his end of the conversation. Which hadn't been much. Obviously, Kellan hadn't liked that there hadn't been much progress in the investigation. Then again, it'd only happened six hours ago, and the CSIs were still processing the scene.

Kellan's phone rang again, something it'd been doing throughout the drive, and he mumbled some profanity when he saw the name on the screen. For a heart-stopping moment, Gemma thought it might be Eric, but then she saw her handler's name on the screen. Amanda had already called once when they'd still been at the police station, and Kellan had let it go to voice mail, but he answered it now, and he put it on Speaker.

"Have you figured out who leaked Gemma's location?" he greeted.

"No, but it wasn't me," Amanda answered without hesitation. However, she did sound as frustrated and annoyed as Kellan. "Where's Gemma?" she snapped.

"She's safe." Kellan looked at her and put his index finger to his mouth in a stay-quiet gesture. "I need you to find the source of the leak and prove to me that you fixed it. Then I'll give you Gemma's location."

"That's not the way this works, *cowboy*," Amanda argued. "I'm the one in charge here, not you."

Gemma winced because she could feel Kellan bristling from the marshal's cowboy label and sharp tone. Amanda had never been a warm and fuzzy kind of person, and she was even less so right now.

"Gemma's in WITSEC," Amanda went on, "and that puts this under the jurisdiction of the marshals."

"Only if the marshals can protect her, and you've just proven that you can't." Kellan huffed. "Eric killed another woman last night and left a note for Gemma with her address. He's coming after her, and I'd rather make sure that no one wearing a badge is feeding Eric info to help him do that."

That silenced Amanda for a couple of seconds. "Is this about Rory?" Amanda came out and asked.

It was a question Gemma had expected. Rory was Marshal Rory Clawson, and Kellan's then fellow deputy, Dusty Walters, had been investigating the marshal for the murder of a prostitute whose body had been found in Longview Ridge. Dusty hadn't been able to find any evidence other than hearsay before Eric had gunned him down.

"Why would it be about Rory?" Kellan challenged.

"Because I figure you're holding a grudge against Rory because you weren't able to pin bogus charges on him. You still haven't been able to pin those charges on him," Amanda emphasized. "Or maybe you've got a wild notion that he aided Eric in some way."

Kellan didn't waste any time firing back. "Did he?"

Amanda made a dismissive sound. "This isn't over. You will turn Gemma over to me," the marshal added before she ended the call.

It sounded like a threat, and Gemma was certain they'd be hearing from her again soon. Maybe though, Amanda wouldn't try to put her in a new WITSEC location until they had some answers about this latest attack.

"Do you trust her?" Kellan asked when he put his phone away.

Gemma opened her mouth to answer yes, but she stopped. The truth was, she didn't know Amanda that well at all. They'd only met twice in the months that Amanda had been her handler.

"I don't have any reason *not* to trust her," Gemma settled for saying.

"Other than someone compromised your location, a location that only a handful of people knew, and Amanda was one of them." Kellan paused, and then he huffed even louder than he had when he'd been talking to Amanda. "I just don't want to make another mistake."

Gemma could have said those same words to him. If she'd just lived up to her reputation of being a top-notch profiler, she could have stopped him.

"I owe you," Kellan added a moment later.

That got her attention, and Gemma turned in the seat to face him. "You owe me?" she repeated.

Again, that was something she could have said to him. She'd been the one to mess up, not Kellan. But before she could press him on that, his phone rang again, and this time it wasn't Amanda. It was Unknown Caller on the screen.

"Eric," she whispered on a rise of breath.

Owen must have thought it was him, too. "I'll try to trace it while he's on the line." Owen quickly handed his brother a small recorder, and Kellan clicked it on before he hit the answer button.

"So, I guess you're both still alive and kicking?"

Eric asked the moment he was on the line. "If Gemma had died, my little bird would have told me."

"And who exactly is that little bird?" Kellan snapped.

"Someone in a very good seat for birds." Eric chuckled.

Maybe a marshal or a cop. But Gemma tried not to react to that because this could be just another of Eric's taunts. The word was probably already out that she'd survived, and he could have heard about it through any means from gossip to even a news report. Then again, maybe he knew she wasn't dead because he'd had no intentions of killing—yet. Not until he'd made her suffer.

"Sorry, but I need to keep my bird's name to myself for now," Eric added a moment later. "Might need him…or *her* again."

Kellan's eyes narrowed. Obviously, he also hated these games that Eric loved to play. "I'm guessing you blew up Gemma's house just in case there was any evidence left behind. That tells me you were actually in it."

"I was," Eric admitted, causing her skin to crawl. "It was fun to see how she's living her life these days. So much security! You could practically feel the worry when you stepped into the house."

Three bullets could do that, and it twisted away at her that just by hearing his voice, he could pull that old fear from her.

"I left that little microphone so I could talk to you," Eric admitted.

"You mean so you could try to make us believe you were still inside," Kellan snapped. "But you weren't. No way would you have risked getting blown up, because you're a coward."

"Sticks and stones," Eric joked, but there was just enough edge to his voice that made Gemma wonder if Kellan had hit a nerve.

At one time Eric had wanted to be an FBI agent. Or so he'd led her to believe. And maybe that was true. If so, that coward insult would have stung.

"Too bad you didn't blow up her neighbor's house where you had your hired thug shoot at us," Kellan went on. "It wasn't very smart of him to leave a spent shell casing behind. Sometimes there are fingerprints on those."

It was a bluff. If the CSIs had indeed found something like that, they would have mentioned it in the calls Kellan had made to them. Still, it got a reaction from Eric.

Silence.

She doubted this would send Eric into a rage or panic, but maybe it would rattle his cage enough for him to make a mistake.

"If there really is a casing," Eric said, his words clipped, "then I suppose we'll just have to wait and see."

"Oh, there's a casing all right," Kellan assured him, "and if we use it to ID the shooter, then there'll be a trail to you."

"No, there won't be. But good luck wasting your time with that."

"It might not be a waste of time," Gemma reminded him. And it earned her a glare from Kellan. But she finished what she intended to say, and she made sure her voice was as steeled up as she could manage. "You believe you covered your tracks, but maybe you didn't. You're not perfect. You were in a panic the night Caroline and I found out what you were, and you took us hostage, remember? That wasn't the well thought out actions of a cocky killer."

Eric paused for a long time. "I remember," he snapped. "And I'm sure you do, too. All that research we did together on Geo-Trace, and you didn't have a clue."

She hadn't. She, Eric and Caroline had worked for two years on Geo-Trace, the name of their project for profiling and predicting specific areas of cities where violent crimes were most likely to occur. It could have helped law enforcement if Eric hadn't been manipulating the data. He'd done that by murdering his victims in those predicted areas.

"Why did you do it? Why did you kill all those people?" Gemma asked Eric, earning her another glare from Kellan.

Yes, those were questions that could wait, and Eric likely wouldn't even give her an honest answer, but maybe by keeping him on the line, Owen would be able to trace the call.

"That's a conversation for another time," Eric snarled.

"Not really. My guess is that you were in love with me and wanted to impress me."

"Don't flatter yourself, sweetheart. I never loved you. It was never about you."

There'd never been any hints that Eric had indeed had any romantic interest in her, but it twisted away at her to think that Eric could have done those monstrous crimes because of feelings that she hadn't picked up on. That was yet another layer of guilt she could add to her life.

"Sheriff Slater, are you going to let Gemma do all the talking?" Eric pressed. "I wouldn't if I were you. After all, if it wasn't for Gemma, your daddy and that deputy would still be alive."

"If it weren't for *you*, they'd be alive," Kellan corrected.

"Oh, but you're wrong about that," Eric quickly answered.

Kellan cursed. "Quit playing mind games and tell me what the hell it is you want."

"Always did enjoy your direct approach. So, here's the deal. Now that I'm back on my feet, I'm looking for Caroline. And you should be, too."

"I have been looking for her," Kellan assured him. "Plenty of people have been. Did you kill her?"

"No. Last I saw her, she was very much alive."

Gemma found herself gripping on to the seat, but she shook her head. Eric could be lying, though she wanted that to be true. She had enough blood by association on her hands.

"I've killed a dozen or so people," Eric went on, "but Caroline isn't one of them. Neither was your father or the deputy. Dusty Walters. As much as I'd like to take credit for their deaths, I can't."

Gemma nearly laughed, and it wouldn't have been because that was funny but because it was ridiculous. Wasn't it?

"What the hell are you talking about?" Kellan snarled. "I saw you shoot Gemma, and the bullets that killed my dad came from the same gun."

"Because I found it on the floor inside the house. I picked it up and used it. I didn't, however, use it on

Deputy Walters. You know that because he was shot with a different weapon."

"You had two guns on you," Gemma murmured. At least that had been the most logical theory. For now, she scoffed, "So, you're saying you're innocent?" Gemma didn't bother to take the sarcasm out of that.

But still, something inside her turned a little.

"No, I shot you, all right," Eric admitted, and he sounded so pleased about that. "Wish I'd put the bullets in your head, but that's what do-overs are for. You can have your own do-over, too, Kellan. But here's my advice—find Caroline because she's the one who can tell you who really killed Deputy Walters and your father."

Chapter Four

Kellan wasn't able to shut out Eric's words. They knifed through his head, a violent steady assault that was screwing around with his concentration.

Gemma wasn't helping with his concentration, either, and since they'd arrived at his office, Kellan had been silently cursing her almost as much as he was Eric.

Almost.

Eric was a sociopathic lying snake, and he loved batting around people's emotions. Like a cat playing with a half-dead mouse. That didn't mean Kellan could dismiss what Eric had said, but he also wasn't going to accept it as gospel truth.

So far, there'd been nothing about Gemma he could dismiss. Damn her. He wanted something to make himself immune, and common sense and bad blood sure as hell weren't doing it. It riled him that his body hardened whenever she looked at him. Like now, for instance.

Gemma was in a corner of his office, and their gazes connected when he finished his latest call to the techs who'd tried to trace Eric's call. Kellan had to shake his head. As expected, they'd had no luck with that.

Also as expected, she sighed, lowered her head and got back to work.

She was working on a laptop that Owen had gotten for her so she could start researching some angles about where Eric might have been for the past year. Kellan had warned her to have no contact with her handler, had issued other warnings about hacking—something she was darn good at—or exchanging any communications with anybody. Since Gemma was scared and feeling guilty about Iris's murder, she would probably stick to that, and maybe she'd even be able to find something that would help.

Now that I'm back on my feet... Eric had said.

Maybe that meant he'd been out of commission. That would explain his nearly one-year absence. He hadn't been in jail. Kellan had combed the records for that, just in case Eric had been picked up under an assumed name. He'd investigated any and all possibilities for that and had come up empty.

So, maybe Eric had been hurt and physically unable to kill? Of course, this could be about finances, too. With every law enforcement agency in the state looking for him, he would have needed funds to move around.

Kellan's phone rang again, and he answered it right away when he saw that it was Austin PD. That caused Gemma to send another look his way. Caused Kellan to issue another round of that silent profanity for the bronc-kick of heat he felt behind the zipper of his jeans. Thankfully, it didn't affect his hearing.

"Just wanted you to know that there's still no sign of the shooter," Sergeant Alan Gonzales said. "Or Eric Lang. We'll keep looking though." The update, or rather the lack of it, had probably come because Kellan had left the sergeant two messages to call him.

Kellan was still stewing over the gunman's getaway, and nearly peppered the sergeant with questions about why the gunman hadn't turned up on highway cameras or why no one had spotted him or someone matching his description, but he knew Gonzales. He was a good cop. Still, if Kellan had thought it would get him answers, he would have peppered a good cop with those questions and more. But it was obvious Gonzales had nothing to give him.

He ended the call, taking some of his frustration out on the button on his phone that he jabbed too hard, and he got up to pour himself his umpteenth cup of coffee. Of course, Gemma was looking at him, waiting.

While he gathered his thoughts—and pushed other thoughts aside—he studied her a moment over the rim of his cup. She was as wired as he was, and she'd chewed on her bottom lip so much that it was red and raw. Her fidgeting hands had plowed through her long brunette hair, too. Another sign of those nerves.

She was normally polish and shine with that flawless face and mouth that had always made him think of sex. Today though, her mussed hair tumbled onto her shoulders as if she'd just crawled out of bed, and the only shine came from those ripe green eyes that shimmered from the fatigue of staring too long at the computer screen.

Kellan thought of sex again, cursed again, and forced himself to tell her what she was no doubt waiting to hear. The info he'd just learned from that phone call.

He went across the room toward her. Close enough

to see that her pulse was already skittering against the skin of her throat.

"They didn't find Eric or the shooter." He said it fast, knowing there was no type of sugarcoat that would make it better. It'd left a bitter taste in his mouth, all right. Because it meant Gemma was in just as much danger now as she had been when they'd escaped from her house.

A weary sigh left her mouth, causing her breasts to rise and then fall. If they'd never been lovers, he might have put a comforting hand on her arm. But that was dangerous. Because even though he doubted either of them wanted it, there was a connection between them that went beyond the pain and the hurt of what'd happened a year ago.

"Why did you say you owed me?" she asked.

The question came out of the blue and threw him, so much so that he gulped down too much coffee and nearly choked. Hardly the reaction for a tough-nosed cop. But his reaction to her hadn't exactly been all badge, either.

Kellan lifted his shoulder and wanted to kick himself for ever bringing it up in the first place. Bad timing, he thought, and wondered if there would ever be a good time for him to grovel.

"I didn't stop Eric from shooting you that night." He said that fast. Not a drop of sugarcoating. "You, my father and Dusty. I'm sorry for that."

Her silence and the shimmering look in her eyes made him stupid, and that was the only excuse he could come up with for why he kept talking.

"It's easier for me to toss some of the blame at you for not ID'ing a killer sooner," he added. And he still did blame her, in part, for that. "But it was my job to stop him before he killed two people and injured another while he was right under my nose."

The silence just kept on going. So much so that Kellan turned, ready to go back to his desk so that he wouldn't continue to prattle on. Gemma stopped him by putting her hand on his arm. It was like a trigger that sent his gaze searching for hers. Wasn't hard to find when she stood and met him eye to eye.

"It was easier for me to toss some of the blame at you, too." She made another of those sighs. "But there was no stopping Eric that night. The stopping should have happened prior to that. I should have seen the signs." Gemma silenced him by lifting her hand when he started to speak. "And please don't tell me that it's all right, that I'm not at fault. I don't think I could take that right now."

Unfortunately, Kellan understood just what she meant. They were both still hurting, and a mutual sympathy fest was only going to make it harder. They couldn't go back. Couldn't undo. And that left them with only one direction. Looking ahead and putting this son of a bitch in a hole where he belonged.

She nodded as if she'd reached the same conclusion he had, and Gemma swiveled the screen so he could see it. It was a collage of photos of the crime scene at the Serenity Inn. He'd wanted to give her some time to level her adrenaline and come down from the attack, but it was obvious she was ready to be interviewed.

"I've been studying this," she said, "and Eric could have been telling the truth about some things." She paused. "I hope he's telling the truth about Caroline, that he left her alive."

Yeah. But if she was alive, did that mean she'd been with a serial killer this whole time? That twisted the knot in his stomach. There were things worse than death.

"I know you didn't get a good look at everything in the inn where Eric had you that night. Eric said he picked up the gun from inside the inn. Did he?" Kellan asked.

"It's possible. He'd drugged me by then so everything was blurry around the edges. But, yes, he could have done it. When he stepped into the house, he had his arms crooked around mine and Caroline's necks. Caroline hadn't been drugged so she managed to elbow him as he was backing up with us. She fought like a wildcat."

Kellan nearly smiled. That sounded like Caroline. "If he was telling the truth, the gun would have been on the floor. Eric would have had to reach down to get it."

She stayed quiet a moment, and he could almost see the images replaying in her head. "He staggered when Caroline was clawing at him." Another pause, her forehead bunched up. "They both fell, I think. But only for a few seconds."

He hadn't thought that knot in his stomach could get any tighter. It did. Because a few seconds was plenty enough for Eric to have grabbed a gun and used it to shoot Gemma just as Kellan had been walking through the door. If that had happened though, and if by some miracle Eric had been telling the truth, then that left Kellan with a big question.

Why was the gun there?

Kellan looked at the photos again, letting it play out in his mind, too. "There are some *inconsistencies*." He hated that blasted word, so sterile and detached from the emotion. Still, it was better than saying that there were things that had caused him a year of living hell and to not have a single full night of sleep.

"Dusty was shot with a different gun than my father and you," Kellan said, spelling it out, again, with the hopes the inconsistencies might go away. "We always assumed Eric had two weapons and had possibly even run out of ammo in the one he'd used on Dad and you and that's why he shot Dusty with another one."

She cleared her throat just a little as if trying to clear her head, too. "Neither gun was found at the scene, which means Eric could have taken them with him. I don't suppose either have turned up in a pawn shop or someplace like that?"

"No." He'd been keeping tabs on that because a gun could possibly still have trace or fiber evidence even after a year. "I did put in a request, though, to have the CSIs go through the Serenity Inn again. They'll head there first thing in the morning."

For the first time today, he saw some kind of amusement in her eyes. He doubted it was from actual humor but rather because Gemma would know how that played out. "I'll bet they weren't happy about that. How many times have you had them go through it?" she asked.

"Three." He'd lost count of how many visits he'd made himself. "That hotel was once a house, built in 1880, and people had hidey-holes all over. It has twenty-eight rooms and nearly fifteen thousand square feet. And as if that weren't enough, it sat empty for a decade before Eric got near it. The squirrels and mice could have added even more holes. Easy to miss something in all that space."

Gemma made a sound of agreement, pushed her fingers through her hair again. She opened her mouth, but then closed it as if she'd changed her mind. "Sorry. I was about to attempt a profile. We both know how reliable I am with those."

That bite to her voice was drenched in regret and pain, things he knew plenty about. And while he didn't want to go the profile route, either, he did want to run something past her.

"Rory Clawson," he threw out there. "I know you've been doing hypnosis and therapy to help you remember more of what happened after Eric drugged you, and just wondered if you recalled him being there that night."

"No. No recollection of that," she said without hesitation but then paused. "How did you know about the hypnosis and therapy?"

"I've been getting updates on any and every aspect of this investigation—in case any new evidence came to light." Kellan didn't intend to apologize for it, either. "I want my father's killer caught."

Gemma continued to stare at him as if trying to figure out if that was all there was to it, but she didn't press it. "I've been searching computer records, too, for updates. In case there's any new evidence," she added, emphasizing his own words.

Of course, she had. Because his father's killer was also the same person who'd put three bullets in her. Well, probably. Unless Eric was telling the truth and Gemma had been the only person he'd shot that night.

"I can't hack into Rory's records," she went on. "And, yes, I just tried."

Again, no surprise, but he gave her a warning glare because she'd just confessed to committing a crime. He was ornery enough to consider arresting her but secretly wished he'd had the "moral flexibility" to do the hacking himself. Yes, he wanted the truth, but the badge meant something to him, and it had meant something to his father, too. Buck wouldn't have wanted Kellan or his other sons bending the law even when it was for the sake of finding his killer.

Gemma must have had no trouble interpreting his glare or the way *his* forehead was now bunched up. While looking him straight in the eye, she lifted her hands, palms up, wrists exposed, as if waiting for him to cuff her.

Kellan's glare deepened, and using his free hand, he braceleted those exposed wrists to push them back down. Unfortunately, that involved the touching that he'd been trying to avoid. Touching, that seemed to bother Gemma, too, because her breath hitched a little, and her gaze finally darted away.

"I'm sorry," she said when his grip melted off her. "That put you in a tough position, but I'm not sorry for trying to get to the truth. Eric is out there, *killing.*" Now she shuddered, gave her bottom lip another bite until her mouth stopped trembling. "And he found out where I was, how to get to me. It bothers me that Rory's a marshal and therefore could have gotten access to my WITSEC location."

"That's not the only thing that bothers me about him, but yeah, that's part of it. What bothers me just as much is that I haven't been able to solve the murder of Lacey Terrell, the prostitute Dusty was investigating. He was convinced that Rory was behind that somehow."

Kellan didn't add more because his phone rang again. This time it was Jack, and Kellan went back across the room so he could have at least a little privacy when he talked to his brother.

"Owen just told me what Eric said," Jack blurted out the moment he was on the line. "Did he really say he didn't kill Caroline?"

None of this was a surprise. Not the question and certainly not the desperate emotion that went with it. Jack loved Caroline, and even though all the signs had pointed to her being dead, Jack would never give up, never heal, until they found her body.

"For just a second, think with your badge and no other part of you," Kellan insisted. "Eric is a liar."

Kellan glanced at Gemma to see if she was listening. Maybe she was, but she was also back to working on the computer. Hopefully, not hacking into anything.

"Yeah," Jack snapped. "But there's no reason for him to lie about that."

Sure there was, and it was going to slice Jack, and himself, to spell out what his brother already knew. "If we're focused on finding Caroline, then we'd be looking in the wrong direction—for Eric. No way would he leave her alive if she could be found and lead us back to him."

"Maybe she escaped," Jack insisted.

"Maybe." This was going to slice, too. "But then, she would have found a way to get in touch with you."

His brother's groan was the worst slice of all. Jack was his kid brother, and it hurt to feel him hurting like this.

"I want to talk to Gemma," Jack snarled several

moments later. "I want to work this latest murder investigation with you."

Kellan had anticipated that, too, and had no intention of refusing. "It might hit close to home," Kellan warned him. "The marshals might be involved."

"Rory?" Jack immediately asked.

"Maybe. But also Amanda Hardin. Any idea how and why she became Gemma's handler?"

His brother paused a moment. "No. I would have done it, but I wasn't exactly at my best."

No, because Jack had been in love with Caroline, and she was still missing. His brother had gone a little crazy when they'd found Caroline's blood and then no sign of the woman.

"You're asking if I trust Amanda?" Jack concluded. "I don't really know her that well, but I soon will. Let me see what I can find out, and I'll get back to you."

Kellan thanked him, and he turned, ready to face Gemma's questions about what Jack had said regarding her handler. But it was obvious from her widened eyes that he had his own question.

"What happened?" Kellan demanded.

"Eric," she said, a new kind of quiver in her voice. "I know where he's been for the past year, and I think I know how to find him."

Chapter Five

The fear was gone now. Or at least it had been stomped down for a while and replaced by the relief of what Gemma had found in her computer search.

Now that I'm back on my feet.

Eric probably hadn't even given it a thought about saying that to her and Kellan. It'd been simply a way of starting his latest taunt. But it had opened a big, wide door for Gemma.

She caught on to Kellan's arm, pulling him closer so she could show him what was on the laptop. For just a split second he went stiff, maybe because she'd touched him, but it was possible that she looked a little crazy. He might have thought she was losing it.

And then he saw the screen.

The records from a hospital in Mexico City.

"I started doing hospital searches for the last year. Looking for anyone who fit his description. And, yes, some hacking was involved," she added.

With his eyes fixed on the data, Kellan waved that off, moved out of her grip and went even closer to the screen.

"I figured you'd searched the jails so I excluded those," Gemma added and waited for Kellan to nod.

"So, I decided to go for medical records. Eric obviously used an alias, but that's him." She pointed to the name on the file. Joe Hanson. "The SOB used my last name."

That irritated her, but she pushed it aside, knowing that Eric would have done that with the hopes of her noticing and feeling the sting. Gemma wasn't going to give him the satisfaction.

"Everything fits," she went on. "The age, height, weight and the small sun tattoo on the inside of his right wrist." The tat he'd told her that he'd gotten for his eighteenth birthday. To celebrate, he'd said. But now she wondered if it had a sinister meaning, maybe even to mark his first kill.

Kellan sat down, scrolled through the lengthy record. The notes were in Spanish, which he clearly had no trouble translating. "He went in with a gunshot wound," Kellan said. "Temporary paralysis due to the bullet being lodged in his spine." He looked up at her. "Someone shot him."

She nodded, and even though there were other things she wanted to show him in the hospital records, Gemma pulled up the next file. The police report.

"Eric claimed he had no idea who'd shot him and gave them that fake name, Joe Hanson. He said someone had abducted him and a woman he'd been traveling with. Cassie Marlow."

"The same initials as Caroline. Maybe she shot him," he mumbled, and he continued scrolling. Gemma hadn't gone beyond this point in the file but fully intended to do that as soon as Kellan had skimmed through it.

"Eric didn't give the cops much info," Kellan went on. "Claimed he was blindfolded for the two weeks he'd been held by the so-called kidnapper." The details he had given though eerily mimicked what he'd done to Gemma. Arm around the throat. The drugging. And being shot.

"Eric's too vain to have shot himself," Gemma said. "And even if he had thought this was a good plan, to hide out in a hospital until the heat died down, he wouldn't have risked paralysis."

The sound of agreement Kellan was making came to an abrupt stop. His finger went still on the keyboard, and almost frantically Gemma followed his gaze to see what'd put that stark expression on his face.

"Hell," he said.

Gemma saw it then, too. The detailed report of the Mexican police finding a decomposed body in a car where they'd also found Eric wounded and bleeding. The body of a woman whose throat had been slit.

"Oh, God." Gemma's legs gave way, and if she hadn't sat on the edge of the desk, she would have fallen.

Because the body in the car matched Caroline's description.

Kellan didn't give her any reassurances that it might not be Caroline. No cop's words about needing to wait and see. He simply took her hand and held it.

"That's how Eric murdered his victims before he took Caroline and me hostage and did the shootings at the inn," she mumbled, not able to stop the flow of words that came with the rush of sickening dread. "God, he cut her throat."

Gemma had to fight to keep hold of her breath, had to fight just so she wouldn't scream and pound her fists on the wall. Eric had killed her. He'd killed Caroline.

The tears came, hot and bitter, and the grief was just as fresh as it had been a year ago. "I'm responsible for this. I hired Caroline and Eric. Their paths would have never crossed if I hadn't hired them."

Kellan stood, staring at her, and the grip he put on her shoulders was far from gentle. "Stop it," he said, his voice a low, dangerous warning. No gentleness there, either. "This is exactly what Eric wants. He wants you crying and broken so you'll be an easier target."

Gemma hated to admit that Eric might have succeeded. He couldn't have hurt her more if he'd ripped out a piece of her heart.

Kellan got right in her face. "Don't give in to this. Help me find him." He punctuated each word with anger that had tightened every muscle in his face and turned his eyes to the color of a violent storm. "You said you thought you knew how to find him. Tell me. *Now.*"

Well, he certainly wasn't taking the approach of handling her with kid gloves. Not that she wanted it. Kid gloves weren't going to fix this.

Her hands were shaking when she moved back to the keyboard, and she pulled up the medical files again. The tears were still there, but she tried to blink them away so she could see. She didn't want to miss any of the details here.

"He stayed a month in the hospital in Mexico and then was transferred to a nursing and rehabilitation center here in the States where he learned to walk again." Gemma had to swallow before she could continue. "The center isn't cheap, so he must have gotten his hands on some money. Eric was a trust fund baby, and that wasn't touched, but he could have had other accounts stashed under other names."

"Like Joe Hanson," Kellan mumbled almost absently. He'd put his attention back on the screen now, and he saw the very name that had given her that jolt of excitement. A jolt that was no longer there because it'd been replaced by an emotion of a different kind.

From the bombshell news of the body in Eric's car.

"Maylene Roth," Gemma read. "She's the private nurse Eric hired while at the center. When he was discharged from there *two weeks ago*, the medical staff turned over his care to Nurse Roth. The doctor noted the nurse was very attached to the patient and would stay with him indefinitely."

"*Attached*," Kellan repeated on a heavy sigh. "Either his lover or a groupie."

Gemma agreed, and with every part of her still trembling, she pulled up the final document. "That's the address on record for Maylene." It was in San Antonio. "Eric won't be there, of course, but we can try to track him through her."

She held her breath when Kellan gave her his cop's look, and Gemma figured he was on the verge of giving her a lecture about there being no "we" in the tracking-down process, that this was something only for him and his fellow cops. No lecture though. He stepped out into his squad room and had a short conversation with Owen.

"I ordered a background check on Maylene and will have the cops go to her address," Kellan told her when he came back into his office. "Not a quiet, just-checking-on-you approach, either. Full sirens and SWAT gear. The chances are slim to none that either of them will be there, but it'll send a message to Eric that we're on to him and that I'm willing to use his friend to get to him."

Good. It was exactly the kind of game that Eric would play, and if Eric had any "attachment" to Maylene, it might rattle him. Then again, Gemma had to wonder if Eric even had enough normalcy inside him to rattle. As a profiler, she'd interviewed dozens of serial killers, but none of them had had such a perfect cold mask as Eric did.

Kellan took out his phone. "I'll make arrangements for you to go someplace safe," he said. "But first I want to work on getting whatever info I can on the body that was found in Eric's car."

"I can probably access autopsy records—"

"No. Let me do it. And don't mention this to Jack. Not yet."

She wouldn't, not until they had more info. Proof, she amended. Best not to give Jack a double dose of grief, one from hearing about the body and another when Kellan managed to get an ID. Then, Gemma could grieve right along with him.

"Where did you have in mind for me to go?" she asked.

Kellan didn't get a chance to answer because of the voices that came from the squad room. Not Owen, but it was someone Gemma immediately recognized.

Marshal Amanda Hardin was walking straight toward them. "Have you lost your mind?" Amanda immediately snapped.

Since Amanda was volleying glances at her and Kellan, Gemma thought the question was aimed at both of them. Amanda was clearly upset, her posture stiff, her mouth in a flat line. Like the other times Gemma had seen the woman, she was wearing black dress pants, white shirt and her marshal's badge. Unlike the other times, Amanda looked frazzled with her hair mussed and the dark circles under her eyes.

"I'm busy," Kellan answered, and in the same slick way she'd seen him draw his weapon, he closed the laptop, no doubt so that the marshal wouldn't see what they'd been researching, and he positioned himself between Amanda and her.

That told Gemma loads. That Kellan wasn't going to trust Amanda. Good. Because Gemma didn't, either.

Kellan's response and the protective move certainly didn't improve Amanda's mood, and her narrowed gaze flew to Gemma's. "I didn't think I'd need to spell this out for you, but you're acting like an idiot," the marshal said. "You're in grave danger. Eric Lang is at large, and yet here you are in the very place that Eric will expect you to be. And you're with a town sheriff who has no authority to interfere with WITSEC."

Amanda flicked a glance at Kellan.

"Guess you're the idiot and I'm the interfering local cop," Kellan grumbled to Gemma. Despite everything, she had to fight back a smile.

Amanda noticed that, too, and shot them both glares. The marshal paused several moments, obviously trying to rein in her temper. It worked, sort of. When she spoke again, her voice was slightly more level.

"I've already arranged for a safe house," Amanda told Gemma. "You need to come with me. I'm not giving you a choice about that. I'm not going to allow you to stay here where you'll be an easy target."

In the past year, Gemma had thought she'd lost the

backbone and confidence that she'd once had. Eric had done that to her. But now she felt a little of that backbone return, and Gemma stepped out to Kellan's side to face the marshal head-on.

"No," Gemma said.

There were plenty of emotions that zinged through Amanda's eyes. Concern might have been in there, but Gemma saw a lot of anger. "No?" Amanda repeated like a challenge.

"No," Gemma repeated like a declaration. "I'm not going with you. I voluntarily placed myself in WIT-SEC, and now I'm removing myself. That means you're no longer my handler, and you can go."

The color drained from Amanda's face, and Gemma had no idea what emotions she was witnessing now. What the heck was this about?

It took the marshal a hard breath before she recovered enough to look at Kellan. "If she stays here, Eric will kill her."

Kellan didn't jump to deny that, probably because he knew that Eric would indeed come after her again.

"*You* could get her killed if she stays with you," Amanda added.

Kellan lifted his shoulder, but Gemma thought there was nothing casual about that shrug. "Eric got to the last safe house you set up for Gemma. The one *you* had set up for her," Kellan reminded the marshal. "It's up to Gemma if she wants to take a risk like that again."

"I have no intention of going anywhere with you," Gemma told Amanda.

Amanda's now hard gaze lingered on her a couple of seconds before it slid to Kellan. "Are you two sleeping together again? Because it's obvious you're not thinking with the right parts of your bodies right now."

Kellan's glare and huff weren't casual, either. He merely looked past Amanda and at Owen. "Escort Marshal Hardin out of the building." Kellan stepped back and closed the door in Amanda's face.

Kellan then turned to Gemma. "If you want to change your mind and go with her—"

"No." She didn't have to think about that, but she did want to give some thought to the way Amanda had gone pale when Gemma had told her she was leaving WITSEC.

Gemma had heard some snippets of Kellan's conversation with Jack, and Kellan had asked his brother something about why Amanda had become her handler. Gemma very much wanted to know what Jack had had to say.

The door opened, and for a moment Gemma thought that Amanda had returned to continue an argument that she stood no chance of winning, but it wasn't the marshal. It was Owen. One look at his face, and Gemma knew something was wrong.

A moment later, Owen confirmed just that.

"There's been another murder."

Chapter Six

Milton Oswald.

An hour ago, the name had meant nothing to Kellan, but it sure as heck had some meaning now. That's because from everything found at the scene, he was their missing shooter, the very person who'd tried to gun Gemma and him down.

According to the preliminary report he'd just pulled up, the man was basically a thug with a mile-long record.

And now he was dead.

Oswald's body had been found just inside the Longview Ridge jurisdiction, and Kellan figured that was intentional. Now he had a murder investigation that would tie up not only a team of deputies and himself but also the CSIs.

It wasn't just the stretch on the manpower and resources though. It was the emotional toll of it, and the note left at the scene was certainly a whopping big toll. Not just for Kellan but for Gemma.

From the sound that Gemma made when she looked at the report on Oswald, she tried to bite back a groan. She failed. Kellan cursed and wished he hadn't viewed the photo that the deputies had just sent him with their initial report. The gruesomely clear picture of the man sprawled out on the ground in front of the Serenity Inn.

In that photo, Oswald's skin was already white, indicating he'd been dead at least a half hour. His lifeless eyes had started to sink back in his skull. With the blood, it made it seem as if he was wearing some kind of sick Halloween mask.

In contrast, Gemma's eyes were filled with life. And probably the same dread and disgust that he was feeling as her gaze skirted over the screen.

Kellan tried to close the file, but Gemma caught on to his hand, stopping him. "This is Eric's doing," she said, touching her fingers to the image of the man's neck and the slit that had almost certainly been his cause of death.

Yeah, that was his signature, all right. But they hadn't needed the cut to confirm that it was indeed Eric. That's because the snake had left them a note pinned to Oswald's shirt.

Here's your missing shooter, Sheriff Slater. Now Gemma and you can sleep better tonight knowing he's not out there to harm you. Sweet dreams.

Kellan knew that the only one who'd sleep better was Eric. That's because Oswald was no longer a loose end.

"Who found Oswald's body?" Gemma asked. "How did they find it?"

"An anonymous 911 call. One of my deputies lives close to there and was on his way to work. He went to the scene and had no trouble spotting it."

Judging from the volume of blood, Eric had killed

him there, maybe by luring the guy to the scene with the promise of payment. Kellan should have considered that Eric would go back there.

Kellan eased her hand away from the keyboard, and this time he managed to shut down the file. She wasn't as pale as the dead guy, but seeing the picture wasn't helping her color any.

It occurred to Kellan that the paleness worried him. Maybe more than it should. Because that kind of concern meant his focus was shifting away from Eric and on to her. Something that he knew could have the worst consequences.

Because that's what'd happened the night his father had been killed.

He'd been so homed in on saving Gemma that he had almost certainly missed signals that could have saved his father. Maybe saved her, too, from getting shot.

Doing something to correct that focus shift, Kellan stood to get yet more coffee. And put some distance between Gemma and himself.

"There's a recording of the person who called in Oswald's death?" she pressed, though he figured she'd noticed his not subtle shift of position.

Kellan nodded. "It was a woman. She refused to identify herself when the dispatch operator asked for her name."

"Maylene," Gemma concluded in a rough whisper.

That was his guess, too, and Kellan had passed that on to the deputy team who'd be primary on this case. Since this was now a homicide investigation, that would make the woman a person of interest. Of course, it might make her dead because Eric might think of her as another loose end who should be permanently silenced, but there was nothing Kellan could do about that now.

However, there was something he could do about Gemma.

Something she wasn't going to like. Hell, he didn't like it, either, but no scenario he could come up with would be ideal.

He stepped out of the office first, to have a quick chat with Owen in order to set things in motion, and then Kellan went back in to lay things out for her.

"I'm going to take you to the ranch," he said, and he just continued despite the head shaking. "We'll be there in about ten minutes."

She went still. There'd been no need for him to tell her how far away the place was. Gemma knew because she'd been there.

And she'd been in his bed.

Gemma didn't ask if that was a wise decision. It wasn't. But it was the best of the worst options they had. He couldn't turn her over to the marshals, and a safe house would stretch the manpower of the sheriff's office to the breaking point—which would please Eric to no end.

Kellan made a quick check over his shoulder where Owen gave him a nod. "Come on," he told Gemma, picking up the laptop and putting it into the small suitcase that Owen had gotten for her.

Owen had also managed to get her a replacement phone along with some clothes and toiletries. Kellan handed her the bag so it'd free up his hand in case he needed to use his weapon.

Gemma started walking with him, but she shook her

head again. "Doesn't Owen live on the grounds with his daughter? You can't take me there. This could put her in danger—"

"It's fine," Owen volunteered. "She's going away with her nanny for a few days."

That couldn't be easy on Owen. His brother's wife had died in childbirth, crushing him, and Kellan believed the only reason Owen had made it through that darkness was because of his little girl. Owen would miss her, desperately, but he wouldn't do anything to risk her safety and neither would Kellan. That's why he'd sent a reserve deputy with the nanny. Owen was too valuable to lose, but if things heated up, Kellan would have no choice but to send him to guard the child.

However, Kellan was certain that Eric wasn't after a child. Eric's target was standing right next to Kellan.

When they reached the front door, both Owen and Kellan glanced around the area and drew their guns despite it only being a few feet to the cruiser. Kellan didn't see anything, but there were plenty of places for someone to hide on Main Street.

After Kellan gave him a nod, Owen went out ahead of them, throwing open the back door of the cruiser before he hurried to get behind the wheel. Kellan hurried, too, pressing his hand on Gemma's back to keep her low until they were both in the back seat. As soon as they were in, Owen drove off.

Kellan didn't let down his guard. The cruiser was bullet resistant, but he was also concerned about someone following them. Eric had to consider that Kellan would take Gemma to the ranch, but there was no need to hand Eric that info on a silver platter.

"The hands are putting down the strip spikes on the road like you asked," Owen said when they reached the end of Main Street. "Eli is on the way there, too. Once he's in place, I can go back to the office and help with the murder investigation."

Eli was a Texas Ranger and would do just fine as backup without Kellan having to tie up any more of his deputies. There was the added benefit of having three lawmen brothers. Too bad he couldn't use Jack for this, but he might be having his own demons to face when they ID'd the body in Eric's car.

"I'm having the CSIs put up two surveillance cameras at the Serenity Inn," Kellan went on, mentally going through the list of things he'd need to check on once he had Gemma settled. Then he could focus on finding Eric before he struck again. "It's a long shot that Eric would go back there, but he could if he's in the mood to play more games."

Of course, that would also mean another dead body.

"I'll keep doing computer searches on Maylene to find out anything I can about her," Gemma added, obviously going through her to-do list, too. "What about the raid on her house? When will that happen?"

Kellan checked his watch. "Any minute now." It was anyone's guess though as to how long it'd be before the cops found anything. If Maylene wasn't there, then the entire house would have to be processed to find any evidence of not only Maylene's link to Eric but any proof that he'd actually been to her house.

Gemma turned to look out the window when Owen took the turn to the ranch. Even though the sun was just starting to set, there was still plenty of light for her to see the stretch of pastures and the Angus cattle that grazed there. It looked peaceful, and Kellan wanted to keep it that way.

She dragged in a long breath when Owen came to a stop in front of the house. Maybe preparing herself for the run inside or maybe because of the jolt of memories she was about to face.

Kellan got out ahead of them, unlocking the door to the house and checking to make sure there were no signs of a break-in. None. The security system immediately triggered, and he entered the code before he motioned for Owen to get Gemma inside. He reset it as soon as they were inside with the door locked.

Gemma came to a halt in the foyer, her attention going straight ahead to the large framed picture that hung on the wall facing the door. His parents. It was one of the last photos they'd taken of them together before his mom had gotten cancer and passed away ten years ago. It wasn't a posed shot but one of them standing by the corral, their hands linked while they watched Jack working with a new horse. All three were smiling.

"It's nice," she said, her voice barely a whisper. "Very nice."

The picture hadn't been there a year ago when he and Gemma had been lovers and his father had still been alive. It was possible it brought back memories of that night. Sometimes, it did for Kellan, but in his case, it brought on more good than bad.

Owen volleyed a few glances at them, and Kellan didn't think it was because of Gemma's reaction to the picture. It was probably because the foyer was zinging with emotion, and while it wasn't the blasted heat between Gemma and him, emotion of any kind could lead to trouble.

"I need to grab a shower so I'll be ready to go back to work when Eli gets here," Owen said, heading up the stairs.

Kellan shot him a scowl and hoped that this wasn't Owen's way of giving them some privacy.

"I'll put your suitcase in the guest room," Kellan told her, taking the bag from her. She'd had it clutched in front of her like a shield. "If you're hungry, just help yourself to whatever you find in the fridge."

Gemma nodded and released a quick breath and dragged in another one as if she'd been holding it too long and was suddenly starved for air. Just a breath, Kellan assured himself. Not the meltdown, adrenaline crash he'd been expecting from her. Still, instead of just heading up the stairs, he set down the suitcase and looked at her.

"I need a truce with you," she said, surprising him.

Even though he wasn't sure what she meant, he nodded and was ready to point out that a truce was already in place. She was in his house, under his protection, and they were working together to find Eric. Yes, there were still plenty of bad feelings between them stemming from both of them sucking at their jobs and that in turn causing his father's death. Still…

Gemma stepped right into his arms, her body landing against his. He got that quick jolt of heat that was mixed with, yes, those emotions. Talk about a lethal combo.

"I take meds," she whispered with her mouth close to his ear. "Some of them are to stave off panic attacks, and I'm due a dose very soon." Her voice trembled when she added that. "I'm not telling you this so you'll feel sorry for me or baby me, but I can't take them right now because they fog my head and I won't be able to work. So, you might hear me tonight…when the nightmares come."

Well, hell. Kellan would have had to be a cold-hearted bastard not to react to that, and before he could even try to come up with a different solution, his arms went around her.

"If you hear me tonight," she went on. "Don't come in the room. I'll be okay."

He seriously doubted the okay part or that she wouldn't need meds to get her through the night. Kellan considered having Owen pick her up a prescription and then he could demand that she take the damn pills, but he knew that wouldn't do any good. Nightmares couldn't kill, but Eric could, and she was as determined to find him as Kellan was.

"Can I do anything to help?" he asked, easing back from her so he could see her.

She gave him a slight smile, but it didn't make it to her eyes, and she stepped out of his grip. "You're doing it. I need this truce." She hiked up her chin then, clearly trying to look a lot stronger than she felt, and she picked up her bag. "I can put this in the guest room. I know the way." She did. In fact, Gemma probably knew every inch of his house.

Every inch of him, too.

Not exactly the right thought to settle the nerves jangling just beneath his skin. Those nerves caused him to jolt a little when the sound of his ringing phone shot through the foyer. Gemma immediately stopped and waited for him to look at the screen.

"Rory Clawson," Kellan told her.

While he didn't especially want to talk to the marshal, this could be related to the investigation. More likely though, Rory was going to try to browbeat Kellan into persuading Gemma to go back into WITSEC. As far as Kellan was concerned, there was zero chance of that happening until he knew every single detail of how Eric had found Gemma.

Kellan took the call, putting it on Speaker, and he immediately heard Rory's greeting. "Sheriff Slater. Kellan," Rory amended.

Over the past year, Kellan had had several conversations with the marshal, and unlike Amanda, Rory's attitude was laid-back, just as it was now. Kellan had no intention of aiming for laid-back.

"What do you want?" Kellan asked, and he thought he heard Rory make a heavy sigh.

"Amanda said she'd gone by your office, that she saw Gemma and that Gemma looked shaken up."

"What do you want?" Kellan repeated. He kept his tone just one notch short of being hostile, but that wouldn't last if Rory was wasting his time.

"Please tell Gemma how sorry I am about Eric finding her. I'm glad you were there to get her out."

"Yeah, she's glad about that, too." And that had more than a smidge of sarcasm. "How did Eric find her?" Kellan snapped.

"Maybe through Oswald, the dead triggerman."

Kellan certainly hadn't expected Rory to say that, even if it was a possibility. Judging from Gemma's suddenly wide eyes, she felt the same.

"Why Oswald?" Kellan pressed.

"I'm sure it'll come up when you're deeper into the murder investigation, but he was a criminal informant for the Austin cops," Rory explained. "And he was also a hacker. I'm betting that's the reason Eric hired him."

Kellan bet the same thing. Well, if this was true. He doubted Rory was lying to him about something that would be easy to verify, but Kellan intended to verify it anyway. Maybe the marshal was innocent and had had no involvement with the dead prostitute and sex trafficking that Kellan's father had been investigating, but Kellan had always felt in his gut that there was a connection.

"If I find out anything else about Oswald or Eric, I'll call you," Rory said. There seemed to be some weariness in his voice now. "Keep Gemma safe," he added as he ended the call.

Kellan stared at the phone a moment before he looked at Gemma to get her take on that conversation. "You think Amanda and Rory could be playing a version of good cop, bad cop?" she asked.

"That's possible. Or maybe Rory just knows there's nothing he can say that will make me trust him. Not right now, anyway." Kellan tipped his head to the stairs. "Why don't you go ahead and get settled. I'll make a pot of coffee and start a deeper background check on Oswald."

This time, Gemma hadn't even had time to take a step before his phone rang again. Kellan thought it might be Rory calling to add something he'd forgotten. But it said Unknown Caller on the screen.

"Eric," Gemma said, pressing her hand to her heart and moving closer.

Since there was a high probability it was indeed Eric, Kellan hit the record function on his phone and took the call, again on Speaker. He didn't say anything though. He just waited for the caller to say something.

"Sheriff Slater?" a woman asked.

Definitely not Eric. "Who is this?"

"I can't stay on the line," she said without answering his questions. "Eric could find me."

That got his attention. "Eric's after you?"

"Yes, and I can't risk him finding me. He'll kill me, Sheriff Slater. He'll murder me like he did the others." Her voice broke, and she made a hoarse sob. "I need to get away, and I want your help to do that. I'll call you again."

"Tell me where you are, and I'll send deputies to you. I can keep you safe."

The woman only sobbed again. "I'll call you when I can," was her answer.

"Wait," Kellan said before she could hang up. "Who are you?"

"I'm Maylene Roth. God. Oh, God. I should have never trusted Eric."

And the line went dead.

Chapter Seven

Oh, God. I should have never trusted Eric.

Maylene's words went through Gemma's head, repeating along with the ache that pulsed at her temples. Actually, she was aching everywhere, but the pain in her head was making it especially hard to think. Still, she forced herself—again—to concentrate while she paced the floor of the guest room.

The woman had sounded terrified. And maybe she was. But it was just as possible that Eric had put her up to making that call and that anything she told them would be a lie to cover for him. After all, the medical report had said Maylene was *attached*.

She glanced at the door that she'd purposely kept slightly ajar. She'd done that in the hopes that if Maylene called back, then she'd either be able to hear Kellan's phone ringing or that he would come and get her. Since his bedroom was just across the hall, it wouldn't be a long trip for him to make.

But there'd been no phone ringing. No other whispered cop conversations like the earlier ones in the evening between Owen and Eli after he'd shown up to relieve his brother. There was only the dull, throbbing silence and the fatigue.

Gemma shifted her attention to the laptop on the nightstand. It was still running a probability program to help her narrow down possible locations for Eric. Even if it gave her results though, she wasn't holding out hope that it would be in any place where they could get to Eric in time to stop him from killing again. Still, they didn't have a lot of options.

Sighing and silently cursing, Gemma dropped down on the bed. Her legs were just too tired to keep pacing, something she'd been doing for the past two hours since she and Kellan had finally called it a day and put aside the investigation to get some rest.

As many steps as she'd taken, she was surprised she hadn't put ruts in the hardwood floor. She'd certainly put a huge dent in her already drained energy levels, and her body couldn't keep going like this. It was already past midnight, and she had to try to sleep.

As much as she dreaded the thought of it.

Maybe, just maybe, the dreams would give her some peace tonight.

Gemma snapped to a sitting position when she heard a phone ring, and she stood when Kellan came hurrying into the room. He had his phone extended for her to hear.

"Maylene," he said to the caller. "Where are you?"

"It's not safe. I can't tell you." The woman sounded even more terrified than she had before.

"If I don't get to you, Eric could kill you." In contrast, Kellan's voice was calm. Nothing calm about his face though. The muscles in his jaw were at war.

"Yes, Eric can kill. He killed that woman in Mexico."

That caused Gemma to go even closer to the phone, though she could hear Maylene just fine.

"What woman?" Kellan asked.

Maylene made the same sobbing sound she had with the earlier call. "He called her Caroline."

Gemma had thought she had steeled herself up enough to hear that. She hadn't. And she had to sit down on the bed. Kellan kept his cop's face, but Gemma knew that beneath his tough exterior, that had to hurt because of his brother Jack.

"I could end up like Caroline if I stay with him," Maylene went on. "That's why I have to get away from him. That's why I need your help."

"Just tell me where you are," Kellan insisted.

"I can't. Not until I'm sure it's safe, and I can't stay on the line in case someone's trying to trace this. I just want you to be ready when it's time for you to help me. I'll call you right back."

"No. Wait," Kellan snapped, but he was talking to the air because Maylene had already ended the call.

Kellan cursed, squeezed his eyes shut and then scrubbed his hand over his face. Gemma totally understood that frustration because it could be hours before Maylene spoke to them. If at all.

"Unknown number," he said, adding more profanity. "Even if Maylene's using a burner cell, she's not staying on the line long enough for me to trace it."

No, and Gemma doubted that was by accident. Maylene wasn't going to let them find her until she was ready for that to happen. Maybe that wouldn't be too much longer.

Kellan turned off the recorder function on his phone, walked closer to the bed and looked down at her. Well, actually he looked at her clothes. She was still wearing the same outfit she'd had on earlier. So was he, but his shirt was unbuttoned,

He took hold of her chin, angling her face to examine her eyes. "Will it do any good if I tell you to try to get some sleep?" he asked, but he immediately pulled back his hand and waved that off. "How are you holding up?"

Maybe this concern was part of the truce they'd reached. Or because he was worried about her having a panic attack that she'd warned him about.

Gemma considered saying that she was okay, but she wasn't that good of a liar. "My stomach is in knots because of what happened to Caroline. I'm scared for Maylene. For us. For anyone who crosses Eric's path. I'm upset. Tired. And…" She certainly hadn't meant to go quiet when she looked up at Kellan, but her attention landed on his bare chest.

Really? She was feeling this now? Gemma gave a hollow smile, a sigh and shook her head.

Kellan could have pretended he didn't know what she meant, but maybe he wasn't in the mood for lies, either. "Tempting," Kellan said. "But I think we both know if I put my arms around you right now, it won't stop there."

It wouldn't. The sex between them had been good. Darn good. And coupled with the spent adrenaline, fatigue and worry, it wasn't wise to add attraction to that mix. That's why it surprised her when he eased down on the bed next to her. Definitely not a good idea, but at least they were not face-to-face, no longer making that deep eye contact that only lovers could make. Instead, they were looking straight ahead.

He reached out again, this time not touching her

chin but running his thumb over her bottom lip. As much as Gemma knew she should stop this and guard her heart, she felt herself leaning right into that touch. She would have done more than lean, too.

If Kellan's phone hadn't rung.

He snapped away from her, his expression as surprised and frustrated as hers, and then Gemma saw Unknown Caller on the screen. As he'd done with the other calls, he hit the recorder before he answered.

"Sheriff Slater," Maylene said. She said something else that Gemma couldn't understand. That's because the woman was sobbing. "Meet me tomorrow at noon. Serenity Inn. Please come because that's where I plan to lure Eric. Kill him for me. Please. Before he kills all of us."

KELLAN TRIED TO shut out the chatter and noise in the squad room so he could volley his attention between the live feed from the surveillance camera at the Serenity Inn and the medical examiner's report for Oswald.

He'd printed out the report to free up his computer so he could use full screen for the surveillance camera. He wanted to see something—in either the report or at the inn. To find something. He wanted a blasted smoking gun that would give them Eric on a silver platter.

There sure as heck was nothing in the report or onscreen that would do that.

But maybe Maylene would come through for them four hours from now as she'd said. Maybe she could indeed lure Eric there at noon. However, it was just as possible that this was a trap or a wild-goose chase. Still, a trap could yield them Eric if they played this right.

Kellan had started the "playing right" by already

having three deputies in position near the inn. When it got closer to noon, he'd go out there, as well. Wearing Kevlar and armed to the hilt. And if he got lucky, this would all come to an end today.

He got up from his desk to pour himself another cup of coffee but decided against it. He was already a tangle of nerves, and coffee wasn't going to fix that. Nothing was, except for bringing both Eric and Maylene into custody.

Gemma looked at him when he sank back down behind his desk, and she raised an eyebrow. "What, eight cups is your limit?" she asked. She managed a slight smile to go with that.

"Trying to cut back." No smile for him, but it was light enough to ease just a bit of that tension.

The strain on her face wasn't easing anything though. Gemma had likely gotten as little sleep as he had, and she had passed on the coffee, making him wonder if she'd given up caffeine because it interfered with her usual meds.

Meds that she still hadn't taken.

Maybe once this situation with Maylene was resolved, he'd be able to coax her into taking not only the meds but also a nap. *Alone*. He made sure he mentally repeated that to his body.

His body didn't seem to be listening though. And that was the reason he forced his attention off her and back to the report.

"I got some more info on Maylene," she said, sipping the herbal tea that she's ordered from the diner. "She and Eric were classmates at an expensive private high school. Maylene flunked out."

Gemma turned the computer screen so he could see

a picture of Maylene when she'd been a teenager, and he mentally compared it to more recent ones that he'd pulled up from DMV records and high school transcripts. She hadn't changed much. A plain face with no makeup and straight brown hair.

"I can see if they actually had classes together," Gemma went on, "but it wasn't a large school."

So, the pair had known each other for a while and came from similar backgrounds. Well, other than the fact that Eric had never flunked out of anything and likely wouldn't have with his high IQ. But Maylene wasn't stupid. After all, she had a nursing degree, so maybe there was some other reason she'd left the school. Maybe that reason was Eric.

Kellan was still mulling that over when Jack came in, a tray of take-out cups in one hand and a huge box of doughnuts in the other. The box was open, and the deputies flocked to it like a mini-swarm, each of them snagging one or two as Jack said, "Help yourselves." Once they were done, he set the box on the small table where Gemma was working.

"Woman does not live by herbal tea alone." Jack flashed her a smile and plucked another cup of tea from the holder. "There's an apple fritter in there with your name on it."

He hadn't been joking about that. The apple fritter did indeed have a napkin placed over it, and Gemma's name was written on it.

"Thanks." She rose to brush a kiss on Jack's cheek.

Such a simple gesture caused Kellan's stomach to clench. He didn't especially want a chaste peck from Gemma, but it was a reminder that she no longer had that ease with him. No longer felt it was her right to kiss him whenever she wanted.

And vice versa.

"Is this some kind of bribe?" Kellan asked him when Jack put the coffee and drinks on the edge of Kellan's desk.

"No. Just lucky timing. As I was coming in, I saw Amanda pull into the parking lot. I figured a chocolate-glazed doughnut might make the visit easier to tolerate."

No. It wouldn't. And Kellan had one thought about the woman's visit—what the heck did she want now? He wouldn't have long to find out because at that moment, Amanda came through the front door, her attention going straight to him.

"If the subject comes up," Jack added, "Amanda pressed to become Gemma's handler. In fact, she called in a couple of favors to make sure it happened."

Interesting and not actually a surprise since Amanda seemed to have taken the duty personally and with more than the usual fervor. The question was, why had she done that? Was it because of Rory?

Jack glanced at the computer screen with the feed from the Serenity Inn. "Want me to keep an eye on that while you tell the marshal to go to hell?"

Kellan debated his options and nodded for Jack to take a seat behind his desk. "This won't take long. And don't let her see the screen." He glanced at Gemma to tell her the same thing, but she was already closing her laptop.

"I'm busy," Kellan snapped the moment Amanda came in.

She nodded, and there was none of the raw anger

that'd been on her face the previous day. In fact, the look she gave both of them seemed to be some kind of apology, but if so, Kellan wasn't going to buy her "good cop" act.

"This won't take long." Amanda turned her attention to Jack as if she might ask him to leave, but then she reached behind her and shut the door.

"I'm busy," Kellan repeated, his voice sharp.

She nodded but stayed put. "There are some things I need to tell you. Things that may or may not come up during your investigation."

Kellan hadn't thought there was anything the marshal could say that would allow this meeting to go on, but he'd been wrong.

Amanda dragged in a long breath, shoved her hands into her pants' pockets. "I volunteered to be Gemma's handler. That'll come out sooner or later."

"It already has come out," Kellan assured. He didn't ask her why, something he very much wanted to know, but instead gave her a moment to flick a glance at Jack.

Jack looked up from the computer screen and smiled at her.

Amanda's expression seemed slightly less apologetic when she shifted back to Kellan. Maybe because she thought revealing that detail herself would earn her some brownie points. It wouldn't, and Kellan made a circling motion with his finger for her to continue.

The marshal did, after another long breath. "Rory and I are lovers, but I suspect you already knew that."

Kellan tried not to look surprised, though Gemma's eyes widened. Jack obviously hadn't known, either, or he would have already spilled a tidbit like that.

"Yes, I let my feelings for Rory get in the way of

how I handled myself yesterday. I was angry that you *might* have a vendetta against Rory because of what happened to your father."

Her body language and the way Amanda had said that *might* let him know that she did indeed believe there was a vendetta.

"Is there a point to all of this?" Gemma asked. "Did you think if you stayed close to me that I'd tell you if Kellan found evidence to prove that Rory murdered the prostitute?" She was both impatient and tough.

Good. Kellan figured it was all an act, but he liked having the marshal taken down a notch. And no, it wasn't because of the power play that she'd tried to make by forcing Gemma back into WITSEC. It was because he simply didn't trust Amanda.

"Yes, there's a point," Amanda continued. "It's not about Kellan. It's not even about Rory." She paused, muttered some profanity. "It's about Eric."

Again, Amanda had surprised him. "What about him?" Kellan pressed.

Amanda didn't jump to answer, and her forehead bunched up. "First of all, I didn't withhold evidence. I wasn't even sure if it all connected." She paused before her eyes went to Gemma's. "I believe Eric murdered a dear friend of mine. Her name was Callie Wellman."

That obviously meant something to Gemma because Kellan saw the spark of recognition even as she shook her head. "Callie Wellman is a missing person I tried to link to Eric. I couldn't."

"Neither could I," Amanda said quietly.

Kellan knew there was a long list of missing women that the FBI, and obviously Gemma, had researched to try to find out if they were part of Eric's body count.

Kellan had studied that list, but there had been dozens of names, and he hadn't committed them to memory.

"Why do you think Eric killed her?" Kellan asked Amanda, and depending on how she answered, he'd decide if she'd withheld evidence.

Amanda took her hands from her pockets so she could drag one through her hair. "Callie told me that she'd met someone. He was a student at the college. She said he was some hotshot criminal justice guy and that she was going to meet him for coffee. That was two years ago and also the last I heard from her." Another pause. "She was...*is* like a sister to me."

Kellan wanted to point out that there were hundreds of criminal justice students, and that the odds were slim of it being Eric. But if Amanda had the instincts to go along with her badge, then this could be one of those unexplainable gut feelings that had pointed him in the right direction too many times to count.

Of course, that hadn't worked the night his father had been murdered.

Nor had it worked for Gemma when Eric was working right next to her.

"I'm sorry," Amanda went on, still talking to Gemma. "I became your handler so I'd get first dibs at finding Eric. I figured that eventually he'd try to come after you, and I could catch him."

A bad feeling immediately flashed through Kellan's head. "Did you leak the location of Gemma's WITSEC house so Eric would be able to get to Gemma?" He had to speak through clenched teeth.

There was steel and ice in Amanda's eyes when she looked at him. "No. Of course, not." It sure seemed as if she wanted to add more. Probably something that included some curse words, but instead she turned and stormed out.

Kellan would have gone after her, to grill her about that, but his phone dinged with a text message, and he saw it was from Gunnar Pullam, one of the deputies he had posted in the woods near Serenity Inn.

A woman just arrived in a four-door sedan. The license plates are smeared with mud. Can't confirm if it's Maylene or not, but she'll soon be in camera range.

Kellan hurried to the desk. Gemma, too, and along with Amanda, they looked at the camera feed. Despite the meeting still being three and a half hours away, a woman walked into view.

It was hard to see her face because she was wearing huge sunglasses, and her hair was tucked beneath a baseball cap. Actually, it was hard to see her body, too, since she was wearing baggy pants and a loose men's shirt.

With slow, cautious steps, the woman went closer to the inn. Closer to the camera, too, and when she looked up, Kellan had no doubt who this was.

It's Maylene, he texted to Gunnar. Kellan had studied the woman's picture enough to know her despite the attempts to hide her hair and face. "Hold your position, but stop her if she tries to leave."

"You're hoping she was able to lure Eric there," Gemma said in a hoarse whisper.

Kellan risked glancing at her. She certainly didn't look so strong and tough now, and that herbal tea didn't stand a chance against nerves like this. He would have liked to have given her some kind of reassurance, but Kellan had no idea how to manage that. Maybe, though, Eric would show up, and he could end this.

While he continued to watch the screen, Kellan took the Kevlar vest from the small closet behind his desk. That certainly didn't ease Gemma's nerves, but she had to have known that he would go there.

"What's your plan?" Jack asked him.

"You'll stay here with Gemma. I'll go to the inn and park nearby on that old ranch trail." No need to tell Jack which one because they both knew that area like the backs of their hands. "If Eric shows, I'll arrest him. If he doesn't, I'll arrest Maylene and get her to tell me where Eric is."

It was simple enough, but all three of them—and the deputies on scene—knew that plenty could go wrong.

"Keep your eye on Maylene and call me if there's any change in her position," Kellan added, and he headed for the door.

"Wait," Jack called out.

Jack motioned for Kellan to come back over to the computer screen. When he did, he saw Maylene looking directly up at the camera that was on the roof of the front porch.

Kellan cursed, expecting her to run, but she didn't. With her attention as fixed on the camera as he was fixed on her, she caught on to the bottom of her shirt and lifted it.

"Something's on her stomach," Gemma immediately said.

Yes, there was, and Jack used the computer keys to

zoom in on it. And Kellan soon saw the words written there in bold letters.

Don't come here. It's a trap.

OF COURSE, KELLAN went anyway.

From the moment Gemma had seen Maylene's message, she had known that Kellan would go to the Serenity Inn. There was no way he would stay tucked away in the sheriff's office while his deputies risked a trap by bringing the woman into custody.

Unlike Gemma.

He'd had no trouble tucking her away, and with a repeated warning for Jack to "watch her," Kellan and Owen had hurried out of the squad room. There'd been no verbal goodbyes, but Kellan had given her a quick glance from over his shoulder. Eye-to-eye contact. Coming from Kellan, it was almost as potent as a kiss.

Even after the cruiser was out of sight, Gemma stood in the doorway and tried to rein in her fears. Impossible to do, and she might have stood there indefinitely if she hadn't felt the hand on her shoulder. Jack. With the gentlest of touches, he eased her back into the office and shut the door. Probably so that she wouldn't be in the line of sight of the windows.

Only then did Gemma realize this could be a reverse trap. Eric and/or Maylene could have planned to get Kellan and as many deputies out of the building so that Eric or one of his henchmen could come after her.

"Anything new on the investigation?" Jack asked her. He immediately went back to checking the computer screen.

Gemma doubted there was something about the case

that he didn't already know. Well, with the exception of Maylene saying the body in Eric's car was Caroline's. But that info wasn't going to come from Gemma. That meant Jack's question was to distract her.

"No." She went to the computer to watch.

Maylene was still on the screen, but she was no longer looking up at the camera. She had moved to the side of the porch and had crouched down next to an overgrown shrub. Not exactly concealed, but at least she wasn't out in the open.

"Maybe she's waiting for Eric," Gemma said. Or she could just want it to look that way. Ditto for her "trap" warning. It could be real or just part of a sick plan to kill Kellan, and a Kevlar wasn't going to save him from a head shot.

With that thought eating away at her, the minutes crawled by, making her wish that she could hear the conversation on the police radio. If she did that though, she wouldn't be able to watch what was happening on the screen.

"If it bothers you to look at the place, you can wait on the other side of the room and I'll tell you what happens," Jack offered.

He was thinking that the inn would trigger the bad memories of her own shooting. And it did. But right now, it was triggering more concerns about the present than the past.

"I can do the same for you," Gemma said. "It has to bother you to see this place, too."

Jack made a sound of agreement. "I could say that about the entire town." He shrugged. "But home is home."

Yes, and despite everything that'd happened, she'd missed living here. Missed the people.

And she'd missed Kellan.

God, had she missed him.

She checked the time. Only three minutes had passed. But since the inn wasn't that far from town, it wouldn't be long now before Kellan and Owen got to the trail. After that, it would be a short walk to the inn itself.

"Are you still in love with Kellan?" Jack's question came out of the blue.

Gemma took her eyes off the screen a moment to flash him a flat look. "*Still?* That implies I was in love with him before things…well, just before."

"Yeah, it does. Are you still in love with him?" Jack flashed a cocky grin to go along with that repeated question, and Gemma wasn't sure if he truly wanted to know or if he was again trying to distract her. She suspected the latter.

The distraction wasn't working. Worse, the flashbacks were coming, and they were blending with the thoughts of Kellan being there. Of Maylene being there, too. Because if the woman was truly innocent and on the run from Eric, then she could be in grave danger.

Jack's phone dinged with a text message. "Kellan's on the trail and heading to the inn," he relayed after reading it. "Owen's about to call. He'll keep his phone on so we'll have audio."

His phone immediately rang, and even though Owen didn't say anything, she could hear the sounds he made while he moved. Could hear his already heavy breathing, too.

Gemma automatically moved closer to the screen. "Kellan and Owen will be coming from this direction?" she whispered, tapping all the way to the right.

"Probably. I doubt he and Owen will split up. They'll probably try to use the trees for cover until they make it to Maylene." Jack moved closer, too, until they were huddled together. "I couldn't tell if she was armed."

Neither could Gemma. Nor did she know if the baggy clothes were usual for the woman or if she was using all that bulk to hide a weapon. The way Maylene had hunkered down, she could have already drawn that weapon and been ready to try to use it on Kellan and his brother.

When her lungs started to ache, Gemma released the breath she didn't even know she'd been holding, and she got just a slight jolt of relief when she saw Kellan at the bottom of the screen. Owen was only about five feet away, and both of them were firing glances all around.

Maylene must have seen them, too, because she levered herself up just a little. She shook her head. Frantically shook it.

"Get down!" Maylene shouted.

That was the only warning Kellan and Owen got before the explosion ripped through the yard.

Chapter Eight

Kellan heard Maylene's shout, and he instantly dropped down into the shallow ditch on the side of the walkway that led to the Serenity Inn. Good thing, too, because the blast came just seconds later. It was deafening, the sound roaring through him; beneath him, the ground shook.

He immediately glanced over at Owen and said a quick prayer of thanks when he saw that his brother was shaken but okay. Now he had to make sure the same was true for his other deputies. And Maylene.

"I don't see anyone," Owen said, coughing from the dust and debris that the explosion had kicked up.

Neither did Kellan. Not even Maylene. Maybe since the woman had given them that warning, she'd managed to get away from the blast, but it was too risky for Kellan to go looking for her.

He made the calls to the deputies while Owen phoned for a bomb squad. God knew how long it would take them to get there, but in the meantime he could seal off the area as much as possible in case there was a second bomb.

"We're both okay," Kellan heard Owen say several

long moments later. *It's Jack*, he mouthed to let Kellan know who was on the other end of the line.

Kellan was about to curse when he realized the explosion would have been on the camera feed and Gemma would have seen it. But before he could get out a single word of profanity, his phone dinged with a text message. It was from Unknown Number.

You might want to check on Gemma, the message said. Poor thing. She's at your office with only a deputy and your brother to protect her. Think that'll be enough to stop me from getting to her?

Eric. The snake was going after Gemma.

"Come on," Kellan told Owen. His brother didn't question it. He just started running back toward their vehicle while Kellan barked out orders to the other deputies to secure the area and call the Texas Rangers for backup. Like the bomb squad though, the Rangers wouldn't be there for a while.

Kellan didn't have to tell Owen to keep watch. They both did. Because Kellan was well aware that this threat to Gemma could be a trap.

The moment they were back in the cruiser, Kellan got them moving while he stayed on the phone with Gunnar to spell out to the deputy that he didn't want him or anyone else going near the inn. Again, it could be another trap with yet more explosives. It was also the reason he'd turned on the security alarm for the cruiser before he'd ever started on the ranch trail. That way if Eric or someone else had tried to tamper with the vehicle, the alarm would have sounded.

"Jack knows there could be trouble at the sheriff's

office," Owen relayed when he finished the latest call with their brother.

Kellan didn't doubt that Jack would be ready, but he wanted to kick himself for letting things come to this. He should have anticipated that Eric would do something so he could try to get to Gemma. She was the target.

"Still no sign of Maylene," Owen added after reading a text that had almost certainly been sent by one of the deputies on scene. "But she could be under the debris."

Yeah. She could be dead. In fact, she probably was. Kellan didn't know the exact spot where the explosion had been planted, but it might have been impossible for Maylene to get away. And it wasn't hard to figure out why Eric would want her dead. The woman was just another loose end for him.

Thankfully, there was no traffic on the rural road that led into town, but Kellan didn't let down his guard. He continued to keep watch, along with sending up some prayers that he wouldn't be too late.

The miles crawled by, and it seemed to take an eternity before he finally reached the sheriff's office. Kellan braked to a quick stop, and with his gun still drawn, he hurried inside with Owen right behind him. He also hit the button on his keypad to activate the security on the cruiser. He didn't want anyone trying to tamper with it, and someone might try even though it was parked directly in front of the eyes of cops.

Kellan's heart skipped a couple of beats when he found the place empty, but then he spotted Jack peering out from his office. His brother was in there with

Deputy Clarie McNeal, and Kellan immediately knew they had positioned themselves in front of Gemma.

"No Eric and no hired thugs," Jack quickly let him know.

Kellan felt the jolt of relief, but it didn't last because he saw Gemma. She was pale and shaking. Ready to lose it. Jack and Clarie must have realized the same thing because they both stepped out, moving back into the squad room so that Kellan could go into his office. Before he could even get the door shut, Gemma launched herself at him, landing in his arms.

She didn't speak. Didn't cry as far as he could tell. Gemma just buried her face against his neck and held on. Now he felt the trembling even more. Her breath was coming out in short shallow bursts, and her heart thudded against his chest. Definitely not the concern of someone who was a casual friend, but there'd never been anything casual between Gemma and him.

"I'm all right," he assured her, because he had no idea what else to say. It wasn't enough. Nothing would be enough. "So are the deputies."

He eased back to finish the update about Maylene and maybe come up with the right thing to say, but Kellan made the mistake of meeting her eyes. He saw the tears she was blinking back and the concern—for him. But there was only a flash of that before the air changed between them, and his gaze drifted lower, to her mouth.

Hell.

They were practically wrapped around each other. Her breasts were pressing against him—which meant other parts of them were pressing, too. Not good with the emotions zinging around them. Especially not good with that whole change-in-the-air thing. Everything went still, as if waiting for something to happen.

And what happened was the kiss.

Before he could talk himself out of it, his mouth went to hers, not a gentle gesture of comfort. Not this. It was fast, hard and filled with heat and need. Much too hungry, considering they were both coming down from the shock of the explosion—and that they shouldn't be doing this.

Kellan mentally repeated that *hell* several more times, but he didn't stop. In fact, he made things worse by cupping the back of her neck so he could angle her and deepen the kiss. Yeah, he was stupid, all right. Stupid and worked up.

She made a sound that came from deep within her throat, not exactly from pleasure, either. It was need, raw and edged, and it knifed through him. Kellan was certain it was doing the same to her.

Her fingers, no longer trembling, pressed into his sides, gripping hard as they moved up his back and into his hair where she fisted a handful. Holding on to him. While the kiss raged on.

When she finally broke for air, Gemma kept her face against his, and he could feel the muscles of her forehead bunched up. Her breath gusted against his neck, and with a voice with hardly any sound, she said his name.

"Kellan."

He'd heard her say it that way before. It'd been on that slick rise of heat that came with sex. So much emotion. Too much, and she must have sensed that because she pulled back, putting some space between their bodies. Slowly, she released the grip that she had on his hair. Then her hand brushed across his shoulder and down the length of his arm before she stepped back.

"We can't pretend this doesn't matter," she whispered.

For just a handful of words, they packed a punch. And while they were true, Kellan figured this was the worst time possible for him to admit that he'd just crossed a huge line. She wasn't a job. Heck, maybe she never had been. But if he said that to her now, then he was going to have to tell her something else. That he was too involved with her to be objective, that he should turn her and this investigation over to someone else.

But that wasn't going to happen.

The truth was, even with the line crossed, he didn't trust anyone else. She kept staring at him, no doubt waiting for him to say that, but the moment ended when there was a knock at his door. Both knew this could be critical information, maybe even news of an impending attack. That's why Kellan quickly threw open the door, but it wasn't Jack, Owen or Clarie.

It was Rory.

Since Kellan was so not in the mood for this, he was ready to tell the marshal to get lost, but Rory spoke before he could say anything.

"I think I just saw Eric," Rory blurted out. The man was out of breath, and he put his hands on his hips as if steadying himself.

"Where?" Kellan snapped.

"He was just up the street. I was on my way here, and I saw a man in the alley next to that antiques store. I stopped, and the guy started running. I went after him, but he had too much of a head start on me." Rory shifted his attention to Gemma then. "I'm sorry. But it was Eric, and he was only a few blocks from here."

Kellan wasn't surprised, but he was riled. Not just because he'd figured Eric would come here but also because he hadn't gotten Gemma some place safe. There were too many buildings crammed onto Main Street. Too many places for Eric to hide and launch an attack. Heck, he wouldn't even have to get close to the sheriff's office because he could possibly get one of his henchmen to set explosives as he'd done at the inn.

"I can help you move Gemma if you like," Rory offered.

Kellan gave him a flat look. "No thanks," he said at the same time that Gemma simply said, "No." And she moved to stand next to him, arm to arm.

Rory nodded as if that were the answer he'd expected. "I do have something that might help with your investigation," he added a moment later. "Or it could be just white noise." He paused. "Your dead gunman, Oswald, was once lovers with Lacey Terrell."

Beside him, Kellan felt Gemma's arm muscles tighten. Kellan had a similar reaction. There was no need for Rory to explain who Lacey Terrell was. She was the dead prostitute Kellan's father and Dusty had been investigating at the time of their own murders. Dusty's top suspect was none other than Rory.

"Like I said, it could be white noise," Rory continued, "but knowing how Eric operates, he could have picked Oswald because he knew it would stir up the connection with Lacey."

That was possible, anything was when it came to Eric. The same might be true of Rory though.

Or Amanda.

If either of them had anything to do with Gemma's attack, they could have reasoned that using Oswald might make them look innocent. After all, they wouldn't be stupid enough to use someone who could go back to the very heart of Buck's and Dusty's murders. But, of course, Rory and/or Amanda could have done it to throw a monkey wrench in the investigation.

"I'll keep looking for any other connections to Oswald," Rory went on. He checked his watch. "I plan to call Lacey's friend Tasha Murphey and find out if she's recently seen or heard anything from Oswald."

Tasha Murphey was someone else who didn't need an explanation. That's because as Lacey's best friend, Kellan had interviewed the woman several times over the past year, but Tasha hadn't been able to give him anything new. Still, that didn't mean he was going to nix Rory talking to her. Even though Kellan didn't trust Rory, the marshal might uncover something they could use.

"Thanks for the info," Kellan told Rory, and he made sure his tone had a definite goodbye to it.

Rory got the message, though he did give one pleading look to her before she shook her head. The marshal finally walked away, and Kellan kept his eyes on him until he was out the door.

"Once we're sure that Eric's out of the immediate area, I want to move you back to the ranch," Kellan immediately told her. "You can say no, but—"

"I'm not saying no," she interrupted. "I don't want to stay here, not with Eric so close."

Good. They were on the same page, and Kellan motioned for Jack. "Rory said he spotted Eric up the street. He also told me that Oswald and Lacey were lovers."

That got a raised eyebrow from Jack. "You believe him?"

"Yeah. On both counts. That's why I'm taking Gemma back to the ranch. You're driving."

Jack nodded without hesitation. "What about Owen?"

"He'll stay here with Clarie." Kellan checked the time. "The Rangers should be here soon to help with the team out at the inn. Maybe help here, too. I'll alert the ranch hands to make sure everything is secure there."

Since the cruiser was still parked right by the front door where Kellan had left it, he motioned for Gemma to stay back while he went to the door. Jack came, too, and together they looked out, up and down the street. Most of the buildings were one-story so that helped, but Kellan knew there could be a gunman on one of the roofs. That's why he took several moments to check for any glints of metal or any other sign that something wasn't right.

"I'll get in the back seat with Gemma," Kellan told his brother.

That earned him another of Jack's famous raised eyebrows. Jack could carry on a good chunk of conversation with that particular expression.

"Keep that thought to yourself," Kellan grumbled.

Which, of course, only caused Jack to smile. The smile faded, however, when Kellan got Gemma moving. Jack suddenly became all lawman, and Kellan knew he'd do whatever it took to keep Gemma safe.

His brother went out first, unlocking the cruiser and getting it started. Kellan went next. He opened the door, rushing Gemma inside, all the while bracing himself for shots. But no one fired at them, thank God.

Jack took off, going in the opposite direction of the inn and where Rory had last spotted Eric, but Kellan had no way of knowing if they were heading toward trouble or away from it. That's why he kept watch, along with ignoring the glances Jack was giving him in the rearview mirror. His brother no doubt knew that things were heating up again between Gemma and him. Jack probably had some worries, too, as to how this would affect not only the investigation but Kellan himself.

Kellan was wondering the same thing.

We can't pretend this doesn't matter, Gemma had told him after that scorching kiss. And she was right. But dropping the pretense wasn't going to help when it came to keeping his focus.

"There's a truck ahead," Jack said, causing Kellan's attention to shift from the side window to the front windshield.

Kellan immediately saw it. An older model with the red paint blistered and rusted in places. It wasn't unusual for a truck to be out here. After all, this was ranch land, but it wasn't a vehicle he recognized. Plus, Kellan didn't like the way it was just creeping along, going a good thirty miles under the speed limit.

Jack didn't have a choice but to slow down. This was a road with plenty of curves and blind spots, and this stretch was the worst part of the trip. His brother couldn't risk a head-on collision by trying to pass the truck.

With his gun still in his hand, Kellan took out his phone and texted Owen to run the license plate. While he waited, Kellan glanced at Gemma to make sure she was okay, and in that glance he saw her eyes widen, causing his attention to snap back to the truck.

Hell. What now?

There was the flash of brake lights, the sound of tires screeching on the asphalt as the truck came to a stop. Jack hit his brakes, too. Almost immediately, the driver of the truck threw open his door, barreled out and ran toward the ditch.

"Get out of here now!" Kellan shouted to his brother.

But Jack was already doing that. He threw the cruiser into Reverse and hit the accelerator just as the driver scrambled into the ditch. Kellan didn't have time to figure out why he'd done that.

Because the blast tore through the truck.

Chapter Nine

Everything seemed to happen at once. The ear-splitting blast, immediately followed by the blazing pieces of the truck raining down on them and the road. The safety glass on the windshield held, but it cracked and webbed so that it was impossible to see.

"We got company," Jack belted out. He jammed on the brakes again, slamming all three of them in their seats.

Gemma's heart was already in her throat, already pounding, but that only got worse when she looked behind them and spotted the SUV. It, too, had come to a stop, not directly behind them but sideways so it was blocking the road. Two men got out, one from the front seat and the other from the back. Both aiming guns at the cruiser.

The first of the shots slammed into the glass.

Cursing, Kellan pushed her down on the seat. "Call for backup," he told Jack. "And if you can manage it from cover, keep an eye on the guy in the ditch."

Gemma certainly hadn't forgotten about him, but the full impact of what could happen hit her like a fist to the stomach. That man was no doubt a hired gun, and he could also start shooting, trapping them in the cross fire. It would take a while, but the bullets could soon rip the cruiser to shreds, and then she, Jack and Kellan would be killed.

That twisted away at her heart.

"It's me they want," she reminded Kellan. "I could try to negotiate with them and stop them."

Kellan gave her an icy glance that could have frozen the sun. "Not a chance. You're staying put."

He sounded exactly like the cop that he was, but Gemma wasn't giving up. She would do whatever it took to save Kellan and his brother. After all, they were only in danger because of her, and she had enough blood on her hands.

Gemma was ready to try again when her phone rang, and she saw Unknown Caller on the screen. She showed it to Kellan, hit the answer button and put the call on Speaker.

"Gemma," Eric immediately greeted. "In a bit of a fix, are you?"

She gathered every ounce of breath and courage that she could manage. "Call off your thugs."

Eric chuckled. "I think not. They're not done playing with you yet. Are you scared?" he taunted.

"Of course, I am. I'd be stupid not to be scared, but at least I'm not a coward…like you," she added a heartbeat later. "But then being brave was never your strong point, was it?"

Gemma knew that would hit a nerve. And it did. Definitely no more laughter from him, and she didn't need to see Eric's face to know there would be a flash of hot anger in his eyes.

"I don't need to be the one to actually pull the trigger to end you," Eric spat out. "Or your lover. How is Kellan, by the way?"

She hated her own flash of anger, hated even more that he could carry through on this. A coward's bullet could still be deadly.

Gemma looked up at Kellan, but he had his attention focused on the gunmen behind them. Jack's attention was ahead, and he automatically flinched when a shot blasted into the front windshield.

"That came from the guy in the ditch," Jack relayed.

So, the cross fire had begun.

"Kellan is fine," Gemma said to Eric. It was a lie, of course, but she refused to give Eric the satisfaction of knowing that he had just orchestrated her greatest fear. Not her own death. But Kellan's.

Eric laughed again. "I doubt that. Tell me, will you kiss him goodbye before he bleeds to death in your arms?" He didn't wait for an answer. "I told my men to save you for last. Wouldn't want you to miss anything."

With that, Eric ended the call.

If Kellan had any reaction to what he'd just heard, he didn't show it. His voice wasn't the only thing that was all lawman now. So was his expression and every iron-hard muscle in his body.

The shots continued, each of the bullets eating their way through what was left of the glass. Now, Kellan glanced at her. "Stay down," he repeated, and in the same breath, he made eye contact with Jack in the rearview mirror. "Hit the accelerator and aim for the men. When they scatter, I'll deal with them."

Gemma felt a new slam of fear, as she had no idea if it was a good plan or not. Maybe it was the only plan they had.

"No!" she said when Kellan lowered his window.

But he ignored her. "I'll take care of the one in the ditch first," he told Jack. "Move now."

Jack did. The tires on the cruiser squealed as it sped backward. She immediately heard the shouts from the men who'd been in the SUV. Shouts and more gunfire. Kellan didn't even look back at them. He took aim and fired, sending three shots ahead.

"Got him," Kellan growled.

Just as Kellan said that, she heard, and felt, the thud on the back of the cruiser. There was a screech of pain, and the shots stopped. So did Jack, but it was so he could throw the cruiser into gear and get them turned around. Kellan fired again, only one shot this time, and it was followed by his raw profanity.

"Want to go after him?" Jack asked.

Kellan shook his head. "No. Get us out of here. I'll send someone after him."

So, one of them had gotten away, but it was hard for Gemma to be sorry about that right now because of the relief flooding through her. Cautious relief. Because Eric could have set another trap for them along the way.

Kellan looked at her, their gazes connecting, and things silently passed between them. She could see that he was already blaming himself for this. She was doing the same, but apologies and reassurances would have to wait. He pushed the button to raise his window, and then he called Owen.

From the front seat, she heard Jack breaking more of the glass. No doubt because that was the only way he could see through the windshield. Once he'd done that, he sped up, hurrying them back toward town. She doubted Eric was still there, but Gemma prayed there weren't any other gunmen. With the shape the cruiser was in, they wouldn't have much protection against bullets.

"The Rangers will come out and assist," Kellan relayed to Jack once he'd finished his call with Owen. "I want them to take over processing this crime scene, too. And the one at the inn."

Good. She didn't want Kellan out in the open to do something like that. Also, the Rangers had more men and resources to get it done faster. Info gathered from those scenes could help them piece all of this together.

"Eric will use you to get to me," Gemma said to Kellan, but she had to clear her throat and repeat it because her voice cracked and was practically soundless.

"He'll use whatever he can," Kellan argued. "He's desperate, and that means he'll make a mistake."

She prayed that was true, but he'd literally gotten away with murder for too long. The best way to stop him would be to set some kind of trap, where she'd be bait, but she doubted it was the right time to bring that up to Kellan.

"You know the drill," Kellan said to her several minutes later. "Move fast and go straight to my office and stay away from the windows."

Yes, she did know, and while she was thankful they were all in one piece, it twisted at her insides to know that this wasn't the end.

The moment Jack stopped the cruiser, Kellan had her out and running through the door that Owen had already opened. Like Jack and Kellan, Owen also had his gun drawn, and there was plenty of concern on his face.

"We have a visitor," Owen told them the moment

they were inside. "I searched her and put her in the interview room."

"Who?" Kellan asked, taking Gemma by the arm so he could lead her into his office.

Owen dragged in a long breath before he answered. "It's Maylene, and she says that she can help you catch Eric."

KELLAN SUDDENLY HAD a dozen questions, but he started with the simplest one first. "You're sure it's Maylene?"

Owen nodded. "It's the same woman who was on the security camera footage from the inn. She's not hurt," he added, obviously anticipating what Kellan would ask next. "Just a few nicks and cuts on her face and hands. She refused medical treatment."

Kellan couldn't force her to see a doctor, but the minor injuries were a surprise. The last time he'd seen Maylene, she'd been plenty close to that blast.

"Please tell me you checked her for weapons," Gemma said. She was no longer shaking, not on the outside anyway, but Kellan figured she was about to have a whopper of an adrenaline crash. It certainly felt as if he was.

Owen nodded again. "And I have Clarie standing guard outside the interview room so that she doesn't try to leave." He volleyed glances at Kellan and Gemma. At Jack, too, who'd already moved across the room to start the string of calls and follow-ups that would need to be done. "Are all of you okay?"

"We weren't hurt," Kellan settled for saying. "I had to shoot two men. A third one got away."

"Yeah, Jack told me that when he called for backup.

The Rangers should be out at the scene any minute now. They'll look for him."

Kellan didn't doubt that, but finding the gunman probably wasn't going to happen. The guy had too much of a head start on them. But maybe they wouldn't need a hired thug if they had Maylene. Of course, there were no guarantees that the woman was actually there to help.

"How did Maylene get away from Eric and get here?" Kellan asked.

"She said she managed to run and hide until she thought it was safe to come out. Sam Willard gave her a lift. He picked her up when he saw her walking near his place."

That was possible. Sam's horse ranch wasn't that far from the inn, but it put a knot in Kellan's stomach to think that the elderly man could have given a lift to a killer. Or at least a killer's accomplice.

"While you were out, you got a call," Owen went on. "From Tasha Murphey. It's small potatoes in the grand scheme of things, but she said she needed to talk to you, that she was upset about Rory contacting her."

Kellan hadn't forgotten about Rory saying he would call Tasha about her possible connection to Oswald, but he didn't have time to deal with her now. Once he'd gotten what he could from Maylene, then he needed to figure out a safe way to get Gemma back to the ranch.

"I want to see Maylene," Gemma insisted. "I want to talk to her."

Kellan had been expecting this, and Gemma was no doubt expecting his response. "I can't let you sit in on the interview. You know that. It could compromise anything she says, and I don't want her slipping through any loopholes."

"Neither do I, but I need to see her," Gemma blurted out, but then she stopped and steadied herself with several deep breaths. When her eyes came to his again, she wasn't exactly calm, but it was better. "You'll have cause to hold her."

"Yeah," Kellan assured her. "At minimum she's a person of interest in the attacks. She's not going anywhere."

"Actually, I'd like to say the same for you," Owen spoke up, and he looked straight at Kellan. "Just minutes ago someone tried to murder you, and you had to kill two men. I don't think it's a good idea for you to try to interview a woman who might have had some part in that."

Kellan opened his mouth to argue with him. He was the sheriff, and it was his job, period. But then Owen made another glance at Gemma, and Kellan thought his brother might be telling him that he should be making sure that she didn't fall apart. She wouldn't. Stubbornness alone would keep Gemma on her feet, would keep her pushing in this investigation. But she was human, and soon, very soon, she was going to come down from the attack.

"You take the interview with Maylene," Kellan told Owen, "but I want to introduce myself, and I'll watch from the observation room."

"I'm watching, too," Gemma insisted.

Kellan didn't even try to nix that. Yes, there was a good chance that Maylene would say something to upset Gemma even further, but at least she would be with him so he could keep an eye on her. He doubted that Eric would send gunmen into the sheriff's office, but Kellan didn't plan on taking any chances. He didn't want to let her out of his sight. And no, it didn't have anything to do with that kiss.

He hoped.

Kellan stayed ahead of Gemma as they walked to the interview room, and when they reached it, Clarie stepped aside and went back into the squad room. Maylene immediately got to her feet, and Kellan saw the nicks and cuts Owen had mentioned. Her shirt and hair also had smears of dirt and soot.

"Sheriff," Maylene said, but she barely spared him a glance before her attention went to Gemma. "I'm so sorry."

Maylene's voice was barely louder than a breathy whisper, and she went to Gemma as if she might hug her or something. Kellan didn't let that happen. He stepped to the side, blocking Maylene from getting closer. The woman looked up at him, her shoulders slumping as if disappointed that he hadn't trusted her to get near Gemma.

"Deputy Slater will interview you," Kellan said, keeping his tone as official and as devoid of emotion as he could. That was hard to do though, since part of him wanted to get to the truth.

"I don't want to talk to your brother," Maylene protested. "I want to talk to Gemma and you." But it seemed to Kellan that she added him as an afterthought. "I can help you get Eric."

"So you said. How?" Kellan asked.

Maylene certainly didn't jump to answer. She pushed her hair from her face, made a low sobbing sound and pressed her hand to her mouth for a moment. "Eric wants me dead now. The explosion proves it."

No, it didn't. Eric could have had multiple reasons for setting that blast, and he wouldn't have cared what kind of collateral damage he caused. That included Maylene being blown to bits.

"Eric knows I betrayed him," Maylene said several moments later. "He won't forgive me for that. He'll try to kill me again, and when he does, when he comes after me, you can catch him."

"And how do you suggest that I make him come after you?" Kellan asked, but he immediately waved that off. Even if Maylene allowed herself to be used like that, it didn't mean she wouldn't be leading them into a trap. "Where's Eric?" he demanded.

She looked him straight in the eyes. "I honestly don't know. That's the truth," Maylene quickly added. "He doesn't trust me, and he's not going to tell me where he is."

"You were a fool to trust him," Gemma muttered. "So was I."

Maylene nodded. "And I regret it as much as you do. He'll kill us both if he gets the chance."

Finally, Maylene had said something that had Kellan in complete agreement. "Give your statement to the deputy," Kellan repeated.

"Are you arresting me?" Maylene asked before he could walk away.

"Have you committed a crime?" Kellan fired right back at her.

Maylene frantically shook her head. "Eric tricked me. I didn't know what he was. I swear I didn't. But I know now, and even though I haven't done anything wrong, I want you to arrest me. That will stop him from getting to me until I can figure out how we can catch him."

Kellan gave the woman no assurances of an arrest, protective custody or something else. That would be up to Owen, depending on what he learned in the interview.

He and Owen changed places in the doorway, and Kellan led Gemma to the observation room so they could watch behind the two-way glass. Thankfully, someone had put a chair in there because he immediately had Gemma sit.

"I'm okay," she said as if defending herself.

Kellan just gave her a flat look. "You're not. You look ready to collapse, but a chair is the best I can do right now. You want a drink of water?"

She shook her head, and he got a little suspicious when she dodged his gaze. When he shifted his position, he saw the reason she was avoiding eye contact. She was blinking back tears.

"Hell." He reached for her, but she moved away from him.

"Touching's a bad idea right now. A hug wouldn't stay just a hug."

True, and that was the only reason he didn't pull her into his arms. That and if he was holding Gemma, it would make it darn hard to concentrate on what Maylene was saying.

Which wasn't much.

The woman was still arguing that she wanted him and not Owen to do the interview. If she kept it up, Kellan would have to go back in there, but he was hoping

Maylene would settle down and spill whatever there was to spill.

When Kellan heard the footsteps in the hall, he stepped in front of Gemma again and put his hand over his weapon. No threat though. It was Clarie.

"We have another visitor," Clarie said. "Tasha Murphey."

Kellan groaned softly. Obviously, the woman hadn't waited for him to return her call which he wouldn't have done for a while. He'd wanted to deal with Maylene and the explosion before talking to Tasha.

"She said it's important," Clarie added, "but she's not here to see you. She claims that Maylene called her and told her to come. She's here to see her."

"Maylene?" he and Gemma said in unison.

Clarie shrugged and nodded. "If we play connect the dots, Tasha and Lacey were friends. Lacey was murdered but was also lovers with Eric's gunman Oswald. You think it's a coincidence that Tasha knows Maylene?"

There was an easy answer to this. No. It wasn't a coincidence, and Kellan headed toward the squad room so he could have a chat with Tasha.

Chapter Ten

Gemma didn't ask for permission to go with Kellan. She just followed him, and it didn't take her long to spot Tasha even though she'd never actually met the woman. Gemma had done a background check and saw photos of Tasha. She'd also read the statement she'd given to Kellan's father and Dusty when they'd been investigating Lacey's murder.

Tasha was still by the reception desk where Clarie had no doubt left her, and unlike Maylene she stayed put as if she wanted to be as close to the door as possible. With her police record for prostitution, theft and drug possession, it was highly likely that the woman wasn't comfortable in a police station.

Also highly likely that Tasha was still turning tricks.

Gemma hated to judge a person by their clothes, but Tasha's micromini leather skirt, bloodred cropped top and sex-against-the-wall heels definitely looked more suited for seedy bars and dark street corners than a *voluntary* visit to a small-town sheriff's office.

Jack was near the reception desk, too, but he must have sensed this conversation would go better without him, because he went into Kellan's office. He didn't shut the door though, and Gemma suspected he was not only listening but that he was also ready to come to back up if this visit turned bad.

"I called you," Tasha snapped the moment Jack was gone, and she aimed that comment and a stony look at Kellan. "Why did you set Rory on me?"

Kellan held his ground, giving her that cold cop's stare in return. "I didn't. It was his idea to get in touch with you so he could ask you about Oswald." He paused. "Do I need to clarify who Oswald is?" Now there was a touch of sarcasm in his voice.

"No. He was Lacey's man for a while." A muscle twitched in Tasha's heavily made-up jaw. Actually, several muscles were twitching, and the wild almost unfocused look in her eyes made Gemma wonder if the woman needed a fix. "But Rory would have known I didn't have anything on Oswald. He would have known I hadn't seen Oswald in months."

"And how would Rory have known that?" Kellan said.

"Because the marshals have been spying on me, that's why," Tasha said without hesitation.

Kellan went a step closer. "Why would they do that? And why would Maylene call you to come here?"

Tasha huffed as if the answer was obvious. It wasn't, and that's why Gemma stared at the woman. Tasha noticed the stare, too, and she narrowed her eyes.

"I know who you are," Tasha spat out. "You're spying on me, too?"

Gemma shook her head. "I have no reason to do that."

Tasha glanced around, then scrubbed her hand over her face, smearing her mascara and makeup even more than it already was. "I'm just punchy, that's all. Look, I don't want to get involved in this."

When she didn't add anything else. Kellan made a circling gesture with his finger to indicate he wanted her to continue.

"Maylene," Tasha clarified after more of those glances around. "I don't want to get involved with her."

"How do you know her?" Kellan pressed.

Now there was some hesitation, and Tasha chewed on her bottom lip before she went on. "We grew up together. Our mothers were friends. And no, I don't want a lecture about squandering away my life and not living up to potential."

Gemma knew that Tasha's parents were wealthy, but she certainly hadn't come across any connection between Maylene and her. Of course, she hadn't been looking for that, not with so many other threads of information to investigate.

"Eric and you grew up together, too?" Gemma asked.

"No." Tasha couldn't say that fast enough. "Maylene met him when she went to the private high school. By then I was…on a different path."

Yes, to juvie for drug possession and shoplifting, followed up by repeated trips to rehab. "Maylene and you have stayed in touch though," Gemma pointed out.

Tasha lifted her shoulder. "She only calls me when something's wrong." She rolled her eyes, huffed. "Well, I've got my own problems, and I want you to get Rory and the marshals off my back." Her voice got louder with those last words, and she directed her anger at Kellan.

Kellan studied her a moment. "What do you think the marshal wants with you?"

Again, Tasha made an "isn't it obvious" sound. She opened her mouth, closed it, and she was clearly trying to figure out how much, or how little, to say. When her gaze came back to Kellan's, there was some fire in her eyes.

"Get Rory and that she-bitch marshal off my back, and I'll tell you," Tasha bargained.

"You mean Amanda?" Kellan questioned. "What does she have to do with this?" he included when Tasha nodded.

"Amanda would do anything to protect her man, wouldn't she?" Her expression was both cold and flat. "They're lovers. You know that."

Kellan didn't deny it, but he did take a couple of seconds before he responded. "I'll call Rory and Amanda and tell them not to contact you again."

"I want more." She aimed her red polished finger at Kellan. "I want you to threaten Rory and his marshal cronies. I want you to do whatever it takes to get them to back off. I mean *really* back off. I don't want them following me or prying into my life."

That was a whole lot of emotion in her voice, and Gemma didn't think it was her imagination that the woman was scared. Maybe she had a reason for that if Rory and Amanda were dirty.

"All right," Kellan finally agreed. "I have plenty of friends who are Texas Rangers. I'll have them work through some of their contacts and make sure Rory or any other marshals don't hassle you again. Now, tell me why it's so important that I do this?"

Tasha took her time answering. "Because I don't want to end up dead like Lacey."

Gemma and Kellan exchanged glances. "You think Rory or the marshals had something to do with that?"

A burst of air left her mouth, a sick laugh that wasn't from humor. "You're a cop. You figure it out."

"It'd be easier to do that if you tell me why you're so afraid." Kellan's voice wasn't so sharp now, and he stooped down a little to be on the same eye level as Tasha. "Has Rory ever threatened you?"

"No." Tasha glanced away again, looking at everything but Kellan. "He wouldn't have to. I know that tangling with him could get me killed."

Tasha turned as if she might walk out. Or rather might try to do that. Gemma was certain Kellan wasn't going to let her go. He stepped forward, but Tasha whirled back around.

"By the way, you didn't hear this from me, and if you press it, I'll deny I said it," Tasha added, her hard eyes now drilling into Kellan's. "But Rory was having sex with Lacey. No, not just sex," she amended. She blinked back tears. "Lacey was in love with him, and I think… I *thought* he had feelings for her, too."

Gemma choked down the groan that nearly escaped from her throat and then reminded herself that this could all be the delusions of a drug addict. Or a flat-out lie. But those tears that slid down Tasha's face certainly looked like the real deal.

Kellan didn't have much of a reaction, either. There was only a slight change in his lawman's expression. "When did this affair happen?"

Tasha glanced away again. "It was still going on right up until the time Lacey was murdered."

Now there was a change in Kellan. He cursed under his breath. "You have proof?"

"Nothing that a cop would call proof, but Lacey told me, and I believe her. She had no reason to make up something like that, and I could see her feelings for him. It's hard to hide it when you love someone that much."

That hung in the air for several uncomfortable moments.

"Does anyone else know about this?" Kellan asked.

Tasha lifted her shoulder. "Maylene found out. I'm not sure how, but she thought you should hear about it. Lacey didn't spread it around, because she didn't want to hurt Rory. She knew something like sleeping with a confidential informant could cost him his badge."

It could, but it could do more than that right now. It could cost him his freedom if he was arrested. And that could happen. Well, it could if Tasha was telling the truth, because as a minimum it would mean that Rory had withheld evidence in a murder investigation.

"Was Lacey afraid of Rory?" Kellan went on.

"No." Tasha didn't hesitate. She blinked and stared at him. "You don't get it, do you?" Tasha shook her head. "It wasn't Rory who killed her. I can't prove it, but it was Amanda who killed Lacey."

KELLAN COULDN'T IGNORE his dull, throbbing headache any longer. As soon as he finished his shower and dressed, he popped two ibuprofens and chased them down with water that he drank straight from his bathroom faucet. A good night's sleep would no doubt do more than the pills, but he figured the best he would be able to manage was some catnaps.

It was Amanda who killed Lacey.

Those were the words that kept going through his head, and they sliced through with the images of Gemma's too pale face and her fear when they'd been under fire in the cruiser. He'd seen more of that fear when he and Clarie had finally driven Gemma back to the ranch. This time without incident, thank God. He doubted though that their safe arrival at his house would help her sleep any better than he would.

No.

And he'd gotten proof of that before his shower. That's when he'd heard her stirring in the guest room across the hall. Pacing was his guess. Worrying. Trying to figure out what they were going to do now that they had not one but two marshals as suspects.

Jack would help them with that. *Was* helping, Kellan silently amended. Shortly after Tasha's bombshell, Jack had driven back into San Antonio so he could start looking into the woman's allegations.

His brother wouldn't take the bull in the china shop approach. Jack would use some of his charm and finesse to try to get to the bottom of it, but word would eventually get back to Rory and Amanda that Jack was asking questions. And if they didn't get wind of it, the pair would soon know when Kellan dragged their butts in for questioning. Just because a person wore a badge, it didn't put them above the law, and in this case, those badges could have been the reason his father and Dusty were murdered.

One of the reasons, anyway.

Eric could have been solely responsible, and since the snake was still at large, that meant yet more precautions had to be taken. Maylene was in a holding cell at the sheriff's office, officially as a material witness, but if the woman was telling the truth about being on the run from Eric, then she had a Texas-sized target on her back.

Tasha probably had a target on her, too, but she'd refused protective custody. She'd also refused to stay at the sheriff's office after telling him about Amanda. Probably because she didn't trust him. Or any other cop for that matter. Now he needed to figure out if Tasha was lying…or if she'd just blown his investigation wide-open. To do that, he'd need to bring the woman back in for a full interview, but first he wanted to see how far Jack could get with this through his own sources.

Still toweling his hair dry from his shower, Kellan came out of his bathroom and stopped. Gemma was obviously no longer pacing in the room across the hall because she was now sitting on the foot of his bed. Her hands were in her lap, one of her bare feet tucked behind the ankle of her other, and the long look she gave him held far more interest than it should have.

"I started to call out to you to let you know I was in here," she said. "Just in case you were going to walk out here naked."

Well, he wasn't naked, but he wasn't fully dressed, either. He'd pulled on jeans and a shirt, but the shirt wasn't buttoned, and his jeans weren't zipped the whole way. He didn't fix that now because it seemed like closing the barn door after the horse was already out. Besides, Gemma had seen him all the way naked before.

And he had also seen her without a stitch of clothes.

Probably not something he should recall right now, especially not with such detailed memories of all the interesting parts of her. The most interesting though, was that face, but he had no intentions of admitting it.

"I didn't come in here for sex," she added a moment later.

Man, she had a way of off-balancing him. She always had. "Did you need to borrow my toothbrush?" he asked, just to try to keep things light. But it was a losing battle because being light didn't stand a chance around them.

"I, uh, just didn't want to be alone." Gemma frowned and then glanced away from him.

Yeah, he got that. He didn't especially want that, either, but it wasn't exactly safe having them together like this. No bullets flying. No open laptop, jammed with the details of the investigation. No other people in the room.

And then there was the bed.

It was a huge temptation, but that didn't stop Kellan from going to her and sinking down next to her. "Will you get some sleep if I'm in the bed next to you?" he bargained.

"Maybe." Her gaze came back to his and then slipped lower to his chest—which she had no trouble seeing because his shirt was still unbuttoned. "No," she amended. She plowed her hands through the sides of her hair and groaned. "I honestly didn't come in here for sex. We never had that kind of relationship, and I couldn't use you like that. No friends with benefits for us."

No. Neither one of them was the casual-sex type. There'd been feelings and emotions. There'd been lots of caring for each other. And that had all gone to hell in a handbasket after his father's murder and her nearly dying.

"I could give you a pass and just say—use me," he joked. Well, it wasn't completely a joke. Kellan was sure the smile that he flashed didn't quite make it to his eyes.

Her smile didn't make it to her eyes, either. She stared at him as if trying to figure out what to do, and then she surprised him when she lifted her top. Not in some "come and get me" sexual gesture. She only exposed her stomach.

Which was plenty enough.

The scars were there. The ones from her surgery to remove the bullets that Eric had fired into her.

"I just need to get this out in the open," she said, studying him. "I need to see in your eyes that this isn't going to keep tearing us apart."

Kellan wasn't sure what she saw when she looked at him, but he seriously doubted it was an expression that could make her believe the scars didn't matter. They did. They mattered *a lot*. Not because they marked her otherwise perfect body. He could deal with that, but he would always know that he'd been unable to stop it from happening.

"Yes." Her voice was a whisper now, and she looked away. "Eric got past you to do this, and he got past me to kill God knows how many people. Maybe your father. Maybe Dusty. But even if he didn't kill them, there are plenty of others, and I didn't stop it."

She blinked hard, and Kellan knew the tears were just seconds away from falling. Knew, too, the risk of pulling her into his arms, but he did it anyway, and he brushed a kiss on her forehead. That was possibly the biggest mistake he could have made. Because a gentle kiss like that wasn't fueled by heat but by the very emotions that had first landed them in bed for the noncasual sex.

"Is this too much for you?" she asked, her voice shaking.

"It will be if you put your hand inside my shirt." Kellan thought he did a better job of smiling that time, because she laughed.

Gemma eased back, their eyes connecting. "I know your hot spots, and this isn't one of them." She eased her hand to his arm and gripped lightly.

She was wrong. Every part of him was ready to be aroused right now. Even that arm she touched. But she was right about knowing the prime ones.

"You used your profiling skills on me when you found my hot spots," he reminded her. It was stupid to discuss this with her, with the air starting to crackle between them and that shimmer on her face. "You identified possible target areas, then narrowed them down by trial and error."

Even the "errors" had felt darn good.

She made a sound of agreement, lifted her shoulder, and he was glad using the word *profiler* hadn't put the shadows back in her eyes.

Gemma reached up, brushed her fingers against the base of his ear. "Here."

Yeah, that would indeed become a hot spot if her mouth got involved in this. Kellan considered just letting her take this to the next level. That's what his body wanted him to do, but he knew his body rarely made good decisions about this sort of thing. That's why he gave her another of those chaste kisses. This time on her cheek. Then, he gathered her into his arms and moved her farther up the bed and to the pillows.

"I want you to get some sleep," Kellan said. "Let's see if we remember how to spoon."

Her eyebrow came up, letting him know that spooning wasn't going to do squat for this ache that was spreading through both of them. But it might give her a chance to get some much-needed rest. He'd rest better, too, knowing that she was right there in case something went wrong. Well, he would rest better that is if he managed to forget that this was his former lover next to him.

Kellan risked pulling her against him, her back to his front, and he felt the immediate protest from that stupid part of him that wanted this to be a whole lot more. Before he could even have an argument with himself, his phone buzzed, and just like that, he went on full alert when he saw Jeremy Cranston's name on the screen. Jeremy was not only one of his top hands, Kellan had put him in charge of security for the ranch.

"Boss, I'm by the cattle gate, and I think you need to get out here and check this out," Jeremy said the moment that Kellan answered. "A woman just came walking up the road, and before she passed out, she insisted on seeing you." He paused. "She had a gun, but I took it from her."

That was not what Kellan had been expecting to hear. "A woman? Did she say her name was Tasha Murphey?" If so, she could be in danger.

"No, sir. This woman claimed she didn't know what her name was, but I sure know it." Jeremy paused. "Boss, it's Caroline Moser, the woman we all thought was dead. But she's alive, all right. Well, for now anyway. I've already called for an ambulance, but you need to get down here fast because I think she's hurt real bad."

Chapter Eleven

Gemma was plenty close enough to Kellan to hear exactly what his ranch hand had said. The shock hit her first and then the words sank in.

"Caroline," Gemma repeated. "She's hurt. I need to go to her." And she would have run out the bedroom door if Kellan hadn't stopped her.

"This could be a trap," Kellan calmly reminded her. He kept hold of her hand while he continued to speak to Jeremy. "You're positive it's Caroline?"

"Yes, sir. I've seen her plenty of times when your brother used to bring her here to the ranch."

Jack had indeed brought Caroline here, because they'd been in love. But then Eric had taken Caroline hostage, and no one had seen her for the past year. Maylene had told them about the body in Eric's car, but if Caroline was here, that meant she was very much alive.

But maybe not for long.

"How bad is she hurt?" Gemma blurted out. "Has she been shot?"

"I don't think so," Jeremy answered. "She's got a bunch of cuts and bruises all over her, like somebody beat her up, and she was talking, well, crazy before she passed out. Something's wrong, no doubt about that. Should I put her in my truck and drive her up to your house?"

"No. Don't move her. I'll come down in the cruiser."

"I'm going with you," Gemma insisted the moment Kellan ended his call.

He let go of her so he could put on his boots and holster, but he looked at her, his mouth set in a hard line. She knew he was about to tell her no, that he wanted her to stay safely tucked away while he took all the risks.

"Please," Gemma added. "Caroline's my friend. I'm the reason Eric kidnapped her." And God knew what the monster had put her through if he'd actually had her all these months.

Kellan stared at her, huffed, and then he nodded. Gemma didn't give him a chance to change his mind. She hurried across the hall to the bedroom, put on her shoes and then raced down the stairs right behind him.

"Clarie, you'll drive us," Kellan told his deputy once they'd reached the foyer. "Gemma will stay in the cruiser with you while I see what's going on down at the cattle gate."

Kellan had to disengage the security so they could leave without setting off the alarms, and then he rearmed it when they were on the porch. Probably because he didn't want anyone using this as a chance to sneak in the house while they were gone. But if that was the plan, then Caroline wasn't in on it. No way would she help Eric. Well, unless Eric had managed to brainwash her or something.

Gemma quickly pushed that thought aside.

No need to borrow trouble when they already had

enough of it. It was best just to speak to Caroline and try to figure out what was going on.

It was already past midnight, but there were plenty enough security lights on the property that Gemma saw the three trucks that were by the cattle gate that stretched across the road. Clarie pulled right in the middle of the other vehicles, probably so that Gemma would have even more protection. A sniper would have to get through lots of metal to get to her.

"Stay here," Kellan warned Gemma. He drew his gun and stepped out, walking toward the trio of hands who were crouched down around the woman who was lying on the ground.

Gemma moved to the edge of her seat, and thanks to the cruiser headlights, she saw her. Her heart slammed against her chest and her breath went thin.

God, it *was* Caroline.

But Jeremy had been right about the cuts. There was blood on Caroline's too pale face, and she was moving her head from side to side, the way a person did when they were in pain.

"Put down the window for me," Gemma instructed Clarie. Gemma couldn't do it herself because the windows and locks were controlled from the front.

Clarie obviously wasn't happy about that, but the deputy knew that Caroline was Gemma's friend. That's probably why she lowered the window just a fraction.

"Caroline?" Gemma called out to her.

Caroline's eyes went wide, and when she looked at the men surrounding her, she tried to scramble away from them. Kellan stopped her from doing that by taking hold of her arm.

"Stay away from me," Caroline yelled on a gasp. "I'll hurt you if you touch me."

Gemma pressed her fingers to her mouth. Mercy, she sounded terrified, and Caroline was certainly in no shape to fight back. Kellan moved back from her, and the other hands didn't touch her. However, they did corral her in with their bodies so that she couldn't run.

"Who are you?" Caroline asked, volleying wild glances at them.

"You know who I am." Kellan kept his voice calm. "I'm Sheriff Kellan Slater. You came here to see me, remember?"

Her eyes widened again, and while her gaze fired all around, Caroline shook her head as if baffled by that. When she moved, Gemma could see what appeared to be a scar on her head along with some fresh bruises. It was possible Caroline had some kind of injury that was affecting her memory.

"She had this in her pocket with the gun," Jeremy explained, and he passed a piece of paper to Kellan.

Kellan looked at the note and then held it so that Caroline could see it. "You have my name written here. See, it says Sheriff Kellan Slater."

Not simply Kellan. That caused the knot in Gemma's belly to go hot. Because Caroline wouldn't have used his title. Kellan was her friend, and she would have called him by his first name.

"Why did you want to see me?" Kellan asked Caroline. "Where have you been all this time? And where's Eric?"

Each question seemed to confuse Caroline even more, and she looked on the verge of panicking until her attention landed on Gemma. "Help me, please," Caroline said to her.

"Unlock this door," Gemma ordered Clarie.

Clarie muttered some profanity, but she didn't disengage the locks until Kellan gave her the go-ahead nod. As soon as she had the door open, Gemma scrambled to her.

"You'll be okay," Gemma assured her. She took Caroline's hand and tried not to react to all the injuries she was seeing on her friend. She stayed quiet a moment, giving Caroline some time to settle. "What happened to you?" Gemma asked.

Caroline opened her mouth, closed it, and this time when she shook her head, it wasn't a frantic, panicked motion. There was confusion and pain, and a hoarse sob tore from her mouth.

Clarie hurried to the cruiser and came back with two plastic evidence bags. One for the note and one for the gun that Jeremy had taken from Caroline. Gemma took a quick look at both. She didn't recognize the gun, but the writing on the note appeared to be Caroline's. It had not only Kellan's full name and title but also his address—an address that Caroline knew well. Or at least she had a year ago. She shouldn't have had to write it down.

"Can you tell us anything about what happened to you?" Gemma whispered to her.

"I don't know," Caroline said. "I don't know." She just kept repeating those three words while she collapsed into Gemma's arms.

In the distance, Gemma heard the ambulance siren, and she knew she only had a couple of minutes before the medics whisked Caroline away. It was obvious her friend needed medical attention, obvious, too, that she'd experienced some kind of extreme trauma, but Gemma knew this might be her last chance to say anything to Caroline before the doctors, and then Kellan, took over. Kellan was going to want to question her.

"I'm so sorry," Gemma told her. She felt the tears threaten, and she tried to blink them back. "I didn't see Eric for who he was. How bad did he hurt you?"

Caroline pulled her hand away from Gemma and studied her. Or rather she tried. From the rapid blinking of her eyes, she could tell Caroline was having trouble focusing. "I know you?" she asked, and yes, it was a question.

Gemma nodded. "We're friends."

There was nothing on Caroline's battered face to indicate she believed that. "Someone wants me dead. Is it you?" This time it was a question, and it was aimed at Kellan.

He tapped his badge. "I'm a cop, and no, I don't want you dead. I want to protect you."

Again, there was no hint that Caroline believed him. The stare she gave him was long and hard, but her gaze fired away when the ambulance turned onto the ranch road and came toward them. Gemma expected Caroline to fight the medics as she'd done with Kellan and the hands, but she kept her attention on Kellan while they put her on a gurney and then into the ambulance.

"I want to go to the hospital with her," Gemma told Kellan.

"Not in the ambulance," he said as if he'd been expecting her to make that demand. "We'll follow it to the hospital." He took her by the arm and got her in the cruiser, and as soon as the ambulance took off, Clarie pulled out right behind it.

Gemma tried to keep it together, but this time when the tears threatened, she wasn't able to hold them back. Nor was she able to stop the sound in her throat when the sob broke.

"No, you're not responsible for this," Kellan snapped. His voice was tough, all cop, but he was gentle when he wrapped her in his arms.

But she was responsible, and just like that, all the memories came flooding back. Not just of Caroline's kidnapping but her own shooting. And Buck's and Dusty's murders.

"Once she heals, Caroline will be able to give us answers," Kellan said. "She saw things that went on that night."

Yes, she had. In fact, Caroline was their best bet at finding out the truth, but Caroline's repeated words came back to haunt Gemma.

I don't know.

Kellan eased her away from him. "I need to call Jack."

Gemma's stomach tightened because she knew it would be a mixed bag. Jack would be beyond relieved that Caroline was alive, but it was going to crush him when he saw her injuries. He would blame himself for not being able to protect her.

Kellan took out his phone. However, he almost immediately tossed it aside and drew his gun. Gemma felt the instant punch of adrenaline, but it was dark and she didn't know what had put that alarm all over Kellan's face.

Then she saw the SUV.

It was parked on the side of the road with its lights off. It didn't stay that way. Once the ambulance sped past it, Gemma heard the roar of the engine.

And the SUV came right at them.

"LOOK OUT!" KELLAN shouted to Clarie.

His warning hadn't come in time, but thankfully Clarie jerked the steering wheel to the right to avoid a head-on collision.

The SUV still bashed into them though, ramming into the side of the cruiser. The slash of metal against metal, and the impact was enough to send them exactly where Kellan didn't want to go.

To the ditch.

He could tell from the way the cruiser sank that their tires on the passenger's side were now bogged down. Clarie threw the cruiser into Reverse, trying to get them out, but Kellan wasn't holding out hope that would happen. After all, the SUV hadn't gone in the ditch with them.

"Call Owen and tell him what's happening. Then, call Jeremy," Kellan said, passing Gemma his phone. "I need their help. Tell him I want the hands to approach with caution."

That last reminder was a necessity because Kellan figured this was going to be another attempt to kill them. Later, he'd curse himself for that and try to figure out if Caroline had been bait to draw them out. If so, it'd worked because here he was on an open road with Gemma once again in danger.

Beside him, Gemma made the calls, and while Kellan knew that Jeremy and the others would come right away, it would still take about five minutes for them to get there. Too long, and he doubted whoever was in the SUV would wait that long to make a move.

He was right.

The SUV turned around and came at them again from behind, ramming into the driver's side door again. It was the only saving grace in this. Gemma was on the other side of the cruiser, and if bad turned to worst, she could be able to get out and take cover in the ditch. In case that happened, he passed her his backup weapon.

In the near darkness, her eyes met his. She was scared, of course, but he saw a whole lot more. "If they get past us, they could go after the ambulance." Her voice was a ragged whisper. "They could kill Caroline."

Yeah, and Kellan figured that was the plan. Of course, there could be other hired thugs waiting ahead to intercept the ambulance. That's why he'd wanted Gemma to call Owen. His brother would respond from the other direction and might be able to stop another murder from happening. In the meantime, Kellan had to do the same here.

"Get down on the floor," he told Gemma when the SUV started turning around, no doubt to come at them again. It'd be an attack from the front this time. "Clarie, lower my window."

Both Gemma and the deputy did as he ordered, and Clarie put down her window, too. She'd obviously given up on getting out of the ditch and took his cue about trying to stop whomever was behind the wheel of the SUV.

When the SUV sped forward, Clarie ducked down so that it would give Kellan a clear shot, but the deputy fired, too. Together, they sent double rounds straight into the SUV windshield, cracking the glass into a spiderweb, and then they immediately pulled back when the SUV crashed into them. The SUV stopped, side by side with the cruiser.

The moment seemed to freeze.

Kellan could see the driver. The bulky shouldered guy had blood on his head, but his hands were firmly on the wheel. But it wasn't the driver that caused the moment—and Kellan's heart—to stop. Judging from Gemma's gasp, she saw it, too. Their reactions were for the man in the back seat.

Eric.

Kellan certainly hadn't expected Eric to be personally involved in an attack, but it was him, all right. He'd seen that face enough in his nightmares. However, Eric wasn't sporting his usual cocky grin.

He looked…afraid.

But that couldn't be right. Eric wasn't the *afraid* type, but Kellan didn't have time to consider what else might be on the killer's mind. That's because the driver let go of the wheel and drew a gun. Someone on the other side of Eric, someone who Kellan couldn't see, thrust a gun into Eric's hand, too.

Kellan didn't let either of them get off any shots. "Take out the driver," Kellan barked to Clarie, and she fired, her bullets slamming into the man.

But not killing him.

Groaning in pain, the man hit the accelerator.

All of that happened in the blink of an eye. Kellan had already taken aim at Eric, and he double tapped the trigger.

Just as Clarie's shots had done, the bullets crashed through the passenger's side window, and Kellan didn't miss, either. Before the SUV sped away, the last thing Kellan saw was the blood as Eric slumped back on the seat.

Chapter Twelve

Gemma was doing everything possible to rein in her emotions. Kellan already had enough to worry about without being concerned she might fall apart. She wouldn't, but it was going to take an effort to tamp everything down.

Caroline was being examined so Gemma didn't know how bad things were with her friend, but even if she made a full physical recovery, it didn't mean she would be okay. But she was alive, and Gemma latched on to that as a much-needed silver lining in all of this.

She took several long, steadying breaths while she sat in the private waiting room of the Longview Ridge Hospital. Kellan wasn't sitting though. He was at the door, keeping watch, while he was talking on the phone with a Texas Ranger who was in pursuit of Eric and the men in the SUV.

Well, hopefully he was in pursuit.

Maybe the Ranger had even managed to capture them. Or better yet, maybe Eric was dead.

Gemma had seen the blood and the shock on Eric's face after Kellan had shot him. What she hadn't seen was the last flicker of life as death claimed him. And since Eric was like a cat with nine lives, he might have figured out a way to survive two bullets to the chest. After all, she'd survived three.

Kellan ended his latest call, but when he didn't turn to her right away, she knew the news wasn't good. "The Rangers didn't find Eric," she said.

Now he turned sideways so that he could keep watch in case anyone came up the hall toward them. "Not yet. They're calling in another team to help them. In the meantime, I'll keep a deputy with Caroline."

Yes, because if Eric was indeed alive, he might try to kill her. Of course, it was possible that Caroline had served his purpose by drawing Gemma out—a thought that sickened her. It would sicken Caroline even more if and when she realized that was what had happened.

Gemma stood when she heard the footsteps. Her first thought was this was the doctor, coming to update them, but the person was running, and since Kellan didn't draw his gun, she figured it wasn't a threat.

It was Jack.

"I want to see Caroline," Jack immediately blurted out. "Where is she?" His breath was gusting, and there was a sheen of sweat on his face.

"You can't see her. Not yet." And as Kellan had done to Caroline earlier, he took hold of his brother's arm.

Jack cursed, slung off his grip and started back down the hall. Kellan only sighed and motioned for Gemma to follow him. He didn't move out of the doorway until she was by his side, and he didn't run. But then he had an advantage over Jack because he knew where Caroline was. Since Jack didn't, he raced down the hall, opening every door. By the time he made it to the last examining room, she and Kellan had caught up.

Clarie was in the room, and she was in midreach for

her weapon. However, she stopped when she saw them. The deputy was next to the door, and Caroline was on the bed with a doctor and nurse hovering over her. Both snapped toward them, and the doctor scowled.

"I told Kellan that the patient couldn't have visitors yet," the doctor said. Gemma knew him. He was Dr. Michael Gonzales, and while he didn't look very happy about being interrupted, he must have realized that he wasn't going to be able to stop Jack. Good thing, too, because Jack merely pushed him aside and went straight to the bed.

"Caroline." That one word was heavy with emotion, and for a moment she thought Jack might scoop Caroline up in his arms. And he probably did want to do that, but there was no place on her body that wasn't bruised or cut. "Caroline," he repeated.

Jack picked up her hand, gently lacing his fingers through hers, but Caroline shook her head and tried to recoil. Since the bed was narrow, she couldn't go far.

"Who are you?" she asked.

Jack stared at her and then threw a glance over his shoulder at Kellan and Gemma to see if they had an explanation. However, it was Dr. Gonzales who spoke.

"Caroline has a head injury," he told Jack. "Two of them actually." He pointed to the scar on her forehead. "That one's healed, but she has another on the back of her head."

The healed one was likely given to her by Eric, when he'd taken Caroline and Gemma hostage. Heck, Eric had probably given her the most recent one, too.

"My guess is the blunt force trauma caused memory loss," Dr. Gonzales went on, "but I'll need to run some tests on her to see what's going on."

Because Jack was now the one who looked ready to lose it, Gemma went to him and put her hand on his arm.

"She didn't know who we were when she got to the ranch," Gemma whispered.

Apparently, Caroline still didn't remember, judging from the wild, frightened look in her eyes.

Jack stood there, casting uncertain looks at all of them before his attention settled on Caroline. "I'm Jack. Marshal Jack Slater," he added. "Remember?"

Caroline's reaction was to back even farther away from him, and she might have fallen off the bed if the nurse hadn't caught her.

Gemma saw the hurt all over Jack, and she knew this wasn't about the things that Caroline might not be able to tell them about the attack. This was personal because he was in love with her.

"I don't know," Caroline said, and just as she'd done at the ranch, she repeated it.

Kellan stepped closer. "A serial killer named Eric Lang took you hostage. Do you remember anything about that?"

Caroline volleyed more of those glances at them, and Gemma couldn't tell if she was actually trying to remember or if her memories were so horrific that she had pushed them away—permanently.

Find Caroline because she's the one who can tell you who really killed Deputy Walters and your father, Eric had said. Well, they had found her, and it was obvious that Caroline wasn't going to be able to give them any answers. Not tonight anyway.

"Do you remember anything?" Kellan tried again.

He tipped his head to Gemma. "Anything about when you worked with her?"

Caroline studied her again but only for a few seconds. "I don't know. I don't know." Except this time, she got louder with each word. More agitated, too, and she batted away both the doctor and nurse when they tried to settle her down.

"Wait outside," the doctor snapped to Jack. "After I've finished my exam, I'll come out and talk to you."

Jack wouldn't have gone on his own, and that's why she and Kellan got on each side of him and led him out the door. Even then he kept looking back at Caroline, kept muttering and swore under his breath.

Once they were in the hall, Jack's cursing turned to groans, and he put a hand on each side of his head and squeezed hard. "What the hell happened to her? How'd she get to the ranch?"

"I don't have the answers you want, but it's my guess that Eric brought her there. When he called yesterday, he said he was looking for her, so that could be when she escaped. Or else he lied about that and has had her this whole time. Eric could have dumped Caroline at the end of the road by the ranch because he thought it'd lure out Gemma."

Jack lowered his hands and looked at her. "And it worked."

Gemma shook her head. "Whatever happened, Caroline didn't do it voluntarily."

She wouldn't mention the possible syndromes a person could go through after being held captive a long time. Especially captive by someone like Eric. As a lawman, Jack could no doubt fill in the blanks on his own.

"Besides," she went on. "I don't think Eric was lying about that. I believe Caroline had indeed gotten away from him." She paused. "I know that doesn't explain the note she had with her."

"What note?" Jack snapped.

Gemma shook her head. "Kellan's name and address."

"Caroline's alive," Gemma reminded Jack. Reminded herself, too. "She'll heal. She'll get back her memory." And she prayed that wasn't wishful thinking.

Jack scrubbed his hand over his face, and she could practically see the thoughts firing through his head. "I'm not leaving her here alone, and no, I don't want Clarie to stay with her," he added when Kellan opened his mouth to say something. "I'll stay here with her until she's released from the hospital, and then I'll have her moved to WITSEC."

"The danger might be over," Kellan explained. "Eric could be dead."

Jack paused as if considering that. "I'm still staying with her. I can't leave her."

Kellan didn't argue with that, probably because he knew it wouldn't do any good. Gemma wasn't sure she believed in actual soul mates, but if it existed, that's what Jack and Caroline were. That's why it had to eat away at him that she didn't remember him.

The door to Caroline's room opened, and Dr. Gonzales stepped into the hall. "I don't think her injuries are life threatening," he said right off. "My biggest concern right now is the head injury. It could have caused some swelling on her brain, and that in turn could be the reason for her memory loss."

"So, it could all come back." Jack sounded relieved and cautious.

"Too soon to tell. The good news is there are no signs of sexual assault, and she's been well fed. Slightly dehydrated, but the IV will fix that."

The no sexual assault wasn't a surprise to Gemma. Eric hadn't been into that. He'd been satisfied enough to commit murder.

"She has defensive wounds," Jack pointed out. "Her hands are cut and bruised."

The doctor nodded. "Yes, I would say that she managed to fight her attacker, but she took some licks, too. There are bruises on her stomach and ribs."

Some of the color drained from Jack's face.

"Probably punches from one of Eric's thugs." Gemma hated that she'd said that aloud, but when all three men looked at her, she continued. "Eric couldn't beat Caroline in a fight. Not a fair one anyway. She's had self-defense training." She turned to the doctor. "Was she drugged?"

He nodded. "I don't know with what yet, but I've drawn blood, and it'll be tested." The doctor checked his watch. "I don't want you to question Caroline tonight. My advice is all of you should go home, get some rest and come back in the morning. *Late* in the morning," he emphasized.

"Jack's staying," Kellan said before his brother could.

The doctor's eyebrow came up. "Caroline got agitated when she saw you. I think she'd be more comfortable with Clarie in the room."

"Then I'll wait here outside her door so that she won't see me," Jack insisted.

Dr. Gonzales made a suit-yourself sound and strolled away while making notes on a tablet.

"I'll have Gunnar go with Gemma and me back to the ranch," Kellan said, taking out his phone.

Gemma nearly protested, but she wasn't sure exactly what she wanted him to do differently. They couldn't question Caroline, and she didn't especially want to go to the sheriff's office. It was late, nearly three in the morning, and like her Kellan was probably feeling the bone-weary fatigue from the adrenaline crash.

"Call me if there's any change or if you need anything," Kellan added to Jack.

They exchanged a glance that could only pass between brothers before Kellan took out his phone. While he made the call to Gunnar, he took her back to the private waiting room where they'd been earlier. Even though Gemma couldn't hear the conversation he was having with his deputy, she guessed from the way Kellan's forehead bunched up that it wasn't going well.

God, she hoped it wasn't more bad news because Gemma was afraid she wouldn't be able to take it. Her body suddenly felt as if it were made of glass, the kind of glass that would break with a touch.

Kellan finished his call, cursed and put his phone away. "Maylene's family sent in a team of lawyers. They convinced a judge to spring her from jail so she can have a psychiatric evaluation. We have no choice but to release her."

Gemma's mind was whirling, and it took her several moments to see the big problem with that. "Eric. If she's working with Eric, she can go to him. And since she's a nurse, she can help him. If she's not working with him, it'll be easier for him to have her killed."

Kellan nodded and gave a sigh of acceptance. She saw the fatigue then. Even more than there had been just minutes earlier. "Gunnar's on his way and will go with us to the ranch. I'm not sure how long I can spare him though."

She understood. So many irons in the fire. And Gemma was about to tell him that when she heard the voice. Not Gunnar. But rather Amanda. Gemma wasn't sure whose groan was louder—Kellan's or hers.

"What kind of game do you think you're playing?" Amanda snapped when she appeared in the doorway. A doorway that Kellan kept blocked because he didn't step aside.

"You don't want to get in my face right now, Amanda," Kellan warned her.

"Funny that you should say that, because getting in my face is exactly what you're doing." Amanda's mouth was in a flat line. "You're having your people investigate me. How dare you!"

Gemma knew this was tricky territory for Kellan because he probably wasn't going to want to spill what Tasha had told. Plus, there was no proof of it. That's why Jack had been looking into things. Obviously though, Amanda had gotten wind of what was going on. Or at least she was aware that someone was digging into her personal life.

Kellan dragged in a long breath, put his hands on his hips. "I'm having you investigated because you withheld information about Eric murdering your friend. By your own admission, you manipulated the system to become Gemma's handler, only to have her WITSEC location breached. I tend to get testy when things like that happen."

Gemma didn't miss what Kellan *hadn't* told the marshal. Nothing about the possibility that Amanda might have murdered Lacey because she'd been jealous of her lover—Rory—having sex with the prostitute. Gemma would have liked to know how Amanda would react to that, but it would be a risky ploy to bring it up.

Because it might send Amanda or Rory after Tasha.

"I didn't have anything to do with the leak at WIT-SEC," Amanda practically shouted at Kellan, but then Gemma immediately saw her trying to rein in her temper. And then she saw why.

Rory came up the hall and appeared in the doorway.

Great. Now they had to deal with two marshals. Two marshals that neither Kellan nor she trusted.

"Amanda," Rory said. Definitely not a shout, and he aimed a sympathetic glance at Kellan. "Are you and Gemma okay? I heard you were attacked again. I got concerned when I called your office, and a Texas Ranger answered and told me that you two were at the hospital."

"We're fine," Kellan said, but there was nothing about his tone to indicate that was true. He was as riled as Amanda was.

"Kellan's trying to pin something on us," Amanda snarled, but her voice was much lower now. "He believes we've broken the law." She spun back toward Kellan. "We didn't have anything to do with your father's murder."

"What about Lacey's murder?" Kellan fired back.

Amanda went stiff before even more anger flashed in her eyes. "Not hers, either. We're not criminals."

Kellan made a sound that could have meant anything. "You'll hear this soon enough, but Caroline Moser's resurfaced. She's alive."

Gemma moved closer so she could watch their expressions. If either Rory or Amanda had indeed had something to do with killing Lacey, Dusty or Buck, Gemma figured they wouldn't be happy about a potential new witness. Rory's eyes widened, but if Amanda had a reaction, she kept it to herself.

"How did Caroline get away from Eric?" Rory asked. "And what about that body that was found in Eric's car in Mexico? If that wasn't Caroline, then who was it?"

Kellan shook his head. "I can't answer any of that."

"Can't or won't?" Now it was Rory who snapped.

"Both," Kellan readily admitted. "Caroline was injured. I'm not sure how yet, but because Eric is still at large, she's in protective custody, and I haven't been able to question her."

Rory and Amanda exchanged glances, and Gemma figured they were trying to figure out a way around Kellan so they could get to Caroline. That wasn't going to happen because Jack wouldn't let either of them get near her.

"Eric," Rory repeated on a frustrated sigh. "I called a Texas Ranger friend on the way over here, and he said there was no sign of the SUV. You're positive it was Eric?"

"Yes," Gemma answered before Kellan.

Rory stayed quiet as if waiting for more, but Gemma followed Kellan's cue and didn't add anything.

"The Ranger told me you thought you'd shot Eric," Rory went on, looking at Kellan.

Either that was news to Amanda or else she thought

it was a good time to fake surprise. "You shot him? Is he dead?"

Kellan lifted his shoulder. "I won't know until they find the SUV."

And even then, they might not. Yes, the CSIs would be able to measure blood loss, but unless Eric's actual body was in the vehicle, it didn't mean he was dead. Or alive, for that matter.

Another of Eric's hired help could have gotten Eric to a doctor or hospital. That was the reason that one of the calls that Kellan had made was to get out the word to inform him of any patient showing up with gunshot wounds. Gemma also made a mental note to do some computer searches to see if she could figure out how Eric was paying for all this "help."

"Instead of investigating me, we should be working together to find Eric," Amanda threw out there. "I want to talk to Maylene. Please." Amanda's mouth was still tight when she added that last word. "You know why it's important for me to find Eric."

"I do," Kellan admitted. He didn't mention Amanda's dead friend, but Gemma suspected that Rory knew all about it. "But even if you could talk to Eric, that doesn't mean he'd tell you the truth."

"He would," Amanda insisted. "He'd want to brag about it."

Yes, Gemma had to agree with the marshal on that, and that's why it niggled away at her that Eric had denied killing Kellan's father and Dusty. And that Eric had been so adamant that Caroline knew the truth.

Maybe Eric hadn't been the only killer at the inn that night. One who might be more dangerous than Eric simply because they didn't know who he or she was. One who could hide behind a badge. At least Eric had been forthcoming that he had committed murder.

"Better the devil you know than the one you don't," Gemma muttered. She certainly hadn't expected to say that aloud. Or for it to get Amanda's and Rory's attention.

Rory obviously picked up on the meaning because now there was some anger in his eyes. "Amanda's not dirty," he assured her. Which, of course, assured her of nothing—especially when Rory brushed a loving hand down Amanda's arm.

"I'm going to help the Rangers look for Eric," Rory said to no one in particular. "You need a ride?" he added to Amanda.

The marshal shook her head and kept her attention fixed on Rory as he walked away. She only returned her attention to Gemma when Rory was out of sight.

"You're in love with him," Gemma concluded.

"Yes." Amanda said it quietly and with what Gemma thought might be some regret. "I hadn't intended for it to happen." But she immediately waved that off as if she'd just admitted too much.

Kellan must have picked up on that, too, and he obviously wasn't going to let Amanda off the hook. "It must have hurt you when you found out Rory was having sex with Lacey."

The surprise flashed through Amanda's eyes, but she quickly recovered. "Yes," Amanda repeated. "How did you find out?"

"A source," Kellan settled for saying.

"A source," she muttered, already turning to leave. She said the rest of it as she walked away. "Yes, it hurt when I found out."

Just as Amanda had done with Rory, Kellan kept his eyes on the marshal, and he cursed under his breath. "She just gave herself motive for murder."

Delores Fossen

150

Chapter Thirteen

Considering everything that had gone on, Kellan figured he should count it as a major achievement that he'd finally gotten Gemma safely back to the ranch. He'd managed that without anyone firing a single shot at them or trying to blow them up.

Too bad it wouldn't last.

That was the thought that kept repeating in his head as he paced across his bedroom floor while he waited for updates. *Any* updates. He had so many threads of this investigation going on right now that sooner or later something was bound to break. Maybe it would break in Gemma's and his favor. Caroline's and Jack's, too.

Jack was mentally in bad shape, what with Caroline not remembering who he was or what'd happened the night their father had been murdered. But at least Caroline was alive, so there was hope that her memory would return. Kellan just hoped when it did that she'd be able to deal with whatever the hell she'd been through all these months.

He'd left his bedroom door open so he could hear Gemma in the guest suite or Gunnar if he called out to him from downstairs. Kellan didn't hear a sound from either of them, but he considered going across the hall to check on Gemma.

He groaned.

It wasn't a good idea for a man to lie to himself, and if he went to her, it would be for sex. That reminder was enough for him to stay put and sink down onto the foot of his bed. He wasn't the only one with too many "threads." Gemma had them, too, and she didn't need the added complication of rolling around on the sheets with him.

He knew he wouldn't get any sleep, so Kellan didn't even try that. Instead, he took his laptop from the nightstand so he could see if there were any answers to his emails about Amanda.

Now that the marshal with the constant bad attitude had confessed that she knew about Rory's affair with Lacey, it meant Kellan needed to find anything to prove that Amanda had killed the prostitute. He'd have to do an interview with her and check her alibis, not just for the night of Lacey's murder but also his father's and Dusty's. It was a mountain-sized understatement that Amanda wasn't going to like that much.

Of course, there wasn't much about any of this Kellan liked, either, so they'd be in the same boat. Still, he didn't have a choice about what he had to do. If there was a link, he had to find it. Ditto for Maylene. The woman's lawyers might have convinced a judge to free her, but there were lots of unanswered questions. Including the big one.

Was Maylene a killer?

Better the devil you know than the one you don't, Gemma had said about Amanda and Rory, and Kellan agreed. He could add Maylene in there, too, of suspects who possibly hadn't been up-front with them. Maylene seemed vulnerable and innocent, but he needed to backtrack and see if it was all just an act. If so, that made a very dangerous woman. Even more dangerous than Amanda or Rory because Maylene could team up with Eric.

Kellan had silenced his phone, but it dinged with an incoming call, and when he saw Jack's name on the screen, he put his laptop aside and went to his bedroom door to close it before he answered.

"I don't have anything new on Caroline," Jack immediately volunteered, and Kellan could hear that the no-change was worrisome for his brother. "I'm calling about the missing SUV."

Before Kellan could respond to that, his door opened, and Gemma stepped in. "I heard your phone," she blurted out.

Obviously, she hadn't been asleep if she'd heard such a soft sound. "It's Jack," he let her know. "I'll put the call on Speaker so you can hear him." It was a risk because this could be bad news, but one way or another Gemma would have to know. He couldn't keep even the god-awful stuff from her since she was the target.

"I called the Rangers to ask for an update, and I learned they just found an SUV matching the description of the one that crashed into you." Jack paused. "It's *the* SUV," he added a moment later. "The driver's dead. No ID on him yet. And no signs of Eric, either. However, there was blood in the back seat."

Kellan's stomach clenched. It would have made things so much safer if Eric had been dead, though part of Kellan didn't want the man to have such an easy way out. He wanted Eric locked up in a cage for the rest of his life. That could still happen, but now they'd have to find him—again.

He looked up at Gemma to see how she was handling this. Not well. The worry was right back on her face, and she looked exhausted. With a heavy sigh, she sat down next to him and buried her face in her hands. Because there was nothing Kellan could say to her to make this better, he just slipped his arm around her.

"There have been no reports from hospitals about anyone showing up who matches Eric's description," Jack continued a moment later. "Nor are there any unaccounted-for doctors or nurses or ones who've been reported missing."

Yes, Kellan had checked for that, too, because Eric had kidnapped before and would likely do it again. Still, it was possible a kidnapping had happened, and no one had noticed that the person was gone. If Eric needed medical attention, he would figure out a way to get it even if he had to kidnap, and then kill, again.

"Caroline's having an EEG and some other tests done now," Jack went on. "I'll call you when I have the results." He hesitated again, then cursed. "She called me *Marshal Slater*."

Kellan knew that had to be hard to hear since Jack and Caroline had been lovers. *Marshal Slater* definitely wasn't intimate. He was about to remind Jack, though, that it could all be temporary, that Caroline might regain her memory before the night was out, but he didn't like lying to his brother any more than liked being lied to himself. So, Kellan settled for saying, "I'm sorry."

It wasn't nearly enough, but just as it had been with Gemma, there was nothing Kellan could say that would ease Jack's pain.

"Thanks," Jack mumbled before he ended the call.

Other than to drop her head on his shoulder, Gemma didn't move when he slipped his phone back into his jeans pocket. He steeled himself up in case she was about to go through all the things that had gone wrong. Or worse, all the things that *could* still go wrong.

But she didn't.

When she looked up at him, he saw the stillness in her eyes. Behind that stillness, though, was no doubt a whole lot of worry, but she somehow managed to tamp it down.

"You obviously weren't sleeping if you heard my phone beep," he said and risked brushing a kiss on the top of her head.

"No." She lifted her shoulder. "I was debating if I should come over here and have sex with you."

Oh, man. That wasn't a good thing for him to hear, not with his body in knots and his nerves humming. Gemma's shrug let him know that she understood it wasn't a good thing for her to say.

However, it was the truth.

"Sex won't fix anything," she added, her voice a breathy whisper. "And I don't want to settle for kissing or just spooning."

She didn't dodge his gaze. Didn't look embarrassed or uncertain about the moment. Or about anything else. She just looked at him as if waiting for him to make the next move.

Kellan had a short debate with himself. A totally unnecessary debate. Gemma was offering him sex, and he wouldn't turn it down, period. She was right. It wouldn't fix anything except maybe the most important thing of all. It would ease this need that was clawing its way through him. It would dull the ache. And it would remind him that she was everything that he'd ever wanted.

Kellan didn't make her wait long. He pulled her to him and set things into motion with a kiss.

GEMMA HADN'T EXACTLY been subtle with her offer of sex so it wasn't a surprise when Kellan took her up on it. But what was a surprise—a shock, actually—was that something as simple as a kiss could heat her in an instant from head to toe. But then, Kellan had always managed to do just that.

She wound her arms around him, already fighting to get closer. Already needing the kiss to be so much more. She wanted him hot and fast. Something rough that would do a quick cooldown of this scalding heat.

Something where she wouldn't have to think.

But she did think. And she knew that Kellan would regret this because for him it would mean a loss of focus. A complication. Sex would do that for her, too, but resisting was no longer an option.

Her body burned against his. Her mate. That's what the primal pulse inside labeled him, but her heart was telling her that he was so much more.

Gemma made a sobbing sound when she broke for air, and it must have alerted him that something was wrong because he stopped and pulled back. He brushed her hair from her face, but what he didn't do was ask her if she wanted to put an end to this. Well, he didn't ask with words, but the question was there in his gun-metal-gray eyes.

She took in that look in his eyes. His face. Yes, his

face could always do it for her even if the need hadn't already been at the surface.

"I want you," she settled for saying.

Still, he continued to study her for several moments. Things passed between them. It was like those unspoken conversations he'd had with his brothers, but this was a different kind of chat.

The kind of chat between lovers.

When Kellan lowered his head and kissed her again, it wasn't that urgent, out-of-control fire as the other one had been. This was long, slow. Thorough. Surprisingly gentle. She didn't think he was giving her a chance to change her mind, either. No. This was what he wanted from her, and she was going to give it to him. Or rather let him have her this way.

He slipped his hand into her hair, easing her head to an angle so he could deepen the kiss. He touched his tongue to hers. Also gently. Still no urgency. And that caused the taste of him to slide right through her.

The heat slid up a notch when his hand went to the front of her shirt. Gemma tensed only a second when she remembered her scars. But Kellan had already seen them. In fact, he'd seen all the worst things about her, and yet he was still kissing her. Still giving her this gentleness when there'd been no such gentleness in her life for a long, long time.

With that same gentle coaxing he was doing with his mouth, his hand went under her top. Over those scars. And into her bra. He pushed it down and ran very clever fingertips over her nipples.

He knew the sensitive things about her, too, and he was doing an incredible job of stoking the heat higher and higher. Still, Gemma resisted the onslaught until his hand went in the other direction. With that same slow ease, his hand trailed up her thighs. He didn't even put those clever fingers inside her panties. He just brushed against them, and she was toast.

The restraint inside her snapped, and the next sound she made definitely wasn't a sob. It was a throaty groan. She caught the flash of his smile—yes, a smile—before she claimed his mouth and pushed him back on the bed.

Now she was rough and couldn't help herself. Everything inside her was past the simmering and had gone to a full boil. She had to have him now.

Kellan didn't resist when she pinned his wrists to the bed and used her other hand to go after the buttons on his shirt. Her own hands were shaking so it wasn't a graceful effort, but the moment she had his shirt open, she went after his chest. And she showed no long, lingering restraint that he had with her mouth.

He let her take him as she kissed her way down his body, but when her mouth made it to the front of his jeans, she felt the same snap that had just gone through her. He groaned, too. Then he cursed, mixing her name in with that profanity.

And in a flash, he had her on her back and was on top of her.

Now she saw it. His eyes had a storm in them and he was as hard as stone, his erection straining against her. His grip was far from gentle when he shoved up her skirt and rid her of her panties.

Gemma felt his jeans brush against the inside of her thighs and considered getting them both naked so she could feel even more of him. She quickly discarded the idea, though, when he put his fingers inside her and nearly caused the climax to come on like a flash fire.

She fought it, wanting to hang on to this for as long as she could. Which wouldn't be long. That's why she battled against his clever touches to get him unzipped and freed from his boxers. Then, she was the one cursing when he stopped to grab a condom from his nightstand drawer.

The moment he had it on, he plunged into her, filling her until she thought that she might burst. The pleasure came—rough and raw. *Thorough.* That was the one word that kept repeating in her head as he thrust into her.

Her mate. *Hers.*

She rose as he lowered himself. Again and again. The rhythm, primal now. And fast. Then, even faster. Until the coil inside her was so hot, so vicious, wound so tight that she couldn't hold on any longer.

Kellan kept his eyes on her. They were blue and narrowed now. Sizzling like fire created by some warrior pagan god. And he watched her, doing exactly what he wanted to do while he sent her crashing right over the edge.

He watched her do that, too.

Her vision blurred. And dazed and quivering, with her body closing like a fist around him, she could only hold on as he emptied himself into her.

Chapter Fourteen

Kellan had been certain that he wouldn't sleep, not after Gemma had come to him with her *offer*. But he'd been wrong about that. Maybe it was just sheer fatigue, great sex or the combination of both, but he'd closed his eyes and drifted off.

With Gemma curled up next to him.

Hours later, she was still there with her face pressed to the curve of his neck. She was naked now though. They'd managed to get their clothes off for the second round of sex that'd been just as great as the first, and then she'd obviously managed to sleep, too.

Kellan didn't want to wake her, but it was nearly six, and despite having gotten barely an hour of sleep, he had to get his day started. There were phone calls to make, persons of interest to interview and paperwork to complete. All of which he wanted to ditch when he looked down at Gemma.

A sensible man would kick himself for taking her as he'd done. But he hadn't been anywhere near sensible. Taking her a second time was proof of that. The fact that he wanted her again was more proof that he didn't need.

He eased away from her, surprised that the movement didn't cause her to stir and wondered if it had. It was possible she was actually already awake and was puzzling over what'd happened as much as he was. Also like him, she could use some time to think.

Kellan took his phone and gun, choosing to do his thinking in the shower, but with everything else he had to do, he kept it short, and he didn't find any answers in the scalding hot water. Of course, that was asking a lot of a mere shower.

He spent less than five minutes total, managing to change into some fresh clothes and brush his teeth. Then, he checked his emails on his phone, scanning through the sparse updates that he found there before he went back into the bedroom. He figured it was time to wake Gemma so they could go to his office, but the bed was empty.

Alarm shot through him.

He drew his gun, but then he heard the shower running in the guest room across the hall, and he released the breath that he'd sucked in. Even though it was highly likely that nothing was wrong, he glanced into the guest room anyway. She'd left open the adjoining bathroom door, and he saw Gemma's silhouette behind the opaque glass of the shower stall.

His body clenched, and it wasn't alarm that shot through him this time. It was need, and Kellan might have done something stupid and acted on that need if his phone hadn't rung. Jack's name popped up on the screen so Kellan went back into his bedroom to take the call.

"Is everything okay?" Kellan immediately asked.

Jack greeted him with a groan, and for such a simple

sound, Kellan still heard the weariness. "No one tried to kill us, so that's good," Jack said.

It was indeed good. "You're still at the hospital?"

"Yeah. I sent Clarie home so she could get some rest."

Kellan wanted to point out that Jack needed rest, too, but it wouldn't do any good. If their positions had been reversed, Kellan would have stayed at the hospital, as well.

"The doc got back some of the test results," Jack went on. "There's no sign of brain swelling, which means the memory loss is from mental or emotional trauma rather than the injury."

Kellan was thankful that there wasn't that kind of physical damage because it meant Caroline could recover, but the trauma told them that she'd been through hell and back. There was no way to give Jack any comfort about that so Kellan didn't even try.

"There were traces of drugs in her system," Jack continued. "Barbiturates, and there were two recent needle marks so Dr. Gonzales thinks that's how the drugs were administered." He paused. "Along with other defensive wounds, there was bruising around the injection sites."

Which likely meant someone had administered the drugs by force. Not a surprise, but it added to an already gruesome picture. Caroline had tried to fight whomever had done this to her, but she'd lost. Partially anyway. Yes, the person had managed to drug her, but she'd gotten away.

"If you find Eric, I want a shot at him," Jack added a moment later.

There was a thick layer of anger coating the exhaustion and worry. Not a good combination. But Kellan was pretty sure that his brother didn't mean an actual shot as in putting a bullet in the snake. Still, with Jack's emotions running this high, it was too big of a risk to take.

"I'd rather you stay with Caroline. She needs you just in case there are any more hired thugs out there." It was playing dirty, but Kellan knew it had worked when Jack cursed.

"Catch the bastard," Jack growled, and he ended the call.

As Kellan put his phone away, Gemma hurried into the room. She was toweling dry her hair, and he could tell from the way the side of her top was hiked up that she'd dressed in a hurry.

"Anything?" she asked, tipping her head to his phone.

"No brain damage for Caroline." He kept it at that and hoped she wouldn't press for details. To help his chances with that, he went to her and brushed a kiss on her mouth.

There was suspicion in her eyes when she met his gaze. "I figured you'd be trying to put up a wall between us. Conflict of interest, loss of focus, etc."

"I tried," he admitted, and when he lingered a moment with the next kiss, Kellan forced himself to step back. He cursed, something he'd been doing too much of lately, and it wasn't helping. "I need to wrestle a bull," he grumbled.

Her eyebrow lifted, and amusement flirted with the bend of her mouth. "Is that a metaphor?"

He shook his head. "Taking down a bull would burn off some of this...restlessness." That wasn't anywhere near the right word for it, but Gemma knew what he meant.

"I watched you do that once," she said. "Years ago." More of the amusement came, this time to her eyes, and he was glad to see it. If talking about the past lessened her fear and worry, then he was all for it. "It was...*interesting.*"

He got the feeling that wasn't the actual word she meant, either. That maybe what she'd seen had been arousing. Or maybe that was just what a certain part of his anatomy wanted him to believe.

Thankfully, he didn't have to deal with the temptation because his phone rang. He pulled the cell from his pocket, and just like that, he became all cop again. That's because of what he saw on the screen.

Unknown Caller.

There'd only been two people who'd recently shown up on screen that way—Maylene and Eric. Gemma obviously knew that, too, because of the soft gasp she made. She moved closer to Kellan, but he went ahead and put the call on Speaker after he hit the record function on the phone.

"Sheriff," the caller immediately said. The voice was weak, more breath than sound.

"Eric?"

"Who else?" Despite the weakness, the killer still managed some cockiness in his tone. "I guess you thought you'd killed me. You nearly did," he added with a cough.

"Don't expect me to feel sorry for you," Kellan snapped. "Where are you?"

"I'll get to that." Eric cleared his throat. "First, tell me about Caroline. I've heard you found her."

"Who told you that?" Kellan countered.

"Oh, you're trying to protect her. How sweet," Eric cooed. "I'm sure your brother appreciates your valiant effort to save the love of his life."

Kellan tried to not let Eric egg him on, but it was hard to hold on to his temper when he wanted to kill this piece of slime. Gemma no doubt felt the same, and she slid her hand down his arm as if to help settle him.

"Caroline was an unfortunate problem," Eric went on. "She got away from me in Mexico."

"Then who was the dead woman we found in your car?" Kellan pressed.

"I'm not sure. She was just some woman who recognized me from the news, and she was going to call the cops. She had a gun, and the bitch actually shot me before I could tackle her. I killed her," he added as if discussing the weather. "Around that same time is when I lost Caroline. That was nearly a year ago, and I didn't know where she was. Not until yesterday when one of my *associates* spotted her right in Longview Ridge." He paused. "She didn't even know who I was."

Kellan had to get his teeth unclenched so he could speak. "So, you drugged her, beat her up and dumped her near the ranch to lure Gemma into the open."

"That's only partly true. I didn't dump her. She got away from us. And as for beating her up, she got in some punches of her own. Our Caroline is no fragile little flower, but she can be beaten down like the rest of us."

The leash snapped on Kellan's rage. "You son of a bitch. So help me God, I will put you in the grave."

Gemma's gentle touch turned into a hard grip, and she yanked Kellan around to face her. Her eyes held both sympathy and a warning. A warning that he knew he needed when he heard Eric laugh.

"Temper, temper," Eric taunted.

"Say another word about beating up Caroline, and I'll let Jack come after you," Kellan taunted right back.

Silence. Then a restrained "yes" from Eric. "I suspect I'd stand a better chance with you than I would with your brother. Though come to think of it, the doctor did have to dig *your* bullets out of me."

So, Eric had seen a doctor. That was a thread that Kellan needed to pull a little harder if he could find out where Eric was.

"And then there's the problem with Gemma," Eric continued. "I'm betting you're not happy with me because of the associates I hired to take care of her."

Kellan didn't fall for the jab this time. "Do you have a reason for calling, or do you just have too much time on your hands?"

"Oh, I have a reason, all right." And this time, it seemed as if Eric's temper was flaring. "After I got the medical attention I needed to stay alive, one of my associates decided to splinter off and conduct some business of his own. He kidnapped me."

Gemma and Kellan exchanged glances, and he wasn't sure who had more doubts about that.

"I figured you wouldn't believe me, but you can check things out for yourself. That associate, Marvin Hiatt, should be at the Longview Ridge Bank right about now. He forced me to give him the key to a safety-deposit box that's loaded with some of my emergency funds."

Kellan was about to ask Eric why he would keep money right up the street from the sheriff's office.

But there was no need. This had been another way of toying with them.

Gemma waited until Kellan gave her the nod, and she hurried out in the hall, no doubt to call one of his deputies to check the bank.

"It's hard to get good help these days," Kellan continued with Eric. "But there are holes in your story. Why would a hired-gun-turned-kidnapper leave you with a cell phone?"

"A mistake on his part. I had three phones with me, and he only found two. He missed the one I had in my boot. I managed to take it out, but I haven't had any luck getting out of the ropes he used to tie me up. Nor is Maylene answering when I try to call her. That leaves you, Sheriff."

"What the hell do you want me to do? Come and rescue you?"

"Yes." Eric let that answer hang in the air. "I popped some stitches when I was fighting with the ropes, and I'm bleeding. A lot. I considered calling 911, but I decided to go right to the source. Unless some of my other sources magically come through to help me, I'm all yours. You just have to come and get me."

A lot of thoughts went through Kellan's head. None good. But first and foremost was that this was a trap.

"Where exactly should I come and get you?" Kellan asked.

"I'll call you back in fifteen minutes. After you've captured Hiatt. I'll tell you. Then, Sheriff, I'll be yours for the taking."

GEMMA HAD HAD no trouble hearing what Eric had just told Kellan. She had no trouble, either, believing this was another sick game. That's why she wasn't holding her breath, waiting for a report from the deputy and Texas Ranger that were on their way to the bank to locate the so-called associate that Eric had told them about.

Judging from Kellan's expression, he felt the same way. Ditto for Gunnar, who was keeping watch from the kitchen window.

Kellan poured himself another cup of coffee while he finished off a piece of toast that he'd started eating as soon as it'd popped up from the toaster. He didn't look overly tense, but she could see the strain in his eyes. A conversation with Eric could do that, leaving you angry and drained at the same time.

"Eat," Kellan told her again. "This could take a while."

She tried a bite of her own piece of toast that had already gotten cold, but she figured it wasn't going to sit well in her stomach. Hearing Eric had drained her, too, along with leaving her muscles tense. Everything inside her twisted and churned, and it only got worse with each passing second.

"Maybe he'll just die," she said, causing Gunnar to make a quick sound of agreement.

But even if Eric did die, Gemma wanted proof of it. She wanted to see his body so that she wouldn't spend the rest of her life looking over her shoulder.

Even though she'd been expecting it, the sound of Kellan's ringing phone still caused her to gasp. He hit answer and put it on speaker.

"This is Griff," the caller said. Griffin Morris, the Texas Ranger that had gone to the bank. "We've got Hiatt."

No gasp this time for Gemma. But the shock caused

her to get to her feet and move closer to Kellan and his phone.

"He resisted, at first," the Ranger explained. "But we caught him coming out of the vault room at the bank where they have the safety-deposit boxes. He had a large amount of cash on him."

"Did he actually confess?" Kellan asked.

"He's volunteered a few things and is claiming he didn't actually kill anyone. He's asking for a plea deal. He wants immunity and in exchange he'll tell us where he left Eric. Said he kidnapped him and tied him up because he knew Eric had a lot more money than he was paying him."

"It could be a trap," Gemma blurted out.

Kellan nodded, stayed quiet a moment. "Have Owen call the DA," he finally said to the Ranger. "No immunity for him, but I want Hiatt offered a lighter sentence contingent on him leading us to Eric. Let me know what the DA says."

Kellan ended the call and looked at her. She figured he was going to try to console her, to reassure her that this could be exactly what they needed to put an end to the danger. But he didn't say anything. On a heavy sigh, he just pulled her into his arms. She might have taken in some of the silent comfort he was giving her if there'd been time. But he had to pull away from her when his phone rang again.

"Unknown Caller," he relayed to her when he saw his screen.

Gemma dragged in a long breath, steeling herself up for another encounter with Eric. But it wasn't him.

"Sheriff Slater," Maylene said the moment he answered. "I just got a phone call from Eric. He told me he was hurt and that he needed my help."

So, Eric had managed to get in touch with her. Or maybe Maylene had been in on this all along. Gemma didn't trust Maylene any more than she did Eric.

"Did Eric say where he was?" Kellan asked.

Maylene wasn't quick to answer that. "I hate him. He ruined my life, and I'm going to kill him."

"Hell," Kellan spat out. "No, you're not. You're going to tell me where he is so I can arrest him."

Maylene made a raw sob. "He won't stay in jail. He'll just get out and ruin other people's lives. He'll kill again. I have to stop him."

Kellan cursed even more. "Where are you, Maylene? And where's Eric?" he demanded.

Again, Maylene took her time answering. "He's in a hunting cabin off Davidson Road, and I'm heading there now. You can't stop me."

"Maylene, wait. Don't do this," Kellan snapped, but he was talking to himself because the woman had already ended the call.

Gemma knew what Kellan was going to do before he even put his phone away. "Get some of the ranch hands to come in the house so they can stay with Gemma and you," he immediately said to Gunnar.

She shook her head and was ready to beg Kellan not to go, but Gemma knew it wouldn't do any good.

"Owen and at least one of the Rangers will go with me," Kellan said, already heading for the door. "I won't try to take Eric alone."

That didn't give her much consolation. "Eric could be armed and waiting for you to show up."

Kellan didn't confirm that, not with words anyway,

but he knew it was a possibility. "I know where this cabin is. It's by the creek with a lot of trees around it. We can use the trees for cover while we close in on him."

She shook her head again. "He could have set explosives."

"I'll call in the bomb squad," he said, and he disarmed the security system to let in the two hands who were there to guard her. "Just stay put."

He opened his mouth, closed it and then pulled her to the other side of the foyer. Kellan stared at her, and she saw in his eyes what he had been about to say. Gemma nipped that in the bud.

"Don't you dare tell me you love me, because you'd be just saying that instead of goodbye," she warned him. "I'm not saying goodbye to you."

Despite everything that was going on, he smiled at her. "All right. I don't love you."

The corner of her mouth lifted; that was as much as she could manage. "Thank you." She caught on to handfuls of his shirt, yanking him to her, and she kissed him. "Swear to me that you'll come back to me."

"I swear," Kellan said, looking her straight in the eyes. "I swear."

He brushed a kiss on her cheek and headed out the door.

Chapter Fifteen

Kellan pulled the cruiser to a stop at the end of Davidson Road and eyed the cabin that was in a small clearing just ahead. It'd been a while since he'd been in this neck of the woods, but it was just as he remembered. Lots of trees with a small creek coiling around the property. It was normally a quiet, serene place.

Not at the moment though.

Since Kellan didn't trust Eric or anyone connected to him, the bomb squad was already on scene. He'd called them as he'd driven away from the ranch and then had gone to the sheriff's office to pick up Owen and Ranger Griff Morris.

The two men of the bomb squad had made good time getting there. They were dressed in bulky gear and were examining the grounds with equipment. They weren't Kellan's men but rather were from the county and responded when the locals needed help. In this case, they'd responded quickly because they knew there could be a serial killer inside.

Gemma knew it, too.

Her image popped into Kellan's head. The stark fear on her face when he'd said his non-goodbye. There'd been nothing he could say to give her any reassurance, and that would continue. Because Kellan knew Gunnar would be monitoring both their cruiser radio and the bomb squad's, which meant it was highly likely that Gemma would be hearing it, too. Kellan wished he could shelter her from that, but he couldn't. However, maybe he could put a quick end to this once the area and cabin were cleared.

"No vehicle other than the bomb squad van," Owen relayed. "No sign of anyone else, either, including Maylene." He handed Kellan the binoculars he'd been using.

Kellan zoomed in on the cabin windows. The morning sun was reflecting off the glass, making it impossible to see inside, but the sunlight gave him an ample view of the grounds.

"Either of you been inside the place?" Ranger Morris asked from the back seat. He, too, had binoculars.

"Once," Owen answered, surprising Kellan. His brother shrugged. "Cal Davidson had a party here when I was in high school."

Cal was Owen's friend, and the cabin belonged to Cal's grandfather, a crotchety man who almost certainly hadn't approved of a party. But the grandfather had passed now, and the place belonged to Cal.

"The only room closed off is the bathroom," Owen explained. "But there are two small storage closets."

Eric, if he was indeed there, could be shut up in one of those. Of course, maybe Hiatt hadn't taken the trouble to hide his captive since he'd perhaps figured he wouldn't be gone that long.

"I don't see any signs that anyone has trampled around the perimeter of the cabin," Griff added.

Neither did Kellan. There was a mix of shrubs and weeds by the windows, and if someone had stepped on them, it would have shown. But he couldn't see the back of the place. Thankfully, there wasn't enough room to park a vehicle back there, but Hiatt or Eric could have left a hired thug there to keep watch. If they'd done that though, the bomb squad would have likely flushed them out.

The minutes crawled by as the bomb squad did their job, and while Kellan knew it was necessary, everything inside him was raring to go. If Eric was in there, he wanted him.

"Hell," Owen grumbled, and Kellan pulled the binoculars from his eyes to see what had gotten his brother's attention.

Maylene.

She was getting out of a small blue car that was parked just up the road from them. He couldn't see a gun, but Kellan had to assume that if she'd managed to get a vehicle, she had also gotten hold of a weapon.

Maylene froze when she spotted them, and even though Kellan couldn't get a good look of her face from the distance, he didn't think she was pleased about him being there.

Welcome to the club.

"You want me to arrest her?" Griff asked.

Kellan was debating how to handle it when Maylene jumped back in her car and sped off. Part of him was glad she hadn't stayed around to complicate things, but that didn't mean she wouldn't be back. In fact, as crazed sounding as the woman had been, she might just go farther up the road, park and make her way here on foot. Kellan would have to keep an eye out for her.

One of the bomb squad guys gave them a thumbs-up, and a moment later Kellan got a text. All clear on the outside. We're heading in now.

Good. That was Kellan's cue to pull the cruiser even closer to the cabin. Close enough that he could easily watch without the binoculars. He got out, keeping behind the cruiser door. Owen did the same on the passenger's side, and Griff got out behind Kellan. All of them already had their weapons drawn.

The bomb squad went on the porch, each of them peering through the windows that flanked the door. Both men shook their head, indicating they didn't see anyone inside.

Kellan cursed and hoped this wasn't all a wild-goose chase.

He waited, watching and holding his breath when the squad checked the front door. They didn't go in that way though. They broke the window and took another look inside.

"There's blood on the floor," one of them relayed to Kellan. "A lot of blood. It looks as if someone got dragged."

That meshed with what Eric had said, but it didn't mean it was true. The blood could belong to another of his victims.

Thankfully, things moved a lot faster then. One of the guys went in through the window, dropping down out of sight. Several minutes later, the front door opened.

"Call an ambulance," the guy shouted to Kellan. "There's a man up in the bathroom. Can't tell who he is 'cause there's blood on his face."

Kellan hurried away from the cruiser and barreled

onto the porch. With his gun ready, he made a beeline for the bathroom.

And he saw Eric.

Just as the killer had said, his wrists were tied with a rope to the sink, and yes, there was blood. Not just on Eric's face where it appeared he'd been beaten, but it was also on his shirt and on the floor. He still had his cell phone clutched in his hand.

At first Kellan thought he was dead since he wasn't moving, but then Eric's eyes fluttered open. "Sheriff, you came." Even now there was a touch of cockiness to his voice. "I trust that you caught Hiatt. And yes, he did this to me."

As much as it twisted at him, Kellan checked for weapons—there were none—and he yanked open Eric's shirt so he could try to slow down the bleeding. It was his job, but sometimes, like now, his job sucked.

"You're wasting your time, you know," Eric said, his eyelids drifted back down, and he dragged in a thin breath. "I'm dying. Funny that it should end this way. Me in a bathroom. You, trying to save me."

Kellan didn't trust himself to comment on that when all he wanted to do was finish beating Eric to a pulp.

"Just in case there is a hereafter, I'll settle up with you," Eric went on. "I didn't kill your father nor that deputy."

"And we're to believe you?" Owen snapped. Only then did Kellan realize his brother was right behind him.

"It's the truth." With his eyes still closed, the corner of Eric's mouth lifted into a smile. "I don't want to take credit for something I didn't do, and I didn't do either of them. In fact, they weren't even killed by the same person."

Nothing could have kept Kellan quiet after hearing that. Maybe this was just another load of bull, but if Eric was clearing his conscience, then Kellan wanted to hear what he had to say.

"Who killed them, then?" Kellan demanded.

Eric opened his mouth, then grimaced. Kellan heard the death rattle in the man's throat and chest. "I'm not the only monster on your turf, Sheriff," Eric said in a ragged whisper. "Save yourself. Save Gemma."

And the moment he'd gotten out those words, Eric Lang took the last breath he would ever take.

GEMMA DIDN'T EVEN try to tamp down the fear that was spiking through her. And she hated that she was tucked away at the ranch while Kellan was out there facing down a killer.

Or walking into a trap.

Either one of those could be deadly.

Eric might be injured. Heck, he might even have been kidnapped by one of his own hired thugs. He could even be dying. But that didn't mean Eric wouldn't use his last seconds on earth to deliver one final blow to her. Killing Kellan would be the ultimate blow. Eric could destroy both Kellan and her by doing that.

That thought hit her so hard that Gemma had to sink down in the chair at the kitchen table. Gunnar was already seated, and he was monitoring the scanner for reports from the cabin. At first, he'd tried to do the "monitoring" through headphones, but Gemma had put a stop to that. As hard as it was for her—she had to hear what was going on.

So far, not much.

Kellan, Owen and Griff were in a holding pattern, and it was as if time had stopped. Just to give herself something to do, Gemma forced herself to her feet and went to the kitchen window to keep watch. She also slipped her hand over the gun that she'd tucked in the back waist of her jeans. That was yet something else she'd talked Gunnar into doing. She doubted that Eric could get to the ranch, but she didn't want to be unarmed if that happened.

When she got to the window, she immediately spotted the ranch hand on the back porch. He was armed with a rifle—as was the one on the front porch. They'd stay in those positions, guarding her, until Kellan returned.

"The bomb squad gave the all clear," Gunnar relayed to her a split second before she heard that static-laced info come through on the scanner.

That was a relief, but Gemma knew this only put Kellan one step closer to going into the cabin and facing, well, whatever he would face there. Maybe Eric. Maybe one of his uninjured henchmen.

When her lungs started to ache, she released the breath she'd been holding and moved to the other side of the window so that she'd have a different angle for keeping watch.

She could see the barn, but there wasn't anyone about. That was because Kellan had put hands on the road to stop anyone from just driving up. It wasn't foolproof though, and they all knew it. There were ranch trails that coiled and cut all around the property, and someone could have parked on the main road and used those trails to get close to the house.

"Kellan's going inside," Gunnar said.

The deputy was watching her now, volleying those cautious glances at her, probably making sure she wasn't about to have a panic attack. She wouldn't. Even though there was plenty of panic inside her, she would keep it together for Kellan's sake. It might cause him to lose focus if he heard she was having trouble.

The conversation she'd had with Kellan started playing in her head. The *l*-word had been part of that, and while it hadn't exactly sent Kellan running, she wouldn't hold him to anything he'd said to her in that moment.

Well, nothing except that "I swear."

He had sworn to her that he'd come back safe, and she latched on to that like a lifeline.

"Kellan's in with Eric," Gunnar told her. "Owen said Eric's bleeding out. Dying."

So, that was true, too. Part of her wanted to be there so she could look the snake in the eyes, so that he could see that he hadn't beaten her, after all. Another part of her just wanted him to go ahead and die, and then Kellan could come back to her.

The static hissed and crackled, and she caught bits and pieces of Eric and Kellan's conversation. Eric said something about Hiatt and settling up. Then, it was as if the static cleared for her to hear—clearly—what he said next.

"I didn't kill your father nor that deputy."

Yes, that was Eric's voice all right, but it wasn't exactly a news flash. He'd said something similar during one of his phone calls. Gemma didn't believe him. Or rather she didn't want to believe him. But if he'd indeed killed them, then this would have been a time for him to brag. After all, he was dying.

"I'm not the only monster on your turf, Sheriff," Eric muttered. "Save yourself and Gemma if you can."

That alone could have put her heart in her throat, but Gunnar drew his gun and hurried to the window. He pushed her aside, but she could still see the barn.

"Do you think that means Eric sent another gunman?" she asked.

"Maybe." Gunnar didn't take his attention off the backyard. "Or it could be Eric's parting shot."

Yes, with just those handful of words, he could rob them of any peace and have them looking over their shoulders.

That might have given her some relief. If Gemma hadn't seen the movement by the side of the barn. For just a split second she thought maybe someone had peered out, so she watched, holding her breath again.

But nothing.

Obviously, every nerve was zinging inside her, and it wouldn't take much for her to see a bogeyman. Not Eric though. He was dead. She wasn't mistaken about Gunnar saying that, but instead of feeling any relief or celebration, Gemma could sense that something was indeed wrong.

There was a strange sound. As if something had smacked against the side of the house. The ranch hand shifted in that direction. So did she and Gunnar, and again, they waited.

Not long this time though.

She felt the jolt of adrenaline as smoke started billowing out from the side of the house. Gemma didn't think this had come from a fire. No. It was pure white and thick, and even though she was no expert, she thought it might be from some kind of smoke bomb. That would explain the strange sound she'd heard just seconds earlier.

Oh, God.

There was no good reason for someone to do something like this. But there was a bad one. Someone had gotten onto the ranch, and that someone was about to launch an attack.

Gemma got confirmation of that when she heard the next sound. One that she had no trouble recognizing.

It was a gunshot.

Chapter Sixteen

Kellan tried not to think. He just drove as fast as he could and hoped if Eric was telling the truth, that he would get to the ranch in time to stop anything bad from happening to Gemma.

I'm not the only monster on your turf, Sheriff.

Of course, Kellan had known that, but he had no idea which monster Eric meant. Or if the man was just blowing smoke during his last seconds alive. Still, Kellan couldn't discount pieces that just didn't add up.

"If Eric didn't kill your father and his deputy, who did?" Griff asked. He was familiar with the case, anyone in the area was, but he probably didn't know the details like Kellan.

"Maylene, maybe," Owen answered. Like Kellan and Griff, he was keeping watch around them on the drive back because one of Eric's assassins could be waiting along the road to do one last bidding for a dead boss. "It'd be a lot easier if it was Maylene," his brother added in a grumble.

Yes, it would be, considering their other two suspects were both marshals who could be hell-bent on covering up the murder of a prostitute. Rory could be doing that because he'd been the one to commit the murder. Amanda, because she wanted to protect Rory or because she'd been so jealous of his affair that she'd murdered Lacey in cold blood. Whatever their motive, if it was either of them—or both—it could mean the danger wasn't over.

Hell, it could be just beginning.

Kellan had already texted one of the hands to let him know to stay vigilant. He hadn't sent the same message to Gunnar though, but that's because it would have alarmed Gemma even more than she already was. Besides, if the hands saw anything, they would alert Gunnar, and his deputy could take things from there.

His phone rang, and when he saw Jack's name on the screen, Kellan took the call and put it on Speaker. "Is it true? Is Eric really dead?" Jack asked the moment he was on the line.

"It's true. But he didn't confess to killing Dad or Dusty."

That caused Jack to curse, something Kellan considered doing. He wanted this tied up in a neat little package, too, but more than that he needed to make sure Gemma was okay.

"I'm on my way to the ranch now and am only a few minutes out," Kellan added. There wasn't any way to tell Jack that Eric had left him with a bad feeling in his gut. Especially since Eric always made him feel that way. "Something's wrong," he admitted. "I have to get to Gemma."

That didn't help Jack's profanity. "You'd better have backup with you."

"I do. You stay there with Caroline. Eric might have left some orders from the grave, and he could have sent someone after Caroline."

"No one will get near her." Jack's voice was low and dangerous, exactly how Kellan felt. "Make sure you do the same for Gemma."

"I will. Gotta go. There's another call coming in." And his heart skipped some beats when he saw Gunnar's name on the screen.

"We've got a problem," Gunnar immediately said.

Yeah, and the deputy didn't have to explain exactly what that problem was. Kellan heard the gunshot.

"Is Gemma all right?" Kellan snapped.

"For now. Just get here as fast as you can," Gunnar insisted, but not before Kellan heard a second shot.

Obviously, Griff and Owen heard the shot, too, because both of them drew their weapons. Getting ready for whatever they were about to face. Kellan readied himself, too, and he pressed down hard on the accelerator, trying to eat up the distance between Gemma and him.

Gunnar didn't stay on the line with Kellan. Probably because the deputy was trying to move Gemma somewhere out of the line of fire. That steadied Kellan, some. Gunnar was well trained, an experienced deputy, but Eric's hired guns had likely honed their "craft," too.

"What the hell?" Owen grumbled when they took the turn to the ranch, and they saw the thick white smoke billowing around the house.

Kellan's first thought was an explosion. There'd certainly been enough of those after Eric had turned up in Longview Ridge. But this was no explosion. Someone was trying to smoke Gemma and Gunnar out of the house.

Ahead of him, the hands that Kellan had left at the gate were already in their trucks, heading for the house.

Good. That meant he'd have plenty of backup. Unfortunately, the hands might not be a match for professionals.

"Call them," Kellan instructed Owen. "Tell the hands to hold back until I get ahead of them."

Kellan didn't slow down while his brother did that. He just kept speeding toward the cattle gate, then past it. Thanks to Owen's call, the trucks pulled off the side, and Kellan sped by them.

There was no sign of Gunnar or Gemma. Also, no sign of the hand who should have been on the front porch. Of course, with that thick cloud of smoke, it was hard to see anything.

Kellan pulled up closer to the house, and he cursed when he spotted the hand. Facedown. Maybe dead. And again, he mentally kicked himself for not being here. He'd let Eric lead him into a trap, after all. It just hadn't been the trap that Kellan had been expecting.

The anger boiled through him, and Kellan wished Eric was alive only so he could kill the bastard.

"Stay in the cruiser," Kellan instructed Griff and Owen.

It took everything inside him to give that order for them to stay put. He needed to get to Gemma—but if they got out, a hired gun could pick them off one by one. That wouldn't help Gemma, and it could get someone else killed.

Kellan pulled off the driveway, crashing the cruiser through the fence and across the yard. Once he got to the side of the house, it was like driving blind because the smoke was so thick. He prayed that he wouldn't run into Gemma or Gunnar, and that's why he pressed down on the horn. Yes, that would alert a gunman, but the odds were the thug already knew they were there.

In fact, that could be the thug's plan.

Eric's plan.

It twisted at him to think that the killer wasn't done with them yet.

Kellan finally made it past the smear of smoke, and he caught sight of the back porch. Again, what he saw there wasn't good. There was another ranch hand lying in a crumpled heap. Worse, there was a second wave of smoke, and this time it wasn't coming from the yard but rather the house. It was billowing out the back door.

Kellan's phone dinged with a text message, but since he didn't want to take his attention off the house, he handed it to Owen.

"It's from Gunnar," Owen relayed. "Gemma and he are coming out the front and they need cover."

Kellan didn't waste a second. He threw the cruiser into Reverse, plowing back through the yard until he reached the front porch. This time he didn't stay inside. He threw open his door. Griff and Owen did the same, clearing the way for Gunnar and Gemma to hurry into the cruiser once they got out.

His heartbeat was thudding in his ears, making it hard to hear, and the smoke was stinging his eyes. Still, Kellan kept watch, waiting—and praying—for Gemma and Gunnar to appear.

The front door finally flew open, and Gunnar came out. The moment he spotted Kellan, he reached back, taking hold of Gemma's arm.

Gunnar had her.

That caused both relief and adrenaline to slam through Kellan, and he ran onto the porch so he could help get her to safety. However, when he reached the steps, Kellan saw something else.

Or rather someone.

A beefy man came up behind Gunnar and Gemma. And with the smoke billowing around her, the guy hooked his arm around Gemma's neck, snapping her back against his chest and out of Gunnar's grip.

And the man put a gun to her head.

FOR JUST A BREATH of a second, Gemma thought she would be able to get to Kellan. She thought they would all be okay and get out of this nightmare. But that all changed—first when she saw the fresh look of terror on Kellan's face.

Then, she'd felt the arm around her throat.

And the gun.

A thousand thoughts and feelings hit her at once, but the one that pierced through that frenzied whirl was that this could get Kellan killed. But Kellan dove for cover. So did Owen, Griff and the hands. Kellan landed on the side of the stone steps, but he immediately shifted his position, levering himself up and bringing his gun.

"Wouldn't do that if I were you, Sheriff," the man behind her growled, causing Kellan to freeze. "That'd be a real bad idea."

Gemma didn't recognize the voice, but then this was probably one of the thugs that Eric had hired. A way of tying up all those loose ends and she was the ultimate prize because she was the one who'd gotten away.

Caroline, too.

And it sent another layer of sickening dread over Gemma that at this very moment one of Eric's goons might be doing the same thing to Caroline as this one was doing to her. At least she could fight back, but Caroline wasn't in any shape to do that.

"Let her go," Kellan snapped. His eyes were narrowed to slits, and every muscle in his body looked primed and ready for a fight. A fight that couldn't happen as long as this snake had a gun to her head.

Gemma needed to figure out what to do about that.

"Not gonna happen," the hit man answered Kellan. "But here's what we're gonna do instead. All of you and any other hands you've got stashed nearby will put down your weapons and back up. If you do that, nobody dies."

Kellan didn't budge. Neither did Gunnar, Owen or Griff. There were also four ranch hands who were behind cover at the backs of their trucks.

"And I'm to believe you about no one dying?" Kellan fired back. "There are two men down, one on the back porch and another just a few feet from you."

"They're not dead. Just stunned and drugged. My boss didn't want any unnecessary collateral damage."

That was laughable. Eric didn't care who was killed in this as long as he got Caroline and her. Maybe Kellan, too. Gemma didn't know how deep Eric's hatred for Kellan went, but Eric could have included him in this cleanup detail.

"My boss only wants the lady here," the thug added. "I'll be taking her for a little ride. I'm to show her something and then let her go."

No one hearing that believed it. Especially not Gemma.

"Guns down," he repeated. "Then, put your hands up so I can see them."

The man jammed the gun even harder against her head. So hard that Gemma couldn't hold back a wince and a soft groan of pain. Then she felt the blood from where the barrel of the gun had dug into her skin.

Kellan saw the blood, too.

He cursed, his grip tightening on his gun. Gemma kept her gaze on him, silently pleading with him not to do anything. Not like this. The thug could literally gun Kellan and the rest down while using her as a human shield.

She felt the blood trickle down the side of her face, and Gemma figured that was the tipping point for Kellan. He couldn't save her, not here anyway. Like her, he had to wait for some kind of opening and pray that this jerk made a mistake. The other hired guns for Eric certainly had.

"Frank, you can come out now," the goon said. "I'm gonna need a little help here."

Gemma cursed softly when she heard the footsteps, coming from behind her, and even though she couldn't see *Frank*, she felt it when he reached in and put a pair of plasticuffs on her wrists.

"Don't make me hurt her to get you to obey," the thug warned Kellan. "I can start putting bullets in her. It won't kill her, but it'll hurt—bad."

Gemma had firsthand experience what it felt like to be shot. And it did hurt. But not as much as seeing that look in Kellan's eyes. He was blaming himself for this. He was reliving the other nightmare of when she'd been held at gunpoint.

With his eyes still locked on hers, Kellan tossed his gun to the side, lifted his hands. One by one, the others followed suit. Almost immediately, her captor started moving with her. Frank was likely watching their backs.

"I'm gonna need a vehicle and keys," the goon said when he reached the steps with her. "I'll take that red truck." Other than the cruiser, it was the one nearest to the house. "And remember, if any of you tries to shoot me, the bullet could go through me and into her. Plus, I'm sure my own finger would tense and I'd end up shooting her in the head. Wouldn't want that, now, would we?"

Gemma tuned him out. Tried to tune out the flashbacks, too, and with each step she took, she tried to figure out how to stop this. She tested the man's reaction by dropping down her weight a little.

"That'd be a good way to get the sheriff killed," he whispered in her ear. "Despite what I just told them, he's the one I'll shoot if you don't cooperate. He's the only one who'll die. I doubt you'd be able to live with knowing you killed him."

She wouldn't, and that's the only reason she stopped. It was best to get away from Kellan and the others. Yes, they would go in pursuit, but once she was in the truck with this snake and Frank, she might be able to cause them to wreck if she threw her body against the steering wheel. It was risky, but anything she did would be.

"Back up," Frank yelled out to the hands. And they did.

When they reached the truck, Gemma heard the engine still running, and the man didn't waste any time shoving her inside through the driver's door. He followed her, shutting the door, and Frank got in from the other side, trapping her in the middle. Only then did she get a look at their faces.

Strangers.

Frank was thin and wiry, and he was loaded down with assorted weapons. The one who'd snatched her was bulky and built like a wrestler, which meant she wouldn't be able to hold her own physically with him. Maybe, though, she wouldn't need to do that if she could send the truck into the ditch.

Gemma tried to get out of the plasticuffs, more as a distraction since she knew they would hold. She wiggled her shoulders.

And the pain exploded in her head.

She hadn't seen the blow coming from the butt of Frank's gun, but she certainly felt it. It blurred her vision and knocked the breath out of her.

"Settle down," Frank warned her. "I don't have orders to kill you, but that doesn't mean I won't."

Despite the searing pain, Gemma latched on to those words. "You expect me to believe Eric didn't leave orders to kill me?"

Frank lifted his shoulder. The gesture was casual enough, but there was concern, or something, in his dull blue eyes when he glanced behind them. Kellan was no doubt already in pursuit.

"I'm supposed to give you a message from Eric Lang," Frank said. "Just carrying out a man's dying wish. I'm to tell you that Eric was telling a fib when he said he didn't kill the sheriff's dad and that deputy. That's the word Eric told me to use—*fib*." Judging from Frank's oily smile, that amused him.

It didn't amuse Gemma, but it was definitely something Eric would have said. "Why did he *fib*?"

"How the hell should I know?" Frank snapped. "The guy was a couple of cards short of a deck if you know what I mean. He said he killed them both and that I should tell you, that you should call the sheriff and let him know, too."

With that, he took out a phone and pressed the button for a number that was already programmed into the phone. Her vision still wasn't clear, and her head was throbbing like a bad tooth, but Gemma had no doubts that Frank was calling Kellan. A moment later, she got confirmation of that.

"Sheriff Slater," he said, his voice as fierce and clipped as she figured his expression would be.

"Tell him what Eric said." Frank passed the phone to her.

"Kellan," Gemma managed after she cleared her throat. She wanted to sound strong with the hopes of making this easier for Kellan. If that was possible.

"Gemma." Not fierce and clipped this time when Kellan spoke. But there was so much worry.

Frank rammed his elbow into her side, obviously his way of reminding her to get on with the message. "Eric apparently told these men that he had indeed killed your father and Dusty."

"Eric wanted to set the record straight," Frank added in a snarl loud enough for Kellan to hear.

"And why would Eric want to do that?" The fierceness was back. "Why would he care what I know or don't know when he's dead?"

"Don't know, don't care," Frank answered. "I'm just the messenger here."

"Yeah, one who kidnapped a woman from my home."

Frank chuckled. "I guess that had to get your goat, what with you being a lawman and all. Don't worry,

Sheriff, you'll get her back in one piece. More or less," Frank added, sneering at her. "My advice would be for you and your fellow badges to back off and let this play out."

There was nothing Kellan would want to play out when hired thugs and Eric were involved.

"You need to make sure Caroline is okay," Gemma blurted out, knowing it could earn her another bashing. Or worse. Still, she had to try. But Frank didn't hit her again. He merely ended the call and put his phone away.

"We're almost there," the driver said, causing Gemma to glance around to see where they were.

And the chill rippled like ice over her skin.

Because this was the road to Serenity Inn.

Oh, God. The last time she'd been here, Eric had nearly killed her.

While she fought to hang on to her breath, Gemma reminded herself that Eric was dead. That didn't help, though, because he wasn't the only one who could murder her and Kellan. Hired guns could do that, too.

The inn came into view, and even though it was daylight, it looked spookier than it had the night Eric had taken her there. Most of the windows had been boarded up, and the ones that hadn't been were just dark holes of broken glass. They reminded her of eye sockets.

The driver went through the side of the yard, or rather what was left of it after the explosion, and as if they'd rehearsed it, both men got out, the driver dragging her after them. A man got on each side of her, and they ran with her into the inn. The moment they were inside, they padlocked the door from within. Since the lock looked new, she guessed they'd been the ones to put it there.

Gemma forced herself to breathe. Hard to do because the stale air inside was clogged with dust, mold and other smells she didn't want to identify. Even in the barely there light, she could still see the foyer floor. And the bloodstains that were there.

Hers.

Outside, she heard vehicles braking to noisy stops. Kellan and the others, no doubt. Frank took out his phone, and she saw him press Kellan's number again. He didn't put the call on Speaker, but she was close enough to him to hear when Kellan answered.

"Tell me what it'll take to get you to release Gemma," Kellan demanded.

"I haven't been paid to negotiate with you, but you should keep yourself and your men back, Sheriff. One more step, and you could all go *kaboom*."

Gemma shook her head, not wanting to believe that, but Frank took out a small device. It was the size of a cell phone and looked like the remote control for a toy car. It had two switches, one labeled Arm, and the other, Execute, was about two inches below it.

When Frank hit the switch and a green light flared on, her stomach went to her knees. But Frank smiled.

"All ready to go now," he said, his thumb moving to hover over the second button. *Execute.* "If I press this, it's gonna be too late for all of us."

The man had just armed a bomb.

Chapter Seventeen

Kellan immediately motioned for Owen, Griff and the hands to stop in their tracks. This could be a bluff, but if Eric was involved in this, then he could have hired someone to set another bomb.

But Kellan was beginning to think that was a big *if*.

Something about all of this wasn't right. If Eric wanted revenge against Gemma, why hadn't his thugs just killed her at the ranch? Of course, maybe Eric just wanted it all to end here, like a sick full circle.

Another possibility came to mind, too. Eric could have left instructions to use Gemma to draw out Caroline so he could finish her off, as well. It wouldn't work. Gemma wouldn't lure out Caroline even if it meant saving herself. Besides, Caroline had no memory of her anyway.

"Why bring Gemma here?" Kellan snapped. He wasn't even sure the hired gun was still on the line, not until he responded.

"Just following orders. And speaking of orders, here's one for you, Sheriff. Start walking toward the inn. Just you. None of your little helpers. I've got my hands on a controller for the bomb, and the light is blazing green. That means it's ready to go, and I've got my thumb over the button that could put you in a lot of pieces."

Kellan looked at the window on the bottom right. It was boarded up, but there was a gap in between two of the boards, and Kellan saw someone peering out at him.

"You said there were explosives," Kellan reminded him. That wouldn't stop him. One way or another he was getting inside so he could try to save Gemma.

No. Not try. He *would* save her. Kellan refused to think differently.

"Oh, there's a boomer out there all right, but you can follow what's left of the stone walkway to the side of the porch. Remember that part about only you coming. If not, the blast goes off and your girl might get hurt. These walls aren't that thick."

That kicked up his pulse several notches, and he felt the slick layer of fear slide over him. It wasn't the first time he'd felt it, but the stakes felt higher than they ever had before.

"You know this could be a trap," Owen warned him. His brother and the rest were behind the cover of their vehicles—where Kellan wanted them to stay.

Kellan nodded, and without ending the call, he slipped his phone in his shirt pocket to free his hands. He started walking. He'd picked up his gun from the yard at the ranch before he left, and he still had it out of his holster. If he got the chance to use it, he would.

With each step, his heart beat faster. His chest went fist tight. And it took everything inside Kellan to fight away the flashbacks from that other night.

He didn't look down at the ground. Didn't want the distraction of remembering the spots where his father and Dusty had died. Kellan just kept walking, and once he made it to the side of the porch, he climbed up.

"What now?" Kellan snapped to the caller.

"Come on in." The welcome was coated with the same kind of mockery that Eric favored, and Kellan heard what he thought was someone disengaging a lock on the front door.

He knew in his gut that if he went, he'd be gunned down.

Kellan slowed, taking a closer look at the gap in the window. No one was peering out at him now, but he could see inside.

Gemma.

She was there in the foyer, much as she'd been the night Eric had taken her. Her hands were still cuffed behind her, and like the big bulky guy next to her, her attention was nailed to the front door. She opened her mouth as if to call out to him, but the thug said something to her. Something probably meant to make her stay quiet. She didn't.

"Kellan, no!" she shouted.

The thug backhanded her, and Gemma's head snapped back. Something else snapped, too. The leash Kellan had on the rage inside him. He took aim through the crack and fired.

Two bullets slammed into the thug's chest.

Kellan didn't wait for him to drop. He ran to the front door, kicking it open and then moving quickly to the side so that the second man couldn't shoot him. But the guy was already running toward the back of the house.

"He was going to shoot you," Gemma said. "And

he's got some kind of device. I'm almost positive it's to set off a bomb. There's a button labeled 'Execute.'"

Kellan didn't have a lot of knowledge about explosives, but Eric had clearly found someone who knew how to blow things up. The proof of that was in the front yard of the inn where there was a gaping hole and debris.

"Owen, tell everyone to stay put," Kellan called out to his brother, and he went to Gemma.

Hell, her face was bleeding, and she was shaking. But she also looked riled to the core. That was good. Much better than a panic attack.

The skinny second man disappeared into a room off a long, dark hall, but Kellan didn't go after him. The thug on the floor was still alive, moaning in pain.

And he was armed.

Kellan did something about that. He snatched up the thug's gun, putting it in the back waist of his jeans, and he moved Gemma away from the man in case he tried to grab her. He didn't want one of the goons getting their hands on her again.

"You came," she said, her breath gusting. "That wasn't very smart."

He nearly smiled. "I swore I'd come back to you, and here I am."

This time when he looked at her, there were tears shimmering in her eyes. Kellan wanted to kiss her, to hold her, but there wasn't time. He used his pocketknife to cut the plasticuffs and then handed her the thug's gun.

"There's really a bomb?" he asked.

"I think so, but it must be outside because I didn't see Frank bring it inside." She tipped her head to the

hall. "That's his name, and he said Eric hired him."
She paused. "I'm not sure I believe him."

"Neither do I."

But that left Kellan with a huge question—who had
done this? And what was he going to do about it? He
couldn't take Gemma back outside, not with the possible bomb, and he didn't want to leave her alone with
the injured thug. If he wanted to catch this Frank and
get answers, then he'd have to go after him and take
Gemma with him. Not that he could have talked her
into doing otherwise.

While keeping watch around them, he took out his
phone to see if Frank was still on the line. He wasn't.
So Kellan sent a text to Owen to let him know that
Gemma was okay, more or less, and that he should call
the bomb squad to get them out there.

Kellan wouldn't have backup until they cleared the
place, and by then Frank could be long gone. If there
was a bomb, Frank would know where it was and get
around it.

"Watch our backs," Kellan told Gemma. He hated
to rely on her for that. She'd just been through a horrible ordeal. A kidnapping. And she was probably having some horrible flashbacks, but he didn't have a lot
of options here.

With his gun still gripped in his hand, Kellan started
moving. There was a large staircase to his right, but
that was boarded off. Not that it would stop someone
from going up there, but he didn't see any footprints in
the thick layer of dust on the floor. All the footprints
led to the hall so that's where Kellan went.

Kellan had been in this hall before, but he cursed
when he saw all the doors. At least a dozen of them.

The other times he'd been in this part of the inn, it had been weeks and even months after his father's murder. There hadn't been the threat of a hired gun ready to strike.

Unfortunately, the hall was even darker than the foyer, and it made it much harder to see the floor. There were dim pockets of light coming from the doors that were open, but most were closed. He didn't know if they'd been that way before Frank's attempted escape or if the thug was hiding behind one of them.

Of course, since each room had windows, it was also possible the man was long gone. Because of the thick shrubs and trees around the place, Owen and the others might not have even seen him.

When Kellan reached the first door, he kicked it open, and waited a heartbeat to make sure he wasn't about to be gunned down. No sound. Nothing. He glanced inside and didn't see a single footprint in the dust so he moved to the next one.

Behind him, he could hear Gemma's still uneven breathing, and when her back brushed against his, he could feel her tight muscles. Maybe she wouldn't hate him too much for putting her through this kind of hell.

Kellan kicked in another door. Nothing there, either. Ditto for the next two. He was about to bash in the door of the fourth when there was some movement at the end of the hall. Someone peered out from one of the rooms, and Kellan automatically took aim at the person.

"Don't shoot," someone said.

Maylene.

Hell, what was she doing here? He didn't like the way she kept turning up where she shouldn't.

Kellan didn't fire, but that was only because the

woman didn't appear to be armed. However, he did make sure he was in front of Gemma.

"Eric's dead," Maylene said, her voice trembling. She seemed to be trembling, too, but Kellan knew that could be faked. "You killed him. Good. I didn't want him alive after what he did. He did horrible, horrible things." Maylene sounded as if she were about to lose it.

"How did you get in here?" Kellan asked her.

"Through the back." She made a vague motion behind her. "Not all the windows are boarded up or locked. I came here because I wanted to see the place where he tried to kill me. He nearly blew me up in that explosion."

"And he still could. There's a bomb nearby. Did you see the man who set it?"

Even in the darkness, he could see Maylene's eyes widen. "No. I didn't see anyone." Her gaze fired around. "We need to leave. We have to get out of here."

The woman turned as if ready to bolt, but someone reached out from behind her and put her in a choke hold. Just as the thug had done to Gemma back at the ranch.

Seeing that felt as if someone had slugged Kellan in the gut, but he kept his hand steady. Took aim. But he didn't have a clean shot, not with Maylene in the way.

Maylene shrieked, but the sound was strangled, no doubt because the man was already cutting off her oxygen.

"Let her go!" Kellan tried, and he sent a warning shot at the man, aiming the bullet into the ceiling above the guy's head.

The man was behind Maylene, but Kellan saw his gun snake out. And the man fired.

Kellan pulled Gemma into the room in the nick of time because the bullet slammed into the doorjamb.

"Help me," Maylene called out on the tail of another of those shrieks.

Kellan wasn't sure if this was a trap or not, but he couldn't just let the woman be murdered in front of him. He leaned out to send off another warning shot, and that's when he saw the face of the man who was holding her. Not Frank.

Rory.

EVERYTHING SUDDENLY WENT so still that Gemma thought it was as if everything, including her body, had simply stopped. Her breath. Her heart. Even her thoughts.

The moment just froze.

Rory stood there, his arm curved around Maylene's throat, his gun aimed at Kellan and her. And in that moment she knew why it'd come to this.

"You killed Lacey," Gemma said, her voice carrying like a whispered echo in the empty inn.

"Then you murdered my father and Dusty to cover it up." Kellan's voice wasn't exactly a whisper. More a dangerous growl.

"No. Not your father." Rory spoke calmly. He didn't sound especially angry despite the fact he was on the verge of killing a woman. "But Dusty, yes. I'm sorry about that. Sorry it had to go down that way."

Strange that he would admit to one murder but not the other. But if Rory hadn't murdered Buck, then who had? Eric had denied it, as well.

"The only thing you're sorry about is getting caught," Kellan spat out.

"Yes," Rory admitted. He was calm. Too calm. And that was even more chilling. He wasn't killing in some crazed haze like Eric. This was ice-cold and calculated.

There was only a thin thread of light in that part of the hall, but Gemma caught Maylene's eyes and saw the terror in them.

"Is Maylene part of this?" Gemma asked.

"No. She's not what you'd call an organized thinker. Eric used her."

Gemma glared at him. "And you didn't?"

Rory certainly didn't deny that, so maybe he'd lured Maylene here. It wouldn't have taken much. She wasn't just an unorganized thinker, the woman was almost certainly mentally unstable.

"Amanda's helping you." Gemma threw it out there, hoping it would hit a nerve. By God, she wanted to know who was involved in this so they could be punished.

"No. Not Amanda." Rory didn't hesitate, but the moment he answered her, he shoved Maylene forward, took aim at her.

And he fired.

The bullet slammed into Maylene. She screamed, a hoarse pitiful sound that told Gemma the shot hadn't killed her. Not yet anyway. But she was in pain. Worse, that scream might send Owen, Griff and the hands running into the inn, and they could set off the explosives. If that happened, they could all be killed.

Rory didn't wait around. The moment Maylene hit the floor, he turned and ran back into the room where he'd been hiding.

"He's not getting away." Kellan took off after him, the sound of his cowboy boots slamming against the hardwood floor.

Gemma went with him, keeping watch behind them in case they were ambushed. After all, Frank could still be around, and if so, she needed to get that remote control from him and try to deactivate the bomb.

"Stay behind me," Kellan warned her as they reached Maylene.

The woman was moaning and had her hand over her shoulder, and while there was blood, Gemma prayed it wasn't life threatening. There was no way they could get an ambulance out there, not until they'd secured the area. Whenever that would be.

"Put some pressure on the wound," Gemma instructed the woman. It wasn't enough, but at the moment it was all she could do. She needed to make sure Kellan wasn't about to be ambushed.

Kellan peered into the room where Rory had disappeared, and he immediately cursed. Gemma soon saw why. The window in this room wasn't boarded up.

It was wide-open, the tattered remains of old white curtains fluttering in the breeze. It looked like a ghost.

Since there was some light here, she could also see the footprints in the dust. A lot of them, making her wonder if this was how Frank had escaped, too. But she soon saw that he hadn't. Frank was on the floor, in one of the shadows in the corner of the room.

"Stun gun," Rory said, causing Gemma to snap to attention, and she frantically tried to pick through the darkness and find him.

Rory was in the opposite corner from Frank. Sitting there, his back wedged against the wall. He had his gun in his right hand, and it was pointed directly at Kellan. The remote control for the bomb was in his lap, the fingers of his left hand hovering over the button with that sickening label.

Execute.

Gemma's first instinct was to shoot him, but she couldn't do that, not with him holding that remote.

He could blow the place up.

"You did more than stun him," Kellan said.

Gemma had a closer look, and she saw the syringe sticking out of Frank's neck. It had been rammed into him like a knife, and she thought maybe it had killed him. She couldn't see any signs that he was breathing.

It was impossible for her to feel sorry for the monster on the floor who'd kidnapped her and brought her to this place. Not under Eric's orders, either. But Rory's. However, seeing him sprawled out on the floor like that was proof that Rory was capable of killing. He'd already admitted to that, but it turned her stomach for it to be right in front of her.

"He was about to escape out the window, and he saw me. I could see it in his eyes that he knew what was going on, I couldn't leave him alive. He would have eventually blackmailed me the way Eric did." Rory's forehead bunched up, and he winced as if the impact of what he'd done was hitting him hard.

Good, Gemma thought. She didn't want any of Eric's insanity or cockiness. She wanted Rory to understand every bit of the misery he'd caused.

Misery that wasn't over yet.

She nearly reminded him that his other henchman was still alive. Well, maybe he was. But hearing something like that might send Rory even farther over the edge. If that was possible.

From out in the hall, Maylene moaned, but it sounded as if the woman hadn't moved. Maybe if Maylene had put some pressure on the gunshot wound, it would be enough until the medics could get to her.

"You need to put down your gun and that controller," Kellan told the marshal. "You're not going to get out of this alive."

"No," Rory readily agreed. He kept his eyes locked with Kellan's. "It was never supposed to go this far. I don't expect you to understand, but it was never supposed to go this far."

Kellan cursed. It was raw and mean. "You son of a bitch. You killed people. You just shot a woman out in the hall. And you brought Gemma here to kill her. Why? She had nothing to do with Lacey."

But Kellan stopped, went still. "You were going to pin all of this on Eric. His sick orders from the grave. Mop up. You were going to stand back with blood on your hands and let Eric take the fall."

Rory made a sound of agreement. "Both Frank and his partner thought they were working for Eric. They told you exactly what I instructed them to tell you. I figured if you believed Eric was behind this, that he had killed your father and Dusty, that you'd let it go."

"Never," Kellan assured him. "I would have kept digging."

"Yes. I know." Rory dragged in a long breath. "You and Gemma just wouldn't let it go. Dusty, your father and you kept digging and digging, Eric, too."

"Eric?" Gemma challenged.

No sound of agreement that time. It was more of a

quick hollow laugh. "A year ago, Eric contacted me a few hours before he kidnapped you, said that he'd worked it all out. That he knew I'd killed Lacey and tried to cover it up so Amanda wouldn't find out. But it wasn't like that. I didn't plan to kill her. It just happened when she tried to blackmail me."

"You think that excuses what you did?" Kellan snapped. "It doesn't."

"No. It doesn't. But Eric used it. He said he'd go to you with some so-called proof. Something that I left behind at the scene of Lacey's death. Eric lured me here to the inn that night, and that's when I shot Dusty. I thought I was shooting Eric." His gaze came to Kellan's again. "But not your father. I swear on Amanda's soul that I didn't kill him."

Kellan certainly didn't jump to say he believed him. Neither did Gemma. But he hadn't sworn on his own soul but rather Amanda's. So, maybe Rory didn't have that death on his head.

Gemma glanced at the syringe in Frank's neck and wondered if the drugs inside it had been meant for her. Re-creating the scene of what Eric had done to Caroline and her a year ago. Just one more piece of a pretense put together so a killer could get away with what he'd done.

"Eric had given Dusty proof of my affair with Lacey," Rory continued. His eyes were blank, the look of a man who'd been defeated. "That's how Eric lured me here that night. He wanted me to kill you, your father and Dusty." He glanced at Gemma. "He was going to save Caroline and you for himself."

That wasn't a surprise. Eric loathed her. Caroline, too, because they'd been the ones to expose him for the monster that he was. Still, he was no more of a monster than Rory. Because Rory had sworn to uphold the law, and here he was taking it into his own dirty hands. In that moment, she despised him more than she did Eric.

"You didn't have to involve Maylene in this," Gemma said, glancing over at the woman.

"Yes, I did, because I couldn't be sure what Eric had told her." Rory looked up at Kellan then. "I didn't kill Eric, but I wanted to. God, I wanted to. It's a nice touch that he got betrayed by one of his own men."

Yes, it was. If Eric had lived though, she doubted he would have been amused by it. He would have murdered Hiatt in a brutal way.

"You gave Eric the location of my WITSEC house?" Gemma asked. Not that it mattered, but it would tie up that one loose end in her mind.

Rory nodded. "*I* was the breach in WITSEC. Whatever you do, don't try to pin any of this on Amanda."

"That's exactly what I'm going to do," Kellan replied. "That's why you're going to put down the remote and your gun so I can take you into custody. You can confess to everything and by doing so, you clear your girlfriend's name. If not, I'll go after her and find a way to connect her to your crimes. I'll put her behind bars for the rest of her life."

Gemma could see what Kellan was doing. He was trying to goad Rory into making sure Amanda didn't get hurt in this.

But she would anyway.

If Amanda loved Rory as much as she claimed, this was going to destroy her. And when Gemma looked in Rory's eyes, she saw that he knew exactly that.

"Please don't do that to her. Please," Rory said. "Tell her I'm sorry." He moved both of his hands.

In the same motion, Kellan lunged at him. But it was too late. Rory hit the button on the remote just as he fired a bullet in his own head.

Chapter Eighteen

Kellan's heart stopped dead. He automatically lunged at Gemma, wrapping his arms around her waist and pulling her to the floor so he could try to use his body to protect her.

They hit, hard, the jolt of the impact slamming through him, but Kellan shoved aside the pain and braced himself for the explosion.

It didn't come.

He held his breath, waiting, wondering if the bomb was on a timer. Maybe. If so, the threat was still there, and it was possible that the sound of the last gunshot would cause Owen and the others to come closer. Kellan took out his phone, to call them and tell them to stay back, but then he saw the controller still on Rory's lap.

Rory was clearly dead, his head now slumped to an obscene angle against the wall, and his eyes blank and lifeless. There was blood spatter everywhere, including on the controller, but it didn't cover the lights.

The green light was off.

Kellan had a closer look, and he realized that Rory hadn't executed the bomb. He'd turned it off.

The breath of relief swooshed out of him, but there'd be no real relief until he had Gemma safely away from this place. There could be another way to set off the bomb, one that didn't involve the controller. A marshal—especially a dirty one—would have seen to that. Rory had obviously changed his mind about blowing them up, but there could be other hired guns out there waiting to do the job. They wouldn't have gotten the "memo" that their boss had just offed himself.

Kellan pulled her to her feet, and that's when their eyes met. Definitely not relief, either. Or shock, something he had expected.

"We have to get out of here," she said.

He wasn't going to argue with that, but when he glanced at Maylene who was lying in the doorway, he knew leaving wasn't going to be easy. The woman was bleeding, and unlike Gemma, there was some shock.

"Frank was going to leave out the window," Kellan reminded her.

Or rather that's what Rory had told them. Kellan didn't like to put any stock in anything Rory had said, but judging from the position of Frank's body, it made sense. And if it was a safe enough way for him to escape, then they could use it, too.

"Are you hurt?" Kellan asked Gemma, and it twisted at him that he hadn't already asked, or checked for himself. He'd soon remedy that when he had her safe.

"I'm okay. Let's get Maylene out the window."

Kellan figured the okay wasn't anywhere close to the truth. Her face was bleeding, and the bruises were already forming on her cheek. Still, Gemma moved fast when they went into the hall, got on each side of Maylene and hoisted the woman up.

He kept watch because the hired thug was still in the foyer, but Kellan didn't see the man as he and Gemma made their way to the window. It was a risk because he could end up hurting Maylene more than she already was, but they couldn't stay inside. Thankfully, Maylene cooperated, but she did let out a long whimpering sob when she saw Rory.

"He shot me," Maylene said. "Why? I never did anything to him."

Since Kellan didn't have an answer for that, he just stayed quiet and eased Maylene out the window. "Don't move," he told the woman. "There could be explosives out here."

In hindsight, he should have figured out a gentler way of telling her that because he had to latch on to Maylene to keep her from running. Kellan held on to her while he climbed out. Gemma was right behind him, and she landed on her feet right next to him.

"Kellan?" he heard Owen shout. There was plenty of concern in his brother's voice.

Kellan sat Maylene on the ground and took out his phone. Owen answered on the first ring. "We're out of the house, and in the backyard. Gemma and I are… fine." He used Gemma's answer only because he didn't want to get into the truth.

"Good." Owen blew out a breath. "Stay put. The bomb squad just got here to do a scan. There's an ambulance here, too."

Since Kellan hadn't heard any sirens, it must have made a silent approach, but he was glad it was there. Maylene's injuries didn't appear to be life threatening, but she needed help. That's why it was so damn hard to stand there and wait.

"There's another hired gun in the foyer," Gemma said, leaning in closer to the phone. Closer to Kellan, too. He wanted to pull her into his arms. Wanted her against him. But he needed to keep his hands free in case he had to defend them. "Maylene's also been shot, and she's in the backyard with us."

"I can try to get to you," Owen offered.

"No." Kellan couldn't say that fast enough. "Make sure the grounds are clear first. The thug Frank said the walls of the inn weren't that thick, meaning that the bomb was outside." Well, unless there were others.

Owen didn't sound relieved now. He cursed. "How bad did things get in there?"

Bad. But Kellan didn't say that aloud, either. "It was Rory. He killed Lacey and Dusty. Rory did that to cover up his affair with Lacey." Kellan had to pause. "Rory just killed himself."

Silence. Followed by more profanity that was raw and punched up with emotion. "And Dad? Did Rory kill him, too?"

"He said he didn't." Kellan hated to add this next part. "And I believe him."

The words had hardly left his mouth when Kellan heard the footsteps behind them. He immediately turned, putting Gemma behind him, and he saw Amanda making her way toward them. She had drawn her gun, but she held it down by her side.

Kellan's first thought was that she'd come there to finish the job that Rory had started, but then he saw her eyes. They were red from crying, and there were fresh tears on her cheek.

"Is Rory here?" Amanda asked, her voice trembling. "I tapped in to the GPS, and I know he came here. I found his car on a trail." She made a vague motion to the right, but she never took her gaze off Kellan.

"Put down the gun, Amanda," Kellan warned her.

She shook her head as if not understanding. Amanda's gaze fired from Maylene, to Gemma and then back to Kellan.

"If you tapped in to his GPS, then you knew something was wrong," Kellan said. "You knew what he'd done to Lacey and Dusty? You knew he was a killer and was ready to kill again to cover his tracks?"

More tears came, and this time her head shakes became frantic. The moment the gun slipped from her hand and fell, Kellan hurried to her to restrain her. He doubted she was an actual accessory to Rory's crimes. Not before the fact anyway. But he wasn't taking any chances. When he put plasticuffs on her, Amanda sank to her knees on the ground.

"Rory's dead," she muttered. It wasn't a question.

"Yes, he killed himself."

Kellan steeled himself to give her details, but he didn't get a chance because he heard a new wave of footsteps.

"It's me," Owen said, and Kellan spotted his brother coming up the trail Amanda had taken. "I saw Amanda making her way back here, and since she didn't set off any explosives, I figured I'd come back and lend a hand."

As Amanda had done, Owen glanced around as if piecing things together, and he cursed softly. Not because of Amanda or even Maylene but when his attention landed on Gemma. "You've been taking some punches lately."

Gemma nodded. "But I'm okay now."

Unlike her earlier assurance that she was okay, Kellan thought this one might be closer to the truth.

"I didn't see any other gunmen," Owen went on, and he looked at Amanda. "Is she under arrest?"

"No," Kellan answered, and since he had his brother's help, he risked slipping his arms around Gemma's waist. "Just being cautious."

Owen made a sound of agreement. "Come on. We can use the trail to get Maylene to the ambulance. To get you and Gemma to the cruiser, too. I'll handle Amanda while Griff deals with the bomb squad."

"There's an injured man in the foyer," Gemma reminded him. "And Frank's in the room."

"Yeah. We'll take care of him once the building and grounds are cleared." Owen went to Maylene, lifting her so he could support her weight. Kellan did the same to Gemma so they could start walking.

Kellan continued to keep watch, but he no longer felt that sinking feeling in the pit of his stomach. Eric and Rory were dead. For now, the danger had passed.

"Jack called," Owen said as they walked. "No change in Caroline's condition. He said he'd call you after you were at the sheriff's office."

Good. Because they needed to talk.

"Caroline will have to stay in protective custody," Gemma muttered.

And Kellan had to nod. Caroline was the only person who could possibly ID his father's killer. That meant she was in danger. Well, maybe she was. Maybe like Rory and Eric, his father's killer was dead, too. Still, it was too big of a risk to take not to keep Caroline under protection. Then, once her memory returned... well, then they'd have to deal with whatever was now trapped in her head.

When they made it back to the front road, Owen

handed off Maylene to a medic who immediately whisked her into the ambulance.

"You should let the medics check you," Owen added to Gemma.

She shook her head. Kellan nodded. He compromised by adding, "Soon."

And the look Kellan gave her let Gemma know that he wouldn't budge on that. He'd come close to losing her, and he had to make sure she was truly all right. First though, he wanted to get her off her feet before she fell flat on her face.

Kellan threaded his way through the medics, bomb squad, Griff and the hands who were still around, and he led Gemma to the cruiser. He got her in the front seat but didn't drive. That's because he wasn't sure he was steady enough to do that. Not yet. She wasn't the only one who was shaken.

He reached for her, to pull her into his arms, but he was surprised when she stopped him.

"You're not going to apologize," Gemma said, and she sounded a lot stronger than he'd expected. "Eric was a bastard. Rory was a bastard. And they both failed."

She put her hands on the sides of his face, forcing eye contact even though he had no intention of looking anywhere else. "You swore to me that you'd come back, and you did." Her breath shuddered now, the nerves showing. "You did," she repeated, the shudder making it to her voice.

He nodded. "I have this thing about keeping my promise to a woman I've seen naked." It had the intended effect.

It made her smile.

Kellan smiled, too, when he eased his hand around the back of her neck, pulled her to him and kissed her. There it was. That kick of both comfort and heat. It slid right through him, healing all the raw parts of him. She probably wouldn't believe him if he told her the effect she had on him, so he went in a different direction.

"I love you," he said. "And, no, that's not a good-bye," he quickly added. "I have this thing about saying 'I love you' to a woman whom I, well, love."

Gemma stared at him. And stared. Before she smiled again. "I love you. And I have this thing about making sure it lasts a lifetime."

He felt another surge of comfort and heat, this one like an avalanche. It was exactly what Kellan wanted. "You swear?" he asked as he pulled her to him for another kiss.

"I swear," Gemma answered, and her mouth met his.

* * * * *

UNDERCOVER ACCOMPLICE

CAROL ERICSON

Prologue

He ducked into the cave and swept the beam from the weak flashlight around the small space. Releasing a frosty breath, he slid down the wall of the cave into a crouch and faced the entrance, balancing his weapon on his knees.

After he'd helped Rafi and the others fight off the intruders who'd attacked their village, he took off for the hills—but not before he'd arranged another meeting with Pazir.

The last time he'd tried to meet with Pazir, it had led to the death of an army ranger, the possible death of one of his Delta Force team members and his own decision to go AWOL. He hoped for a better result this time.

A bush outside the cave rustled and he coiled his thigh muscles, getting ready to spring. His trigger finger twitched.

A harsh whisper echoed in the darkness. "Denver? Major Denver?"

He rose slowly, his jacket scraping the wall of the cave, the light from his flashlight illuminating a figure on hands and knees at the cave's entrance. "If you have any weapons, toss them in first. If you're not alone…you soon will be."

Pazir sat back on his heels and tossed a small pistol

onto the dirt floor. He rummaged through the clothes on his body and flicked a knife through the air. It landed point down on the ground.

"That's all I have." Pazir continued forward on his knees, his hands in the air. "I had nothing to do with the ambush at our previous meeting. I barely got out of there with my life."

"The other Delta Force soldier? Asher Knight? Do you know what happened to him?"

"He survived."

Denver almost sank to the dirt again as relief coursed through his rigid muscles. "You know that for sure?"

"I know that he and the others are challenging the story that's out there about you."

"They are?" Denver's spine stiffened, and he lined it up against the cave wall again.

"Your men are loyal to you, Denver."

"But they haven't cleared me yet?"

"They're getting close. My sources tell me there's a battle raging about your guilt in the highest levels of government."

"You have good sources, Pazir." Denver gestured with his weapon. "Sit. What else have they told you? What do you know about those weapons at the embassy outpost in Nigeria? What do you know about the car bomb at the Syrian refugee camp?"

"Al Tariq."

Denver cleared his throat and spit. "Too small. I know that group and there's no way they could pull off what they're doing."

"They're the front group in the region. They're being used to do some of the grunt work. They're being used to track you down."

"By whom? Who's behind this and what do they want?"

"As far as I know, it's an international group, moles from different government agencies working together. They want weapons, and they're close to getting their hands on a nuclear device."

Denver swore, finally loosening the grip on his weapon. "That's what I was afraid of, and now you've just confirmed it."

"Has to be more than a rumor, Denver."

"I wanna know who's at the top. It's not good enough to finger Al Tariq."

Pazir scratched his beard and squatted across from Denver. "I know Al Tariq wasn't responsible for kidnapping that CIA agent."

"That female?"

"She was getting too close to the truth—just like you."

"They released her."

"She escaped."

"And you think the people who kidnapped Agent Chandler are the same ones pulling the strings for Al Tariq and trying to get their hands on this nuclear device?"

"I know it, Denver. Don't ask me how."

"Then I need to figure out who kidnapped Chandler."

"From here?" Pazir threw out one arm.

"I have to stay in hiding. You don't."

Pazir snorted. "I can't exactly run around the globe and travel to Washington, either."

"No, but you can get a message out for me, can't you?"

"Yes." Pazir reached into his pouch and pulled out a piece of flatbread. He ripped it in half and thrust one piece at Denver. "You want me to try to send a message to Agent Chandler?"

"I want you to send a message to one of my Delta Force team members. Hunter Mancini worked with Chandler on a covert mission once, and they got…close. You get a message to Mancini, and he can contact Chandler. Maybe she has some insight into who held her and what she was working on, but she's afraid to say anything."

"I can do that." Pazir pulled a pencil and pad of paper from his bag. "Give me the details."

As Denver chewed through the rough bread, he rattled off instructions to Pazir for contacting Mancini. "I don't have to tell you not to let this fall into the wrong hands."

"I give up nothing."

"Shh." Denver sidled along the wall of the cave and peered out the entrance. "We're not alone."

Pazir lunged for his weapon. "We'll fight them off together."

"You go." Denver grabbed a handful of Pazir's jacket. "I'll distract them. Get that message to Mancini if it's the last thing you do."

Chapter One

Sue slipped the burner phone from the inside pocket of her purse. She swiped a trickle of sweat from her temple as she reread the text and ducked into the last stall in the airport bathroom. Her heart fluttered in her chest just like it always did before she made a call to The Falcon.

He answered after one ring. "Seven, one, six, six, nine."

The numbers clicked in her brain and she responded. "Ten, five, seven, two, eight."

"Are you secure?"

The altered voice grated against her ear as she peeked through the gap between the stall door and its frame at several women washing their hands, scolding children, and wheeling their bags in and out of the bathroom, too concerned with their own lives to worry about someone reciting numbers on a cell phone.

Their nice, normal lives.

"Yeah."

"You got the name of the barbershop wrong. There's no Walid there."

"That's not possible."

"You misheard the name...or they purposely fed you the wrong one because they made you."

Sue swallowed and pressed her forehead against the cool metal door. "They didn't."

"Because they would've killed you when you were with them?"

"That's right." Sue yanked off a length of toilet paper from the roll and stepped in front of the toilet to make it flush automatically. "I've been doing this for a while. I'd know."

"That's what I like about you, Nightingale. You're a pro. You've already proven you'll do anything for the cause."

She swallowed the lump in her throat and sniffed. "Next move?"

"We need the correct barbershop."

"I can't exactly call up my contact and ask him."

"You'll figure it out. Like I said, you're a pro."

The Falcon ended the call before she could respond.

Sighing, she pushed out of the stall and washed her hands. On her way out of the bathroom, she almost bumped into her stepmother.

"Where have you been? We need to get to our gate. I can't wait to get out of this place. I hate D.C."

Sue dropped to her knees in front of her son, regretting that she'd spent their last precious minutes together on the phone with The Falcon—regretting so much more. She grabbed Drake's hands and kissed the tips of his sticky fingers, inhaling the scent of cinnamon that clung to his skin. "Be a good boy for Gran on the airplane."

Drake batted his dark eyelashes. "You go airplane, too, Mama?"

"No, cupcake. Just you and Gran this time, but I'll visit you soon."

Linda fluttered a tissue between the two of them. "Wipe your hands, Drake."

"That's not going to help, Linda. He had a cinnamon roll for breakfast. He's going to have to wash his hands in the restroom." Sue waved her hand behind her at the ladies' room.

Pursing her lips, Linda snatched back the tissue. "Cinnamon rolls for breakfast? You spoil him when he's here. I'll get him a proper lunch once we get through security, if he still has any appetite left."

He will unless you ruin it.

Sue managed to eke out a smile, as Drake was watching her with wide eyes. "Nothing spoils Drake's appetite. He could eat a horse and ask for dessert."

"We don't eat horses, Mama." Drake giggled and Sue pinched the end of his nose. "Give me another hug."

Drake curled his chubby arms around her neck, and Sue pressed her tingling nose against his hair. "Love you, cupcake."

"Love you." Drake smacked his lips against her cheek. "Can I live here?"

"Not yet, my lovey, but soon." Blinking the tears from her eyes, Sue straightened up and placed Drake's hand in her stepmother's. "Give my love to Dad."

Linda sniffed as she yanked up the handle of her suitcase. "I don't know why some people have children if they can't be bothered to take care of them."

"Linda." Sue ducked toward her stepmother and said through clenched teeth, "I told you. This…arrangement won't be forever, and I don't appreciate your talking like that in front of my son."

Linda's pale eyes widened a fraction and she backed up. "I hope you're not going to be landing in trouble every other month, or you'll never have Drake with you. You were right to leave him with your sister. Children need stability. You should give up this crazy job and find yourself a husband to take care of you, a father for Drake, and settle down like your sister."

Sue opened her mouth and then snapped it shut. She'd promised herself not to argue with Linda—besides, her stepmother had a point. As it stood now, Sue couldn't keep her son with her and raise him properly—even if The Falcon had allowed it.

And he hadn't.

"It won't always be like this. I plan to transfer to another position, and then I can have him with me all the time. I'll contact you tonight for some face-to-face with Drake. Ask Dad. He knows how to do it."

"I know, I know. Your father knows everything."

"Thanks, Linda. Safe travels." Sue blew a kiss to Drake as her stepmother hustled him toward the line for security.

She waved until they got to the front of the line. Knowing her father would be stationed at the airport in South Carolina to pick them up was the only thing that allowed her to turn away and leave the airport. Drake lived with her sister, Amelia, and her family, but they were in the Bahamas and Sue hadn't wanted Drake to go along, so she sent him to Dad and Linda.

Linda could take care of Drake's physical needs and keep him safe, but she trusted only Dad to meet Drake's emotional needs. Her stepmother didn't have the capacity for that job, as Sue suspected she trash-talked her to Drake whenever she got the chance.

If Sue had one more incident like the one she'd faced in Istanbul, she had no doubt her stepmother would move against her to take Drake away from her completely and declare her an unfit mother.

Sue clenched her teeth and exited the airport. She'd

just have to make sure she didn't have any more of those close calls.

After she fed her parking receipt into the machine and the arm lifted, Sue flexed her fingers on the steering wheel of the car and glanced in her rearview mirror. With Drake's visit over, she could finally breathe... and find out who was following her. The possibilities were endless.

She navigated out of the airport and drove straight to her office. She had to confront her supervisor, Ned Tucker, about her suspicions. She'd already been debriefed after the kidnapping. Why was the CIA still dogging her? And if it wasn't the CIA, maybe Ned could help her figure out who it was. She hadn't wanted to tell The Falcon about this new development.

He thought she was a pro who could handle anything. She could, but handling everything on her own all the time had gotten old. Sometimes a girl just needed a shoulder to lean on. She'd had that shoulder...once.

She rolled up to the parking gate of the office and held her badge out the window.

The security guard waved her through, and she parked her car. Slipping her badge lanyard over her head, she marched toward her office building. She'd taken the day off to drop off Drake and Linda at the airport, but she couldn't wait any longer to get to the bottom of this mystery tail.

She punched the elevator button and almost bumped into one of her coworkers coming out.

Peter held up his hands. "Whoa, what's the hurry?"

"Sorry, Peter." She stepped to the side.

"Thought you were out today."

"Half day. I need to talk to Ned."

"I think he needs to talk to you, too."

"Why? Was he looking for me? He knows I'm out today."

Peter shrugged. "You might wanna turn around and go home."

"Why?"

Peter pivoted away from her and called over his shoulder, "Take someone's advice for once, Sue."

If Peter thought his cryptic warning would send her home, he didn't know her very well. She dropped her hand from holding open the elevator doors and stepped inside.

Good. If Ned wanted to talk to her, maybe he wanted to explain what the hell was going on.

The elevator deposited her onto the fifth floor, and she badged the door to the cubicles. The hum of low voices and keyboard clicks created a comforting welcome.

As she turned the corner to her row, she stumbled to a stop. A man she didn't know was hanging on to the corner of her cube and Ned's head bobbed above the top.

She bit the inside of her cheek and continued walking forward.

At her approach the stranger turned, and his eyes widened. "Chandler."

She stopped at the entrance to her cubicle, her gaze darting from Ned to a woman sitting at her desk, accessing her computer.

"Wh-what's going on here, Ned?"

Her boss ran a hand over his bald head, his forehead glistening with sweat. "I thought you were out today, Sue."

"So, what? You figured you and a couple of strangers could get into my computer in my absence?"

The guy to her right straightened up and pulled back

his shoulders. "Ms. Chandler, we've noticed some irregularities on your workstation."

"Irregularities?" She shot a look at Ned, who refused to meet her gaze. "I don't understand."

The woman sitting in front of her computer twisted her head around, a tight smile on her face. "I found another one."

"Another one what?" Sue stepped into her cube, hovering over the woman seated at her desk.

The man placed a hand on Sue's arm. "Perhaps it's best we talk in Ned's office."

Sue had noticed a few heads popping up from other cubicles. She lifted her own chin. She knew damn well she didn't have any irregularities on her computer. The Falcon would make sure of that—unless these were communiqués from him.

"Let's go, then." She shook off the man's hand and charged out of her cubicle and down the aisle to Ned's office in the corner.

She reached Ned's office before the two strangers, with Ned right behind her. She swung around, nearly colliding with him. "What's going on, Ned?"

"They received an anonymous tip about you forwarding classified emails and documents to your home computer."

"What? You know I'd never do anything like that. I've been in the field myself. There's no way I'd put anyone in danger."

"I know that, Sue." His gaze darted over his shoulder, and then he sealed his lips as the two investigators approached.

Sue shuffled into the room as Ned sat down behind his desk. "Take a seat, Sue."

"That's okay. I'll stand." Folding her arms, she squared her shoulders against the wall.

The two investigators remained standing, too.

The woman thrust out her hand, all business. "I'm Jackie Templeman."

Sue gripped her hand and squeezed hard, her lips twisting as Jackie blinked.

The man cleared his throat and dipped his head. "Robert Beall."

He didn't offer his hand and she didn't make a move to get it. She folded her arms across her chest and asked, "What did this anonymous email say?"

Templeman shot a glance at Ned. "To check your emails."

"You have no idea who sent it?"

"No." Templeman shook her head. "That's why it's anonymous."

Sue smirked. "Got it. So, you believe every anonymous email you receive and rush in to do an investigation?"

Templeman hugged her notebook to her chest, as if guarding state secrets. "Not everyone."

"Oh, I see." Sue shoved off the wall and plopped into the chair across from Ned. "Just the ones about me."

Beall finally found his voice. "Because of your...um... the incident."

"Funny thing about that incident." Sue drummed her fingers on Ned's desk. "You'd think the Agency would be kissing my...rear end, considering a leak on their part led to my kidnapping in the first place."

"And then you escaped." Templeman tilted her head.

"Yeah, another reason the Agency should be nominating me for a medal or something instead of combing through my computer."

"You escaped from a group of men holding you in Istanbul." Templeman's delicate eyebrows formed a V over her nose.

Sue snorted. "I guess that's hard for *some* people to believe, but *some* female agents aren't pencil-pushing computer geeks. Some of us know how to handle ourselves."

A smile tugged at Beall's lips, but he wiped it out with his hand.

"Besides, I was debriefed on that incident and the case was closed. You still seem to be using it to go after me."

"The point—" Templeman straightened her jacket "—is that we *did* find anomalies on your computer. Enough for us to confiscate your machine and suspend you."

"Suspend?" Sue jumped from the chair. "Is that true, Ned?"

"Just until they can figure out everything. I think there has to be a mistake, and I told them that. We already know those emails implicating Major Rex Denver and sent to a CIA translator were fakes. I'm confident that this investigation is going to find something similar with these emails and you'll be in the clear, Sue."

"Suspension starting now?"

"Yes, we'll accompany you back to your cubicle if you want to take any personal items with you." Templeman pushed past Beall and opened the door.

"I don't have anything there I need." Sue smacked her hand on Ned's desk. "Let me know when this is over, Ned."

"Of course, Sue. Don't worry."

As she stepped through the door, Templeman tapped her shoulder. "Badge."

Sue whipped the lanyard over her head and tossed it at Templeman's chest, but it slipped through the investigator's fingers and landed on the floor. The woman couldn't even make a good catch. No wonder she had a hard time believing Sue had escaped her captors.

Sue strode out of the office, not looking right or left. When she stepped out onto the sidewalk, she took a deep breath of fresh air.

Maybe she sent her son away early for nothing. Maybe her senses had been on high alert because the Agency *had* been tracking her. Now that they'd made their move and suspended her and confiscated her computer, they'd back off.

The thought didn't make her feel much better. The CIA didn't trust her, and being falsely accused made her blood boil. Of course, if the Agency knew about her work with The Falcon, the accusations might not be false. She didn't have to worry about that, though. The Falcon would have her covered.

As she waited for the elevator in the parking garage, her phone buzzed and she squinted at the text message from her friend, Dani Howard.

Dani knew she'd sent Drake back home and figured Sue needed some cheering up. Dani had no idea how much cheering up she needed.

Sue texted her friend back. I'm up for cocktails tonight. What the hell did she have to lose at this point?

SUE SPOTTED DANI already sitting at the bar, and she squeezed between the people and the tall tables to reach her. "This the best you could do?"

Dani gave her a one-armed hug. "I just got here five minutes ago. Haven't even ordered a drink yet."

Hunching over the bar, Sue snapped her fingers and shouted, "Hey."

The bartender raised his hand. "Be right with you."

A minute later he took their order for two glasses of white wine.

Dani sighed as she flicked back her hair. "It must be your commanding presence that gets their attention. Did you see Drake off okay today?"

"I did." Sue rolled her eyes. "Of course, I had to put up with Linda's jabs."

"Our mothers should have a contest to see who can outshame the single moms." Dani picked out some pretzels from the bowl of snack mix on the bar and popped one into her mouth.

"Stepmother. At least Fiona's dad is in the picture."

"You say that like it's a good thing."

"Okay then, at least Fiona lives with you and you're not in constant fear of losing custody of her."

Dani folded back the corners of the napkin the bartender had tossed down when he took their order. "You know I'm planning to drive down to Savannah, and I'd be happy to drop in on Drake for you. Text me your parents' address, and I'll see if I can make the detour—just a familiar face from where Mom lives might make a big difference."

"That would be great, but I don't want to put you out."

"Happy to do it." Dani snatched their glasses from the bartender's hand and handed one to Sue. "Drink."

Sue took a big gulp of wine, but there wasn't enough alcohol in the world right now to drown her sorrows.

"Stop beating yourself up. You're saving the freakin' world." Dani tilted her head. "I suppose you can't tell me about this hush-hush assignment of yours."

Not only did she not have a hush-hush assignment, she didn't have any assignment—unless she counted the one to get the name of the right barbershop.

Sue put a finger to her lips and swirled her wine in the glass. "No questions about my job."

"Don't even ask about *my* job...except for the new resident who started his rotation." Dani winked.

"Not another doctor. You need to date outside the medical field."

"I need to date and I may have just found the answer to our prayers." Dani tilted her head to the side and twirled a strand of her red hair around one finger.

Sue put her glass to her lips and shifted her gaze above the rim toward a table to Dani's right, where two men had their heads together. "Are you sure they aren't gay?"

"Not the way they've been eyeing us for the past few minutes." Dani drew back her shoulders and puffed out her ample chest. "Besides, they have a table, and we're stuck here at the bar getting squeezed out."

One of the men had noticed Dani's move and he sat up, nudging his buddy.

An evening with Dani always ended in the company of men, and for once, Sue welcomed the distraction. She smiled at the eager suitors.

One of the guys raised his glass and pointed to the two empty chairs at their table.

"And score." Dani wiggled her fingers in the air. "I get the blond unless you have a preference. I'm just thinking about cute little strawberry-blond siblings for Fiona."

Sue's gaze shifted to the dark-haired man as she pushed away from the bar. At least he was her type. "Go for it, Dani."

The two men jumped from their seats and pulled out the chairs for her and Dani. She and Dani did a little dance to get Dani seated next to the blond.

He spoke first. "You two looked so uncomfortable

packed in at the bar. It seemed a shame to let these two chairs go to waste."

"Thank you. I'm Dani and this is Sue." Dani's southern accent always got more pronounced in front of men, and they seemed to eat it up.

Dani's future husband pointed to himself. "I'm Mason—" and then he pointed to his companion "—and this is Jeffrey."

They all said their hellos and launched into the inane small talk that characterized meet-ups in bars. Sue had no intention of winding up with Jeffrey or anyone else at the end of the evening and tried to keep her alcohol consumption to a minimum.

She failed.

Mason, or maybe it was Jeffrey, ordered a bottle of wine for the table, and then another. Although Sue continuously sipped from her glass, the liquid never dropped below the halfway point, and by the time she staggered to the ladies' room on her second trip, she realized the men had been topping off her wine.

She'd have to put a lid on that glass when she got back to the table.

As she wended her way through the crowded bar, she stumbled to a stop when she saw Jeffrey alone at the table. She clutched her small purse to her chest and took the last few steps on unsteady legs. "Where are Mason and Dani?"

"They left—together." Jeffrey lifted one shoulder.

Sue sank into the chair, snatching her phone from the side pocket on her purse. "Whose idea was that?"

"I think it was mutual." Jeffrey held up his hands. "Don't worry. I know we didn't hit it off like they did, and I have no expectations."

She scowled at him over the top of her phone. "I hope not."

Dani picked up on the first ring. "Hey, Sue, did Jeffrey tell you I left with Mason?"

"He did. Are you okay?"

"I'm fine." Dani giggled and sucked in a breath. "I'm sorry. I shouldn't have left you there with Jeffrey."

"That's okay. As long as you're all right. Do you have an address where you're going?"

"The Hay-Adams."

"Okay. Be careful."

Dani ended the call on another giggle and Sue shoved her phone back into her purse.

Jeffrey raised one eyebrow. "Your friend okay? Mason's a good guy."

"He'd better be." Sue raised her phone and snapped a picture of Jeffrey. "Just in case."

A spark of anger lit Jeffrey's eyes for a second, or maybe she'd imagined it. Then he tucked some bills beneath his empty glass. "Can I at least see you home?"

She shook her head and then clutched the edge of the table as a wave of dizziness engulfed her brain. She took a sip of water. "I'm fine, thanks."

"Really? You don't look fine. The booze was flowing as fast as the conversation tonight. You look…woozy."

Woozy? Someone had stuffed a big cotton ball in her head to keep her brain from banging around. After the day she'd had, she'd wanted to let loose, tie one on. Now she had to face the consequences.

"I didn't drive. I can just hop on the Metro, one stop." She staggered to her feet and grabbed the back of her chair. She'd be paying for her overindulgence tomorrow morning for sure.

Jeffrey jumped from his chair. "Are you positive I

can't help you? I can walk you to the station or call you a taxi or rideshare car."

She narrowed her eyes and peered at him through a fog. Why was he so insistent? Why didn't he just leave her alone?

She raised her hand and leveled a finger at him. "Stay right where you are."

Jeffrey cocked his head and a lock of his brown hair slipped free from the gel and made a comma on his wrinkled brow.

Had she made sense? She tried to form another word with her thick tongue, but she couldn't get it to cooperate.

She resorted to sign language, raising her middle finger. Would he get the picture now? "Whatever." He plopped back into his chair. "Just be careful."

She swung to the side, banging her hip on the corner of the table, jostling all the empties. Putting her head down, she made a beeline for the door.

Once outside, she gulped in breaths of the cold air but couldn't seem to revive herself. Walking should help. She put one foot in front of the other and weaved down the sidewalk. Oncoming pedestrians gave her a wide berth, and a few made jokes.

Oh, God. Was she a joke? A drunk joke? She placed a hand flat against the side of a building and closed her eyes.

She hadn't been this drunk since college days, and she didn't intend to make the same stupid mistakes she'd made back then.

She shoved a hand into the pocket of her leather moto jacket and fumbled for her phone. Jeffrey had been right about one thing—she should call a taxi.

After she pulled the phone from her jacket, it slipped

from her hand and bounced twice on the sidewalk before landing in the gutter.

She dropped to a crouch and stuck her hand over the curb to feel for the phone. The effort proved too much for her and she fell over onto her side.

Good thing her son couldn't see her now, passed out like a wino in the gutter.

She flexed her fingers toward her phone but lead weights had been attached to their tips—and her eyelids. DC Metro would pick her up and she'd lose her job for sure.

"Sue? Sue? You're coming with me now."

An arm curled around her shoulders and pulled her upright. Jeffrey. He'd followed her out to finish what he'd started.

She arched her back, but her gelatinous spine sabotaged the act and she collapsed against Jeffrey's chest.

He had her.

"It's all right. I'm taking you to my hotel."

Her lips parted and she uttered a protest, but just like everything in her life lately, the situation had already spiraled out of her control.

Her mind screamed resistance, but her body had already succumbed.

SUE STRETCHED HER limbs and rubbed her eyes, the silky, soft sheets falling from her shoulders. Then the memories from the night before tumbled through her mind in a kaleidoscope of images.

She bolted upright against the king-size bed's headboard, yanking the sheets to her chin to cover her naked body.

Had Jeffrey raped and abandoned her at the hotel? Was his name even Jeffrey?

The bathroom door crashed open and a large man stopped cold on the threshold. "God, you look beautiful even after the night you had."

Sue's mouth dropped open as she took in the man at the bathroom door, towel hanging precariously low on a pair of slim hips.

The man she'd betrayed and who still haunted her dreams...and it sure as hell wasn't Jeffrey.

Chapter Two

The look on Sue's face shifted from shock to disbelief, to horror, to pain and to a whole bunch of other stuff he couldn't figure out. And that had been his problem with Sue Chandler all along—he'd never been able to figure her out.

Those luscious lips finally formed a word, just one. "You."

He spread his arms wide. "In the flesh. Did you expect me to leave you in the gutter, like you left me?"

"As I recall, it was a luxury hotel." She patted the pillow next to her. "Somewhat like this one—and all I did was check out."

"Details, details."

She pointed at him. "Your towel is slipping. Not interested in seeing that package—again."

The years hadn't softened Sue Chandler one bit. He held up one finger. "Give me a second."

As Sue turned her tight face away, he crossed the room to his suitcase, tugged a pair of briefs from an inside pocket, dropped his towel and pulled on his underwear.

"There." He turned toward the bed. "Decent."

Her gaze flicked over his body, making him hot and hard, as only Sue Chandler could do with one look from her dark eyes.

The twist of her lips told him she'd noticed the effect she had on him.

"Maybe not decent enough." He yanked open a dresser drawer and pulled out some jeans. He stepped into them, feeling less cocky under Sue's unrelenting stare, but he had the upper hand for once.

"Now, are you going to tell me what you were doing last night stumbling along the streets of DC close to midnight?"

"I live here." Her jaw hardened. "What are *you* doing here and how did you happen to find me?"

"You're not exactly hard to find. You work for the CIA and live in DC, and I knew you weren't on assignment, not after…"

"You know about my kidnapping?" She drew her knees to her chest beneath the sheets, clasping her arms around her legs.

"Several special forces knew about it and were actively planning your rescue." He tilted his head to the side. "But you didn't need rescuing."

"Don't go throwing any parades. The kidnappers were not that bright." She blinked. "Is that why you're here? Have you been following me?"

"Whoa, wait." He tossed his towel onto the foot of the bed. "I followed you from your place to the bar last night. That's it. I just arrived yesterday."

She sank back against the stacked pillows. "Why'd you follow me? Are you here on official duty, or something? I've already been debriefed by the Agency."

"Official duty? Really? What would a Delta Force soldier have to do with the kidnapping of a CIA agent?"

"Don't try that 'Who, me?' stuff with me, Mancini. You didn't seek me out to profess your undying love. You had three years to do that—and not a peep."

He reached into the closet and jerked a shirt from a hanger, leaving it swinging wildly. "You're not gonna pin that on me. I got the message loud and clear that you were moving on. Did you expect me to chase after you?"

Sue opened her mouth and then snapped it shut. Then her eyes widened and she gathered the covers around her body. "I'm naked. How did I get naked?"

"I took your clothes off—sorry." He gestured to a pile of clothing in the corner of the room. "Yours were dirty. I didn't think it was sanitary to put you to bed in filthy clothes."

"How thoughtful." She snorted. "I fell on the sidewalk. I'm sure you could've brushed the dirt from my slacks and left my underwear alone."

He cleared his throat. "You vomited all over yourself when I got you to the room."

"Oh my God." She covered her mouth with both hands. "I don't know what happened last night. I—I apologize."

"Nothing I haven't handled hundreds of times before with my buddies. I'm sure we can send your clothes to the hotel's laundry or dry cleaning. I already cleaned off your boots and jacket."

"I don't know what to say. I'm embarrassed. I'm not sure what came over me. I did have a lot of wine last night, but I've never felt that way before."

"I'm thinking the fact that you upchucked saved you."

"Saved me from what?"

"Whatever was in your system."

"You mean besides the alcohol?" She twisted a lock of dark brown hair around her finger, not looking surprised at all. "What do you know? Why are you here in DC?"

He swallowed against his dry throat. He had to concentrate, but remembering Sue naked in bed had his thoughts scrambled.

Should he pretend he was here for her instead of trying to explain the real reason? He met those dark, shimmering eyes that seemed to see into his very soul. He couldn't lie to Sue—not that she'd believe him, anyway.

"I got a message from Major Denver."

"Major Rex Denver? AWOL Delta Force commander?"

"You know as well as I do that he isn't and never has been working with any terrorist organization against the US government. One of your own translators proved the emails she'd received implicating him were phony."

"I've heard all the stories, but if he's innocent, why won't he come in? Why is he sending messages to you instead?"

"He doesn't feel it's safe yet. He's already been the victim of a setup, and he doesn't trust anyone."

"Yeah, I understand that." Sue bit her bottom lip. "What was the message? What are you supposed to do?"

"Contact you?"

"What? Why?"

"He believes the people who kidnapped you belong to the same group he's trying to bring down, the same group that he believes is planning some kind of spectacular attack."

Sue clenched the sheets in her fists. "Why does he think that?"

Hunter's pulse jumped. Again, no surprised looks from Sue. "Something his informant told him. Why? What happened during that kidnapping? Did they ever give you any reason why they snatched you?"

"Wait." She massaged her temple with two fingers. "I can't take all this in right now, especially not huddled under the covers with no clothes on. I need a shower. I need breakfast. I need clothes."

"The shower's all yours. I can send your clothes out

to the laundry right now, if you're okay with eating room service wearing my sweats and T-shirt." He took a step to the side and slid open the closet door. He reached in, his hand closing around the fluffy terrycloth of a hotel robe. "You can wear this into the bathroom."

"Thanks."

She uttered the word between clenched teeth, almost grudgingly, but he'd take it at this point. Her reception of him had been chillier than he'd expected, especially since she was the one who had ended their brief affair by leaving him in his hotel room with no note, no phone call, no explanation.

He placed the robe across her lap, dropping it quickly and jerking back. Being close to Sue again had proven to be more difficult than he'd expected when he first got Denver's message. Undressing her last night and putting her to bed had been an exquisite torture. His hands lingering on her smooth flesh had screamed violation, so he'd made quick work of it.

"I'm going to bag your stuff and call housekeeping. I'll put a rush on it, so your clothes will be ready by the time we finish breakfast." He pinched the strap of her lacy bra between two fingers and held it up. "Anything need special attention or dry cleaning?"

"Everything is machine washable." She flicked her fingers in the air. "Turn around, please."

Not like he hadn't already seen every inch of her beautiful body.

"Yes, ma'am." He turned his back on her and stuffed her clothing into the hotel's plastic bag for laundry, as she rustled behind him.

She slammed the bathroom door before he even rose from the floor with her bag of clothing dangling from his fingertips.

Blowing out a breath, he wedged a shoulder against the closet. He knew it wouldn't be easy reconnecting with Sue after what had happened in Paris, but she couldn't completely blame him for not contacting her, could she?

They'd met at a party of expats. He knew she was CIA, and she knew he was Delta Force on leave. They'd approached their relationship as a fling and had been enjoying each other's company until she'd turned cold. He'd assumed at the time it was because she knew they'd have to end their Paris idyll once he got deployed, even though he'd been ready to ask her to wait for him.

Maybe it hadn't been the wisest decision for him to get involved with someone so soon after separating from his wife, and maybe she got that vibe from him, although he hadn't gotten around to telling her about his wife. He hadn't wanted to open that can of worms until he'd gotten a signal from Sue that they had some kind of future. Once she'd shut that down, he'd shut down, too. He didn't need any more women in his life who couldn't accept his military career.

He pushed off the closet and grabbed the phone by the bed. He requested a laundry pickup and then room service, ordering eggs, bacon, the works. From what he'd seen of Sue's body last night, she still must work out and burn calories at a ferocious rate. With Sue's dedication to running, kickboxing and Krav Maga, he'd had no trouble imagining her escaping from a gaggle of hapless terrorists—even though others did.

He'd heard rumblings that Sue faked her kidnapping and miraculous escape but hadn't heard about any motive. Why would she fake a kidnapping in Istanbul? Glory? Sue wasn't like that. Didn't need that. The woman he'd met in Paris kept her head down and got to work. No nonsense. No drama.

And that's how she'd ended their affair.

The bathroom door swung open, and Sue poked her head into the room. "Can they do my clothes?"

"They haven't picked up yet, but they assured me they could have them ready by noon. Is that okay?" He glanced at the clock by the tousled bed. "You don't have to get to work?"

"I have a few days off. That's why I was out last night with my friend."

"When your friend left the bar with that guy, I thought maybe…" He shrugged.

"You thought I'd be leaving with someone, too?" She tucked a lock of wet hair beneath the towel wrapped around her head. "Queen of the one-night stands?"

"What we had wasn't…"

He choked to a stop as she sliced a hand through the air. "Don't want to discuss it."

"Housekeeping." The sharp rap at the door had him pivoting to answer it. He handed the bag to the woman. "I was told the clothes could be returned by noon."

"That's what I have on the order, sir."

By the time he turned back to the room, Sue had grabbed what she needed from his bag and retreated to the bathroom.

He ran a hand across his mouth. He didn't understand her anger at him. He hadn't been the one who abruptly left Paris without a word, without even a note on the pillow.

She'd hurt him more than he'd cared to admit, but he'd chalked it up to being dumped and accepted it as a sign that he shouldn't have gotten involved with someone so soon after Julia left.

Maybe Sue had expected him to run after her, pursue

her, but he hadn't had the energy at that time for games and he'd let her go without a fight—clearly his loss.

She emerged from the bathroom again, yanking up the waistband of a pair of gray sweats that swam on her.

"I can turn up the thermostat in the room if you just wanna wear the big T-shirt."

"That's all right. I don't plan to run any marathons, or even leave the room."

The next knock on the door brought breakfast, and Hunter added a tip and signed the check. He lifted the cover on the first plate. "Eggs, bacon, hash browns. Is that okay?"

"Toast?"

"Under this one." He plucked a cover from a rack of toast. "Coffee?"

"Please."

She'd exchanged her ire for a cold civility. He couldn't decide which stung more. Over the years, he'd built up some ridiculous significance to their fling—Sue just set him straight.

He poured her a cup of coffee and nudged the cream and sugar toward her where she'd taken up a place across the table from him.

She dumped some cream into her coffee, picked up the cup and leveled a gaze at him over the rim. "Where did you sleep last night?"

His own coffee sloshed over the side of his cup. "The sofa."

"That small thing?"

"My legs hung over the edge, but I've had worse."

All the questions that must be bubbling in her brain and *that* one came to the surface first?

"Look, this is what happened." He slurped a sip of coffee for fortification. "I'd followed you to the bar from your place. I watched the entrance, waiting for you to come out, and I was going to approach you then."

"Why not sooner?"

"I told you, I'd just arrived in the afternoon, and I didn't have your address right away. Figured you'd be at work, anyway. By the time I got around to finding your place, you were on the move. I didn't want to interrupt your evening. I thought about leaving you a note, but…"

"You figured I might not contact you."

"So, I followed you to the bar and waited."

"How'd you know I was with Dani? A woman? You mentioned seeing my friend leave with a man."

He cleared his throat. "I went into the bar."

"You were watching me inside the bar?" She stabbed at her eggs with a fork. "Creepy."

His lips twitched. "Sorry. I didn't stay long. Then I waited outside and saw your friend leave."

"Just in time to see me staggering out."

"Scared the hell out of me."

"Why?"

"It didn't look…normal, and I knew you weren't a big drinker, or at least you weren't in Paris." There he was, acting like some big expert on Sue Chandler.

"It didn't *feel* normal." She dropped a half-eaten piece of toast onto her plate. "If that guy I was with, Jeffrey, drugged me, what did his friend do to Dani? And why would they want to do anything to either of us?"

"Before we try to answer that second question, why don't you give Dani a call?" He crumpled his napkin next to his plate and grabbed her phone off the charger. "I found your phone charger in your purse and took the liberty of hooking you up."

"Thanks. Seems like you thought of everything."

"Except that change of clothes." He dropped the phone into her palm.

While Sue called her friend, Hunter shook out his napkin and listened. Everything sounded okay on this end. Maybe he'd been wrong about Sue being in danger.

She ended the call and tapped the edge of the phone against her chin.

"Everything okay?"

"Dani's already home. Seems Mason was the perfect gentleman. She passed out in his hotel room, and he checked out before she woke up. He left her a note telling her to order anything she wanted from room service and to take her time. And she woke up with all her clothes on…which is more than I can say for myself."

"Maybe Dani passed out before she had a chance to hurl all over herself."

"Don't remind me." She made a face and stuck out her tongue.

"That's good, then. Dani is safe at home with her virginity intact."

Sue covered her lower face with her napkin and raised her eyebrows. "I wouldn't go that far."

"But she's all right."

"She is."

"You don't sound relieved."

"I am relieved, but I'm puzzled." She swirled her coffee in the cup, staring inside as if looking for answers there. "Why did we both have such strong reactions to a couple bottles of wine? Dani knows how to get her drink on. I've never seen her more than a little tipsy, and I haven't gotten sick on booze since my college years, when we'd get an older classmate in our dorm to buy us a bottle of cheap rum and we'd mix it with diet soda."

"Now *I'm* feeling sick." He dusted toast crumbs from

his fingertips into his napkin. "I don't know why you're confused. Just because Dani wasn't assaulted, thank God, doesn't mean the two of you weren't drugged."

"For what purpose? I just told you, Mason didn't molest Dani, and I passed out in the gutter like a common drunk."

"And I rescued you."

"What?" Her eyebrows created a V over her nose. "Rescued me from what?"

"I think I rescued you from Jeffrey." He held out his hand as Sue began to rise from her chair. "Just wait. Did you think he was going to haul you out of the bar in front of witnesses? Did he suggest walking you out or to your car?"

"Yes."

"Maybe he planned to make his move then."

"What move?" Sue hugged herself. "Now you're scaring me."

"I'm not sure, Sue. Those two men, Mason and Jeffrey, or whatever their names are, zeroed in on you and Dani. They slipped you some something and Mason was charged with getting Dani away while Jeffrey was supposed to take care of you."

"'Take care of'? What the hell are you talking about, Mancini?"

"You were kidnapped once and you escaped. What did your captors want with you? Did you think that was going to end just because you escaped?"

This time she did jump up from her chair, and it tipped backward with a thump.

"That was Istanbul. This is DC." She twisted her napkin in front of her.

He raised one eyebrow. "You ever hear of travel by airplane? It's a newfangled invention."

She fired her napkin at him. "Why are you joking? This is serious. You're trying to tell me the people who kidnapped me in Turkey are trying to recapture me here?"

"It's a strong possibility, especially in light of the message Denver sent me."

She stalked to the end of the room, spun around and stalked back. "You said you arrived in DC just yesterday afternoon?"

"Yeah, why?" His heart thumped against his rib cage. He recognized that look on her face—the flared nostrils, the pursed lips, the wide eyes, as if to take in everything in front of them.

"I felt—" she rubbed her upper arms "—like I was being followed the past few weeks. That wasn't you?"

"Nope, but it must've been someone. Your instincts are sharp." He rose from the chair and stationed himself by the window.

"They usually are." She aimed a piercing look at him from her dark eyes and he almost felt the stab in his heart.

He cleared his throat. "Then I think it's clear what we need to do."

"It is? And who's this *we*?"

"Me and you. We need to figure out why you were snatched in the first place and what it has to do with Denver." He rubbed his hands together, the thought of being with Sue, of working beside Sue, making his blood sing.

"I don't think so, Mancini."

"What? Why? Major Denver's life might depend on it, not to mention your safety."

"You and I working together? Spending days and nights together? Heads together?"

"Yeah." He couldn't stop his mouth watering at the prospect, especially when she put it like that.

"We both know that's a prescription for disaster."

"Why is that?" He folded his arms and braced a shoulder against the window, knowing damn well why she thought his idea stunk but wanting to hear it from her lips.

"I… We…" Her cheeks sported two red flags.

He'd never seen Sue flustered before. Could he help it if it gave him a prick of satisfaction?

A knock on the door broke the tension between them, and he silently cursed the hotel staff as Sue crawled back into bed.

The knock repeated, accompanied by a male voice. "Housekeeping. Laundry."

Hunter stepped away from the window, his gait slow. Once Sue got her clothes and got the hell out of here, he'd never see her again. He knew how she operated.

Denver had pegged the wrong man for the job if he wanted intel out of Sue. She wouldn't give him the time of day—even after what they'd shared three years ago.

He swung open the door. "Right on time."

The hotel worker charged into the room with Sue's clothes bagged and draped over his arm. As he brushed past Hunter, the plastic covering the clothing crinkled.

Hunter staggered back. "Whoa."

Before Hunter regained his balance, the clothes slid from the man's arm…revealing a weapon clutched in his hand.

Chapter Three

Sue stared down the barrel of the .38. Her jaw tensed, along with every other muscle in her body.

Hunter made a slight move, and the man with the gun leveled it at her head. "Stay back or I'll take the shot, and it doesn't have to end this way. We just want to talk to her."

"Who's *we*?" Hunter's voice came out in a growl that made the hair on the back of Sue's neck stand on end.

"You need to get lost. You don't want to be involved with her—trust me." The man's lips curled into a lopsided sneer.

Sue's hands tightened into fists around the bed covers. She not only had to stop this guy from shooting her or abducting her; she had to stop him from outing her to Hunter.

With his words, the man had made it clear he didn't have the slightest idea he had a member of Delta Force looming behind him. Good. They'd use that to their advantage. She had to hope the same thought had occurred to Hunter at the same time.

In one movement, Sue yanked the covers over her body and rolled off the bed, toward her would-be kidnapper's knees. She barreled into his legs at about the same time she heard the whiz of his gun's silencer right over her head.

The man grunted and kneed her in the side of the face. Then she felt him go down with a thud, followed by a sickening crack. She yanked the bedspread from her head and came eye to bulging eye with the intruder as Hunter choked off his breath.

The sleeper hold worked like a charm, and the man slumped to the side, his weapon inches from his useless hand.

Panting, Sue scrambled to her feet. "Good work. I thought you'd take advantage of the situation."

"And I'm glad you made that situation possible, even though he could've shot right into those bunched-up covers and hit some part of you." Hunter crouched beside the unconscious man and thumbed up one of his eyelids.

"What now? He's going to come to any minute." And she didn't want this guy talking. Sue dropped to her knees and reached across Hunter, grabbing the gun by the silencer.

The man's lids fluttered and he coughed. His eyes widened and his body bucked.

Sue brought the butt of the gun down on the back of the man's skull and he pitched forward again, a stream of blood spouting from his wound.

Hunter cocked his head. "That's one way to handle it."

"I'm the one he was aiming at. I didn't want to take any chances." She put two fingers against his neck. "I didn't kill him."

"We definitely don't want to leave any dead bodies behind." He pointed at the gun, dangling from her fingers. "You wanna take care of that?"

Rising to her feet, Sue kicked aside the last of the covers wrapped around her ankles and headed for the bathroom. She grabbed a hand towel from the rack and wrapped the gun in its folds.

She returned to the bedroom, placed the gun on the nightstand and knelt across from Hunter, who was rummaging through the man's pockets. "Any luck?"

"A little cash and…this." He held up a cell phone. Then he dropped it and tapped her cheek with his fingertip. "What happened? The side of your face is all red."

"He bashed me in the face on his way down." The throbbing of her cheekbone turned into a tingle under Hunter's gentle touch. "I'll get some ice on it. Phone."

"I'm assuming you have no idea who this guy is or what he wanted?" Hunter's blue eyes narrowed like a jungle cat's.

Had the man's words advising Hunter not to get involved with her registered with Hunter?

She shrugged. "No clue, but I'm guessing he's connected to Jeffrey from last night or maybe the kidnapping in Istanbul or maybe even my suspension from the CIA."

Hunter's head jerked up from the cell phone. "You didn't tell me you'd been suspended. Why?"

"Anonymous tips and emails. Sound familiar?"

"Same tactics used against Major Denver." He scratched his chin with the edge of the phone. "This is getting more and more tangled."

You have no idea, Hunter.

She nudged the inert form on the carpet with her knuckle. "How much time do you think we have?"

"That was a hard blow to the head. I think you bought us fifteen minutes at a minimum." He jabbed his finger at the pile of clothes on the floor. "At least he brought your laundry."

"And look how you tipped him."

He held up one hand. "I just choked him out. You're the one who delivered the lights-out."

Sue ripped the plastic from her slacks and blouse and clutched them to her chest as she backed up toward the bathroom. "I'm going to get dressed, and then we need to leave. I'm not going to explain this situation to hotel security."

"Neither is he." Hunter made a move toward his suitcase parked by the door. "I'll put the Do Not Disturb hanger on the doorknob to buy him some time. When he comes to, he'll want to hightail it out of here."

"You're right." She tapped her cheek. "Can you grab some ice from the machine for my face while I'm getting dressed?"

"I'm on it."

As she stepped into her slacks, she heard the door open and close, and she eased out a sigh. Who the hell was that in the other room? Was The Falcon right? Had she been made?

She wouldn't put those strong-arm tactics past the Agency, either, so it could be someone following up on her suspension. Her life was becoming more complex than usual—and the appearance of Hunter Mancini had just added to the mayhem. But what sweet mayhem.

Those blue eyes of his held the same hypnotic quality she hadn't been able to resist in Paris—even though hooking up with Hunter had broken all the rules. She hadn't given a damn then, and she didn't give a damn right now.

She needed someone on her side. Someone she could trust. Someone she could reach out and grab—unlike The Falcon, a nameless, faceless contact spitting orders at her.

The banging of the door made her jump. She smoothed

the blouse over her hips and straightened her spine. Time to get to work.

She exited the bathroom and almost ran into Hunter, dangling a bag of ice from his fingertips.

"You looking for another black eye?"

"I don't think I'm going to get a black eye, but I can see a bruise forming on my cheek." She took the bag from him and pressed it against her face with a shiver. "You have toiletries in the bathroom."

"Thanks, I'll grab them, and then we'll get out of here."

"Did you check his phone?"

"Password protected." He patted the pocket of his button-up shirt. "We'll figure it out."

Sue stepped over their conked-out guest on the floor on the way to her boots. Perching on the edge of the bed, she pulled them on. "You have everything? Do you need to check out?"

Hunter stuffed his toiletry bag into his suitcase, along with the wrapped-up gun, and zipped it. "I'll call the hotel later and tell them I had a change of plans. I don't want housekeeping coming up here anytime soon, not until our friend wakes up and gets out of Dodge."

"Do you have another place in mind?" She strode to the credenza and grabbed her purse, her own weapon stashed in the side pocket.

"Your place?"

Her head whipped around and she swallowed hard. "No."

"From the outside, the place looks big enough for the two of us." He drew a cross over his heart. "I promise not to undress you and put you to bed anymore—unless you need it."

She snorted. "I'm not going to need it, and staying at

my place would be a bad, bad idea. You don't think these goons…whoever they are…know where I live?"

"Your building looks secure and we're both armed." He tipped his head at the man on the floor. "I think we can handle anything that comes our way."

Hunter wouldn't be able to handle anything in that townhouse.

"I think it would be best if you found yourself another hotel." She hitched her purse over her shoulder. "I may even join you."

Hunter's blue eyes darkened. "Does this mean you're gonna work with me to figure out if the guys who snatched you are the ones working against Denver? 'Cause you were dead-set against that before this guy came along and pulled a gun on you."

"Exactly. He made me change my mind."

"Maybe I should thank him—or at least make him more comfortable." Hunter returned to the bathroom and came out swinging a hand towel.

He crouched beside the man and wrapped the cloth around his head, pressing it against his wound. Then he jerked back.

"We need to leave—now."

"Is he coming around?" Sue lunged for the hotel door and plucked the hanger from the handle.

"His color is coming back. It shouldn't be too much longer now." He stepped back from the body on the floor and grasped the handle of his suitcase. "Lead the way."

Sue held the door open for him as he wheeled his suitcase into the hallway. She eased the door closed and slipped the Do Not Disturb sign onto the handle.

When they got to the elevator, Hunter punched the button for a floor on the parking level.

"You have a car?"

"A rental. Do you have any suggestions for my next stop?"

"Is money a consideration, or no?" Her gaze flicked over his expensive suitcase, black leather jacket and faded jeans, which told her nothing except the man was still hotter than blazes.

"No." He lifted one eyebrow toward the black hair swept back from his forehead.

"Then I'd suggest the Hay-Adams. It's in the heart of everything, too crowded for us to stand out, too busy for us to be accosted at gunpoint in the parking lot, too expensive not to have security cameras everywhere."

"That's where your friend, Dani, was taken last night."

"Exactly. Maybe we can do a little research on those two guys from last night." She patted her purse. "I didn't tell you I took a picture of Jeffrey."

"A selfie of the two of you?"

Her brows snapped together. "Insurance in case he raped and murdered me."

"Quick thinking. I didn't get a good look at either one of them when I snuck into the bar last night for surveillance."

"Not very good surveillance, then." She clicked her tongue.

"I didn't want to out myself by staring."

The elevator dinged, and Hunter jabbed at the button to hold open the doors. "After you."

Once he loaded his bag into his rental car and pulled out of the parking structure, she directed him to the next hotel. He maneuvered through the busy streets like a pro, and they left the car with the valet in front of the hotel.

She hovered at his elbow as he checked in, drumming

her fingers on the reception desk. She'd played up her fear over returning to her own place, as there was no way in hell she could have him inside her townhouse, but she'd have to explain somehow that she felt perfectly safe returning home on her own. She couldn't stay in this hotel with Hunter—not again.

She had very little self-control when it came to this man—and she needed her self-control.

"Thank you, Mr. and Mrs. Roberts. Let us know if you need anything." The clerk smiled as she shoved a key card toward Sue.

Sue blinked and then swept the card from the counter and pocketed it.

As Hunter wheeled his suitcase toward the elevator, she hissed into his ear, "Who the hell is Mr. Roberts? Or Mrs. Roberts, for that matter?"

"That would be us, dear." He winked at her. "You're not the only one who knows how to play spy. I have a whole new identity for my stay in DC. I told you that I'm not here on official duty and I don't want my actions to be tracked."

"You have all the credentials?" She tilted her head. "Driver's license, credit cards?"

"I do. Mr. Roberts even has a passport."

She held the elevator door open for him as he dragged his suitcase inside. "I feel so humbled now that I know how easy it is for anyone to fake a new ID."

"Spare me." He nudged her shoulder. "As if you don't know all about that. Half the time the Agency can't locate someone, it's because he or she adopted a new identity."

"Just like I'm sure Jeffrey on my phone is not really a Jeffrey."

"He must've followed us back to my hotel and notified the second shift...if he was in on it."

"I'm pretty sure that was no coincidence—passing out and then the attempted abduction this morning. They didn't expect you to be there, that's for sure."

The elevator settled on their floor, and they exited. Sue got her card out when they reached the room and slid it home. She poked her head inside before widening the door for Hunter and his bag. "Just making sure nobody is here before us."

"They were good last night, but not that good." He wheeled his suitcase into the corner and then bounced on the edge of the king-size bed. "Plenty of room for the two of us—your side and my side."

No time to burst his bubble now. She curled her lips into a perfunctory smile. "Should we get to work on the phone now before it's deactivated?"

"Do you have any tricks of the trade to find out or bypass the password?" He fished the would-be kidnapper's phone from his pocket and tossed it onto the bed beside him.

"I might have a few tricks up my sleeve." She wedged a knee on the bed and scooped up the phone. "In the meantime, why don't you have a look at Jeffrey's picture just in case? We could send it in for facial recognition—if I were still in good standing with the CIA."

"Yeah, I was counting on you having all the Agency's resources at your disposal. Now I'll just have to do this the sneaky way."

She paused as she drew her phone from her purse, holding it in midair. "Are you telling me you have a contact in the CIA? Someone to do your bidding?"

"Do my bidding? I wouldn't put it like that, but yeah, I have a little helper."

Shaking her head, she said, "That agency has more leaks than a colander."

She tapped her photos to bring up Jeffrey's picture. "Give me your number and I'll send it to you."

"I can just look at it on your phone." He snapped his fingers.

"It's better if we have a copy, anyway." She held her finger poised above her display. "Number?"

"Is this your sneaky way of getting my cell? You could just ask, you know." He rattled off his cell number and she entered it into her phone.

Actually, it was just her sneaky way of keeping him away from her phone. She didn't keep pictures on her cell, but she didn't need Hunter looking at her text messages.

She tapped her screen with a flourish. "There. The picture is on its way. Now, I'll get to work on this phone."

She dragged a chair to the window and kicked up her feet onto the chair across from it. She powered on the stranger's cell, which they'd turned off to avoid any tracking, but turning it back on couldn't be helped.

"This guy your type?" Hunter held up his phone with Jeffrey's mug on the display.

"Tall, dark and handsome?" She snorted. "You could say that."

Hunter brought the phone up to his nose and squinted. "How tall was he?"

"Tall enough." Sue eyed Hunter's lanky frame stretched out on the bed, his feet hanging off the edge.

With a smile curling her lip, she hunched over the cell phone again.

Sue clicked through the phone to access a few of the backdoor methods she'd learned at the Agency for bypassing a password to get into a phone. These worked especially well for burner phones like this one—and she knew a thing or two about burner phones.

She glanced up as Hunter swung his legs off the side

of the bed, hunching over his phone, his back to her. Seconds later, his cell buzzed and he murmured a few words into his phone.

He must've reached his secret CIA contact—one who hadn't been suspended from the Agency. She just hoped he knew to keep her name off his lips.

A few taps later, the gunman's phone came to life in her hand. She slid another glance toward Hunter's back and launched the man's text messages and recent contacts.

Hunter ended his own call and stood up, stretching his arms to the ceiling. "I'm going to grab a soda from the machine down the hall. Want something?"

"Something diet, please." Tucking her hair behind one ear, she glanced up and pasted a smile on her lips.

When the door closed behind Hunter, Sue began transferring the data from the stranger's phone to her own—contacts, pictures, texts and call history.

When she reached the last bit of data, Hunter charged into the room, a can of soda in each hand. "Any luck with that?"

She slumped in her chair, clutching the phone in her hand. "Not yet."

Then she tapped the display one last time to erase everything the man had on his burner phone.

Chapter Four

Hunter snapped open Sue's can of soda and leaned over her shoulder, placing it on the table in front of her. The click of the aluminum against the wood made her jump and flush to the roots of her dark hair as she jerked her head around.

"Did I scare you?" He dropped his hand to her shoulder briefly.

"I didn't realize you were right behind me."

"You were too engrossed in that phone." He opened his own soda and sank to the edge of the bed. "It's a bummer you can't get anything from it."

She placed the phone facedown on the table and spun it around. "None of my tricks are working. Phones are getting more and more sophisticated now and harder to break into. I think the CIA needs to get its cyber division on this to come up with some methods to bypass the new security measures."

"Speaking of the Agency and security measures, my contact thinks he can run Jeffrey's picture through face recognition. If he's on the intelligence radar, we should get a hit."

"He?" Sue twisted the tab off her can. "Is he stationed here in DC?"

"Oh no, you don't. I don't give up my sources, not

even to other sources." He leveled a finger at her. "And that should give you some sense of comfort."

She tucked one long leg beneath her. "Did you ever tell anyone about us? I mean our brief affair in Paris?"

Brief? Had their affair been brief? He'd been so lost in Sue, lost in Paris that the world had seemed light-years away, and he'd felt suspended in time. Ever since then, he'd measured everything in terms of before Sue and after Sue. And everything before seemed to be a pale imitation of what came after.

Under her penetrating dark eyes, he felt a flush creep up from his chest. "I did tell a few people—my Delta Force team. That's all. It's how Major Denver knew to task me with contacting you."

"I see." She braced one elbow on the table and buried her chin in her palm.

"Did you?" He held his breath for some reason.

"No."

The word didn't come out as forceful as the expression on her face. She *had* told someone.

"Our affair was a mistake." She sat back in her chair and crossed her arms over her chest.

Hunter gulped down his soda until it fizzed in his nose and tears came to his eyes. So much for getting Sue into bed tonight.

He wiped the back of his hand across his tingling nose. "Two people, even someone from Delta Force and someone from the CIA, enjoying some R and R in Paris, off duty. As far as I remember, our pillow talk didn't include any state or military secrets. Why is that a mistake?"

She drew her bottom lip between her teeth and hunched her shoulders.

"Oh." He crushed his can with one hand. "You weren't off duty, were you?"

Her eyes narrowed. "You need a haircut."

"What?" He skimmed the palm of his hand over the top of his short hair. "Where did that come from?"

"I know just the place." She sat up ramrod straight and snatched her cell phone from the desk. She tapped her screen and nodded. "It's called T.J.'s Barbershop, and it's downtown."

"Does this have something to do with what happened this morning?"

Sue stood up, tilting her head to the side. "Do you trust me, Hunter?"

Did he? She'd indulged in a fling with him while she was on an assignment in Paris, without telling him, and then left him high and dry in their love nest without a backward glance and disappeared. He never heard from her again. She wouldn't take him back to her place here in DC. And she'd just been suspended from the Agency.

Her dark lashes fluttered as the sun from the window set fire to the mahogany highlights in her hair. Her lips parted, waiting for his answer.

"Yeah, I trust you, Sue."

"Good." She reached across the table and tugged her jacket from the back of the chair. "Haircut at T.J.'s. They take walk-ins and you're going to ask for Walid."

HUNTER DRUMMED HIS thumbs against the steering wheel as he waited for Sue outside her townhouse in George-town. She neglected to invite him in, claiming she'd be just a few minutes.

A few minutes later, true to her word, she appeared on her porch, wheeling one bag behind her, another slung over her shoulder. She waved to someone coming up the steps, clutching a small child by the hand, exchanged a few words with this person and then jogged across the street to his rental car.

He popped the trunk and hopped out of the car.

"Bad idea to leave the car. Parking enforcement love giving tickets on this block." She nudged up the trunk.

"I haven't gone anywhere." He collapsed the suitcase handle and hoisted the bag into the car. "This, too?"

"Got it." She swung her shoulder bag into the trunk on top of her suitcase.

When they got back into the car, he glanced at her as he started the engine. "I suppose you're coming inside with me for the haircut I don't need."

"Of course."

"Are you going to tell me what this is about?"

"I'm pretty sure this barbershop is connected to the group I've been tracking, the same one Denver was looking into before he went AWOL, if his intel is correct."

Hunter's pulse ticked up a few notches. Progress. "You're *pretty* sure, not positive?"

"I got a tip about T.J.'s, but apparently it couldn't be verified."

"And now I'm going to try to verify again. Walid?" He made the turn she indicated onto an even busier street than the one they'd left.

"He's the key." She tapped on the window as they crawled through traffic. "You're going to make a right in a few miles at Sixteenth Street. There won't be any parking on the street at this time of the day, so we'll leave the car in a public lot."

"Are we doing anything in the barbershop, whether or not Walid is there?"

"I am." She dug through her purse and cupped a small black device in her palm.

Hunter raised his brows. "A camera? A bug?"

"Both video and sound. I'm leaving it there, regardless of what happens."

"Do you need me to do anything?"

"A little distraction wouldn't hurt, but don't go overboard and make them suspicious." She poked his thigh with her knuckle. "I know you D-boys like to come in with guns blazing, but this is a little subtler than that."

He raised two fingers. "I'm the height of discretion. I didn't even chase after you after you dumped me in Paris."

"I didn't dump you, Hunter." She folded her hands in her lap. "The affair had run its course. I had somewhere else I needed to be."

"There's nowhere else I wanted to be." He squinted at the brake lights of the car in front of him.

She turned her head to look out the window, her dark hair creating a silky veil over her face. "It was…nice."

Nice? Not exactly the word he'd use for the passion they'd shared, but he'd take it for now.

Rapping on the window, she said, "Next right."

He maneuvered the car around the corner into a bustling business district missing the genteel leafiness of Georgetown but making up for it in sheer energy.

"Is that it?" He pointed to a revolving barbershop pole on the next corner.

"Yeah. Look for a lot."

Almost two blocks away, Hunter pulled the car in to a public parking lot and paid the attendant. As he and Sue trooped up the sidewalk back toward the barbershop, he shoved his hands into the pockets of his jacket, against the chill in the air. Spring had sprung, but nobody had told the DC weatherman yet.

Sue's low-heeled boots clicked beside him. She'd done a quick change of clothes at her place, replacing her black slacks with a pair of black jeans that hugged her in all the right places. Every place on Sue's body was the right place, as far as he was concerned.

When they reached T.J.'s, Hunter swung open the door, causing a little bell to jingle wildly. Three barbers turned their heads toward the new customers.

The one on the end paused, clippers in the air. "Can I help you? Cut?"

"Just a cleanup." Hunter ran a hand over his head, the short ends tickling the palm of his hand. "Edge the neck."

"Sure, have a seat."

As he perched on the edge of a worn love seat, Sue remained standing, facing a rack of magazines, her hand clenched lightly at her side.

Hunter cleared his throat. "Is Walid around? My friend recommended Walid."

Did two of the barbers stop clipping at the same time?

"Walid?" The man on the end who'd welcomed him shook his head. "He doesn't work here anymore. Hasn't been here for a while."

"No problem. Thought I'd check."

"I hope this doesn't take too long, James." Sue grabbed a sports magazine and leafed through it.

"You're the one who wanted me to get the cut, honey. We can leave right now if you want."

The barber in the middle chuckled as he handed a mirror to his customer. "I'm ready for you. Shouldn't take long. Step over to the sink."

The last thing he wanted was some dude washing his hair. He held up his hands and took a step back—right into Sue.

She drilled a knuckle into the center of his spine. "Go ahead, James. I saw a drugstore down the block and I have a few things to pick up. Take your time."

"You're not in a hurry anymore?" He shuffled toward the barber holding out a white towel.

"You might as well get the full treatment." She tapped him with the rolled-up magazine in her hand, and it slipped out of her hand and fell to the floor at the feet of the barber at the first station.

Hunter followed his guy toward the row of sinks, leaving the magazine on the floor.

The first barber set down the hairdryer he'd just picked up and bent over to retrieve the magazine.

Sue reached out, wedging one hand against the magazine rack as she reached with the other. "Oh, thank you."

Hunter figured she'd just placed her device and got confirmation a minute later when she called from the door. "Meet me at the coffeehouse next to the drugstore when you're done."

He lifted his hand before he went under the warm spray.

Thirty minutes later, he managed to get out of T.J.'s with a little off the sides and a cleaned-up neckline. He loped down the street and ducked into the coffeehouse.

Sue looked up from her phone and wiggled her fingers.

He ordered a coffee on the way, when what he really wanted was lunch, and pulled out the chair across from her. "I'm guessing you did what you went to T.J.'s to do."

"Nice cut." She peered at him over the top of her cell phone and then turned it around to face him, showing him a video of the barbershop in real time. "But then I already knew that."

"What did you make of Walid's absence? Do you believe them?"

"I'm not sure, but the fact that they knew Walid was a plus. I know that's the barbershop that featured in my intel." She tapped her phone on the tabletop. "And now I'll have an eye on what goes on there."

"Is that why you dropped by your place—to pick up spy gadgets?"

"That and to change clothes and pack a bag. I meant it when I said I was going to stay with you at the hotel."

"Déjà vu all over again."

She opened her mouth, probably to correct him, but the barista saved him by calling his name.

"My coffee." He pushed back from the table and picked up his drink.

When he returned, she was hunched over her phone again. "Any activity?"

"Plenty, but not the kind I'm interested in." She swirled her cup and took a sip.

"What about the other phone?"

"The other phone?" Her paper cup slipped from her hand and rolled on the table.

He picked it up and shook it. "Lucky it's empty. The phone I took off the intruder."

"I turned that off for now. I'm afraid it can be tracked or pinged." She folded a napkin into a small square. "I wasn't having any luck with the password, anyway."

"We still have his fingerprints on that gun. I'm hoping to get some help with that."

"Yeah, that gun." She dropped her phone into her purse. "Sounds like you have more contacts at the Agency than I do. Maybe your contacts can get me my job back."

"You weren't fired."

"Not yet." She twisted up her mouth on one side. "Now I know how Denver feels."

"You think you're being set up?"

"I don't know what to think." She stuffed her napkin inside her cup. "Are you ready?"

He drained his lukewarm coffee from his cup and stood. "Let's go."

He guided Sue through traffic on the sidewalk, as her phone engrossed her and she barely looked up.

When they got to the car, he opened the passenger's door for her. "I hope you don't walk around the city with your nose in your phone like that all the time."

She held up her cell as she slid onto the seat. "Just when I'm watching surveillance video."

"Do you know what you're watching for?"

"Not really. I'll know it when I see it."

"And then you'll let me know, right?" He caught the door before slamming it. "Right?"

Sue answered without looking up. "Of course."

Hunter scuffed back around to the driver's side. Why did he feel like he just got used in that barbershop? He didn't even need a haircut.

As he got behind the wheel, his phone buzzed. He checked the display. "Perfect timing. My contact has some info on Jeffrey."

"Did he send it through?" Sue finally glanced up from her phone, her eyes shining.

"No. He doesn't want to expose the information by emailing or texting it. He's going to leave it for me in a mailbox."

A laugh bubbled from her lips. "You're joking."

"Why would I be joking? He sent me the address of a vacant house in Fredericksburg, Virginia, and he's leaving the information in the mailbox." He tapped his phone to bring up his GPS and then tossed it to Sue. "Can you enter the address for me?"

"Fredericksburg? That's at least an hour away." She held his phone in front of her face.

"You don't expect him to leave it outside the gates of Langley, do you?"

"No." She turned down the news on the radio. "I take it back. It's an ingenious method of communication. I'll have to remember that ploy for my next covert operation."

"This *is* your next covert operation." He gave her the address of the house and then headed out of town, following the GPS directions south.

The landscape rolled out the green carpet as they hit the highway to Virginia. The recent rains had created a verdant emerald border along either side of the highway that rushed by in a blur.

"Pretty, isn't it?" Sue had slumped in her seat, resting the side of her head against the window.

"I was just thinking that, myself." Hunter glanced at his rearview mirror and furrowed his brow. "That truck's coming up fast on my tail."

"We have two lanes. He can go around." Hunching forward, Sue peered into the side mirror. "Idiot."

"He must've heard you."

Hunter tracked the truck as it veered into the left lane and started gaining on them. He eased off the gas to give the behemoth plenty of room to pass and move over.

As the truck drew abreast of his car, it slowed down.

"Jerk. What does he want? I'm not getting into a road rage situation with him."

Gripping the steering wheel, Hunter glanced to his left and swore. "He has a gun!"

Chapter Five

Sue threw out a hand and wedged it against the dashboard as Hunter slammed on the brakes and the car fishtailed on the road. Her gaze flew to the side mirror and an oncoming car blowing its horn and swerving toward the shoulder.

She hunched her shoulders and braced for the impact. Instead, the car lurched forward as Hunter punched the gas pedal. Her head snapped forward and back, hitting the headrest.

The truck to their left had slowed down when they had, and as the little rental leaped ahead eating the asphalt beneath it, the truck roared back to life.

Hunter shouted, "My gun! Get my gun under the seat."

Sue bent forward, her hand scrabbling beneath the driver's seat between Hunter's legs. Her fingers curled around the cold metal and she yanked it free.

When she popped up, she screamed as Hunter zoomed toward the car in front of them.

He pumped the brake pedal, and their tires squealed in protest. The truck had pulled up next to the car in front of them, veering to the right, almost clipping the left bumper and then jerking back, probably realizing he had the wrong target.

"He's gonna hang back and wait for us again." Hunter's gun nestled in her hand and she slipped her finger onto the trigger.

"You know what to do." Hunter held his body stiffly, pressing it against his seat back.

Sue released her seat belt with a click and leaned into the driver's seat, practically resting her chest against Hunter's.

As the truck drew level with them, she thrust the barrel of Hunter's gun out the open window.

She caught a glimpse of the face in the window, eyes and mouth wide open, before the driver of the truck suddenly dropped back, tires screeching.

The car behind the truck honked long and hard, and Sue retreated to her seat, the gun still clutched in her hand, finger on the trigger. "Someone's gonna call 911 and report this, report our license plates."

"Then it's a good thing that sap Roberts is renting this car and not me."

"Unless the cops respond to the scene and pull you over."

"Not. Gonna. Happen." Hunter cut in front of the car ahead of them and accelerated onto the off-ramp, checking his rearview mirror.

"Is the truck following us?"

"If he can see what we're doing, he will."

They curved to the left, and Hunter blew through the stop sign at the T in the road, making the turn. He pointed at the windshield. "Shopping mall ahead. We're going into that parking structure."

Sue twisted her head over her left shoulder, scanning the road and the off-ramp behind them.

"Is he coming?"

"I can't see around the bend in the road. It's no longer a straight shot."

"Good." Hunter wheeled into the structure and climbed a few levels. He parked between two SUVs, pulling the car all the way in to the parking slot.

He left the engine idling and closed his eyes, drawing in a deep breath. "Should we stay here or go inside?"

"I don't like the idea of being a sitting duck." Her gaze darted to the side mirror for the hundredth time since they'd parked, and they'd been here just about thirty seconds.

"If we head into the mall and they locate the car, they can stake it out. Wait for us."

"We don't know what kind of firepower they have." She licked her dry lips. "They could come up behind us and blast the car. We can't hold them off with one gun."

"Where's yours?"

"It's in my bag in the trunk."

"Bad place for it, Chandler."

She smacked her hand against the dashboard. "I have an idea. I have another camera in my bag of tricks. I can stick it on the back window of the car. That way, we can see if anyone approaches the car while we're inside. If not, and we give it enough time, we'll make our escape."

"I can live with that." He peeled her fingers from his gun still in her grip and wedged by the side of her hip. "I'm packing this and you'd better take yours. We still need to get to Fredericksburg and that mailbox."

She flicked the door handle and Hunter raised his hand. "Hang on. Let me check the area first."

When he finished his surveillance, he tapped on her window. "All clear…for now."

She got out of the car and immediately grabbed Hunter's forearm as her knees gave out.

Curling an arm around her, he asked, "Are you all right?"

"Didn't realize that wild ride had shaken me up so

much." She stomped her feet on the ground. "Just need to get my bearings."

"Take all the time you need." His fingers pressed the side of her hip through her jeans.

"Thanks, and thanks for getting us out of that mess... whatever that mess was."

"I'm not convinced they were going to shoot us."

"Really?" She shifted away from him and tilted her head. "He had a gun."

"So did the guy in the hotel room. He could've shot both of us the minute he walked in with the laundry— had a silencer and everything. He didn't." Hunter tugged on his earlobe. "What do you think they want? An interrogation?"

Sue lifted her shoulders up and down in a quick movement. "I'm not sure, but let's not stand around here any longer than we have to."

He popped the trunk for her and stood guard as she rummaged inside her duffel bag and pulled out her weapon and a small plastic bag containing the same type of camera she'd stuck in the barbershop. Was that where they'd been picked up? Had asking about Walid marked them as hostile intruders?

When she finished, Hunter slammed the trunk closed and said, "I know what I want to do in that mall while we're killing time."

"See a movie?"

"Not a bad idea as long as we get hot dogs and popcorn. I'm starving." He patted his flat stomach. "Evasive driving always works up my appetite."

"I'm glad someone can eat. I feel like I'm gonna throw up." Sue zipped her gun into the side pocket of her purse and strapped the purse across her body.

They took the elevator to the third floor and a pedestrian bridge that crossed to the mall.

The normalcy of people shopping, having coffee and eating made Sue blink. The world still revolved and people still lived their lives while others, like her and Hunter, had to protect them from the harsh truths. She'd been aware of those truths for far too long, thanks to her father.

Hunter tipped back his head and sniffed. "Ahh, mall food—cinnamon, grease, cookies and pizza—what more could you ask?"

"Some real food." She tugged on his sleeve. "There are a couple of restaurants upstairs. We need some privacy."

They rode up the escalator together, which gave her a better view of the indoor mall—and the people in it. Hunter couldn't fool her. Beneath his joking manner— and hers—the tension simmered like a live wire.

She dragged him into a chain restaurant with a five-page plastic menu, and they both ordered ice tea after they sat down.

Sue sucked down some tea, and when she came up for air, she asked, "Do you think they were trying to run us off the road by shooting out our window or tire?"

"Or they were trying to warn you. Maybe someone saw us at the barbershop or the guys at the barbershop placed a call and set someone on us. Where'd you get the barbershop tip?"

She ran a finger across the seam of her lips. "That's top secret stuff. You have your sources and I have mine."

"Yeah, but my source is one of your fellow agents. Who's your source?" Hunter picked up a couple of menus and tapped them on the table before sliding one across to her.

"Can't tell you that." If she started down that road with

Hunter, there's no telling where it might end—probably with Drake.

"Then only you know if the intel about the barbershop is legit—seems that it was, if five minutes after my haircut we're being chased down the highway."

Why would The Falcon tell her the barbershop hadn't panned out? Had someone there recognized her, realizing she probably knew all about the barbershop, anyway?

Hunter pinged her menu and she glanced up.

"Are you feeling better? You're going to order something?"

She ran her fingertip down the page of items. "Probably just some soup."

When the waitress came over, Sue ordered some cream of broccoli soup and Hunter went all out with a burger and fries.

"You haven't checked the barbershop." He prodded her phone with his knuckle. "Maybe we'll see someone making a call or coming inside."

"And let's not forget your rental car." She picked up her phone and tapped the display to toggle between the two camera views. "I'm not going back to that parking lot if there's any suspicious activity going on."

She turned the time back on the barbershop video and hunched forward on the table to share the view with Hunter. "There's you getting your haircut."

"Don't remind me." He huffed out a breath. "You can skip that part because, I can tell you, one other guy came in after me and spent the entire time complaining about his prostate."

"Sounds fascinating." She flicked her fingers at the images. "Did you give him a good tip? Maybe that's why they were chasing us in that truck."

"That's a good sign."

"What?" She stopped the video.

"You can sort of laugh about it after you nearly collapsed getting out of the car."

She smacked the back of his hand. "I didn't almost collapse. My knees were a little wobbly. That's all."

"That's right. You're the badass agent who escaped from a gaggle of terrorists in Istanbul. You never told me about that whole incident, and that's what I should've been asking you about all this time because that's really the connection to Denver."

"Well, we did get sidetracked." And with any luck she'd sidetrack him again. Her so-called abduction was the last thing she wanted to discuss with Hunter...second to the last thing.

Sue clapped her hands together. "Our food's here."

"I thought you weren't hungry." Hunter thanked the waitress and asked for ketchup.

"I recovered." She dipped her spoon into the soup and blew on the liquid.

As they ate lunch, they kept checking back and forth between the two videos on her phone and nobody went near Hunter's rental in the parking lot.

"I guess we lost them." Sue broke up a cracker between her fingers. "I just wish I knew who they were and what they wanted."

"Maybe they just wanted to warn you away from the barbershop."

"How'd they know we were there?"

"They could have their own surveillance devices there if it's a hotbed meeting place for terrorists. They made you when you went into the shop, and someone came out to track you...warn you."

"That's some warning—a gun out the car window."

"No shots fired when they could've easily taken one

at the window." He dragged a fry through the puddle of ketchup on his plate. "Same with the guy in the hotel room this morning. They don't seem very eager to kill you. They want something else from you."

"I can't imagine what." She picked up her phone and studied the display. "I'm okay with heading back to the car now. We want to get to that mailbox before someone beats us to it."

On the ride to Fredericksburg, Sue sat forward in her seat, her spine stiff, her gaze darting between the side-view mirror and out the window.

"I think we're in the clear." Hunter adjusted the rear-view mirror, anyway. "However they got onto us, it wasn't through GPS or we'd have a tail right now."

"If it's GPS, they can afford to keep their distance and ambush us at the mailbox." Her fingers curled around the edge of the seat. "Do you think they put something on your car?"

"When could they have done that? They wouldn't have been able to identify this car at the hotel."

"Unless Jeffrey watched you pick me up from the gutter and load me into your car."

"Didn't happen, and even if they did ID you in the barbershop, which seems likely, they couldn't have known which car was mine or where we parked before we got there."

"So, you think they caught me on surveillance at the barbershop and followed us to our car from there and then tailed us and made their move on the highway?"

"That seems the most probable to me. What they wanted?" He scratched his chin. "I still don't have a clue, but then you haven't been completely open with me, have you?"

Sue's stomach flip-flopped. "What do you mean?"

"Why that barbershop? What do you know about it? Who's there? What are they doing there? Who gave you the tip?"

She released a slow breath through parted lips. "I just can't tell you some of that, Hunter, and some I don't know. Can you be patient?"

"I've waited this long."

He mumbled the words under his breath and she gave him a sharp glance. Did he mean he'd waited long enough for the information or for her?

She felt like she'd been waiting for him, too, but she'd had her orders.

She pinched the bridge of her tingling nose. Hunter was here under an assumed name on unofficial duty. The Falcon didn't have to know, did he?

"Are you okay?" Hunter brushed a hand against her thigh.

Sue blinked. "I'm good. We're almost there."

Hunter followed the voice on his phone's GPS to a leafy neighborhood in an upscale suburb. He spotted the house for sale on the left and drove to the end of the block to make a U-turn.

As he rolled to a stop at the curb, he said, "Sit tight. I'll run around and get it."

"You're driving. I'll hop out and grab it."

"I don't want you to." He put a hand on her shoulder. Goosebumps raced down her arms. "You just got through assuring me we weren't followed from the mall."

"I don't think we were, but why expose yourself?" He grabbed the handle and popped the door. "This is my contact, my setup."

"Knock yourself out, Mancini." She slumped down in her seat just in case his concerns came to fruition.

He bolted from the car and strode to the curb. He

flipped open the mailbox and reached inside. Waving a cardboard tube in the air, he hustled back to the car and tossed the package into her lap. "Got it."

As Hunter peeled away from the curb and punched the accelerator, Sue stuck her eye to one hole in the tube. "There's stuff rolled up in here."

"Can you get it out?"

"Hang on." She licked the tips of two fingers and stuck them inside the cardboard roll. She pressed her fingers against the paper inside the tube and dragged them toward the opening. "I think I have them."

When the rolled-up papers peeked over the edge of the tube, she pinched them between her thumb and forefinger and worked them out.

She unrolled the slick photograph paper first and flattened the pictures on her lap. "It's Jeffrey."

The first photo showed the man who'd chatted her up at the bar last night in conversation with another man, whom she recognized.

She held up the picture to Hunter. "Here's Jeffrey meeting with a known terrorist, proving you were right about him and his motives."

She flipped through a few more pictures in that sequence and turned over another batch. She gasped as her gaze locked onto Jeffrey's companion in the next picture.

"What is it? Who's that?" Hunter pumped the brakes to slow the car.

She knew the identity of the man in the picture with Jeffrey, all right.

But if she told Hunter how she really knew this man, she'd reveal the truth about her real function with the CIA—that she was a double agent, had been one for years and wouldn't be able to help him clear Denver without blowing her own cover.

So, she did what she'd been doing with Hunter ever since the day she met him in Paris—she lied.

Chapter Six

Hunter's gut twisted as he glanced at Sue's face. This had to be bad. Denver?

He careened to the side of the road and skidded to a stop on the soft shoulder. "Show me."

Pinching the photo between her thumb and forefinger, she turned it around to face him. "H-he's a known terrorist."

Hunter squinted at the picture of Jeffrey talking to a man in the shadow of a building, a hoodie covering his head and half his face.

"You recognize him?" He flicked his finger at the photo, hitting it and causing it to sway back and forth. "How can you tell who he is?"

"I just know. I've seen him before…in other surveillance photos." She stacked the picture on top of the others in her lap.

"What does my guy say about these pictures? Any commentary or am I supposed to know what this all means?"

Sue stuck the tube to her eye. "There's a piece of paper in here."

Hunter threw the car into Park as Sue fished the paper from the tube.

She shook it out and started reading aloud. "Face recognition matched with these pictures in our database. The guy with the dark jacket is Amir Dawud, who's gone underground since the bombing in Brussels. We don't know the guy in the…hoodie, but if he's with Jeffrey, he's probably involved in terror activity."

"The entire CIA doesn't know that guy and doesn't have a file on him, but you recognized him from a half-profile shot?"

Sue shuffled through the pictures in her lap and held the photo in front of her again, her head to one side. "Well, I thought it was someone we had ID'd from a previous campaign, but I could be wrong."

"Regardless—" he put the car in drive and rolled away from the side of the road "—Jeffrey is definitely connected to a terrorist organization and his meeting with you last night was no coincidence."

"I'm just glad nothing happened to Dani." Sue busied herself rolling up the pictures and paper again and stuffing them inside the tube.

"I wanna get ahold of one of these guys who keeps threatening you and ask him what he wants." Hunter clenched the steering wheel with both hands. "Did they ever get around to interrogating you when they kidnapped you?"

"No." Sue closed her eyes and sighed. "I guess my connection to Major Denver is tenuous unless we find out what they want from me—and I'm not going to give them that chance."

"This could all be related to your suspension. Do you think someone's trying to set you up at work to discredit any information you might have about Denver?"

"But I don't have any information about Denver." She tapped on the window. "Are we going back to the hotel now?"

"I was, unless you have somewhere else you need to be." He nodded toward her purse on the floor. "You should check the barbershop camera for any developments. Since we left there, we were shot at and almost run off the road."

Sue hesitated before bending forward and plunging her hand into her purse.

He quirked an eyebrow in her direction. "Are you okay?"

Clasping the phone to her chest, she slumped in her seat. "Just tired."

"Do you want me to look?" He held out his hand.

"You're driving. Keep your eyes on the road." She scooted up in her seat and tapped her display several times. "I'll review the footage from earlier—about the time we lost the car following us and turned in to that mall."

Hunter glanced in his rearview mirror. "Nobody tailing us now."

"That's good. It means someone picked us up at the barbershop as opposed to putting a tracker on your car, or something like that." She raised the phone in the air and tilted it back and forth. "They're cutting hair. That's all I see."

"What did you expect to see? What's supposed to be going on at the shop?"

"I'm not sure it's a *what* so much as a *who*."

"And you don't see the *who* there?"

"No."

"And you'd know him if you saw him because you never forget a terrorist's face. You're good."

"I've been at this awhile, Hunter. I've studied pictures, video, been involved in interrogations."

"That's why I think you can help clear Denver's

name." He flexed his fingers on the steering wheel. "If we can match up his contacts with your knowledge of these groups and their personnel, I think we might get a few hits. He seems to think so. That's why he sent me out here to connect with you."

Not that anyone had to twist his arm. He'd wanted to contact Sue so many times over the past few years, but she'd left him and he was done chasing after women who didn't want him.

Sue studied her phone for a few more minutes and then slipped it back into her purse. "Nothing but haircuts."

They drove the remaining miles to the hotel in a silence heavy enough to fog the windows of the car.

Hunter shifted a glance to the side at Sue's profile. She'd had her eyes closed for the past thirty minutes, but she didn't fool him. The pretense of sleep had allowed her to avoid conversation with him. Maybe she'd just shut down, unable to process any more of the information coming at her from all directions.

She'd escaped a kidnapping a few months ago, had just been suspended from her job, narrowly missed another abduction from the bar last night, had been held at gunpoint this morning and had literally just dodged a bullet this afternoon. She deserved the downtime.

He sucked it up, turned on the radio and drove back to DC Metro content with his own thoughts for company.

When he swung into the valet parking area of the hotel, he nudged Sue's arm. "We're here."

She blinked and stretched, putting on a good show. "That went fast."

"I almost didn't want to wake you up."

"Oh." Her cheeks turned pink. "I wasn't really sleeping. Just recharging."

Two valets opened their doors at the same instant,

and Hunter plucked the ticket from his guy's fingers and went around to Sue's side of the car. "Are you sure you're feeling all right?"

"I'm good." She stretched her arms in front of her, flipping her hands up and down. "Look, no visible scratches."

"It's a miracle we got out of that." He rested his fingertips on the small of her back. "When we get up to the room, I'm going to start putting some of this information together."

"We don't have much."

"It's more than Denver has right now."

They swept into the hotel and made it back to their room without incident.

Hunter opened the door cautiously, his gaze scanning the room. "Everything's just as we left it."

"That doesn't always mean it's safe."

"Spoken like a true spook." The door slammed behind them and Hunter threw the top lock. He stood in the middle of the room, hands on his hips, turning in a circle.

Sue threw herself across the bed and buried her chin in her palm. "What are you doing? Planning a remodel?"

"I wish I could repaper these walls."

"Huh?" She widened her eyes, blinking her lashes.

He spread out his hands. "I'd like to tack up the pictures and info we have so far and start making some connections, but I don't think the hotel would appreciate it."

"Whiteboard?"

"I think I'm just gonna have to go digital and create a file on my laptop. I can scan in the pictures we have, add the barbershop, the incidents, and put you and Denver at the top of it all. I'll even add your kidnapping and his setup."

"You're so sure he and I are linked?"

"He is." He flipped open his laptop. "That's all I need."

"Do you want my help over there, or are you better on your own?" She rolled onto her back and crossed her arms behind her head.

"You know what you can do?"

"What?"

"Get back to work on the phone we took off that guy this morning."

"None of my tricks worked earlier, and I'm worried about turning it on. He probably knows we have the phone and they can ping it for our location."

"I get it, but information from that phone could be invaluable." Hunter started a new file and entered Major Denver's name at the top on one side and Sue's name on the other. "Maybe we can try it when we're not at the hotel, and then move on to another location—keep 'em guessing."

"That's an idea." She wiggled her fingers at him. "You keep going. I'm going to make a few phone calls downstairs."

His head jerked up. "I'll be quiet."

"It's not that—CIA business." She shrugged and left the room, her phone cupped in her hand.

Hunter stared at the door for a few seconds after Sue clicked it shut behind her, then returned to his file.

By the time Sue returned to the room, he had all his actors set up in his file and crooked his finger in the air. "Have a look at this and let me know what you think."

The slamming of the bathroom door answered him and he spun around in his chair and called out, "Are you all right?"

"Fine. I'll be right out."

Several minutes later, she emerged patting her face dry with a towel. "How's it going?"

"It's going." He shoved his laptop in front of the empty chair at the desk and kicked out the chair with his foot. "Have a look."

She shuffled toward him, the towel still covering her face. Whipping it off, she plopped into the chair.

Drawing his brows over his nose, he studied her makeup-free face and the red tip of her nose. "Bad news from the Agency?"

"Just that they don't know when they're going to lift the suspension." She draped the towel over her shoulder. "Show me what you've done."

He got out of his chair and leaned over her shoulder, inhaling the soapy scent from her skin. With her hair over one shoulder, the back of her neck exposed damp tendrils of her hair.

His fingers itched to run the pad of his thumb over the soft strands. He reached past her and jabbed his finger at the display. "You and Denver are at the top, with the inciting incident right beneath you."

"The point when Denver went AWOL and my kidnapping in Istanbul."

"Right." He trailed his finger down the screen. "Then we have Pazir, Denver's contact in Afghanistan. The group that grabbed you, Jeffrey and Mason. The gunman whose phone we have. The barbershop. And the two men in the truck."

"What are your initial thoughts? You have to have more than Denver's belief that the guys who snatched me are connected to the group he was investigating before he was set up."

"Denver's word goes a long way with me." He dragged himself away from her realm and sat back down in his own chair. "And then there's the timing. As soon as

Denver makes contact with me to look you up, all these events occur."

"So, your presence here in DC is the trigger and I can blame you for everything?" She began typing on the keyboard.

"What are you entering?"

"My suspension from the CIA. Don't forget." She tapped a key with a flourish and spun the laptop around to face him. "That was in the works before you got here."

"Your abduction prompted that, didn't it?"

"Correction." She held up one finger. "Some bogus emails prompted that."

"Just like for Denver—emails to the CIA." Hunter scratched his chin. "I think someone may have hacked into the CIA's computer system, unless it's someone on the inside."

"It could be both." She stretched out her long legs, crossing them at the ankles. "The only entity I know even remotely capable of that is Dreadworm, but those hackers are not in the game of setting up people."

"We don't know that. They're in it to cause trouble."

"I thought they were in it to shed the light of truth on some dark corners of the government."

He raised his eyebrows. "You sound like a convert."

"I just don't think Dreadworm is responsible for the content of those emails, even if they may have been the conduit." She wound her hair around her hand. "Do you want something to eat? I have to go out anyway to run a few errands, and I can pick up something and bring it back to the room, unless you want to order room service."

Hunter's pulse ticked up a few notches, but he schooled his face into an impassive mask. "Pizza? Chinese? Whatever's easy for you to carry out. Do you need my rental car?"

"No, thanks." She waved her hand. "I can walk."

"Are you sure it's safe out there for you?" She would expect him to ask that, wouldn't she?

"I have my weapon, and I'll take it with me." She tossed her hair over one shoulder and pushed back from the desk. "I—I won't be too long."

"Keep me posted. You should be okay. I don't think they tracked us to this hotel, so nobody would be following you from here."

"Exactly." She grabbed her purse from the bed and hitched it over her shoulder. "Do you trust me on the food?"

"Yeah…on the food."

The hotel door slammed before the last words left his lips—and maybe that was a good thing.

He waited two beats before springing from his chair and grabbing a gray hoodie from the closet. He stuffed his arms into it and zipped it up. Yanking up the bottom of the sweatshirt, he snapped his fanny pack containing his gun around his waist.

He gave the room a last look before slipping into the hallway and heading for the stairwell. He jogged down the nine flights of stairs and peeked through a crack in the fire door, watching the lobby.

He spotted Sue's long stride across the floor, flipped up his hood and edged through the door. He fell in behind her as she exited the hotel, keeping out of sight.

He might trust Sue Chandler with picking out dinner, but that was about the extent of it.

She'd been hiding something from him since the minute she woke up in his hotel room—and he was about to find out what it was.

Chapter Seven

Sue took a quick glance over her shoulder before slipping into the ride-share car she'd ordered on her phone.

Leaning forward in her seat, she asked, "You have the address, right?"

"I know where the park is."

On cue, his GPS spit out the first direction, and the driver pulled away from the curb.

Sue pressed her hands on her bouncing knees. If they needed to talk to her, she'd have to pretend she had no problem meeting with them. Regaining their trust had to be her first step.

She didn't know how she'd lost that trust in the first place. Did they already know Hunter Mancini was in DC and why? Could she help it if the guy rescued her?

She fished her latest burner phone from a pocket hidden inside her purse and placed a call to The Falcon. His phone rang and rang and rang.

She'd have to do this on her own. She could brief The Falcon later. Surely, he'd agree that she had to make this move.

She could be back at the hotel, Chinese food in hand, within an hour, with Hunter none the wiser.

Collapsing against the back seat, she covered her eyes with one hand. Why couldn't she have had the good luck to have met Hunter under normal circumstances? Why couldn't he be a DC doctor? An animal trainer? A ditch-digger?

She'd take any of those over what he was—a Delta Force soldier and a man on a mission.

She ran a hand beneath her nose and straightened her shoulders. She just had to convince Hunter her circumstances had nothing to do with Major Denver's and get him out of her life again...out of Drake's.

Hearing her son's voice tonight had given her strength. She had to do this for him—just as she'd always done everything for him the moment she found out she was pregnant.

"Where do you want me to drop you?" The driver met her eyes in the rearview mirror.

"The road nearest the band shell."

"There's a concert tonight?"

"I'm meeting a bird-watching group there." Not that she owed her driver an explanation of why she wanted to be dropped off near the band shell at Creek Run Park, but she didn't like leaving loose ends—like Hunter Mancini.

The driver pulled over on one of the park's access roads, and she cranked open the back door. "Thanks."

"Be careful out there."

She slammed the door and placed her hand on the outside pocket of her purse that concealed her weapon, putting her one Velcro rip between her hand and the cold metal of her gun.

Another car drove by on the access road, and she held her breath but it kept going. She crept forward on the path that led to the band shell.

Voices echoed from the stage and she drew up behind a tree and peered around the trunk at the band shell.

Clutches of kids...high school kids...were scattered

across the stage practicing dance moves or project-
ing their voices into the night air. A teacher or director
shouted instructions from the seats.

She eased out a breath. At least she wouldn't be meeting her contact in a deserted place in the park—unless
he led her away from the lights and action.

A twig cracked behind her and she spun around, a
gasp on her lips.

"Shh." Jeffrey, in the flesh, held up his hand. "It's
just me."

"Yeah, that's why I'm freaked out." She wedged a hand
on her hip and widened her stance. "Why the hell did
you try to drug me last night and then send some goon
to take me by force?"

"Who's your companion?" Jeffrey slid a hand into the
pocket of his jacket.

"M-my companion?"

Jeffrey tilted his head to the side with a quick jerk.
"Let's walk."

Her tennis shoes squished the mulch beneath her feet,
damp with night dew, as Jeffrey took her arm.

She resisted the urge to shake off the pincerlike hold
he had on her arm, advancing their status as comrades,
two people on the same side.

He led her down a path, away from the performing
teens, away from the comfort their voices brought. As
she started to turn around, he shoved her against a tree
and yanked her purse from her arm.

"Hey!" She spun around and made a grab for it, but
he held it out of her reach and she didn't want to jump
up and down to get it back.

"Do you have a weapon?"

She swallowed. "Of course I do."

He tossed her purse under a bush, several feet away. "Your companion?"

"That guy in the hotel room? He's a friend, an ex-boy-friend." She didn't want to stray too far from the truth. "He followed me and my friend out that night, saw me flailing around in the gutter after you slipped me the mickey and took me back to his hotel."

"If he's an ex, why does he have a hotel room and not a place of his own?" His dark eyes glittered through slits.

She rubbed her stinging palms together, dislodging bits of bark. "He doesn't live in DC. What does he matter, anyway? Why are you guys trying to bring me in by drugging me and holding me at gunpoint? You don't have to put on an act…unless you think someone is watching me here."

The pressure in her chest eased as she blew out a breath. Maybe that was it. They knew she'd been suspended and figured the Agency was watching her. Maybe the assaults were just another staged kidnapping like the one in Istanbul.

"The CIA has suspended you." He pointed a finger at her. "Do they know?"

"Know about us? No." She folded her arms, pressing them against her chest. "Just more follow-up from Istanbul. Is that what this is all about? You think the CIA is onto me?"

A bird chirped from the darkness and stirred some leaves with its night flight.

Jeffrey held a finger to his lips and cocked his head. Then he took the same finger and sliced it across his throat. "If they make you, you're no longer of any use to us."

"Obviously." She straightened her spine against the chill making its way up her back. "That's not what happened. They don't have a clue. Do you think I'd do anything to jeopardize what we have going?"

"How do I know you're not bugged right now?" He waved a hand up and down her body.

She spread her arms out to the sides. "You're welcome to check. I initiated this meeting because I wanted to know why you were trying to take me by force. Do you really think I'd meet with you to try to entrap you?"

Clamping a hand on her shoulder, he forced her to face the tree and shoved her against it again.

The rough trunk bit into her palms again and she sucked in her bottom lip as Jeffrey reached under her shirt and thrust one hand between her breasts. She held her breath as his hands continued their impassionate but thorough search of her body. Thank God she hadn't decided to go rogue and show up with a listening or tracking device.

The Falcon had always given her explicit instructions to show up to meetings clean…but she hadn't been able to reach The Falcon. In fact, he hadn't given her an opportunity to even tell him about her suspension, which made her think he might be behind it.

Jeffrey's strong hands spun her around. "You've made it easy for us. You're coming with me."

"What do you mean? Where are you taking me?" This time she *did* shrug out of his grasp. "I can't just disappear from my life. It's one thing to do that in Istanbul, but it's not happening in DC."

He whipped his gun from his pocket and jabbed her in the ribs. "It's not up to you. We own you."

"I told you. Everything's on track. The CIA doesn't suspect a thing. I haven't been suspended because they're suspicious about any of my activity. That's all you need to know." She wrapped her fingers around the barrel of his gun. "I'll be delivering another piece of information soon."

"You don't get it." He put his face so close to hers she could smell the garlic on his breath. "We don't trust you anymore."

"That's ridiculous. I haven't given you any reason not to. The suspension is not my fault." Her knees began to buckle beneath her, but she widened her stance. Now was not the time to crumble. If she couldn't convince Jeffrey of her loyalty to the cause, he'd take her away and then the interrogation would begin…for real.

"Barbershop." He spat out the word between clenched teeth. "What were you doing at the barbershop? Did you think nobody would recognize you there?"

"I was hoping you would. I was reaching out and Rahid had mentioned the shop at our last meeting in Istanbul. I didn't expect you to try to run us off the road."

"If you knew that was us, why'd you pull a gun?" He nudged her again with his weapon.

"I was with my friend. He doesn't know anything about any of this."

"And then you contacted us with the phone you took off…our guy in the hotel room. Why didn't you do that before the barbershop?"

Sue swallowed. "I couldn't access the phone before. It took me a while to break into it. Give me another assignment. Let me prove myself."

Jeffrey kicked at a rock in the dirt. "This is not what we had in mind for an interrogation. You're coming with me—now."

He shoved her away from him with one hand, while he kept the gun trained on her with the other.

She stumbled and fell to her hands and knees. A wild

thought came into her head to scramble for her purse and get her weapon.

A second later, Jeffrey grunted and crashed onto the ground next to her.

She twisted around and growled at Hunter looming above her, "What the hell are you doing? You just signed my death warrant."

Chapter Eight

"Not now." Hunter crouched beside the man he'd knocked out, the man who'd been threatening Sue, and searched his pockets. He had nothing on him, not even a phone.

Hunter pocketed the man's gun and reached down to grab Sue by the arm. "Let's get out of here before his backup arrives. He must have someone waiting in a get-away car."

Sue threw him off and launched to her feet. "Didn't you hear what I said? If I escape now, they're gonna kill me."

"They were going to kill you, anyway. Don't make me drag you out of here by force—because I will to save your damn life."

She blinked at him, brushed off her jeans and stomped past him. She stopped several feet in front of him and spun around. "Don't kill him, for God's sake."

"I have no intention of killing anyone." He spread his hands in front of him. "But let's get out of here before I *do* have to kill someone."

They tromped down the access road in silence, both breathing heavily. He didn't know what the hell Sue was involved in, but it was putting her in danger and he wasn't going to stand by and watch her get man-handled… or worse.

When they reached the sidewalk bordering the park, Hunter pulled out his phone and ordered a car from the same app that got him here.

Fifteen minutes later, Sue finally broke her silence when they pulled up to an Italian restaurant in Georgetown, not far from her place. "What are you doing?"

"I'm going to eat. I was starving waiting for you to come back with food. I'm also going to conduct my own interrogation—but you'll like mine a lot better than the one you were facing."

Her lips twisted as she got out of the car. "You wanna bet?"

He opened the door for her and the whoosh of warm garlic scent that greeted them made him feel almost comforted. He couldn't help it. The smells of Grandma Mancini's family dinners lived deep in his soul.

He raised two fingers at the hostess scurrying to greet him. "Table for two, please."

She seated them at a cozy, candlelit table with a checkered tablecloth, obviously laboring under some false impression.

Hunter waited until they'd ordered their food and a bottle of Chianti and a basket of garlic bread sat between them on the table before hunching forward on his elbows and saying, "Now, you're going to tell me what the hell is going on."

She plucked a piece of bread from the basket and ripped it in two. "I can't. It's top secret, and I'm not even kidding you."

"I know it's top secret. You wouldn't be meeting with a terrorist in the park in the middle of the night if it weren't. But, hey, you can tell me anything. I happen to have a top secret clearance."

He poured two glasses of wine from the bottle encased in wicker and held one out to her.

She dropped the bread onto a plate and took the glass by its stem. She tipped it at his. "Here's to top secret clearance."

He tapped her glass and took a long swig, the red wine warming his throat.

After taking a dainty sip from her own glass, Sue cupped the bowl with one hand. "What did you overhear?"

"Enough to know you're working with Jeffrey and his cohorts. For whom and how deep is something I aim to discover."

"Why can't you just leave it? Just know that I'm doing my job."

"I can't ignore it. I know it has something to do with Major Denver…and it looks like your assignment has gone haywire and you're in danger. I can't allow that to happen."

"Why is that?" Sue traced the rim of her wine glass with the tip of her finger.

He snatched her hand and squeezed her fingers together. "You know damn well why. I wasn't the one who slipped out of that Paris hotel room in the early morning hours. I wasn't the one who ended our whirlwind affair. I never would've ended it. Those few weeks with you…"

He dropped her hand and gulped back the rest of his wine.

"I—I didn't realize…" Her cheeks flushed the same color as the wine.

"That I'd fallen so hard, so fast?" He snorted. "I thought I'd made enough of a fool of myself for you to figure that out."

"You were just coming out of a marriage—a bad marriage. I figured I was the rebound girl." Her dark eyes glowed in the soft light, making her look nothing like a rebound girl.

"The first couple of days I would've agreed with you, but the more time I spent with you…" He broke off. He was *not* going to open himself up to her again. "Look, I wanna keep you safe. It's the only way I'm going to find out how your group is connected to Denver."

Sue pursed her full lips and nodded. "My cover has probably already been blown. I'm not sure it matters anymore."

They stopped talking when the waitress arrived with their steaming plates of food. She looked up after she sprinkled some grated Parmesan on their pasta. "Can I get you anything else?"

Hunter raised his eyebrows at Sue, who answered no, and he shook his head.

He plunged his fork into his linguine. "I have a question."

"Of course you do."

"Did the Agency suspend you so that you could go deeper undercover with this group?"

"Before I answer that—" she directed the tines of her fork, dripping with tomato sauce, at him "—why did you follow tonight? How did you know?"

"Lots of little things that added up to a great big thing—your reluctance to work on that phone when it could've been a treasure trove of information, your quick ID of the man in the photo with Jeffrey, even though the CIA didn't have a name for him." He shrugged. "The feeling ever since I got here that you've been keeping something from me."

Dropping her lashes over her eyes, she balanced her

fork on the edge of the plate. "Then to answer your question, the CIA *did not* suspend me to allow me deeper access to this group. The CIA doesn't know about this group and doesn't know I'm working with them."

Hunter coughed, almost choking on his pasta. "Who are you working for if not the Agency?"

"It *is* the Agency—they just don't know about it."

"Black ops? Deep undercover?"

"That's right." Sue's shoulders dropped and she stuffed a large forkful of food into her mouth, closing her eyes as she chewed.

"It looks like a big weight just slipped off your shoulders." He cocked his head. "Have you ever told anyone that before? Does anyone know?"

"My dad."

Hunter steepled his fingers, resting his chin on the tips. Sue had told him about her father, the retired spook who had encouraged his daughter to follow in his footsteps, once she'd shown an affinity for languages and martial arts. Hunter wasn't sure he'd urge any daughter—or son—of his to enter the high-stakes and dangerous game of spying, but Sue had taken to it with a flair.

Not that he had children to urge one way or another—his ex had decided, after they were already married, she didn't want any. Julia must've known before he did that their marriage didn't stand a chance.

"He must be proud of you."

"I'm not sure about that." She pushed away her plate and folded her arms on the table.

"You're kidding, right? It's what he wanted for you from the beginning—not only a CIA agent but a double agent, someone working in the bowels of the machinery."

She dug her fingertips into her forearms. "I'm not sure I did things the way he would've wanted me to."

"It's crazy the amount of pressure we allow our families to exert on us." He reached around his own plate and brushed his fingers across the back of her hand. "I'm sure your father thinks the world of what you're doing."

"I've got a bigger problem now, don't I?" She uncrossed her arms, dislodging his hand, and picked up her wine glass, swirling the remnants of the Chianti. "My contacts within this terrorist cell don't trust me anymore—and they're planning to take me captive to interrogate me."

"What about your first kidnapping?" Hunter leaned back in his chair and flagged down their passing waitress. "Check, please."

"What about it?"

"That wasn't real, was it? That was a preplanned meeting with your contacts."

"Ah, you don't believe I escaped, either."

He drilled his finger into the tabletop. "I'm convinced you know how to look after yourself, but it makes sense now. You orchestrated a kidnapping with them to make things look good on your side of the fence. Am I right?"

"You are." Sue whipped the napkin from her lap and dropped it onto the table next to her plate. "But now they want to kidnap me for real, and this time I don't think they're gonna offer me tea and cakes."

"How long have you been working undercover?"

"Over four years now."

Hunter rolled his eyes to the ceiling and counted on his fingers. "You were doing this when we met in Paris."

"I was."

He dropped his gaze to her face. "Is that why…? Never mind."

He snatched up the check the waitress dropped off and reached for his wallet. "You're going to need some protection."

"I thought I had it." She leveled a finger at him. "You dropped poor Jeffrey before he even knew what hit him."

"I mean someone official, someone at the Agency."

"I don't have anyone at the Agency—just my contact. The person who recruited and trained me. He's the only one, as far as I know, who knows what I'm doing. In fact—" she slid her jacket from the back of her chair "—I believe I'm on suspension for the very activities I've been doing undercover, only the CIA doesn't know I'm undercover."

"That's a dangerous game, Sue." He couldn't help the way his heart jumped at the thought of Sue in the middle of all this intrigue—even though he knew better, knew she could handle herself. "You need to contact him right away."

"I tried earlier through our regular channels, and he's not picking up."

"But this has hit critical mass now." He smacked his fist into his palm.

"You don't need to tell me that, although I may have figured a way out, a way to keep working this group."

He raised one eyebrow. He hadn't intended on coming out here and playing bodyguard to a badass spy, who was way more hooked in than he realized, but she'd just pushed his protective instincts into overdrive. "You don't need to keep working with this group. Call it a day and fold your hand."

"This is almost five years of work, Hunter. You don't give up on five years of blood, sweat and tears—and sacrifices. You wouldn't. You can't even give up on Denver. You won't give up on Denver." She shrugged into her jacket and flipped her hair out of the neckline. "Don't tell me what to do."

He held up his hands. Where had he heard that before? "What's your plan?"

"I'll run it past my contact first, but since Jeffrey never saw what hit him and I was just about to go off with him, I can make the case that you followed me without my knowledge—which you did—and were just playing the protective boyfriend."

"Which I was." He felt heat prickles on his neck. "Except for the boyfriend part."

She ignored him.

"I can arrange another meeting for them to pick me up."

"No!" The word was out of his mouth before his brain could stop it. He coughed. "I mean, they're not going to believe you and you know what's waiting for you on the other side of a so-called meeting with these guys. They're gonna want to make you talk and they'll use any means necessary. You know that, Sue."

She lifted her shoulders. "I have to try to salvage my mission."

"Wait and see what your contact has to say. I can't believe he'd be willing to sacrifice an asset like you for a compromised mission."

"I have my burner phone back at the hotel." She jerked a thumb over her shoulder. "I'll try to call him again when we get back."

Hunter had to keep his fingers crossed that this guy was reasonable and would see the futility in having Sue continue with a group that clearly didn't trust her anymore.

Through all this, he couldn't deny that Sue's position

gave her an even better perspective on the web entangling Denver—the same web had her in its sticky strands.

"Let's go, then." He added a few more bucks to his cash on the tray for the tip and pushed back from the table.

When they stepped outside, Sue huddled into her jacket. "The hotel's not far. We can catch the Metro."

"No way." He held out his phone. "I already ordered a car."

As they waited, he rubbed her back. "We don't have to figure this all out here in DC. You're suspended. The Agency doesn't expect you to sit around waiting for them to call you back. We can get out of here, someplace safer for you."

"I need to stay right here. Besides, where would we go?"

"We could go to my place."

She twisted her head to the side. "Colorado?"

The fact that she remembered where he lived caused his mouth to slant upward in a ridiculous smile. "Clean air, wildflowers for days and mountain views for miles."

"I really can't leave DC, Hunter. It's impossible." She waved at the approaching sedan. "This is our guy, right?"

"Yeah." He lunged forward to get the door for her. "Why are you so wedded to DC? You don't even have family here, right? Dad, mom and sister's family all in South Carolina?"

Sue tripped getting into the car and grabbed onto the door. "Good memory. Yes, but I have things to do here."

Good memory? She had no idea the things he remembered about her—the way her brown eyes sparkled when she laughed, the curve of her hip, the hitch in her breath when he entered her.

"Are you getting in or planning to push the car?"

Hunter blinked and ducked, joining her in the back seat. They kept their mouths shut during the brief ride back to the hotel, but once outside the car they both started talking at once.

Tucking her hand in the crook of his arm, she leaned her chin against his shoulder. "There's no use trying to talk me out of anything, Hunter, until I contact The Falcon."

"The Falcon?"

"That's his code name—and I've never told anyone that before."

"Does that mean you're ready to trust me now? Tell me what the two of you have been busy infiltrating all these years?"

She pressed a finger to her lips as they got into the elevator with another couple.

Hunter shifted from foot to foot on the ride up to their floor.

When they got to the room, Sue made a beeline to the hotel safe in the closet. She crouched in front of it and entered the code she'd plugged in earlier. Cupping the phone in her hand, she sat on the edge of the bed with a bounce.

"You just call each other on cell phones?" He sat beside her and the mattress dipped, her body slanting slightly toward his.

She scooted forward to straighten up. "It's a little more complicated than that."

She tapped the display to enter the number and held the phone to her ear. A few seconds later, her body became rigid and she sucked in a quick breath.

Hunter watched her face, as her brows collided over her nose.

"Two, eight, three, five, six." She spit out the numbers in rapid succession.

She jumped to her feet and repeated. "Two, eight, three, five, six."

The phone slid from her hand and she spun around to face him. "He's gone. The Falcon has been compromised."

Chapter Nine

She paced to the window, twisting her fingers in front of her. She chanted under her breath, "This is bad. This is bad."

"How do you know? What just went down?" Hunter leaned forward and scooped the burner phone from the floor. "Was that a code between the two of you?"

"We have a number code that changes for each phone call. We answer calls from each other with random numbers, and the caller returns with the appropriate sequence of numbers based on the original set. It's a calculation The Falcon made up. Nobody knows it but us." She clasped the back of her neck beneath her hair and squeezed.

"What happened this time?" Hunter retrieved a bottle of water from the minifridge and handed it to her.

"When I placed the call, someone said hello with the voice alteration program on. We're not supposed to answer with a hello, but I guess he could've slipped up."

"You've never even heard The Falcon's real voice?"

She shook her head and her hair whipped back and forth across her face. "I have no idea who he is or where he resides—or who else works on the team."

"He answered hello and you threw a random code at him, right?"

"Yes, but he couldn't respond. He paused. He recited

some numbers, but I knew by then I didn't have The Falcon on the other end of the line." She pressed two fingers to her right temple. "I don't know what could've happened."

"Maybe he lost the phone and some random person picked it up and was fooling around."

Digging her fist into her side, she tilted her head. "I know you're trying to make me feel better, Hunter, but just stop. We both know something's wrong. Jeffrey tried to take me in for questioning and now this."

"They could've stolen the phone off him, trying to find another way to reach you."

"How do they know The Falcon? *I* don't even know The Falcon."

The thought of The Falcon, her lifeline, disappearing from the other end of that burner phone suddenly hit her like a sledgehammer and she collapsed onto the bed before her knees gave out beneath her. She flung herself facedown on the mattress and stared at the comforter inches from her nose. "M-maybe The Falcon figured we were made and dropped out of sight for a while."

The bed sagged as Hunter sat beside her. "Sure, that could be it. If he's running a black ops organization, the guy has skills. He's gonna lay low until it's safe for him to poke up his head."

"The timing couldn't be worse. I'm under suspicion at work, and I always thought The Falcon would be able to rescue me if things got too heated. Someone in his position would be able to tell the investigators to back off." She buried her face in the crook of her arm. "What if the CIA actually believes I've been working with this terrorist group and there's no Falcon to bail me out?"

"It's going to be okay, Sue. We're going to clear you and Denver at the same time." He squeezed her shoulder.

"But you have to help me out. You have to give me something—something more than fake kidnappings and barbershops and shadowy black ops commanders. I wanna know what you know."

She squeezed her eyes shut. Should she really tell Hunter what she knew? If she told him her biggest secret, he might walk away from her forever. Last night she would've welcomed that prospect, but now? She'd found her shoulder to lean on.

Rolling onto her back, she sighed. "The group we've infiltrated has ties all over the world. That's why the people I met in Istanbul are connected to a cell here in DC. In the past years, we've become aware that they're planning something big here in the US, but they're being coy."

"This group has tentacles in Afghanistan? Syria? Nigeria?"

"Yes, yes and yes." She narrowed her eyes. Hunter knew more than she thought. "Why did you mention those places?"

"Because Denver has been tied to all those places, as well—he was placed at a bombing at a Syrian refugee center, he was inspecting suspicious arms at an embassy outpost in Nigeria and he went AWOL in Afghanistan—and some believe he's still there."

"It sounds like he's tied into the same structure. Who does he know in Afghanistan? Who was his contact there? Do you know?"

"Pazir—that's the only name I have."

Sue drew her bottom lip between her teeth. "I don't know that name, but I'm going to do a little research tomorrow."

"Thatta girl. Let's meet this thing head-on and be proactive. No point in sitting around waiting for things to happen."

She rolled off the bed and stamped her feet on the carpeted floor. "You mean like intruders, car chases and abductions?"

"Exactly." Hunter formed his fingers into a gun and pointed at her.

"Where's Jeffrey's gun?"

"In my jacket pocket. I'll lock it up in the safe if there's room. In a day or two, I might have as many guns as you do cell phones." He plucked his jacket from the back of a chair. "What did you get off that phone?"

"The number to set up that meeting tonight."

"What did you hope to accomplish by sneaking away to the park to meet with Jeffrey?"

"The chance to convince them that I'm still on their side, maybe persuade them to stop attacking me." She yawned, a heavy lethargy stealing over her body. "Can we pick this up tomorrow? I'm going to brush my teeth and hit the sack."

"We'll be thinking more clearly in the morning, anyway." He grabbed a couple of pillows from the bed and tossed them onto the sofa. "You take the bed, and I'll stretch out over here."

She eyed the sofa, wrinkling her nose. "You're not going to be stretching out on that, Hunter." She patted the bed. "This is big enough for both of us."

His gaze shifted to the bed and his Adam's apple bobbed in his throat. "I don't want to crowd you...or make you uncomfortable."

"It's not like we haven't shared a bed before."

"Yeah, but we weren't sleeping in *that* bed." He thrust out a hand. "Sorry, had to put that out there."

She grinned, a punch-drunk laugh bubbling to her lips. "Oh, I remember."

She turned her back on him and weaved her way to

the bathroom to escape the intensity of those blue eyes. When she'd safely parked herself in front of the sink, she hunched over the vanity and stared at her flushed cheeks.

Must be the Chianti…and the fear. Sharing a bed with Hunter Mancini was a dangerous proposition—no telling where that pillow talk might lead.

She brushed her teeth, wound her hair into a ponytail and washed her face. If he were as exhausted as she was, he'd be out already.

Opening the bathroom door, she peered into the room, spying Hunter in front of the room safe.

He twisted his head around. "You wanna share the combination with me, so I can lock up my weapon collection?"

She reeled off the numbers. "Bathroom's all yours. I'm ready to black out."

Once he secured the guns in the safe, Hunter stepped into the bathroom and closed the door behind him.

Sue let out a breath and stripped out of her clothes in record time. She pulled on a pair of pajama bottoms and a camisole and crawled between the covers.

Hunter had already turned off all the lights except for one over the bed. Sue reached over and flicked it off, leaving the flickering blue light from the TV as the only illumination in the room.

When the bathroom door clicked open, she squeezed her eyes closed and then relaxed her face muscles. She deepened her breathing. As long as she pretended to be asleep, she'd be safe from Hunter…or rather her own desire for him. She'd always be safe with Hunter. She'd known that from the moment she met him in Paris.

He'd been wounded by his ex. She'd cheated on him while he'd been deployed, and Sue's heart ached knowing she'd added to his love battle scars.

Her lashes fluttered and she watched him undress through the slits in her eyes. The glow from the TV highlighted the flat planes and smooth muscle of his body.

He'd stripped to his boxers, and she held her breath as he crossed the room to his suitcase in the corner. He glanced over his shoulder once, then plunged his hand into his bag, dragging out a pair of gym shorts—as if those could hide the beauty of his body and dampen the temptation that coursed through her veins at the sight of him.

He crept past the foot of the bed and tugged at the covers behind her. The bed squeaked as he eased into it.

The mattress bounced a little and it sounded like he was punching pillows. Then the TV station changed from the news to a cooking show, and every muscle in Sue's body seized up.

She'd been hoping he'd fall into an exhausted sleep, but no. The man had more energy than Drake high on sugar at a bouncy house birthday party.

She covered her mouth. She'd been avoiding making those comparisons between her son and Hunter.

A soft whisper floated over her. "Is the TV keeping you awake? I'll turn it down."

"I'm sorry, Hunter."

"Don't worry about it. I can watch the cooking shows without sound—unless it's the light that's bothering you."

She turned toward him, pulling the covers to her chin. "No, I meant I'm sorry that I left you in Paris like that."

He lifted one bare shoulder, and the sheet slid from his chest, exposing his chiseled pecs. "It's all right, Sue. It was a fling—a totally hot, unforgettable fling—and I don't regret it, even though it ended the way it did."

"I—I always meant to look you up later."

"Don't." He lifted a lock of her hair and wrapped it around his finger. "You don't have to pretend."

"I wasn't pretending then—" she scooted closer to his warmth "—and I'm not pretending now."

A low light burned in his eyes, and it sent a shudder of anticipation through her body. She knew they'd wind up here together—the moment she woke up in the bed of his other hotel room. At the time, she didn't know how or where, but she knew she had to have this man again, regardless of the consequences.

His fingers crept through her hair until he loosened the band holding her ponytail together. He pulled it out and scooped one hand through her loose strands.

"As long as you want this now, I'm not even going to ask for a tomorrow."

She placed two fingers against his soft lips. "Let's not talk about tomorrow."

"Let's not talk." He slid down until they were face-to-face. He cupped her jaw and pressed his lips against hers. His tongue swept across the seam of her mouth, and she sucked it inside.

They hadn't even kissed since he'd walked back into her life, so this intimate invasion left her breathless. How many times had she dreamed about Hunter's kisses?

His soft lips carried an edge of greedy urgency, as if he couldn't get enough of her—or maybe he was taking what he could get before she disappeared from his life again.

And she'd have to disappear.

Without breaking his connection to her, he shifted his hands beneath her pajama top and caressed her aching breasts. Would he feel the difference in her body? The new softness since her pregnancy and the birth of Drake?

A sigh escaped her lips as he rolled her nipples between his fingertips. Men didn't notice things like that—

even men like Hunter, who had a surprisingly tender side despite the rough edges.

She placed a hand on Hunter's hip, her fingers tucking inside the waistband of his boxers. Resting her forehead against his, she whispered against his mouth, "I've been waiting so long for this."

He turned his head to the side and growled in her ear. "Same. Never forgot you. Never wanted to forget you."

He slid his hands to her shoulders and pulled her camisole over her head. He dipped his head and let his tongue finish what his fingers started, teasing her nipples to throbbing peaks.

The tingling sensation curled in her belly and zigzagged down the insides of her thighs. She hooked a leg over his hip and rocked against him.

His hands slid into her pajama bottoms and her underwear at the same time and he caressed her derriere. He hissed between his teeth. "So smooth."

She yanked down his boxers and skimmed her hand down the length of his erection. "So smooth."

His breath hitched as he nibbled her earlobe. "Take those off."

"You don't have to ask me twice." She dragged his underwear over his muscled thighs and down the rest of his legs, dropping them onto the floor.

Before he asked, she stripped off her bottoms and tossed them over her shoulder. "Now we're even."

With a smile lifting one corner of his mouth, he encircled her waist with his hands and pulled her toward him.

He always did like her on top first. She straddled him and folded her body to smush her breasts against his chest as he dug his fingers into her bottom.

She laid a path of kisses from the curve of his shoulder

to the side of his neck and his strong jaw. She gasped as his fingers probed the soft flesh between her legs.

As he rhythmically stroked her, she rocked against him, closing her eyes. The passion built from the tips of her toes and raced up her legs, pooling where his fingers teased her and then clawing through her belly.

She caught her breath and held it, every muscle in her body tensing, awaiting her release.

As her climax claimed every inch of her body, her lids flew open and her gaze met the flickering blue light in Hunter's eyes. He plunged his fingers inside her wet core and he rode out her orgasm with her, holding her gaze with his. She couldn't break that connection even if she wanted to—and she didn't want to.

Her body shook and trembled as she came down from her high only to have Hunter enter her slowly and deliberately. He steadied her movement by placing his hands on her hips, guiding her onto his erection as he thrust upward.

They hit their stride and she rode him hard, controlling how deep he went and how fast. He soon tired of her game.

Pinching her waist, he flipped her onto her back and wedged one hand against the headboard as he continued to plunge into her.

Her desire for him burned once again in her pores, and she wrapped her legs around his hips.

He stopped moving and his voice came out in a strangled whisper. "Are you close?"

"Don't wait for me. It feels like you're ready to explode."

"Waited for you for almost four years. I can wait."

His words sent a river of electric current across her

flesh. She arched her back and undulated against him where their bodies met.

He sucked in his breath and braced his hands on either side of her head as he pressed and rubbed against her, his face tense, his jaw tight.

He was a man of steel.

She puffed out a breath, which started the avalanche. Her orgasm rolled through her, turning her muscles to jelly.

Feeling her release, Hunter picked up where he'd left off, driving into her, lifting her bottom off the mattress with the force of his thrusts.

He exploded inside her and kept pounding her until they both lay drained and exhausted.

Totally sated, Sue let out a squeak. "You're squishing me."

"I'm sorry." His body slid off hers, slick with sweat and boneless.

"I can't move."

He rolled his head to the side and opened one eye. "I can barely move."

"Water?"

"I thought you couldn't move?"

She snorted. "I'm afraid if I don't move now, I'll never get up from this bed."

Brushing his knuckles against her hip, he said, "That doesn't sound so bad to me right now. Here, we're in a bubble. Out there..."

"It's a whole different kind of bubble out there, but the night is young—sort of."

His eyebrows jumped. "You mean you're going to require more of me?"

"If you play your cards right." She smoothed her hand

across his damp chest and rolled from the bed. "There's still water in the minibar, right?"

"I can get it."

She swept her camisole from the floor and pulled it over her head. "You stay right there and keep that bed warm."

"Impossible without you in it, and how come you look even sexier with that top on and your bare bottom peeking from the hem?"

"Because you have sex on the brain now." She bent forward in front of the fridge to grab a bottle of water, mooning him.

"You don't play fair, woman." He threw a pillow at her but missed.

"I sure hope you have better aim with a gun than you do with a pillow." She spun around, holding out the bottle of water.

As Hunter grabbed another pillow to chuck at her, a soft knock at the hotel door had them both suspended, the look of shock on Hunter's face surely mirroring her own.

"Wait." He leaped from the bed, snagging his boxers from the floor.

She dropped the bottle of water onto the floor and crept toward the door, hugging the wall in case someone decided to shoot point-blank into the door.

The knock sounded again—louder, stronger.

Hunter appeared beside her, thrusting her behind him as he leaned to the side to peer through the peephole. "It's someone in a dark hoodie. I can't see his face. Too short to be Jeffrey."

A woman's voice called through the door. "The code. Give me a code, Nightingale."

Chapter Ten

Sue pressed a hand against her heart. "It must be some-one working in The Falcon's unit. Maybe she brought news of The Falcon."

Hunter held up his hand. "Hang on."

As he turned to the safe in the closet, Sue called out. "One, five, two, two, seven."

The woman coughed and rested her forehead against the door, but she answered the correct sequence of re-sponding numbers.

Hunter sidled up next to her with a gun pointed at the door.

"She's legit, Hunter. I'm opening the door."

"Slowly." He stood behind the door as she eased it open.

The woman fell against the door with a thump, and as Sue widened the door, the woman fell into the room, landing in a heap on the floor.

"Oh my God." Sue dropped to her knees beside the woman. "What's wrong?"

"I hope she wasn't followed here." Hunter poked his head out the door and then shut it, throwing the top lock in place.

Sue had loosened the woman's sweatshirt and pushed

the hoodie back from her head. She gasped and fell back on her heels. "She's been beaten."

Hunter crouched beside her. "What happened? Who did this?"

The woman's lashes fluttered and her slack mouth hung open, a trickle of blood seeping from the corner.

"I think she lost consciousness."

"Let's get her on the sofa. Get some towels." He slid his arms beneath the woman's small form and lifted her in a single motion.

As he carried her to the sofa, Sue pulled on her underwear and rushed to the bathroom to collect the extra towels. She grabbed a hand towel and ran it beneath the faucet.

Had The Falcon's entire unit been blown wide open? Were they all targets now?

When she returned to the room, Hunter was seated on the floor next to the sofa checking the woman's vitals.

"Is she still alive?"

"Barely." He peeled the woman's blouse back from her chest. "She has multiple wounds. These look like stab wounds."

"God, what happened to her?" Sue pressed a towel against the woman's bleeding head.

"The same thing that would've happened to you had you gone along with Jeffrey tonight."

Sue clenched her teeth as she used the wet towel to clean up some of the blood on the woman's face. "How did she get here?"

"God knows." Hunter clasped his hands behind his neck. "She needs medical attention, Sue. We can't do this here. We're losing her."

"If she wanted to go to the hospital, she would've gone to the hospital—she came here instead."

"Maybe just to warn you, and she's done that." He rose to his feet. "We have to get help. She's somebody's daughter, sister, wife, mother. My God, if this were you, I'd want immediate medical care for you, regardless of any other circumstances."

"Of course, you're right." She smoothed the corner of the towel across the woman's mouth. She might have a son, just like her.

"I'm calling 911, and then I'll call the front desk of the hotel. We can say we don't know her. She came up to our room like this, knocked on the door and collapsed. We don't know anything."

"Does she have ID? Did you check?"

"I didn't." He held up his phone. "You do that while I call."

Sue searched the woman's pockets and scanned the floor inside the room and in the hallway in case she'd dropped something.

When Hunter ended his call, Sue spread her hands. "Nothing. She has nothing."

Ten minutes later, Sue waved at the EMTs as they came off the elevator. "Over here. She's here."

For several chaotic minutes, the EMTs stabilized the injured woman and got her onto a stretcher as the police questioned Sue and Hunter.

The questions continued even after the EMTs had taken away the patient, but Sue had years of lying under her belt and she maintained her ignorance without blinking an eye.

Maybe Hunter didn't have quite the same skills in mendacity as she possessed, but his military training had given him an erect bearing and poker face that was hard to pick apart.

In the end, the cops had no reason to believe she and

Hunter had injured the woman or even knew who she was—and the hotel's CCTV would back them up.

Sue clicked the door closed behind the last of the police officers and braced her hands against it, hanging her head between her arms. "I wonder who she is."

"Hopefully, she'll regain consciousness and tell us… and tell us why she came here." Hunter traced a line down her curved spine. "She must've used every last ounce of her strength to get here and recite that code to you."

Sue turned and nestled her head against Hunter's chest, just because she could. "How did she know I was here? How did she even know about me? The Falcon has never even implied I was part of a group."

"Different plans for different people. Maybe you're the only CIA agent and The Falcon has different rules for you." He squeezed her shoulders. "Let's get back to bed for the remaining hours we have left in this morning."

"We're going to try to see her at the hospital tomorrow, right?"

"I don't see how we're ever going to get any information out of her if we don't—and I'm sure she wanted you to have info or she never would've shown up here." He leaned over her to put his eye to the peephole in the door. "I hope nobody followed her. We've been secure at this hotel so far."

"We *think* we have. How did she find us?"

Hunter yawned and flicked off the light in the entryway. "We'll ask her tomorrow."

On the way to the bed, Hunter peeled off the T-shirt he'd hastily thrown on when the EMTs arrived and stepped out of his jeans and boxers at the same time. He slid his naked body between the sheets and patted the bed beside him. "Has your name on it."

Sue shed her pajamas and underwear and crawled

in beside him. She didn't know if she could do another round with Hunter, but if he wanted her again she wouldn't mind one bit—and she owed him.

Instead, he pulled her back against his front and draped an arm over her waist. He nuzzled the back of her neck. "Would you think I'm heartless if I told you I'm glad that wasn't you bloody and beaten, looking for refuge?"

"No. I know what you mean. You're not happy it happened to her, either, but...yeah." She threaded her fingers through his and planted a kiss on his palm. "I'm glad you're here, Hunter. I've never had a bodyguard before."

"I'm here and I'm not leaving."

She squeezed her eyes shut. *Don't be so sure about that, Hunter.*

THE FOLLOWING MORNING, Hunter slipped from the bed, careful not to disturb Sue. He'd lain awake most of the night as much to soak in feeling Sue's body next to his as to keep watch over her.

He crept to the bathroom and shut the door behind him.

He didn't like the fact that the woman had shown up at their hotel room, hanging on to consciousness by a thread. How did she know she hadn't been followed? She could've led her assailants right to Sue's doorstep.

Or maybe that's what she planned. Who knew where she learned that reciprocal code? Sue had no idea whether or not this woman was connected to The Falcon and the work they were doing.

He couldn't have left a battered woman in the hotel corridor anyway, but he didn't trust her. Hell, he still didn't trust Sue. He knew she'd been hiding something from him. Why not just come out and tell him she was a double agent, a mole embedded with a terrorist group? Why sneak around when they were on the same side… or at least he assumed they were.

Sue had told him she was black ops working for the other side, but what if she were just working for the other side? People turned all the time for money, ideology, revenge. The CIA seemed to have its suspicions.

If he were honest with himself, he didn't know much about Sue's work or life. He'd heard about the CIA father, the overbearing stepmother, the beloved sister. He hadn't fallen for her based on anything she'd told him about herself.

He'd gotten in deep because of the way she made him feel. Rebound. He turned his face to the spray of water in the shower.

He'd clicked with her so quickly because she was nothing like his ex-wife, Julia—except for the secrets and now the lies.

Sue had wanted him at a time when he'd no longer felt wanted. Powerful stuff to resist.

He shut off the water and snatched a towel from the rack next to the shower. Maybe this time, he needed to be the one to walk away—but not before he got everything he could about Major Denver out of her.

She could be lying about what she knew about Denver, too. Once you caught a woman in one lie, you never knew how many more could be on her lips.

The knock on the door caused him to drop his towel. "Did I wake you?"

"Just by not being in bed when I reached for you." Sue knocked on the door and jiggled the handle. "Have you gotten modest all of a sudden? I've seen it all, Mancini… and I'd like to see it again."

He left the towel on the floor and reached over to let her in.

The dark gaze that meandered over his body from head to toe felt like a caress. When she met his eyes, she licked her lips. "Thought we might shower together this morning."

He stepped back, whipped aside the shower curtain and turned on the water again. "Great idea."

As she joined him under the warm spray and he kissed her wet mouth, all his doubts disappeared...or rather receded into one small corner of his brain.

After breakfast in the hotel restaurant, Sue called the hospital, but once the nurse who answered the phone determined that Sue was not related to their visitor from last night, she refused to give her any information at all.

Sue shook her head at Hunter and raised her voice. "I'm the one who called 911. She stumbled to my hotel room."

A few seconds later, Sue slammed the phone to the table, rattling the silverware.

"No luck?"

"She refuses to tell me anything."

Hunter drained the coffee from his cup and clicked it back into the saucer. "If the nurse is that closemouthed, we don't stand much of a chance getting in there to talk to her, even if she does regain consciousness."

"The nurse wouldn't even tell me if she was awake or not." Sue broke a crust of toast in two and crumbled it between her fingers.

"I'm thinking not. If she used the last bit of energy she had to make it to our hotel and give you that code, I think she'd want to talk to you when she comes to."

"Maybe, maybe not, but there are ways to get into hospitals and see patients, whether you're family or not."

"Yeah, I almost forgot…you're CIA." He winked and pulled his laptop from its sleeve and placed it on the table. "You ready to look at everything I have on Denver?"

"Go for it." She raised her hand as the waitress walked by. "Can I get a refill on my coffee, please?"

Hunter brought up the spreadsheet and file he'd been populating since yesterday while Sue had been making her mysterious phone calls and attending her mysterious meetings with terrorists.

He swung the computer toward her. "You and Denver are at the top, and my goal is to connect you by the time we reach the bottom of the tree."

"Have his contacts told him about an impending attack on US soil, too?"

"Yes, that's what he believes is happening. The problem is that the attack is not being carried out by one group—or even the usual suspects. This group is scattered, has no defined leader—and may have connections to the US government."

Sue's heart skittered. "Traitors on the inside?"

"It's the only way to explain the setup of Denver. It's widespread and there seems to be no urgency to clear Denver's name, even when charges against him have been shown to be false."

Sue's phone buzzed on the table beside her, and she shot him a glance beneath knitted brows. "It's my manager."

"Are you going to answer it? Maybe you've been cleared to go back to work."

"I doubt it." She lifted the phone to her ear. "Hi, Ned."

She cocked her head as she listened to the voice on the other end of the line. "What are you doing on the sidewalk in front of my place? I'm not home, Ned."

Sue's eyes widened in her suddenly pale face, and Hunter's insides lurched.

"Okay, okay. I'm at the Hay-Adams in the coffee shop." She ended the call and tapped her chin with the edge of the phone. "Ned's coming over. He wants to talk to me."

Hunter swallowed. "He couldn't do it over the phone?"

"Apparently not."

"He just wants to update you." Hunter shrugged, feigning a nonchalance that didn't match the rumblings in his belly. He tapped his laptop's display. "Did the group you infiltrated ever mention weapons from Nigeria? Apparently, there was a secret stash there that Denver knew about or suspected."

"I'd have to retrieve all my notes, which I pretty much turned over to The Falcon."

"You kept copies?"

"I have copies of all my reports on my laptop. I can definitely go through them with you, and you can tag anything that relates to Major Denver."

They went through another cup of coffee each as they discussed Hunter's spreadsheet, and he really felt that they were making some progress. If they could get to the bottom of this plot and link it to Denver's findings before he went AWOL, the army would have no choice but to exonerate the major.

Sue had been keeping an eye on the entrance to the restaurant, and she lifted her hand and waved at a compact, balding African American man charging toward them.

When he reached their table, Sue stood up and pulled out the chair across from her. "Have a seat, Ned. This is Hunter Mancini. Hunter, Ned Tucker."

Hunter had risen from his chair and stuck out his hand to the other man.

Ned looked him up and down before releasing his grip and taking his seat. "Military?"

"Delta Force. You?"

"Air Force." Ned leveled a stubby finger at Sue. "Are you helping her out?"

"I'm trying. Why?"

"Because she needs it." Ned turned to Sue and covered one of her hands with his. "Sue, what have you been up to? There is no way I believe you've been spying for the other side, but I'm hearing about evidence against you that's giving me pause. Enlighten me."

"You enlighten me." Sue wiggled her fingers at the waitress. "Do you want some coffee, Ned?"

"I'm wired enough as it is." He turned to the approaching waitress and asked her for a glass of water. "I can't tell you much, Sue."

"Bogus emails again? Emailing classified documents?" She pinged her coffee cup. "None of that is true, Ned. It's been planted, just like those emails about Major Rex Denver were fakes."

"It's more than that, Sue." Ned glanced over his shoulder and ducked his head. "The investigators have pictures—pictures of you meeting with known terrorists."

Sue dropped her spoon onto the saucer with a clatter that further jangled Hunter's nerves. Those pictures could definitely be in existence, but who could've taken them?

"That's absurd. Any photos of me with terrorists would be meetings with informants."

Ned wiped his brow with a napkin and then crumpled it in his fist. "Okay, that makes sense, and any of those meetings would be documented as protocol dictates, right? Right, Sue?"

"Of course. Protocol."

"Speaking of protocol." Ned thanked the waitress for his water and downed half the glass in one gulp. "You never saw me here. We never had this conversation. I have my own sources within the Agency and someone gave me a heads-up, but if anyone found out I relayed this info to you, I'd be in almost as much trouble as you're in now."

"I appreciate you're going out on a limb for me, Ned. This is going to come to nothing, but even if it doesn't, I'll leave you out of it." She patted his arm. "Don't worry."

Ned raised one eyebrow to his bald pate. "You're always telling me that like you have some secret guardian angel. I hope you don't mean your old man, because as revered as he is in the Agency, not even he could get you out of this mess if it's true and you don't have the documentation to support those meetings."

"Don't worry." She slid a plate with a half-eaten pastry on it toward Ned. "Have a Danish."

"That's even worse." He patted his rounded belly. "My wife still has me on that diet."

"Thanks for the intel. We can handle it."

Ned rose from the table and said his goodbyes. Then he snatched the Danish from the plate and waved it in the air. "Now you have two secrets to keep."

Hunter watched Sue as she kept the smile plastered to her face long enough for Ned to get sucked into the lobby.

Then she turned toward him and smacked her palm against her forehead. "Who's taking pictures of me at my meetings?"

"The Falcon?"

"And then sending them to the CIA? For what earthly reason?"

"Sue…" Hunter took both of her hands. "The Falcon

is gone…disappeared. Maybe his information was also compromised. Maybe someone else has those pictures and then fed them to the CIA to discredit you."

"Discredit?" She disentangled her hands from his and raked her fingers through her hair. "Those pictures can send me to federal prison. Of course, I didn't document those meetings. They were secret. The Falcon always assured me that he had everything covered—even in the case of an emergency."

"Like this one?"

"Exactly." Sue grabbed her purse and smacked down the lid of his laptop. "Let's get going."

He smoothed his hand over his computer. "If you insist. Where?"

"We're going to talk to the one person who just might know what happened to The Falcon."

HUNTER WHEELED HIS rental car into the hospital parking lot, climbing up to the top floor of the structure. He cut the engine and folded his arms. "Are you sure you know what you're doing?"

Sue had already popped open her door and cranked her head over her shoulder. "We need to get in there and talk to this woman. She knew the code. She knows The Falcon. And she knew where to find me. She probably knows where The Falcon is, too. She's the only hope I have right now…or you can forget about helping Denver. If I'm locked up, you're never going to discover the link."

"I will leave it to your covert ops hands to get us into that hospital room when the nurse wouldn't even tell you if the woman regained consciousness." He yanked the keys from the ignition and opened his own door. "What if she hasn't?"

Sue slid out of the car and ducked her head back inside. "We'll have to come back."

Sue strode into the hospital like she owned the joint. Might as well come in with confidence.

They reached the elevator and she scanned the directory for the correct floor.

Hunter leaned over, touching his head to hers. "Do you know where you're going?"

"When the operator transferred me this morning, the nurse answered with the department—and this is it." She poked at the glass directory with her fingertip and then jabbed the elevator call button. "I just hope this elevator doesn't dump us out in front of the nurses' station."

"If it does?"

"We don't get off on that floor. We'll ride it up to the next."

"Tell me you've done this before." Hunter followed her into the elevator and then held the door for a woman with a tearful, sniffling baby.

Sue nudged Hunter's shoe with her toe. "Something like it."

Hunter ignored her in favor of wiggling his fingers at the baby, who gave him a watery smile and kicked his legs against his mommy's hip.

Sue pressed a hand against her belly. Hunter had wanted children with his ex, but she put him off and then dropped the bombshell that she didn't want kids at all.

When the elevator settled on the woman's floor, she nodded to Hunter. "Thanks for entertaining him right out of his fussiness. You must be a dad."

"Nah, babies just think I'm funny." He touched his finger to his nose and then the baby's. "Must be my nose."

When the doors closed, Sue cleared her throat. "When the doors open on our floor, if you see the nurses' station, press the button for the next floor up and we'll circle back down via the stairwell."

Hunter saluted. "Got it, chief."

"Don't get smart." She elbowed him in the ribs just as the doors whisked open on a short corridor, not a nurse in sight. "We're good."

Sue stepped from the elevator with Hunter close behind her and made a sharp right turn. Seconds later, she tugged on his sleeve and tipped her head toward a door marked Maintenance.

Hunter eased open the door and they both slipped inside the dark room, cluttered with cleaning supplies—and coveralls.

"This is you." She tugged a blue coverall from a hook and tossed it to him. "Slip into that and grab a mop."

"You're kidding."

"I'm not. Do you think the hospital staff knows the entire custodial staff or keeps track of the turnover?"

"What are you dressing up as for Halloween?"

"I'm going to try to snag myself a lab coat." She pinched his cheek. "This will work."

She cracked open the door and put her eye to the space, checking the hallway. She scooted out and checked on the offices and rooms on the corridor before heading upstairs. She had more luck on the research floor where there were no patients.

She lifted a lab coat from a hook just inside a lounge area and stuck her arms into the sleeves. She jogged back downstairs and had even more luck on the way back to the custodians' closet when she ducked into an examination room and swiped a stethoscope from a silver tray.

As she continued down the corridor, she hung it around her neck and then dipped into the maintenance room.

She almost bumped into Hunter, the blue of his coveralls matching his eyes, holding a mop in one hand and a clipboard in the other.

"Hello, doc." He held out the clipboard to her. "Look what I found."

"See, you're catching on. I'll put in a good word for you at the Agency when you get cashiered out of Delta Force."

He leaned on his mop. "You're assuming *you're* going to have a job."

Turning the doorknob, she bumped the door with her hip. She held her breath as two nurses walked by.

She stepped into the hallway and whispered over her shoulder, "Give me a few minutes to find her room. I'll wait in front of her door and you can follow me inside."

Sue tucked her hair behind one ear and peered down at the clipboard in her hand that contained a cleaning rotation schedule instead of someone's vitals—but nobody had to know that.

It took her two passes down the stretch of hall with patient rooms before she located the double room the mystery woman occupied with another patient.

Hunter turned the corner, pushing the mop in front of him. Their eyes met for a split second before Sue crept into the room.

An African American woman hooked up to monitors and devices snored slightly from the first bed.

Sue jumped when the door creaked, and Hunter held his finger to his lips.

Sue said, "Our patient is in the next bed on the other side of the screen."

"Lucky for us, she's out of view of the door. If anyone comes in while we're here, you called me in for a cleanup."

"Got it." Sue tiptoed past the first bed and around the

screen. She grabbed onto the footrest of the other bed where the woman from last night breathed through tubes.

"She looks worse than the other woman." Sue sidled up next to the bed. "Hello, it's me. It's Nightingale. Where's The Falcon? What do you know?"

The woman's eyelids flew open, and Sue jumped backward, gasping and dropping her clipboard.

"What happened?" Hunter materialized by her side, mop in hand.

Sue touched the woman's cool, papery arm. "She's awake."

"She can't talk, Sue." Hunter pointed to the mask over the woman's face.

"She's all I have right now, Hunter." She squeezed the woman's arm. "What can you tell me? You came to our hotel room, and you recited the code. Who are you? Where's The Falcon?"

The woman managed to roll her arm over and blink her eyes once.

"I don't know what you mean. Do you think you can write something?"

"Sue, she can't write. She can't grip a pen."

The woman turned her arm again and blinked.

"She can move her arm." Sue stroked the woman's flesh. "I'm sorry. I don't know what you mean. Maybe you can communicate to the nurses that you want to see me and when you're able to talk I'll come back."

The woman blinked her eyes twice and rolled her arm over again.

"She keeps moving her right arm."

"Maybe it's the only thing she can move right now."

The woman blinked without moving her arm this time and Sue glanced down. "Wait, Hunter."

"What?"

"She has something on her arm." Sue turned the woman's arm, so that her palm was displayed, and squinted at the tattoo on the inside of the woman's elbow.

She skimmed her thumb across the dark blue falcon imprinted on the woman's skin, then raised her gaze to meet the woman's glittering eyes above her mask.

"She's The Falcon."

Chapter Eleven

Before Hunter could respond to this news, the machines keeping The Falcon alive began to beep and whir.

"We'd better get out of here."

He grabbed Sue's hand and tugged, but she seemed rooted to the floor, her mouth working as she mumbled.

"A woman. I can't believe you're a woman." Sue grabbed a handful of white sheet. "Why? Why would you do that to another woman?"

He had no idea what Sue was rambling about, but they had to get out of here. He yanked on her lab coat. "Let's go."

Swinging around, he claimed his mop and pushed it in front of him out the door, almost colliding with three nurses in the corridor on their way to the distressed patient.

He cranked his head over his shoulder and let out a breath as he saw Sue following him. Without waiting for her, he careened around the corner and dumped his disguise in the maintenance room.

He made his way to the elevator, where he found Sue, head tilted back, watching the lights above the car as it descended, the lab coat still over her clothes.

They stepped into the elevator with several other

people and continued to pretend they didn't know each other—not that it would've mattered to these strangers.

When they hit the parking structure, Hunter slowed down to let Sue catch up with him. Her white face and huge, glassy eyes caused his heart to bump in his chest.

He took her hand on the way to the car. "Are you sure she's The Falcon?"

"Positive." She chewed her bottom lip. "Didn't you see her tattoo?"

"Maybe she just got that to mark herself as someone in The Falcon's unit."

Sue turned on him and thrust out her arm, wrist turned outward. "Do you see one of those on me? That was not required—other things were required, but not that."

When they reached the car, Hunter opened the door for her but blocked her entrance into the car. "What's wrong, Sue? Why are you so shocked The Falcon is a woman? You yourself know women in the CIA can be as good as any man."

Her lashes fluttered. "I—I just never pictured The Falcon as a woman. I'm shocked…and I'm shocked that she showed up at my hotel room beaten and bloodied. How did that even happen? She's always worked behind the scenes—giving orders, issuing ultimatums."

Hunter stepped aside and Sue dropped to the car seat, covering her face with her hands.

He closed the door and shook his head on his way to the driver's side. It must be disconcerting to discover someone you assumed was one gender was another. He didn't get the big deal, but maybe it was a female thing—and he'd never voice *that* to Sue.

He slid behind the wheel and smoothed a lock of hair back from Sue's forehead. "At least The Falcon is still alive."

"As far as we know." She peeled her hands from her

face. "She looked bad, and what happened at the end? That didn't sound good."

"How'd you get out of the room with all those nurses rushing in? Sorry I left you, but I figured it would look even weirder for a doctor and a maintenance guy to be in a patient's room while those bells and whistles were going off."

"That's okay. I would've expected you to get out while you could." She powered down the window and took a deep breath. "When I heard them coming, I waited until they were in the room, and then I stepped behind the screen. They never saw me."

"Thank God for that. I wouldn't want to see you accused of tampering with a patient on top of everything else you're going through."

Sue clasped her hands in her lap. "I think my very survival depends on finding a link between the terrorists The Falcon and I have been tracking and the ones Denver was onto. If I can uncover a terrorist plot here in the states, the CIA will have to believe I was working deep undercover—whether or not The Falcon survives."

"Maybe she'll out herself now and the whole operation before she takes a turn for the worse."

"Before she takes a turn for the worse?" Sue flung out her hands. "What were all those beeps and hisses from her machines? That sounded like a turn for the worse to me."

"The nurses were in there in a split second."

"If The Falcon dies..." Sue ended on a sob and covered her eyes with one hand.

"I know she's been someone important in your life, a mentor. Even if you hadn't met her, I'm sure it was hard to see her like that." Hunter rubbed his knuckles on the denim covering her thigh. "Now maybe you can understand what I'm going through with Denver in the crosshairs."

Sue's voice hardened along with her jaw. "The Falcon can rot in hell for all I care. She'd just better not take me down with her—again."

Hunter snatched his hand back and jerked his head to the side. "Whoa. Do you blame her for getting compromised? For comprising your position?"

"I blame her for a lot of things, Hunter." Sue dragged her thumb across her jaw. "And to think, all this time The Falcon was a female—a coldhearted, cold-blooded one."

Hunter braced his hands against the steering wheel and hunched his shoulders. "Why does it matter to you so much that The Falcon is a woman? Professional jealousy?"

He bit his tongue, literally. Did he just say that out loud?

Sue snorted, the nostrils of her longish nose flaring. "Yeah, that's it. Professional jealousy because I aspire to be a cold fish just like The Falcon...or is that a cold bird?"

Hunter gave up on the conversation and concentrated on the road. He didn't want to open his mouth again and blurt out the wrong thing, and Sue wasn't making much sense, anyway.

She descended deep in thought for the rest of the ride back to the hotel, her chin dropped to her chest.

At least she seemed more on board with his agenda, which seemed to have taken second place to all the drama swirling around Sue. But he'd lay odds that her drama was Denver's drama.

By the time they reached the hotel, Sue had climbed out of her funk—mostly.

"Pazir, huh?"

"What?" He pulled the car up to the valet stand.

"Denver's contact is Pazir, some Afghani who's working both sides over there?"

"That's right. Sound familiar now?"

"Not yet, but by the time I'm finished researching him, he's gonna be my best friend in the world." She shrugged out of the lab coat and tossed it in the back seat.

Back in the hotel room, Sue made a beeline for her laptop. "I have most of my files on here. It's secure. Email is encrypted. And my password is my fingerprint."

"All the latest and greatest stuff, but can you get to everything you need?"

"I can, but if your CIA buddy who likes to leave you gifts in mailboxes wants to play, I might need his help."

"I can get him on board. He knows Rex, and he wants to help."

"Rex?"

"Denver."

As Sue attacked her keyboard, Hunter crossed his arms and studied her from across the room. The Falcon's identity seemed to energize her, fueled by her puzzling resentment that The Falcon was a woman.

Sue raised her eyes from her laptop. "What? Why are you staring at me? Shouldn't you be on the phone to your CIA contact to see if he wants to play ball?"

"When we met in Paris, you said you were on assignment, although I didn't know it at the time."

"That's right." She planted her elbows on either side of her laptop, joined her hands and rested her chin on them. "So?"

"I'm not trying to grasp at straws here—or maybe I am—but is that why you had to leave me without a word, without a backward glance, without warning?"

"Technically, I left you word. I put a note on your pillow."

"Cut it. You know what I mean." He wedged a shoulder against the window, wondering again what they were doing in this hotel room instead of Sue's townhouse in Georgetown.

She closed her eyes for a second. "Yes, that's why. Do you think I wanted to leave you? Did last night feel like I wanted to leave you all those years ago?"

His jaw tightened. "The Falcon made you leave me. She's the one who told you never to contact me again."

"Bingo." Sue stared off into space. "I'd already been warned not to get personal with anyone while on a mission, but—" she shifted her gaze to him "—we couldn't help ourselves, could we?"

Warmth flooded his veins, washing away all the doubt and regret that had dogged him since his affair with Sue. After his divorce and his abandonment by Sue, he'd felt toxic.

His shoulders slumped and he sagged against the window.

Sue jumped up from her chair and flew toward him. Wrapping her arms around his waist, she choked, "I never wanted to leave you, Hunter. Never wanted to give up on you, on us, b-but my job depended on it. Maybe even my life."

He rested his cheek on top of her head. "And people think the military demands blind allegiance. Was the job important enough for you to give up…love?"

"I didn't know it was love." She pulled back from him and cupped his jaw with her hand. "Not then. We had a crazy chemical attraction for each other. When we weren't making love, we were talking to all hours of the morning, strolling along the Seine. It was like a magical dream, wasn't it?"

"It wasn't a dream. It was real." He thumped his chest with his fist. "I knew it then. Knew we had something special. The setting, the circumstances might have supercharged what we were feeling, but there was no denying what we were feeling."

"You'd just gotten out of a marriage. I knew it had been hard on you." She brushed her thumb over his lips. "I thought maybe I was just a rebound for you, someone to hold on to and make you feel again."

He raked a hand through his dark hair. "I can understand that. I can even understand slipping away when ordered to by The Falcon, but I can't understand the rest."

Her body stiffened. "The rest?"

"Never calling me, never reaching out." He snapped his fingers. "All it would've taken was one phone call. I would've followed you anywhere. Surely, even The Falcon realizes that CIA agents have relationships, marriages."

Sue broke away from him and stepped back. "I'm more than an agent. You know that now."

"So, once you join a black ops organization, you give up your personal life? I find that hard to believe." He flattened his hands against the cool window behind him.

She pressed the heel of her hand against her forehead. "You might find it hard to believe, but you see how I live—racing from one thing to another, always living on the edge, never knowing whom to trust."

"You're giving up on marriage, kids…love?" He reached out and captured a lock of her hair, slowly twisting it around his finger. "You're made for love, Sue. I see it."

Her cell phone buzzed on the table behind her, and she shifted her gaze to the side as he tightened his hold on her hair.

She jerked her thumb over her shoulder. "That might be important."

Expelling a long breath, he released his hold on her, maybe forever. Her priorities lay elsewhere and he couldn't change that.

She lunged for the phone. "It's the hospital. I'll put it on speaker."

Cradling the phone in her hand, she tapped the display and returned to him by the window, but their connection had been broken. She'd broken it.

"Hello?"

"Is this Sue Chandler?"

"It is."

"I'm calling about the injured woman who came to your hotel room last night."

"Yes?" Sue grabbed his arm.

"She's conscious and she's asking for you. Do you know who she is? She won't tell us her name, she had no ID on her and we can't fingerprint her without her consent. We're going to have to get the police involved, as she was a crime victim."

"I don't know who she is, but I'm curious to find out why she came to my room and why she wants to see me now. Maybe it's just to thank me, but could you hold off on calling the police until I talk to her? Maybe I can discover who she is."

"She just came to in the past few hours after a turn for the worse. She's still not out of the woods, so we have no intention of calling the police yet."

"Okay, I'll be there within the hour. Tell her I'll be there."

"Thank you."

Sue ended the call and then backed up, falling across the bed. "Thank God she's awake and okay."

"It doesn't sound like she's okay. The nurse said she's still in bad shape, but at least she's asking to see you."

He sat on the edge of the bed. "I hope she plans to tell you how she was compromised and can set things right with the Agency."

"I hope she can tell me a lot of things."

They made the drive back to the hospital—a little faster this time and with more confidence. At least he had more confidence. Sue had never had any doubts they could get into The Falcon's hospital room.

This time they checked in at the nurses' station and were given the room number, which they pretended they didn't already know.

The same patient, hooked up to the same machines, in the same position greeted them when they entered The Falcon's hospital room.

Hunter hung back as Sue poked her head around the screen and said, "Are you awake?"

When Hunter heard a slight intake of breath, he followed Sue around the screen. The Falcon didn't look much like a falcon.

The beating had taken a toll on the older woman in the bed. Two dark, penetrating eyes stared out from a worn face, crisscrossed with life's miseries and triumphs.

She rasped out one word. "Nightingale."

She could barely get out that name as it cracked on her lips, and Hunter's high hopes took a nosedive. How much could Sue get out of The Falcon in this condition? The woman looked as if she were on death's doorstep.

Sue dragged a chair over and sank into it while she took the older woman's hand. "What happened? How'd they get to you?"

The Falcon pointed a clawlike hand at the plastic water cup on the bedside table, and Hunter retrieved it for her and held the straw to her lips.

She drank and then waved him away. "Ambush."

"They ambushed you? How did they find you? The CIA doesn't even know who you are. I didn't even realize you were here in DC."

The Falcon coughed. "Whole mission over."

"No." Sue scooted her chair closer. "I don't believe that. I can't accept it. I gave up…everything for this mission."

The Falcon's gaze darted to Hunter and pierced him to his soul. She coughed again, and the beeping on her machines picked up speed. "Over. Too dangerous."

"Tell me what to do. I'll finish it." Sue reached for the water cup again as The Falcon went into another coughing fit.

"Over, Nightingale. Someone inside."

Hunter hunched forward. "Are you telling us there's someone on the inside of our own government working with terrorists against US interests?"

The Falcon placed her thin lips on the straw. When Sue pulled it away, a few drops of water dribbled from the corner of The Falcon's mouth.

"Deep. Someone deep. Major Rex Denver."

"No!" Hunter shouted the word. "He's not involved."

The Falcon reached out, and with unexpected strength, she wrapped her bony fingers around his wrist like a vise. "Someone inside setting up Denver. My shoe, Nightingale."

Sue's eyebrows arched. "Your shoe? What are you talking about? This isn't over, Falcon. I'm gonna see this through."

"Danger. Stop."

"There's always been danger. I'm not stopping now." Sue jumped from the plastic chair and it tipped over. "Why did you do it? Why did you ruin my life if you're going to give up so easily?"

"Necessary."

"Necessary but now it's over?"

Hunter drew his brows over his nose. How did The Falcon ruin Sue's life? If she was talking about their relationship, that wasn't over—and he had no intention of allowing Sue to end it now, black ops or no black ops.

"Had to do it, Nightingale. For the best."

"The best? Really? The best that I gave up the man I loved and our…son?"

Chapter Twelve

A sudden fog descended on Hunter's brain activity. What the hell was Sue talking about? Son? She didn't have a son. They didn't have a son.

Another coughing fit seized The Falcon, and her face turned blue while the machines went crazy.

This time the nurses arrived even faster, and as they swarmed the room and clustered around the bed, Hunter tugged on Sue's arm.

"Her shoe. Get The Falcon's shoe."

Sue turned a blank face toward him as one tear seeped from the corner of her eye.

He dived past her and yanked open the door of a cabinet. He plunged his hand into the folded stack of The Falcon's bloodstained clothes, and his fingers curled around a pair of sneakers. He clasped them to his chest, unnoticed by the nurses and by Sue herself, still rooted to the floor, in a daze watching the medical efforts to save The Falcon's life.

Hunter grabbed her hand and pulled her out of the room, past a doctor rushing in to take their place.

He propelled Sue to the elevator and out to the car, where he tossed The Falcon's shoes in the back seat. He'd deal with those later. There was so much more to deal with in the seat next to him.

His throat tight, he closed his eyes and he took a deep breath. "Sue, what was all that about our son?"

She slumped in her seat and clasped her hands between her knees. "It's true. I'm sorry, Hunter. I got pregnant in Paris and had a son. Drake is almost three."

Her words punched him in the gut and for several seconds he couldn't breathe. For the second time in his life a woman had lied to him about children—but this was much worse than his ex changing her mind about having them. He'd had a son out there for three years and never knew.

A wave of rage overwhelmed him and he punched the dashboard, leaving a crack—like he felt in his heart right now. "Why?"

"Do I have to tell you that after what you just heard?"

He rubbed his knuckles. "You kept my son from me because The Falcon told you to?"

"Yes. I had to. I had to comply."

"Your job was more important…is more important, than anything else in your life?" He snorted. "What a sad life you lead."

Sue sniffed and the tears she seemed to be holding back spilled over and coursed down her cheeks. "You don't think I know that?"

"Where is he now? Where's… Drake?" The unfamiliar name stuck on his tongue and the rage burned in his gut again.

"He's with my dad and my stepmom."

Hunter whistled through his teeth. "That's great. He's with a woman who detests you and a father who groomed you for a soulless, empty career with the CIA. Don't tell me. It was your father's idea for you to go black ops. His little girl fulfilling everything he hadn't in his career."

Sue pressed her fingers against her temples. "Drake

lives with my sister, Amelia, and her family in South Carolina. They went to the Bahamas and I didn't want Drake to go, so he spent some time with me first and then I sent him with my parents."

"Our son doesn't even live with his mother." Hunter bowed his head and rested his forehead against the steering wheel. How did this happen?

He felt Sue's hand on the back of his neck, and he stiffened, his first instinct to shrug her off—this woman who'd tricked him and lied to him at every turn.

But her touch turned to a caress as she stroked his flesh with her fingers. "I'm sorry, Hunter. I thought it was best for Drake to live with my sister while I'm involved in all this. Can you imagine if he lived with me and I failed to return home one night? Or worse, what if I were home with him and someone broke in with a weapon, like how someone stormed our hotel room the other night?"

"Why even have him if you weren't going to keep him?"

Her hand trailed down his back. "There was never any question that I'd have your baby, regardless of how I chose to care for him later. I was thrilled with my pregnancy and never thought about my situation until… I told The Falcon."

He lifted his head. "She's the one who told you to send Drake away."

"Yes."

"Is she the one who told you not to tell me about the baby?" He tried to swallow the bitterness filling his mouth.

"Ordered me. She ordered me to keep quiet and explained the difficulties of raising a child for someone in my position."

"And then she sent you off to Istanbul and Berlin and God knows where else to make the point, right?" He cranked on the car engine, and Sue went back to her own side of the car.

"Do you think she kept me busy on purpose?" She dragged her hands across her face and peered at him through her fingers.

"She must've had a lonely, desolate life herself. She wanted to make sure you had the same." He pulled out of the parking garage so fast the car jumped and Sue grabbed the edge of her seat. "Isn't that why you were so angry when you found out The Falcon was a woman? You could understand a *man* telling you to give up your child, keep him from his father, be a part-time mother. But coming from a *woman*? That must've felt like betrayal."

Sue crossed her arms. "I guess so."

"I'm taking us back to the hotel, or do we even need the pretense now? You did keep me away from your townhouse because there's evidence of Drake all over that place, isn't there?"

"There is and I did." She dropped her chin to her chest. "But that's not the only reason. I really did believe we were safer at the hotel."

"Do you want me to take you home now? Forget this whole thing? Go back to your life?"

She whipped her head around. "Go back to my life? This *is* my life now. Like I told The Falcon, I have sacrificed too much to walk away now. I can't walk away, anyway. I'm under suspension and suspicion at the Agency, and I'm going to be cleared there only when The Falcon speaks up. Besides, didn't you hear The Falcon? There's someone on the inside and that someone is responsible for setting up Major Denver and probably for outing The Falcon's operation."

He nodded and squeezed the steering wheel. "I want to see my son, Sue. I want to meet Drake."

"You will." She traced the corded muscle on his forearm. "Can we wait until this is all over? We can go down to South Carolina together. He's just starting to ask about his father, and I can't wait to introduce him."

"I could've taken him, you know. I could've taken care of him."

"Hunter, you're in the army still getting deployed."

She was right, but he'd be damned if he were going to admit anything. He pulled in front of the hotel and said with a grimace on his lips, "Home sweet home."

She pointed into the back seat. "Don't forget the shoes. Why did you take her shoes?"

"Didn't you hear her? She mentioned her shoes. She distinctly said something about her shoes when half of what she said wasn't distinct at all, but that I caught."

"I'm glad you grabbed them. I was just so consumed by my anger at the time."

"I know how you feel."

They landed in the console, and Hunter picked up one of the small size sixes and shoved his hand inside. He peeled back the insole and ran his finger around the edge of the shoe.

Sue's phone buzzed in the cup holder, and as she picked it up, Hunter picked up the other shoe and repeated the process. "Go ahead."

She glanced at her phone's display. "It's the hospital."

As she spoke in monosyllables, Hunter removed the insole of the second shoe. He peeled up a small piece of paper stuck to the bottom inside of the shoe and unfolded it.

He whispered, "This is it, Sue—The Falcon left an address and a code."

She ended the call and cupped her phone between her hands. "That's good…because The Falcon is dead."

Chapter Thirteen

Sue dropped the phone in her lap and tilted back her head. "Can this day get any worse?"

"I'm sorry." Hunter touched her hand.

He must still be under the impression that The Falcon represented some feminist mentor to her or something, when all she'd felt for the frail woman in the hospital bed was contempt and anger. And now the woman had failed her again.

"How am I going to prove anything to the Agency without The Falcon? I have no idea what umbrella she was under or where she was getting her orders."

Hunter held up a shiny piece of paper pinched between his fingers. "I told you. There's an address and a code on this piece of paper. It was hidden beneath the insole of her shoe. She told you to get her shoes, and this is why."

"An address to what? A code for what?" Sue scooped her hair back from her face. "She left me flapping in the breeze. I'll have no explanation for the investigators when they ask me about those photo ops with terrorists—unsanctioned."

"We'll get there, Sue, and we're gonna start with this slip of paper."

Hunter's blue eyes bored into her, shoring her up, giving her strength. And she'd just rocked the foundation of his world.

"Okay, I'll try to have as much faith in that info as you do." She squared her shoulders. "I'm sorry I didn't tell you about Drake. It was cruel and wrong."

"You were just…" He pocketed the precious piece of paper. "Hell, I don't know what you were doing. You've told me so many lies, I don't know what to believe about you, Sue."

"Just believe I have regrets, and we'll leave it at that for now." She pointed out the window. "The valet has been champing at the bit to park your car and get it out of the way."

"Then let's give him that opportunity. We'll regroup, get lunch and find this address." He patted his front pocket.

Back in the hotel room, Hunter entered The Falcon's address on his laptop. He smacked the table. "It's a storage unit in Virginia. There could be a treasure trove of information in there."

"Why would she keep hard copies?"

"Laptops—" he pinged the side of his "—can get stolen."

"Even if my laptop disappeared, whoever took it would have a hard time accessing any data on it. We have so many layers of security on our stuff."

"Really? Because I'm pretty sure someone used that hacking group, Dreadworm, to access CIA emails to get the ball rolling against Major Denver."

"Maybe, maybe not." She reached into the minifridge and snagged a bottle of water. "If what The Falcon said is true, there's someone on the inside pulling the strings for this terrorist group. He…or she could easily cover his…or her tracks."

Hunter snapped his laptop shut. "Are you ready to head over there now, or do you want to stop and get something to eat?"

"I don't think the storage unit is going anywhere and you look like you could use some food—and some pictures."

"Pictures?"

"Of Drake." She grabbed her purse. "Let's go back to my place before we eat. I have to collect my mail and water a few plants."

"I was going to ask before, but I figured you might not want to carry any pictures of him." Hunter slipped his laptop into its sleeve and tucked it under his arm. "You don't have any pictures on your phone?"

"I don't keep pictures of Drake on my phone—just in case."

"The Agency must know you have a child. You can't keep that kind of information a secret from your employer—especially a government employer like the CIA."

"My employer knows. The pregnancy and birth were covered by my insurance, of course, but I took a leave of absence for five months. None of my coworkers know I have a child. They know I'm close to my nieces and… nephew, but that's it."

"That's crazy, Sue." He rested one hand on her shoulder. "You know that, right?"

"I know, but it makes sense—or made sense for me."

"And it was something The Falcon suggested."

"Working a black ops team is special, Hunter, different. We follow different rules, live different lives." She folded her arms over her purse, pressing it to her stomach. "I'll bet you Major Denver isn't married, is he? No children? No long-term relationships for him. He's not only your Delta Force commander. Someone is using him for intel. He's no different from me."

Hunter blinked his thick, black lashes. "Major Denver's wife and child were killed by a drunk driver. It gutted him. He changed after that, became harder, fiercer and more determined."

"A man with nothing to lose."

"That's right, but you…"

"My mother died from an aggressive form of breast cancer at a particularly vulnerable time in my life. I suffered from depression. I even made a half-hearted attempt to commit suicide, but my father rescued me."

"I had no idea." He touched her cheek. "I'm sorry. How did your father help?"

"I had already shown an aptitude for languages, so he encouraged me, sent me to boarding school in Switzerland for a few years, where I picked up more languages… and a purpose in my life." She lifted her shoulders. "So, your interpretation of my father's grooming me to fulfill his CIA dreams may be true, but it saved my life."

His mouth lifted on one side. "I don't know what the hell I was talking about. I just wanted to strike out at you."

"Understandable and deserved." She took his hand and kissed the rough palm. "Now, let me show you those pictures."

As they got into the car, he leaned over and tapped the phone in her hand. "You haven't looked at the barbershop video in a while. You said Jeffrey admitted we landed on their radar the minute we walked into that barbershop. That means you did have the right barbershop all along. Are you ready now to tell me how you heard about the shop and Walid?"

"Drive." She snatched his phone and entered her address in the GPS, although he probably already had it in there. "When my terrorist contacts pretended to kidnap me in Istanbul, they did so in order for me to pass them information about a raid, which of course was completely made up. The most valuable time I spend with my contacts is when they speak among each other in their own language. They have no idea I know their language, and it's the best way for me to pick up information."

"No wonder The Falcon wanted to keep you on her team by any means necessary. Go on."

"There I was, drinking tea and rubbing a rope against my wrists to prove I'd been held captive instead of turning over intelligence—even if it was fake intelligence." She smoothed a finger over her skin, which had long since healed but looked raw enough after her so-called escape. "They weren't paying much attention to me. They'd already paid me off."

"They thought you were doing it for the money?"

"Oh, yeah. The Falcon had manufactured some gambling debts for me…and several illegal prescriptions for drugs."

"Sue—" the steering wheel jerked in his hands "—would the CIA internal investigators see those things, also?"

"I'm pretty sure they would." She held up one hand. "I know. Don't say it. I already know I'm in big trouble if The Falcon's storage unit doesn't yield any proof of our deep undercover operation."

"I didn't mean to interrupt. Go on. They were ignoring you and talking among themselves without a clue that you could understand everything they were saying."

"That's right. And what they were saying had something to do with picking up materials from a barber named Walid at the shop on that corner. Like a dutiful little spy, I passed that info along to The Falcon. Two days ago, she called me and said the information was false and that there was no Walid at the shop."

"How did she know that?"

Sue spread her palms in front of her. "I was not privy to that sort of information. The Falcon told me it was the wrong barbershop."

"Maybe that's how they made The Falcon…and you. It was some kind of trap. They became aware somehow that you knew their language and they set you up, just like you'd been setting them up with your fake intel."

"Maybe you're right, but it's hard to believe The Falcon would expose herself like that. She was a pro." Sue pressed her fingers against her lips.

"What's wrong?"

"A pro. That's what she always used to call me. She knew she'd asked a lot of me—giving you up for good and then turning my son over to my sister. It was her ultimate compliment, but she was just playing me as surely as she played those terrorists."

"Nice neighborhood you have here." Hunter pointed out the window to the cherry trees lining her block, their pink blossoms preparing to explode with the next spring shower.

"But you've been here before." She tilted her head at him. "Why didn't you come up to my door that night? You'd come to DC specifically to contact me, right? Why skulk around and follow me to bars?"

He pulled up to the curb and put the car into Park. "The truth? I didn't know what I'd find when I got here—husband…children."

She coughed. "Little did you know."

"When you left me in that hotel room, I considered calling you anyway, even though you'd asked me not to contact you. I even looked you up once or twice."

"Let me guess—your CIA friend. Because my address and phone number are not easy to find."

"Don't be too hard on him. I never got your phone number, which is a good thing because it would've been less stressful to place a call or, better yet, leave a voice mail."

"What stopped you from looking me up in person?"

"Pride, I guess. I'd spent enough time trying to make things work with my wife. I didn't want to face any more rejection."

"I half expected you to show up on my doorstep one day."

"And you would've slammed that door in my face?"

"I would've thrown it open and fallen into your arms."

He snorted. "That's not exactly what you did when you woke up in my hotel room."

"Different circumstances." She tapped on the window. "You can't park here. You'll get a ticket. You can park behind my car in the garage."

She directed him around the corner to her parking spot. "You can block me in for now. I'm not going anywhere."

With her key chain dangling from her fingers, she led him through the garage to her back door, which faced an alley. She unlocked the door and pushed it open.

"No killer cats going to spring on me?"

"No, but Drake loves animals and I'm going to get him a puppy…one day." She stepped into the kitchen and wrinkled her nose at the mess on the counter. "I didn't leave…"

Hunter wrapped an arm around her waist and dragged her backward into the alley, hissing in her ear, "Someone's in your place."

Sue arched her back. "I'm done with this. If they're in there, let's find out what they want."

Hunter cocked his head. "I don't hear any doors slamming or cars starting. Wait here and I'll check it out."

"Are you kidding?" She practically ripped the zipper from the outer pocket of her purse, which concealed her weapon.

"At least let me go in first."

She huffed out a breath, her nostrils flaring.

"Humor me." He withdrew his own gun and crept back into the kitchen with Sue's hot breath on his neck.

Leading with his weapon, he crossed the tile floor. The kitchen opened onto a small dining area, the round table adorned with a lacy tablecloth and a vase full of half-wilting flowers. He turned the corner and caught his breath.

Sue swore behind him at the upended drawers and bookshelves in disarray. Colorful pillows from the sofa dotted the floor.

"Looks like they didn't plan to keep their visit a secret."

"Shh." He nudged her shoulder as she drew up beside him.

"If they don't know we're here yet, they're too dumb to surprise us now." She waved her gun around the living room. "There's a half bathroom down here and then two bedrooms and a full bath upstairs."

Hunter glanced at a few photos of a child strewn across the floor, but he didn't have time to look yet.

As Sue placed a foot on the first step, he squeezed past her to take the lead. She'd done enough on her own these past three years. She had nothing to prove.

He made his way up the staircase, then checked both rooms, swallowing hard as he entered the room with the pint-size bed shaped like a car and the puppy-themed border of wallpaper ringing the room.

He checked out the closet, crammed with toys, and then backed out to join Sue in the bathroom, which had also been ransacked.

He wedged a foot on the edge of the tub, brushing aside the shower curtain dotted with red-and-blue fish. "What the hell were they looking for in here?"

"Maybe all my illegal meds."

Sue backed out of the bathroom and returned to her bedroom where she smoothed a hand over her floral bedspread. "Bastards. What do they think I have?"

Hunter crouched down beside the bed and stirred the shards of broken glass on a framed picture of a small boy hugging a rabbit. "He has black hair."

"And the bluest eyes ever—just like his dad." Sue perched on the end of her bed. "This is not how I wanted you to see him."

"But then you never wanted me to see him, did you?"

Biting her lip, she rubbed the back of her hand across her stinging nose. Of course, Hunter wouldn't get over her deception as fast as his casual attitude made it seem he had. The resentment toward her burned deep inside him.

But working with her to clear Denver had to take precedence over any lashing out against her. He couldn't afford to alienate her now. He had to put his work first, too; maybe not to the degree that she'd put hers, but he had to understand what had been at stake for her.

She'd disobeyed direct orders by having a fling in Paris while she was on assignment—and a fling with a military man had just made the infraction worse. She'd doubled down with the pregnancy and her decision to keep the baby—as if she could've come to any other.

When The Falcon had told her to forget Hunter and

keep her baby a secret, she'd finally complied—but what a price she'd paid.

She sighed. "Do you want to help me clean up?"

Cranking his head from side to side, he asked, "Is anything missing?"

"Anything of importance? No. I have my laptop with me, my phones. Anything else?" She shrugged. "Don't care. They didn't come here to rob me, did they?"

He straightened up with the frame in his hand. "Do you have a trash bag for this glass?"

"I'll grab some." When she returned upstairs with two plastic garbage bags, Hunter had another photo of Drake in his hands.

"He looks like a happy boy."

"Amelia and Ben live on Shelter Island off the coast of South Carolina. Drake loves it there, loves his two cousins, loves the beach." Her voice hitched. Did she have to tell Hunter that sometimes Drake cried for his mommy in the middle of the night or that he'd started saying the word *daddy* with alarming frequency? Time enough for that.

"But he'd rather be home with his mother?"

"Here." She shoved a plastic bag at him. "You can dump that glass in here. I'll take care of my clothes."

As Sue yanked open her drawers and folded and re-placed the clothing that had been tossed, Hunter walked around the room straightening the furniture and picking up books, pictures and knickknacks.

Once her bedroom had been put together again, they moved on to Drake's room. The intruders hadn't spared her son's belongings. Whatever they suspected her of hiding, they'd figured that among kids' toys might just be the perfect spot.

This room took longer to set right as Hunter spent

much of his time examining Drake's toys and testing them out. Finally, she trailed downstairs and got to work on the living room.

As Hunter picked up pillows and tossed them back onto the couch, she organized her shelves. Had they been sending her a message by having a total disregard for her possessions? Breaking items? Scattering things across the floor?

She stooped to pick up a frame lying facedown on the floor. The picture had slipped out, but she knew what had been in here.

Sue dropped to her hands and knees and scoured the floor, checking beneath the coffee table.

Hunter tousled her hair as he walked by. "I'll start tackling the kitchen."

Sue passed her hand beneath the sofa and then sat back on her heels, her heart fluttering in her chest. "You know how I told you upstairs I didn't think anything of importance was missing?"

"Yeah." Hunter stopped at the entrance to the dining area, his hand braced against the wall.

"I was wrong."

"What's missing?"

"They took a picture of Drake."

Chapter Fourteen

Hunter tripped to a stop as a shot of adrenaline spiked through his system. "You're sure? Did you check under the sofa?"

She held up an empty picture frame. "It was in here—a shot of him at the beach just a few months ago. It was my most recent picture of him."

When Hunter thought his legs could function properly, he pushed off the wall and joined Sue on the floor. Shoulder to shoulder, they searched the floor for the missing picture.

He even pulled all the cushions off the sofa to check behind them. "We don't know if they took it on purpose or it was stuck to something else they took out of here, or maybe it's still lost in the house somewhere."

Sue remained on the floor, legs curled beneath her. "Why would they take a picture of Drake unless they wanted to know what he looked like?"

"They have no way of knowing where he is, right?" He stretched out a hand to Sue and helped her to her feet, pulling her into his arms.

He'd wanted to remain angry at her for keeping Drake from him and a core of that anger still burned in his gut, but she was the mother of his son. He had a son, and the joy of that reality blotted out every other negative feeling.

"You're going to call your parents ASAP and tell them to keep an extra eye on Drake. Your father, at least, will understand the significance of that, won't he?"

"I'll make him understand." She broke away from him and pounced on her purse, dragging her cell phone from an outside pocket.

"You make that call, and I'll work on the kitchen. Hell, I might even locate that picture. On the beach, right?"

She dipped her head, wide-eyed, and tapped her phone to place the call.

As Hunter banged pots and pans back into what he hoped were their right places, he strained to hear Sue from the next room, but all he got was worried murmurs. He hoped the old CIA man was up to the task.

When she joined him in the kitchen, her face had lost its sharp angles. "My dad's on it. I think it'll be fine. They live in a pretty small town, and it's not like Drake is even school-age and out of their sight."

"That sounds good." He swung open a cupboard door. "Is this right?"

They finished putting the house back together and Sue watered her plants and collected the mail that was at least in a locked mailbox in the front—not that the intruders couldn't have broken into the mailbox. They'd done a bang-up job of breaking into Sue's house and wreaking havoc without raising any suspicion in the neighborhood.

When they were back in the car, Sue turned to him as she snapped her seat belt. "Should we head straight to the storage unit and skip lunch?"

"Are you kidding?" He patted his stomach. "That breakfast seems like a long time ago."

"It was. It's still not daylight saving time and this lunch is more like dinner and it might be dark by the time we get to the storage unit."

"People check on their stuff at all hours of the day and night. I checked their website, and they're open twenty-four hours, as long as you have the code for the gate—and we have it."

"She wrote down two sets of numbers. Do you think one set is for a lock?"

"I hope so, because we don't have a key, and I don't feel like breaking into a storage unit. The company probably has those units under CCTV surveillance, and we wouldn't last long trying to break into her unit."

"Then lunch—or dinner it is. Luckily, the place I had in mind for lunch serves dinner, too, and it's not too fussy, so we can get a quick bite and head out to the units."

They did just that, and as Hunter shoveled the last forkful of mashed potatoes into his mouth, Sue waved down the waiter for their check.

She pulled out her wallet before he could even wipe his hands on his napkin. "I'll get this one."

Hunter dragged the napkin across his face. "You seem like you're in a big hurry now when before you acted like we had all the time in the world."

"Yeah, that was before those lowlifes broke into my place and trashed it, stole a picture of Drake." She waved the check and her credit card at the waiter.

Sensing her urgency, the waiter returned with the receipt in record time and Sue stood up and scribbled her signature. "It's still somewhat light out."

Hunter dragged his jacket from the back of the chair. "Why are you so hell-bent on getting to this storage place before dark?"

"Storage units are creepy enough without having a pack of terrorists dogging your every move."

"There's no way they know where this place is. That

paper was hidden in The Falcon's shoe, and they didn't find it when they searched her."

"I don't know. They seem to be everywhere we are."

As she headed for the door, Hunter gulped down the last of his water and followed her out to the car. He'd already put the storage unit address into his phone's GPS, and he turned it on when they got into the car.

"Just forty minutes away."

Sue cranked her head over her shoulder. "I hope nobody followed us from my place."

"Did you notice anyone? You had your eyes on your mirror the whole way over here."

"I didn't, but then I didn't notice anyone following us from the barbershop, did you?"

"Wasn't looking." He adjusted his own rearview mirror and watched a white car pull out behind them. He eased out a breath when the car turned off. "Now you have me jumpy."

"Good." She punched his arm. "You should be."

"You know, we've been going a mile a minute since I found out I had a son. You were supposed to fill me in at your place, but we were otherwise engaged there, and then we spent our meal talking about The Falcon's storage facility." He drew a cross over his heart. "I promise—no recriminations. I know I don't need to repeat how disappointed I am or...upset."

"That sounds like recriminations to me." She set her jaw and turned her head to stare out the window.

"I'm sorry." He rolled his shoulders. "Did I also tell you how happy I am to have a child? I can't wait to meet him, and I want to play a role in his life—including financial. I'll pay child support or whatever the courts order."

"I hope we don't have to go that route. We can figure this out together without lawyers or courts, can't we?"

"I'd like that. Now tell me about Drake. Does he have a middle name?" His head jerked toward her. "What's his last name?"

"I-it's Chandler. I had to do that, but we can change it to Mancini. I don't have a problem with that."

She slid him a sideways glance, probably to see if he planned to slam his fist into the dash again. He didn't. Drake Mancini.

"Middle name?"

"It's Hunter."

He swallowed the lump that had suddenly formed in his throat. "Thanks for that."

"It was the least I could do."

Then she launched into a history of Drake Hunter Mancini—his likes, his dislikes, his first everythings.

He raised one eyebrow at her. "Does he ask about a daddy?"

"He's practicing the word. Amelia's husband is his father figure—for now—but he calls him Uncle Ben, not Daddy." She twisted her fingers in her lap. "I always figured those questions would come once he started school and saw all the other dads. Now we can avoid that."

Too soon, he took the turnoff for the storage units, located in a light industrial area of Virginia. He'd already memorized the address and the two codes, and as they pulled up to the security gate, he leaned out the window and entered the first code The Falcon had written on that slip of paper.

The gate glided open, and Hunter turned to Sue to share a fist bump. "First hurdle."

Sue pressed her nose to the window glass. "This first row has units in the hundreds. Hers is in the five hundreds."

He rolled to the end of the first row. "Right or left?"

"There's a sign up ahead. Drive forward."

As the headlights illuminated the sign, they both said at the same time, "Left."

Hunter swung the car around the corner. "These are three hundreds and the numbers are getting bigger."

"They just jumped from three to five. This is our row."

Hunter slowed the car to a crawl as Sue called out the storage unit numbers until she recited The Falcon's.

He parked vertically in front of unit number 533, leaving on his headlights. "Just in case the unit doesn't have a light inside."

"Great. We're going to have to fumble around in there in the dark?"

"We'll see." Hunter scrambled from the car, the second code running through his head. He punched it in to the keypad, and the lock on the big silver sliding door clicked on the other side.

He grabbed the handle and yanked it to the side. The door opened with a squeal, and he rolled it wide.

Tipping his head back, he said, "Looks like there's no light source inside."

"Why are they open twenty-four hours if they don't provide lighting in the units?" Sue brushed past him to step inside the chilly space. "Or heating."

Hunter jerked his thumb over his shoulder. "I guess you have to provide your own. You have about twenty cell phones on you now, don't you? We can use all those flashlights."

She tapped the phone in her hand and a beam of light shot out from it. "I have just my own phone right now, but yours and mine should be able to do the trick, and once you move out of the way, those headlights should at least let us see what's in here."

He shoved the door to the end and shifted to the side to allow the lights from the car to flood the unit.

Sue lifted her nose to the air. "At least she didn't stash any dead bodies in here."

"That doesn't mean there aren't a few skeletons in her unit…or her closet." He kicked the bottom box of a stack. "I hope these aren't files."

"One way to find out." Sue attacked the box on the top, lifting the lid and knocking it to the floor. She sneezed. "Kind of dusty."

He sidled up next to her, aiming the light from his phone into the box. "What's in here?"

Sue reached inside and pulled out three passports. She fanned them under the light. "Two US, one Canadian."

Hunter plucked one from her fingers and thumbed it open. "It's not The Falcon. It's a man. Recognize him?"

Sue rubbed her finger across the picture. "Nope."

Hunter flipped open the other two passports. They featured the same man, his appearance slightly altered with glasses, facial hair, different colored contacts…and a different name.

Sue dug through the rest of the box's contents. "Same stuff. Passports, some birth certificates—everything you need to establish a fake identity for purposes of travel."

"These must be all the agents The Falcon used for her black ops missions."

Sue rapped on the second box. "This proves she *did* have black ops missions, anyway, doesn't it? Helps me out."

"Let's keep looking for something more recent." Hunter kicked another box and crouched down to paw through some gadgets. "This is regular spy stuff here— old cameras, listening devices."

"Why would she want me to see all this stuff?" Sue

hoisted the box on top and settled it on the floor. She replaced its lid and dived into the second box. "More of the same."

"It proves she was running an operation, for sure, or several operations."

Sue gasped. "Oh my God."

Hunter spun around. "What is it?"

"My father." She held up a passport in each hand and waved them. "These are my father's. He must've worked with or for The Falcon himself."

"Is there any doubt now he got you into the unit?"

She fired the passports back into the box. "He had to know the price I had to pay. He was allowed to have a family and a home life before opting into that unit."

"You're done with that now, Sue. The Falcon is dead. The mission is over. You need to get your life back."

She waved her arm at the stacks. "And all this is gonna help me. I need my job...and my reputation back."

Hunter tripped over a metal filing cabinet. He flipped it open and rifled through the contents. "This is more like it. Paperwork on some of her missions. Forget the passports and spy gadgets. This is the stuff we need."

Sue stepped over a stuffed suitcase and crouched before another filing cabinet. "At least this one doesn't have two inches of dust coating it."

"Yeah, those are the ones we need to be looking at. I'm sure she directed you to this storage unit for a reason—and it wasn't to find your father's fake passports."

"Okay, minimal dust." Sue's muffled voice came from the back of the unit.

Still in a crouch, Hunter moved two steps to the side and ducked into another filing cabinet. The headlights beaming into the unit flickered.

He called out to Sue. "I hope my car battery's not dying."

"That's all you need. You already cracked the dash."

The lights flickered again and Hunter twisted his head over his shoulder. A flash of light illuminated the space, blinding him.

An explosion rocked the unit and then the sliding door squealed closed—trapping them inside with the blaze.

Chapter Fifteen

The explosion had thrown Sue backward, and she clutched a stack of folders to her chest as she fell to the floor.

As the acrid smoke burned her eyes and lungs, she screamed for Hunter. He'd been behind her, closer to the source of the blast…and now the fire that raged, blocking their exit from the storage unit.

"Sue, are you all right?"

At the sound of Hunter's voice, she choked out a sob. "I'm here. I'm okay."

The boxes provided fuel for the flames and they licked greedily at their sustenance as they danced closer to the back of the unit. Sue flattened her body on the cement floor, the files digging into her belly.

Hunter appeared, crawling through the gray smoke. "Thank God you're not hurt. You're not, are you?"

"No. You?"

"Fine." He even scooted forward and kissed the tip of her nose. "Don't worry. I have a plan."

"The fire's blocking the door, isn't it?" She rubbed her stinging eyes. "What kind of plan could you possibly have?"

"All those spy gadgets I was making fun of?" He

reached behind him and dragged a box forward that looked as if it contained wet suits.

"We're trapped in a room with fire. We're not underwater." Her gaze shifted over his head and her nostrils flared. "It's bad, Hunter."

He pulled one of the wet suits from the box. "These aren't wet suits, Sue. They're fire-retardant suits. They'll allow us to literally walk through flames—if they're not too old and decrepit."

"Why'd you have to add that last part?" She snatched the suit from his hands and shimmied into it while she was on the ground.

"Pull up the hood and put on the gloves." A crash made her jump but Hunter didn't blink an eye. "Hurry! There's netting that drops over the face but cover your face with your gloved hands. Make sure your hair is all tucked in and hang on to me."

Suited up, they crawled across the floor for as long as they could. Then Hunter gave her the command to stand up in the fire.

Sue's mind went blank as she covered her face with one hand and kept the other pressed against Hunter's back. She had a moment of panic when they reached the door, but Hunter yanked it back.

As the air rushed into the storage unit, the flames surged, but Hunter dragged her outside. He pulled her several feet away from the blazing unit and then left her.

Seconds later, she heard the car idling beside her. As she lurched to her knees, Hunter came around behind her and hoisted her to her feet, half dragging, half carrying her to the car.

With her door still hanging open, Hunter punched the accelerator and they sped from the facility. Once outside, he pulled over beneath a freeway on-ramp. "Call 911 from your burner phone."

She reached for the phone on the console, but her thick gloves wouldn't allow her to pick it up.

"I've got it." Hunter yanked off one of his gloves and made the call to 911 to report the fire.

Then he flipped back his hood. "Are you all right? Did you get through okay?"

Sue pounded her chest through her suit. "I think so, but my lungs hurt."

"Mine too. Let's take these things off and see if they worked."

"We're sitting here talking to each other." She reached out and smoothed a thumb over one of his eyebrows. "Outside of some singed hair, I'd say we made it."

Hunter got out of the car and tugged at the suit, kicking it off his legs. He ran his hands over his arms, legs and head. He poked his head into the car. "Do you like that thing so much you plan to wear it?"

Sue hugged herself. "I love it. It saved our lives."

Hunter walked around to the passenger's side and opened the door. "I'll help you."

As she slid out of the car, sirens wailed in the distance. "At least the fire engines are on the way, but the cops are going to wonder why we left the scene. Your rental car is going to be on camera, along with our activities."

"Along with the activities of the people who tossed that explosive device into the unit?" Hunter ripped at the Velcro closure around her neck. "Do you really think they would allow that?"

"What do you mean? You think they disabled the security system?"

"I'm sure of it. They're professionals. There's no way they would be seen on camera—even disguised."

As she stepped out of the suit, Sue ran a hand through her tangled hair, which seemed to have a few crispy ends. "How'd you get that door open? I thought they'd slid it closed, trapping us inside."

"That door won't close without the code. They could slide it shut and maybe they even thought they were locking us in, but you need the code to do that."

"Thank God." She clung to him for a second to steady herself. "I—I thought we were going to die, although really my mind was numb. Looking back, I realize we could've died."

"That's the important thing...but I felt that we were getting so close to finding what we wanted. I suppose if everything's not burned to a crisp, we could try to get back in there."

"We might be okay."

"Yeah, I suppose if you can get us into the hospital room of Jane Doe patients, you can get us into burned-out storage units."

"No, I mean I think we might be okay." Sue pulled up her shirt and gripped the edge of the file folders stuffed into her pants.

Hunter took a step back. "What the hell?"

"You thought we were getting close—we were." She waved the file folders at him. "Do you know how these are labeled?"

"I'd have to get my phone to see. Don't be a tease."

She held the folders in front of her face and kissed the top one. "Denver Assignment."

Hunter wrapped his arms around her and swung her through the air. "I could kiss you."

"Do it."

He set her down and grabbed her face with his hands.

He puckered up and pressed a kiss against her mouth that nearly swept her off her feet again.

Back in the car, she shuffled through The Falcon's notes. "Let's not get too excited. We need to find out how they tracked us to that storage unit. We know they didn't follow us there."

"We also know they didn't have a clue about that place before we got there, or they would've already paid it a visit." He drummed his thumbs on the steering wheel. "They tracked us there."

"They know this car." Sue flipped down the visor and jerked back from her reflection in the mirror. "You could've told me I looked like a raccoon with black circles of ash under my eyes."

He reached across her and grabbed a tissue from the glove compartment. "When would they have had time to bug this car? At the hotel? I don't think they ever knew we were there."

"Maybe not until The Falcon showed up on our doorstep. Don't forget, they know where I live. They could've been bugging your car when you were parked at my place when we were in there cleaning up."

"If they were there when we were, they would've made a move." Hunter scratched the sexy stubble on his chin. "We never found a phone on The Falcon, did we?"

"Nope. We found very little except for that piece of paper in her shoe. Do you think the people who ambushed and beat her have her phone?"

"Makes sense. It also makes sense that The Falcon would have a tracker on every burner phone you picked up, so that she could keep tabs on you."

Sue snatched up the phone in the console, buzzed down the window and tossed it outside onto the highway. "Not anymore."

"It was just a suggestion."

"A damned good one." She patted the dashboard. "But this car is next. Too bad you didn't snag any bug finders in the unit, but I'll get my hands on one and we can sweep this car."

"I'll do one better." He swerved off the highway and pulled in to a gas station. He parked next to the air-and-water station. "Give me some light while I check."

She followed him out of the car and crouched beside him as he scanned the undercarriage. The beam of light from her cell phone followed his hands while he felt for a device.

He rose to his feet, brushing off his jeans. "Nothing."

"They can be pretty small these days. We'll do a more thorough check when we have a device."

"Or I can just swap the car out tomorrow and own up to the cracked dashboard."

"Either way." She pointed to the convenience store. "I need something to drink to soothe my throat. How about you?"

"A couple of gallons of water should do the trick." He coughed and spit into the dirt. "Hotel, right? Unless you want to go back home."

"I'm not going back home until we settle this issue. I feel safer in the hotel—I feel safer with you."

As they drove back to the hotel sipping on their drinks, Sue flipped through the folders on her lap. "It doesn't look like Denver was working with The Falcon, but she definitely knew what he was up to."

"I wonder why she didn't come forward in some way and clear him?"

"We're talking about The Falcon here." Sue gripped her knees. "This is the person who told me to walk away from you forever and then ordered me to send my son away. If it served her purposes to hang Denver out to dry, then she'd do it. The ends justified the means for her."

"I wonder if the hospital and the police identified her yet. Would her fingerprints come back to the Agency?"

"I don't know. If someone's that deep undercover, I can't imagine their ID is going to be easy to ascertain in a situation like this." Sue's fingers curled into her jeans. "It's kind of sad, really. She must have family some-where—even if that family doesn't include a spouse and children."

"She was at least your father's age. Maybe she had the family first, and with her children grown, she went undercover."

Sue shrugged. "Obviously, I'm not the one to ask. I didn't even know The Falcon was female."

Hunter pulled in to the hotel and left the car with the valet. On the ride up the elevator, he asked, "Do you think our arsonists believe we're dead and gone?"

"I'm sure that was their intent. They must've realized when we went to that storage unit that we were after The Falcon's files—and we led them right to it."

"I'm wondering what they were going to use that ex-plosive device for originally. They couldn't have known before they arrived about the storage unit."

"That's why I'm glad we're here." Sue stepped off the elevator. "It's a little more complicated for them to bomb a whole hotel than one townhouse in Georgetown."

As she flicked out her key card, Hunter cinched his fingers around her wrist. "Wait. It's not that difficult to wire one room in a hotel."

She stepped back while Hunter crouched down and in-spected the space under the door. He ran his finger along the seam where the door met the floor and then put his eye to the doorjamb.

"If they think we're dead, they wouldn't be rigging our hotel room, would they?"

"Do they think we're dead?"

Hunter slipped his card into the door and Sue found herself holding her breath as the green lights flashed.

Again, Hunter blocked her entrance, stepping into the room before her. "Looks fine."

Sue followed him in and strode to the window and yanked the drapes closed. "They've upped their game. They're no longer interested in questioning me. They know I've been on the other side all this time, and now they want me dead."

"They also want any information you and The Falcon collected on them all these years. And thanks to your quick thinking—" he drilled a knuckle into the file folder she'd placed on the desk "—you have it and they don't."

Sue rubbed a spot of soot on her jeans. "I'm going to take a shower and wash the smoke and ash away, and then let's see if The Falcon's information can clear me and Denver at the same time."

"And stop whatever this group has planned because that's why both of you got involved in the first place." Hunter pulled out his wallet. "I need another soda. Do you want one?"

"Yes, please. Do you think hot tea would be better?" She stroked her neck and swallowed.

"I don't know about you, but I don't think I could take a hot drink right now."

"You're probably right. Diet for me." She grabbed her pajamas and went into the bathroom.

In the shower, she turned her back to the warm spray and let it pound her neck. She'd been on such a roller coaster these past few days, she couldn't wait for the ride to stop. And when it did, would Hunter be interested in being more than just Drake's father?

Today he'd talked about custody and child support as if they'd be living apart instead of together as a family, which was what she wanted. She'd already wasted too much time with her misplaced priorities, robbing Hunter and Drake both of a relationship with each other.

She loved Hunter. She'd felt ridiculous admitting that to herself years ago when she'd left him. But the years hadn't dissipated her feelings, and when she saw him again in that other hotel room, she knew they were for real.

He'd made it clear—up until the point when he found out about Drake—that he still had strong feelings for her, had never forgotten their time together in Paris. But now?

He seemed to have settled down. The anger had left his blue eyes, but it might return when he met Drake and realized all that he'd missed.

And he'd take out that anger on her—rightly so. She'd been duped, manipulated, and with her puppet master dead, she may also be charged with treason.

The bathroom door cracked open and Hunter stuck his hand through the space, clutching a can of diet soda. "What are you doing in there?"

"Thinking." She shut off the water. "I'll be right out."

She dried off quickly and slipped into her pajamas. Hunter hadn't made a move to join her in the shower or even joke about it. Yeah, that resentment still simmered beneath the surface of his seeming acceptance of her deception.

She entered the other room, drying her hair with a towel. "You should've seen the drain in the shower— black. We're lucky to be alive."

"Amen." He snapped the tab on her soda can and

handed it to her. "I was looking through the files and The Falcon's shorthand is kinda cryptic. I hope you can make more sense out of it than I can. She liked codes, didn't she?"

"Always felt memorized codes were the safest way to communicate." She sat on the bed cross-legged, fluffing a couple of pillows behind her. She patted the space beside her. "Bring those over here and let's have a look. Can you bring our laptops, also? I want to compare any notes I have with hers, and maybe we can fill in more of your chart."

He plucked his T-shirt away from his body. "It's only fair that I shower, too, now that you're all fresh and clean."

"How considerate of you." She crooked her finger. "Can you drop off the files and my laptop on your way to the bathroom?"

He complied and shut the door behind him.

Sue stared at the closed door—another sign that he wanted to keep his distance.

She took another sip of soda, allowing it to pool in the back of her throat, before opening the top file marked Denver Assignment.

As she ran her finger down The Falcon's notes, someone pounded on the hotel door. Her finger froze midpage.

This had better not be another member of the housekeeping staff with laundry.

The pounding resumed before she could even roll off the bed. On her way to the door, her gaze darted to the bathroom, her step faltering.

A split second later, Hunter burst through the door, tucking a towel around his waist. "Don't answer it, especially without your weapon."

He made a detour to the credenza and swept up his

gun. He approached the door from the side, his weapon at the ready. Bracing his hand against the door, he leaned in to peer through the peephole. His shoulders dropped. "It's Ryan."

"Who?" Sue stood behind Hunter's broad back, her arms folded, hands bunching the sides of her pajama top.

"Ryan Mesner, my CIA contact."

With his gun still raised, Hunter eased open the door. "You're alone?"

"Not for long. Let me in, Hunter. This is important."

Hunter swung open the door and a tall man with cropped dark hair and a full beard pushed past him.

He leveled a finger at Sue. "Are you Sue Chandler?"

"Yes."

"You'd better get the hell out of here. CIA internal investigations is on its way—and they're prepared to charge you with treason."

Chapter Sixteen

Sue's legs wouldn't move. Her brain wouldn't work. The only thing racing through her mind was that if she were arrested, she'd lose Drake. She couldn't lose Drake.

"They're on their way now?" Hunter dragged some clothes from his suitcase and stepped into a pair of jeans underneath his towel, dropping it to the floor.

"They were just at her place in Georgetown, and now they're triangulating her cell phone."

Sue lunged across the bed and ripped her phone from its charger. She turned it off and stuffed it into her purse.

Hunter pulled a shirt over his head and stuffed his feet into his shoes. "Do they know she's with me?"

"As far as I know they do not, but they've been questioning Ned Tucker. Does he know about you?"

"Ned won't tell them anything. If they went to my place first, Ned didn't tell them I was at this hotel. He's not going to tell them about Hunter."

As she and Hunter shoveled their clothes and toiletries into their bags, she turned to Ryan. "Why are you doing this for me? I don't even know you."

"I've had to watch Major Rex Denver, the most honorable man I know, get dragged through the mud and set up. I'm not going to stand by and watch it happen again to someone who might be able to clear his name."

"And we're not going to allow you to take the fall for this, Ryan. Get the hell out of here now." Hunter clasped Ryan on the shoulder and gave him a shove toward the door.

As Ryan grasped the door handle, Sue grabbed his arm. "Is there any way they can track you here or find out you warned me?"

"I don't have my phone on me, I took a taxi over here and paid cash, and I made sure my face was hidden as I went through the hotel—just in case they decide to check the footage."

"You're a good agent, Ryan. Thanks—you won't regret this. I'm no traitor."

"Neither is Major Denver." He flipped up his hoodie and slid out the door.

"The files." Hunter tipped his head toward the bed. "For God's sake, don't forget those files."

Sue gathered them up and shoved them into the outside pocket of her suitcase. She waited at the door with their bags, as Hunter cleared out the safe and gave the room a once-over. "If they decide to run prints on this room, they're going to ID me."

"Maybe you should stay here and wait for them. I can knock you on the head, and you can pretend you know nothing about any of this." Her voice hitched in her throat. "Drake's going to need one parent who's not in federal prison."

"Nobody's going to prison, and I'm not gonna allow you to bash me over the head." He joined her at the door and held it open. "Now let's get the hell out of Dodge."

They avoided the lobby on their way down to the car and Hunter waved off the valet to load their bags in the trunk himself.

As he pulled away from the hotel, he said, "I'm returning this car now. I don't want anything to be traced back to me, but we can't use your car, either."

"Thanks to The Falcon, we have some options. I've never had to use it before, but there's a safe house near Virginia Beach. I think we'll find everything we need there for a quick getaway."

"How far is Virginia Beach?"

"About four hours."

"We can't drive for four hours in this car. The rental car company most likely has a GPS on this vehicle, and once the CIA shows up, they'll track the car for them."

"I have a plan for that, too." She held up one of her many burner phones. "I'm going to call a friend of mine to pick us up at the airport after you leave the car there. She'll let us have her car and she can take a taxi home."

"Is this Dani from the bar?"

"Dani's on a road trip. This is another friend who owes me and I'm about to collect, big time."

While Hunter drove to the airport, keeping one eye on his rearview mirror, Sue placed a call to her friend.

Jacqueline answered after three rings, her voice sleepy and befuddled. "Hello?"

"Jacqueline, it's Sue. I need your help."

Her words worked like a slap to the face. Jacqueline's voice came back sharp and urgent. "Anything."

"Meet me at Reagan as soon as you can. I'll be at parking lot D, the main entrance. Bring your junker. I'm going to take that car and you'll take a taxi home. I'll pay you for everything—the car, the ride home, your time."

"I'll do it and you don't owe me a dime. You know that, Sue. I'm leaving now."

"And if anyone comes by later and asks you about me…"

"I never got this call."

Sue closed the phone and tossed it out the window. "Like you said—Jeffrey and his gang probably have The Falcon's phone and she may have put trackers in all my burner phones."

"What did you do for this woman that she's willing to leave her home in the middle of the night, drive to the airport and give you her car?"

Sue lifted her shoulders. "I saved her life."

She directed Hunter to the parking lot where he plucked a ticket from the machine. He parked on an upper level, and they emptied the car.

Hunter pulled a T-shirt from his bag and wiped down the inside of the car for good measure. "They don't have to know you were in this car."

Sue grabbed his wrist as he stuffed the shirt back into his suitcase. "You don't have to do this, Hunter. I can take it from here."

"I'm not leaving you to finish this on your own." He kicked the side of her suitcase. "Besides, you finally have what I came here seeking—information about Denver, and I'm not giving up on that, either."

She pressed her lips against the side of his arm. "I knew you were someone I could count on the minute I met you. I'm just sorry you couldn't count on me."

"I'm counting on you now. I'm counting on you to get us out of this mess and to that safe house."

They dragged their bags and the rest of their gear to the elevator and got off on the ground level. They stationed themselves near the parking arm, turning away each time a car rolled through.

Thirty minutes later, a small compact flashed its lights and pulled to a stop in front of them.

"That's her?" Hunter squinted into the back window.

"That's Jacqueline."

Jacqueline hopped out of the car and ran to Sue. She threw her arms around her, and Sue hugged her back with all her might.

"Thank you so much, Jacqueline."

She flicked her long fingernails in the air. "What else would I do when you call?"

"Jacqueline, this is my friend—no names, just in case."

Jacqueline extended her hand. "Bonjour, no name."

Hunter sketched a bow and kissed her long fingers, befitting the Frenchwoman. "Bonjour. What exactly did Sue do to warrant this loyalty?"

"This?" Jacqueline flicked back her dark hair. "This is nothing compared to what she did for me. She saved my life."

"Okay, I won't ask." He held up his hands. "Could you please open the trunk...if it opens?"

"The remote doesn't open it anymore, but there's always the old-fashioned way." Jacqueline shoved the key into the trunk and lifted it.

As Hunter loaded their bags, Sue took Jacqueline's hands. "Everything still okay with you?"

"Perfect." Jacqueline lifted her delicate brows. "I won't ask the same, but it looks like you have a big, strong man on your side now."

"I do. I'll call you when this is all over."

"Is it ever over for you, Sue?" Jacqueline shook her head. "You give too much."

"This time you gave to me and saved *my* life." She kissed Jacqueline's cheek. "Now call up a car so you're not waiting out here alone. We can't wait with you."

"I'll be fine. I've faced worse than a dark corner at night, and you know it."

They hugged again and Hunter waved. He got behind

the wheel of the little car that could, and Sue slipped into the passenger's seat.

Sue directed Hunter back to the highway, heading south, and they drove in silence for a few minutes before he turned to her. "Are you going to tell me how you saved her life, or is that top secret, too?"

"Jacqueline was seeing a dangerous, violent man. The more she tried to get away from him, the more ferociously he went after her, and protective orders did nothing to stop him because he had diplomatic immunity here. But I finally stopped him."

"How?"

"I knew he'd been supplying information about some of his country's dealings to sources who were then using that intel against his country to strike favorable deals." She shoved her hands beneath her thighs. "I told his country."

"What happened to him?"

"I don't know. He disappeared and Jacqueline never heard from him or saw him again."

Hunter whistled. "Do you think he was killed? Was it one of *those* countries?"

She glanced at him out of the corner of her eye. "*Any* country can be one of those kinds of countries."

"I suppose you're right. The US has had our share of spies working against us, but it looks like we're dealing with corruption at the highest levels here. I guess anything is possible." He held out his phone to her. "Are you going to put the address in my GPS or am I going to drive blindly into the night in a car that's on its last legs…wheels?"

"There is no address, or at least not that I'm aware of, but I have the directions up here." She tapped her forehead.

"Then take me home, but when we stop for gas, I'm

going to need some coffee and some food. We haven't had anything to eat since that late lunch, and we've been through an explosion and a whirlwind escape from the hotel."

"Let me know if you want me to drive." Sue curled one leg beneath her. "I hope The Falcon's files have enough to prove my innocence. Someone at the Agency *has* to know what she was doing. With all the money and support we had, she couldn't have been running a rogue operation."

"And her black ops contact at the CIA can't be our insider, or he never would've allowed her to compile the information she got."

Sue shivered. "That's a scary thought—the one person who can verify The Falcon's existence is the one working with this terrorist group."

"I have a feeling the insider is terrified of black ops groups like The Falcon's. Those groups are the very ones that could uncover a leak or a spy within."

"There's just one problem."

"What?"

"Why hasn't this person stepped forward yet?"

"The Falcon just died this afternoon. Her contact may not even know that yet." Hunter squeezed her knee. "It'll be okay, Sue. I'm not gonna let this end any other way—I've got a son to meet."

They drove through the night, stopping for gas, coffee and snacks. As they began to head east, toward the coast, Sue studied the road signs and the landmarks.

She'd never been to this safe house before, but The Falcon had drilled its location along with countless other details into Sue's head for so long, she felt as if she'd been this way before.

"Here, here, here." She hit the window with the heel of her hand. "Turn right here."

"Are you sure?" Hunter turned the wheel, anyway. "It looks dark and deserted. I hope you're not directing me right into the water."

"The isolation is the point…and the water is farther out with a few more houses scattered out there." She hunched forward in her seat, gripping the edge of the dashboard. "Turn left at the big tree. It should be a gravel road—not quite unpaved."

The little car bounced and weaved as they hit the gravel, but the headlights picked out a clapboard house ahead with a wooden porch.

"That's it. I think you can park around the back."

The car crawled around the side of the house and Hunter cut the engine. "Let's leave the stuff in the car so we can check it out first. I suppose you know where to find the key."

"Exactly." She took his cell phone because she was running out of ones of her own and she hadn't had a chance to charge the temp phone she'd picked up at the gas station. She turned on the flashlight and stepped from the car.

Several feet from the house, she spotted the rock garden and she lit up the ground below her to avoid tripping over the uneven surface. She counted three rocks from the left and crouched before it, digging her fingers in the dirt to tip it over.

Bugs scurried at the invasion while she sifted the dirt with her fingers. "Got it."

She pulled the key free from its hiding place and wiped it clean on the thigh of her jeans.

She returned to Hunter waiting by the car, his gun drawn. She pointed to the weapon dangling by his side. "Expecting company?"

"You never know."

She held up the key in the light. "I think this works on the back door, too."

Hunter dogged her steps as she walked to the back of the small house and unlocked the back door.

She pushed open the door, clenching her jaw. Something had to go right. This had to work. Creeping to the front of the house with Hunter right behind her, she held the phone in front of her. She sniffed, the musty odor making her nose twitch.

Hunter voiced her thoughts. "Hasn't been used for a while, has it?"

"Doesn't smell like it, but then I think this particular place was sitting in reserve for me and I never needed it…until now." She twisted on the switch for a lamp centered on an end table and a yellow glow illuminated the comfortable furniture.

"Looks more like my nana's place than a spy hideaway." Hunter picked up a throw pillow, punched it once and dropped it back onto the sofa.

"That's the point." Sue wandered into the kitchen and flicked on the light. "It's supposed to be stocked—with all kinds of things."

Hunter crowded into the kitchen next to her and tugged open the fridge. "Not much in here. Bottled water, which I could actually use right now."

Sue reached past him to open the cupboard door. She shuffled through some cans of food and freeze-dried pouches. "This is more like it. Stuff for the long haul. I don't know how often these safe house supplies are replenished."

Hunter leaned over her shoulder and picked up one of the packets and threw it back into the cupboard. "Ugh, looks like an MRE. I'll pass on these for the local pizza joint."

Sue returned to the living room and turned in a circle, her hand on her hip. She'd seen this room and knew just where to look.

"Do you have a knife on you?"

Hunter reached for his belt and produced a switchblade. "What do you need?"

Sue knelt in front of the fireplace and lifted the braided rug. She placed her hand on the wood slats and rocked back and forth. When she felt some give, she pounded the board with her fist. "Here. Try here."

Hunter crouched beside her and jimmied the blade of his knife between the two slats. When he got a lip on one, he pulled it up to reveal a cavity in the floor.

He scooted onto his belly and put his face to the space. "There's a canvas bag in there, along with a few spiders. We'll need a bigger space to bring it up."

Sue curled her hand around the next slat and yanked it free. They had to dislodge one more before they were able to lift the bag from the space beneath the floor.

Hunter swung it out and plopped it onto the floor.

Sue eyed it, wrinkling her nose. "Are those spiders gone?"

"Badass spy like you worried about a few spiders?"

"Yes."

Hunter kicked the bag a few times. "That should do it. Are you sure it's not booby-trapped?"

"Why would there be a booby-trapped bag in a *safe* house?"

"I have no idea how you people operate, but just in case, I'll let you open it first."

"What a man." She pinched his side.

Leaning over, she unzipped the bag and peeled back the canvas. She clicked her tongue as she ran her hands through the stacks of cash. "Nice. Having all this means never having to use your credit card."

She dug in deeper and pulled out a gun. "Untraceable I'm sure."

Hunter dived in next to her and withdrew handfuls of minicameras, GPS trackers, a small flashlight. "This is a mini stash of the same stuff she had in the storage unit."

"Minus the fire suits." Sue rubbed her arms and looked around the room. "I hope we don't need those here."

Hunter scooted back, sitting on the floor and leaning his back against the sofa. "We can stay here for a few days and catch our breath. Really look over The Falcon's files on Denver and this whole assignment and get your name cleared once and for all. Get you back to Drake where you belong."

"Which reminds me." Sue held up one finger. "I need to get that phone charged so I can call my parents tomorrow morning, just to make sure everything's okay. I suppose I'm going to have to tell my father that I'm under investigation. I'm sure the CIA investigators are going to pay them a visit."

"Maybe not. They might be afraid of tipping off your parents and having them shield you and hide you."

"Funny thing is? They probably wouldn't."

"It's late, Sue. I'm going to bring in our bags and then you're going to get some sleep."

"You, too."

"Yeah, of course."

She narrowed her eyes. "Right. You have no intention of sleeping, do you? You're going to be on guard all night long."

"I'll catch some shut-eye. Don't worry about me." He stood up and made for the back door.

Sue zipped up the bag and dragged it next to the fireplace. The day's events caught up to her and she sank onto the sofa. She didn't even blink when Hunter came through the back door, hauling their suitcases.

The sofa dipped as he sat beside her, pulling her against his chest. "Do you think the beds are made up?"

She murmured against his shirt, "I don't care at this point. I'm going to fall asleep right here."

He kissed her temple. "Stay right here."

Sue must've drifted off. It seemed like hours later when Hunter returned and took off her shoes, lifted her legs to the sofa and spread a blanket over her body.

He sat back down in the corner and shifted over so that her head nestled on his lap, as he stroked her temple.

A smile curved her lips. Whatever happened now, she could endure it as long as Hunter stayed right by her side.

Chapter Seventeen

Her lashes fluttered, and she reached for Hunter. When her hand met the sofa cushion instead of the warm flesh she'd expected, she bolted upright.

"I'm in here." Hunter waved from the kitchen across the room. "I'm making oatmeal if you're interested, but we have to skip the bananas, blueberries, almonds, brown sugar and everything else that makes it remotely tasty."

"Breakfast?" Sue rubbed her eyes, running her tongue along her teeth, which she'd been too tired to brush last night. "I didn't even realize it was morning."

"You slept soundly."

"Did you sleep at all?" She gathered her hair into a ponytail.

"A little." He held up the burner phone she'd bought yesterday. "It's fully charged, and better yet, it's not being tracked by The Falcon."

She yawned and shrugged off the blanket. "I wonder who pays the utility bills for this place to keep the gas, water and electricity running."

"Probably comes from some supersecret spy slush fund."

She joined him in the kitchen and watched him stir hot water into some instant oatmeal. "Not bad. I'll have some of this coffee first, though."

She leaned her elbows on the counter and plucked the phone from the charger. She entered her father's cell phone number, although at this point it might be worse talking to him than Linda.

"Hi, Dad."

Hunter held a finger to his lips. He didn't want her to give Dad the lowdown on her situation in case the CIA hadn't contacted them yet.

"Hi, Sue." Her father didn't even ask her about the new phone number. He knew. "Drake's just fine, although he misses his…cousins."

Sue's shoulders sagged. For a minute, she thought Drake had been missing her. "I hope you're keeping him busy. He likes blocks and he loves riding his tricycle."

"He sure is an active boy." Dad cleared his throat. "We had a surprise this morning."

"Oh?" Sue's heart picked up speed.

"A friend of yours named Dani Howard called and asked if she could stop by for a visit. Says her daughter plays with Drake there in DC?"

Sue patted her chest and sucked in a breath. "That's right. She told me she was driving down to Savannah to visit her folks and said she'd stop in to see Drake."

"Okay, just checking. She's going to call back, and I'll tell her it's fine."

"Thanks, Dad." She threw a quick glance at Hunter, pouring a cup of coffee. "Sh-should you put Drake on the line? I'll say a quick hi."

"He's outside on that trike already, Sue. Maybe later. This a new number for you?"

"For the time being. Don't program it in your phone or label it."

"I know better."

Sue's mind flashed back to her father's fake passports in The Falcon's storage unit. *I bet you do.*

"Okay, then. Just keep me posted. Everything else… all right?"

"Everything's just fine. We'll have Drake back at Amelia's just as soon as they return from the Bahamas."

"Maybe he'll be returning to me instead."

Hunter's hand pouring the condensed milk jerked and he splashed milk on the counter.

Her father paused for several seconds. "Why would you say that? Mission over? Won't there be another?"

"We'll talk about it later. Just keep my little boy safe." She ended the call and tucked the phone into her purse.

"Drake's okay?" Hunter shoved a cup of coffee at her.

"He's fine. Apparently, he's always just fine without me." She blew on the coffee before sipping it.

"You meant what you said to your father? That Drake will be going back home with you?"

"The Falcon's dead. These assignments, this lifestyle I have is too dangerous for a parent. As soon as I'm clear, I'm done."

He scooped up a spoonful of oatmeal and studied it. "I'm not arrogant enough to tell you what to do, but I think it's a good idea—if you can manage it."

"I have to get out of this mess first, or Drake will be visiting me behind bars—both of us."

After two more tastes, Hunter gave up on the lumpy oatmeal and dropped the bowl into the sink. "Who's driving down to Savannah and stopping in to see Drake?"

"My friend Dani Howard. She has a daughter around Drake's age."

"Is she the one you went out with the night you ran into Jeffrey?"

"Same. Thank God he left her alone. Jeffrey's cohort must've had orders not to hurt her."

"Does Dani know what you do for a living?" Hunter rinsed out the bowl and held out his hand for hers.

"I'm willing to give it a try." She yanked the bowl back and held it to her chest. "Dani? Yeah, she knows I'm with the Agency but not much more, of course."

"And what does she do?"

"She's a nurse." Sue wrapped her hands around her bowl and walked to her suitcase. She unzipped the outside pocket and pulled out the file folders she'd rescued from fire and mayhem.

"I think it's time for me to have a good long look at these and try to decipher The Falcon's notes. They're my only chance right now."

She brought the files to the kitchen table, and as she dropped them, the contents spilled out of one of them. She pinched a newspaper clipping between two fingers and she waved it in the air. "From a French newspaper, but it looks old. Probably nothing to do with Denver."

"You read French, don't you?"

"Oui, oui." She pulled up a chair and scooted under the table. She brought the article close to her face, translating out loud a story about a bombing in a Paris café that took the lives of four people, one a child.

When she finished reading, Sue pressed the article to her heart. "How awful. This sounds familiar."

"It's all too familiar." He leaned over her shoulder and plucked up another article. "Looks like it could be the same story."

She took it from his fingers and scanned it. "Yes, the same story, different newspaper or maybe a follow-up."

Straddling the chair next to her, Hunter asked, "Why

was she keeping this story in particular? She must've worked a lot of these types of cases."

"Maybe she has more articles on more cases, but I didn't happen to pick those up."

"But these were filed in the same cabinet as the Denver material." Hunter rubbed his chin and shuffled through the folder. He slid another article toward him with his forefinger. "This one has an accompanying picture."

He squinted at the two women and one man, grim-faced, looking away from the camera. "What's this one say, Sue?"

Her gaze flicked over the words. "They're the victims, or the victims' family members."

"Sue," Hunter bumped her shoulder with his as he ducked over the article. "Doesn't that look like a young Falcon? And I don't mean the bird."

"What? No." She smoothed her thumb across the pinched face of a woman, her sharp chin dipping to her chest. "This one?"

"Exactly." He circled her face with his fingertip. "You said The Falcon didn't have a family. How'd you know that?"

"When she was telling me how I needed to leave you and then give up Drake, she implied that this job and a family didn't mix. I just assumed she was speaking from experience."

He tapped the picture. "Maybe she *was* speaking from experience. Maybe she lost her daughter in that explosion."

"And her husband." Sue pressed a hand against her roiling belly. "The child killed in the blast had the same last name as one of the men who died."

Hunter blew out a breath that stirred the edges of the clippings. "It makes sense, doesn't it? If she lost her own family to a terrorist attack, maybe one that was directed at her and her loved ones, she'd want to warn you away from that possibility."

"I feel sick to my stomach."

"I wonder why she put this personal stuff with the Denver notes."

"Maybe it's more than personal. Do you think The Falcon has been tracking this group for—" she glanced at the date on the newspaper "—twenty years?"

Hunter pointed at the articles. "Did they ever find out who was responsible? Or more likely, did anyone take credit for the attack?"

Sue flipped through the rest of the articles. "Nidal al Hamed's group claimed responsibility. That group is the precursor to Al Tariq, but more importantly al Hamed's son broke away from Al Tariq a few years ago to form his own organization—an international organization that finds common bonds with terrorists across the globe, no matter what their agenda."

"The Falcon's entire investigation could be a personal vendetta."

"You can frame it that way, but this group has hurt more than just The Falcon's family."

"Nidal's dead, right? What's his son's name?"

Sue cranked her head to the side, her eyes as big as saucers. "Walid. Walid al Hamed."

"From the barbershop." Hunter slapped his hand on the table.

"It's not an uncommon name. Don't jump to conclusions."

"Could the leader of this new group be hiding out in plain sight in the middle of DC, mere miles from CIA headquarters?" Hunter swung his leg over the chair and paced to the window, the drapes firmly pulled across them.

"And this could be the same group Denver is tracking. The two investigations must converge somewhere in here." She fanned out the pages of the Denver folder on the table.

"You worked with The Falcon, knew her fondness for codes. Get on it, girl." Hunter strode toward his laptop on the coffee table. "I'm going to research something else that's been bugging me."

"What?"

"How long have you known Dani Howard?" Hunter sat on the sofa and flipped open his laptop.

The pen Sue had poised over a blank piece of paper fell from her fingers. "What? Why? I've known Dani for almost two years."

"Where did you meet her?"

Sue forgot about the articles and her research and turned around, fully facing Hunter. "At the pediatrician. We both had our kids in at the same time. Drake had an ear infection. Why are you asking these questions about Dani? You were probing me about her before when I got off the phone."

"I just thought it was unusual for her to take a detour from her trip to Savannah to see your parents. I mean, if you were there, I could see it."

"Sh-she just thought a familiar face from home would be nice for Drake."

"Why? He's at his grandparents', and excuse me for saying this, but isn't he more at home in South Carolina than he is here?" He held up a hand. "I don't mean to poke at you or criticize."

"Yeah, but I didn't think her offer was weird. Do you?" She scooted to the edge of her chair, her heart beating double time. "How long have you been thinking about this?"

"It niggled at me after your conversation with your father." He tapped his keyboard, and without looking up, he asked, "Whose idea was it to go out that night and who picked the bar?"

"Dani, but she was always the one issuing the invitations and she goes out more than I do, so it's only natural for her to pick the spot."

"And who noticed the two men that night?"

Sue sprang from her chair, gripping her arms, her fingers digging into her flesh. "Stop it. You're scaring me."

"Who noticed the two men, Sue?"

"Dani." She locked her knees so they'd stop wobbling. "Of course she did. That was her thing."

"Was it also her thing to leave with men when you two were out together, or was that an unusual move for her that night?"

"It was atypical, but that was a different kind of night. We were drugged. I don't think she realized what she was doing." Sue pressed a hand against her forehead. "This is crazy. She has a young daughter. I've been in her home. She has pictures of…of…"

Hunter glanced up sharply from his laptop. "Of what?"

"Of her daughter."

He hunched forward on his elbows. "And what else?"

"I don't know." She sat next to him on the sofa. "Maybe it's what she didn't have, or maybe you're just making me crazy for no reason at all."

"What didn't she have?"

"She had pictures of Fiona but nobody else—no family photos. I know she didn't get along with her mother." She flicked her finger at the computer screen. "What have you been looking up?"

"Did a general search of Dani Howard, and I didn't find much. What hospital does she work at?"

"She doesn't work at a hospital. She works for a medical group."

"Do you know the name of it? I'll look it up." He gestured to her phone on the kitchen counter. "Call it."

"It's Mercer Medical. I've picked her up there before." She jogged across the room to grab her phone.

"Out front or did you go inside?" His fingers moved quickly across his keyboard.

Sue licked her dry lips. "Outside only, but she had a lab coat on."

"You mean like the one you stole in the hospital yesterday? Call." He swung his computer around to face her. "The website doesn't list any personnel."

"I know Dani. You don't. I think you're on the wrong track here." She entered the number on the website with trembling fingers.

Hunter said, "Speaker."

She tapped the speaker button just as someone picked up the phone. "Mercer Medical, how may I direct your call?"

"I'm trying to reach a nurse there, Dani Howard."

The pause on the other end seemed to last a lifetime. "What doctor does she work for? He?"

"Dani is a she. Dr. Warner."

"She doesn't work for Dr. Warner. Is she new?"

Sue squeezed the phone in her hand. "C-could you check. Maybe it's not Dr. Warner. Could she be in another office?"

"I'll check, ma'am, but this is the only Mercer office in the DC area."

Sue heard some clicking on the other end, which sounded like pickaxes against rock. Her gaze met Hunter's, but if she expected reassurance, what she saw was grim confirmation instead.

The receptionist came back on the line. "I'm sorry, ma'am. There's no Dani Howard here. Perhaps you…"

Sue didn't hear what she should perhaps do because she ended the call and dropped to the edge of the coffee table. "Oh my God. What have I done?"

"You've done nothing." Hunter placed a steadying hand on her bouncing knee. "Call your father right now and warn him against Dani. He'll know what to do."

Sue went back to her phone and called her father for the second time that morning, this time putting the call on speaker for Hunter.

"Hello?" Leave it to Dad to know not to assume it was her calling just because it was the same number from this morning.

"Dad, it's Sue again."

"Don't worry. Drake is fine."

She flattened a hand against her fluttering belly. "I need to tell you something very important. That woman who's supposed to come by…"

"Yeah, Dani. Nice girl."

The blood in Sue's veins turned to ice. "She's there? Dad…"

"No, they're not here. Dani and her little girl Fiona took Drake to the park down the street."

Chapter Eighteen

A sharp pain pierced the back of his head, but Hunter didn't have time to succumb to it. Sue had dropped the phone and let out a wail.

Her father was shouting into the phone. "Sue? Sue? What's wrong?"

Hunter scooped up the phone. "Mr. Chandler, I'm with Sue right now. Dani Howard isn't who she says she is. When did they leave? Can you catch up to them?"

Sue's father swore. "We didn't know. How were we supposed to know? They left over thirty minutes ago."

"Did you see her car?"

"Of course I did. Who the hell are you, anyway?"

"I'm Sue's…friend. I'm trying to help her, and she needs help. The Falcon is dead and Sue's been implicated. She has no one to vouch for her and now they've taken Drake."

"The hell they have. I'll get him back. You tell my little girl. Tell her I'll get him back. I'm going out right now. Our town isn't that big. Someone must've seen them."

"While you do, stay on the phone with me and tell me everything you remember about Dani and her car."

As Mr. Chandler gave him the details of Dani's visit, Hunter squeezed Sue's shoulder. She hadn't moved since getting the news from her father, except to drop her head in her hands.

Sue's stepmother interrupted her husband.

"What are you saying, Linda? Phone number?"

"What is it, sir?"

"My wife said that snake, Dani, left her a new phone number for Sue. Said she'd lost her phone on the road and picked up a temporary one. She wanted Sue to have the number." Chandler snorted. "I'll bet she did."

"Give me the number. It's probably the contact phone for Sue's instructions."

Sue's father recited the number to him. "What do they want with Sue, anyway?"

"I think they just want Sue."

Sue moaned. "They can have me as long as they let Drake go."

Sue's father yelled into the phone. "Don't be ridiculous, Sue. Do you know what they'll do to you? Someone who betrayed them? Someone who has information about them?"

"I'd rather have them do it to me than Drake."

Hunter knelt beside her and brushed the hair from her hot face. "We'll get him back. Don't worry. Your father gave me some good information."

Mr. Chandler said, "I'm already in my car. I'm going to find her. I'll keep you posted."

Hunter ended the call and ran his hand over Sue's back. "We're going to rescue him, but we'll play along. Call Dani now. She won't be expecting you to call her for a while—not until your parents notify you that she never brought Drake home."

Sue straightened her spine and pulled back her shoulders. "Catch her off guard."

"Exactly."

Sue snatched the phone from his fingers and tapped in the number as he recited it to her from memory. He didn't have to tell her to put it on speaker.

This was his son—a son he'd never even met. He'd go to hell and back to bring him home.

"Yes?"

A woman answered the phone. There was children's laughter in the background, and Hunter ground his teeth. What kind of a mother could kidnap a child from another mother?

Sue's nostrils flared and her cheeks flushed. "Where's my son, you bitch?"

Dani drew in a sharp breath, audible over the line. "That was fast."

"You've had him for half an hour. You can't be far. My father's out looking for you."

"How did he find out?" Dani laughed. "I guess he's a better CIA operative than you are. You didn't have a clue for almost two years."

"Why would I think another *mother* would be plotting against me?"

Dani clicked her tongue. "Oh, Sue. You don't have to play the outraged mother with me. You're never with Drake anyway, but I hope you care enough to turn yourself over to us to keep him safe."

"Keep your commentary to yourself and tell me what I need to do."

"I'll call you back with instructions. I really didn't expect you to call so quickly—and make sure your parents know that if we detect any police involvement, you'll never see Drake again."

Sue covered her mouth with her hand but didn't let the fear seep into her voice. "Why did you move in on me two years ago? Did Walid al Hamed's group suspect me then?"

The silence on the other end of the line proved that they'd been right about Walid's group being behind the plot.

Dani cleared her throat and recovered. "Nobody knew for sure, but you really should've been spending all that money we'd funneled to you. Once we realized someone was checking out that barbershop, we knew we had you…and your boss, too."

"You killed her."

"We left her for dead. She must've been a tough old bird. We never imagined she'd pull herself together and go see you. And we never imagined you'd get out of that storage unit alive."

"I guess you underestimated both of us."

"Who's your sidekick? Who's helping you?"

Sue reached out and squeezed Hunter's hand. "I work alone. You should know that by now."

"It doesn't matter who he is. You'll be on your own for sure now. Any interference and Drake is gone."

"What does that mean, *gone*?" Sue's body seemed to vibrate.

"You don't want to find out. I'll be in touch."

Dani cut off the call, and Sue's shoulders rounded. "They're going to interrogate me—torture me to find out what I know about the organization, and then they're going to kill me."

Hunter laced his fingers with hers. "Do you think I'm going to allow that to happen? We'll find a way to get Drake back and keep you safe."

"We have to be able to use The Falcon's files to lure them into a change of plans. They don't know what we have, if anything, from that storage unit."

He pushed off the sofa and pulled her along with him. "Then let's get back to those files and see if we can trade anything for Drake."

Sue shuffled the papers from The Falcon's personal folder and closed it, setting it aside. "That's The Falcon's motivation for bringing down this group and now I have my own personal reasons."

"Then let's do it." He slid her notebook and pen in front of him. "What do those notes say about the group Denver is investigating?"

"Looks like The Falcon picked up on Denver's activities a while ago. There was a bombing at a Syrian refugee camp designed to derail the negotiations between the Syrian government and the rebels—it worked. So, Walid's group is all about fomenting dissent in the Middle East...and Africa." She tapped the paper with her finger. "Denver discovered a cache of weapons at an embassy outpost in Nigeria. He's putting these events together like nobody else is and The Falcon is paying attention."

"Someone else was paying attention, too, and that's why he was set up. There has to be someone on the inside."

"At what level?" She skimmed her fingertip down a list of agencies and names. "The Falcon was on that track, also."

"Walid's group, which doesn't even have a name, is dependent on this insider and they're desperate to keep him a secret."

"Then we need to pretend we know who this insider is and that we have the proof to bring him down—and we'll do it unless we get Drake back."

"That won't work, Sue. We can't offer the people who took Drake any insurance that we didn't pass along this info to someone before we collect Drake, or any assurance that we didn't take pictures of the proof with our phones." He rubbed a circle on her back. "The only thing we have as a bargaining chip—is you."

Sue folded her arms and buried her face in the crook of her elbow. "Then it has to be done. My life for Drake's. It's a no-brainer."

"It's a no-brainer that you're going to show up, but I'll figure out a way to get you both out alive." He put his head close to hers and his warm breath stirred her hair. "I found you again and discovered we have a son together. Do you seriously think I'm going to let anything come between me and everything I ever wanted?"

She raised her head and kissed his chin. "How did I ever let myself get talked into leaving you and keeping Drake from you?"

Tapping the notebook with his knuckle, he said, "This is how. The work. Your work."

"And where has that work gotten me? Estranged from you, Drake kidnapped, my career and my very life in jeopardy."

"Make it worthwhile."

"You mean instead of wallowing in self-pity?" She picked up the pen and resumed her examination of The Falcon's notes.

"I know what your problem is, and it's not self-pity." He stood up and made a move toward the kitchen. "You need to eat something. You never finished that awful oatmeal. I'll make us something else awful."

While Hunter banged around in the kitchen, Sue put together a time line of all the events that linked Major Denver with their undercover work with Walid. "It's here. This is it, Hunter. Walid's group is the same one Denver has been tracking and the same one The Falcon had me infiltrate. But for what purpose?"

"What purpose?" He walked toward her carrying two bowls of something steaming.

She sniffed the air. "Chicken noodle soup? Drake loves noodles."

"Must be genetic. This stuff is homemade, straight from the can." He set the soup at her elbow, a spoon already poking up from the bowl. "What purpose are you talking about?"

"The connection between Denver's investigation and the one I was doing with The Falcon is evident, but I don't know why either investigation is so important. This group—" she thumbed through the pages "—really hasn't been up to much of anything. Outside of the Syrian bombing and another in Paris, the group has been operating under the radar."

"Denver seems to think they're plotting something big, and obviously The Falcon thought so, too."

"In the US." Hunter blew on his soup before sucking a noodle into his mouth. "Yeah, I know that."

She shifted her gaze from Hunter's lips and glanced down at the page in front of her. "The Falcon does have *GB* several times on the page. Could there be an impending attack in Great Britain, also? It just doesn't make sense in the context of her notes, which really couldn't be more confusing if she tried."

"GB?" Hunter dropped his spoon and snatched the notes from her hand. "That's what the military calls sarin gas."

Sue choked. "My God, Hunter. That's it. A weapon in the context of these notes makes so much more sense than a place. They're planning a sarin attack. But where?"

She scrambled through The Falcon's notes again, drawing a blank. Slumping in her chair, she dropped the notes onto the table. "Do you think these are enough to clear me with the CIA? There are references to the people I met and why. The Agency can't accuse me of collaborating with the enemy once they see The Falcon's notes. Someone has to come forward at some point to claim The Falcon. She didn't work in a vacuum."

"They'll go a long way toward proving your innocence."

"Then maybe I should turn myself in now. Maybe they can help us get Drake back."

"That would be the worst thing we could do for Drake right now. If there's an insider, and these notes—" he smashed his fist against the papers "—indicate there is, how long do you think it's gonna take him, or her, to report back that the Agency is aware of the kidnapping?"

"Not long at all." She plowed her fingers through her hair and dug her nails into her scalp.

Her cell phone rang and she froze.

Hunter picked up the phone and checked the display. "It's your father."

Sue lunged for the phone. "Dad?"

"I couldn't find her, Sue. I don't know where she took him, but he's gone."

"We'll handle it, Dad. I'll get Drake back."

"At what cost?"

"Whatever it takes."

When her conversation with her father ended, Sue finally picked up her spoon and took a few sips of soup. She'd hoped that The Falcon's notes would contain a blueprint to clear her, clear Denver, give her something to use to bargain with Drake's kidnappers, ID the mole and map out the plan for Walid's attack. It only hinted at some of those things, leaving the rest just out of her grasp.

She cared only about Drake now. His safety was more

important than all the rest. It always was and she hadn't been able to see that until now.

Her phone rang again, and when she looked at the calling number, she inhaled her soup so fast it went up her nose. "It must be Dani."

She put it on speaker and answered. "Yes?"

Dani answered, a slight accent creeping into her voice that Sue had never noticed before. "Are you ready?"

"I'm ready for anything."

"You'd better be." Dani spoke away from the phone in a muffled voice and then continued. "We're going to pick you up on a street corner in DC at midnight tonight. If anyone follows us or we see any police presence, helicopters, drones or any other suspicious activity, your son will disappear."

"Are you bringing him with you when you pick me up? How will I know he's safe?"

"We'll let you video chat with him on the phone before we pick you up. We'll even let you see him before... before we take you away for interrogation."

Hunter jumped up from the table, his hands clenched into fists.

Sue met his gaze. "How do I know you'll let him go once you have me?"

"You'll just have to trust us. We're working out a plan for your father to pick the boy up."

"I need more than that." Hot anger thumped through her veins and she pressed two fingers against her throbbing temple.

"What choice do you have, Sue? Are you going to be at the meeting place tonight or not?"

Hunter came up behind her and stroked the side of her neck.

Sue took a deep breath and swallowed. "Of course I'll be there. Give me the instructions."

As Dani reeled off the steps, Sue wrote them down on a piece of paper. When the call ended, she dropped her head to that paper and banged her head on the table. "What are we going to do? There's no way to find out where they're going to take me. You can't follow us. She already said they're going to divest me of any cell phones, purses, bags, and they're even leaving clothes for me to change into so I can't sew anything into my clothing. And I don't even know if Drake will be safe at the end of this. They might kill us both."

Hunter braced his hands on the table, his head drooping between his arms. "That's not going to…"

His head jerked up. "Where's the bag from the floor with all the cash?"

"By the fireplace." She jerked her thumb over her shoulder. "Why?"

Crossing to the fireplace in three long strides, he said over his shoulder, "The Falcon had every conceivable spy tool in that storage unit. She also had some in that bag."

"GPS tracker? They'll find it, Hunter."

He knelt before the bag and dived into it, dragging out stacks of money and throwing them over his shoulder. His hands scrabbled through the items in the bottom of the bag, and then he sat back on his heels, with a smile that showed all his white teeth.

"Got it. God bless The Falcon."

"What do you have?" Sue sprang up from her chair like a jack-in-the-box and launched herself at him.

He waved the package in front of her nose. "You're going to swallow the GPS."

Chapter Nineteen

Hunter tugged his hat lower on his forehead as he watched Sue across the street in her ill-fitting jeans and baggy T-shirt. She still looked incredible, regal even, as she awaited her fate—and Drake's.

They'd made the four-hour drive back to DC that afternoon and had lain low in a chain hotel outside the capital until it was time to leave. They'd come separately, he in a disguise, so nobody would make the link between him and Sue.

She'd followed their instructions to the T, picking up a bag at the front desk of the specified hotel, changing into the clothing in the bag, stashing her own clothes, along with any personal items, in the bag and checking it back in with the bellhop.

Now she waited on that corner with no guarantee that her sacrifice would spare Drake. *He* was her guarantee. He finally had the family he'd dreamed of having and he wasn't going to let it—or them—slip out of his grasp so easily.

He brought up the GPS app on his phone and entered the code for the tracker in Sue's belly. She appeared as a stationary green dot.

Sensing movement, Hunter shifted his gaze from his phone to the street. A blue van pulled up alongside Sue and she hopped in. Just like that, she disappeared from his sight, and a wave of panic clutched at his innards for a few seconds until he got his bearings.

They could search her all they wanted; they'd never find the tracker. But he—and they—had to act quickly. It was good for only a few hours, and he couldn't be seen following the van.

He swallowed the fear bubbling up from his gut and paid for his coffee and apple pie. He hobbled out of the twenty-four-hour café and made a sharp turn toward the parking garage where he'd left the car borrowed from Sue's friend.

Nobody knew that car. Nobody knew the bearded man in the Nationals cap with the slight paunch and the stiff leg. He limped toward the elevator, passing a few tourists out on the town, maybe going to their nighttime monuments tour.

When he got behind the wheel of the car, he checked his phone again. Sue and the van were headed out of the city, south toward Virginia.

He followed their path. At this rate, he'd be pulling in to the destination ten minutes after they did. If her captors acted quickly and whisked her or Drake away as soon as they got there, he didn't stand a chance. They didn't even know if Drake would be waiting at the location. He might be somewhere else completely.

He pounded his hands against the steering wheel. He couldn't let himself think that way. He had to be Delta Force right now. He had to remove the personal feelings from this mission and focus on the objective. Rescue the targets and kill the enemy, if necessary.

With his phone propped up on the dashboard, he followed the green bull's-eye. Forty-five minutes passed before the van made a move off the highway. Hunter checked the map and saw farmland. A rural area would expose him, but it would expose them, too.

And he had all the gear he needed to conduct a raid—Delta Force–style.

When the target stopped moving, Hunter caught his breath. He was eight minutes out. As he continued to drive, he pulled up another map on his phone and switched to a street-view image. The location of the green dot matched up to what looked like a barn of some sort.

His mind clicked into action. A barn—high ceilings, wooden structure, possible fire hazard, maybe a hayloft, horse stalls. Places for concealment.

He parked his car a half mile out, hiding it behind a clump of bushes. He secured his backpack, the weight of his equipment solid on his shoulders. He stumbled onto a dirt access road—no trees or cover-up to the structure, but high grass, high enough to conceal a man in a crouching position.

He waded into the grass, hunching forward, his pack bouncing on his back. The vegetation whispered beneath his feet, and he could imagine it said "Sue, Sue" with every step closer to the barn.

Just as he was close enough to emerge from the grass and hit the ground in an army crawl for the ages, Hunter almost plowed into a man standing on the edge of the grass.

Hunter fell to the side just as the guard cocked his head. Hunter circled around to the side, grateful for the wind that kicked up and fluffed the grass, making it sigh.

The man on duty didn't know which way to look, and when he cranked his head in the other direction, away from him, Hunter made his move.

He came from the side, hacked his hand across the

man's windpipe to silence any cries, shoved his gun beneath his left rib cage and pulled the trigger.

The silencer made a whooshing sound and the man collapsed to the ground, his blood already soaking the dirt. "That's for Major Denver, you bastard."

Hunter searched him for a walkie or cell phone and found the latter. Hopefully, Hunter would be in that building before anyone decided to check with the guard on watch.

Stashing the dead guard's weapon in his backpack, Hunter dropped to the ground and crawled toward the barn. He paused next to the van and hitched up to his knees.

He pressed his ear against the side of the van, which rumbled with the sound of a radio. Damn—someone waited inside. He'd never make it to the barn without being seen.

He scanned the ground and scraped his fingers through the dirt to collect some pebbles. He tossed these up in the air and they showered down on the top of the van. Then he scrambled beneath the van and held his breath.

The driver's door opened and one booted foot landed in the dirt. Another followed, and the driver emerged from the van, facing it, probably trying to see the roof.

As the man's boot heels eased up off the ground, Hunter rolled out from beneath the van and bashed the guard in the kneecaps.

The man gave a strangled cry and swung his weapon down to point it at his surprise attacker. The same look of shock was stamped on his face when Hunter shot him. "That's for Sue, you bastard."

His path now cleared to the barn, Hunter returned to the ground and snaked his way to the building. When he heard the high, clear tones of a child's voice, his heart lurched.

He was here. His son was here.

The barn's windows were too high to see into and he couldn't charge through that swinging front door without knowing the situation inside first. He crawled around to the side of the building and swung his pack from his shoulder.

He rummaged through the contents, feeling each item with his fingers, identifying each gadget from memory. When his fingertip traced around a small, round object encased in plastic packaging, he withdrew it from the backpack.

This little device could be his eyes inside the barn, give him some situational awareness. He slit the package open with his knife and programmed the spy cam into his phone. He rose, creeping up the side of the barn, and swung his arm at the window above him a few times to judge the distance.

As long as this didn't land on someone's head, he should be able to slip it inside without anyone knowing they were being watched.

Saying a silent prayer, he tossed the minicam through the window and into the barn. He held still for several seconds, his muscles taut. No screams, shots or people came from the barn, so he turned to his phone and brought up the app.

The camera had landed almost against the wall, but it gave him a clear view of a small area encircled by farm equipment—and made his heart ache.

Sue sat on the floor with Drake, his dark head against her shoulder. Were they allowing her to say goodbye to her son before they tortured and killed her? Would they do the same to Drake?

A cold dread seeped into his veins as he thought about all the ways they could use Drake to get Sue to talk. But he was here now—watching everything they did.

Sue and Drake sat on the farthest side away from the door. A woman, he assumed Dani, and a man, who looked like Jeffrey, stood close to the door. They both had weapons, but they hung loosely in their hands. They figured their trusty guards would warn them of any trouble.

Hunter eyed the van with the dead man next to it, just feet from the front door. The construction of the barn wasn't very solid, and a heavy vehicle wouldn't have too much trouble crashing through that door.

Would Dani and Jeffrey react to the van's engine starting? Why wouldn't the guard start the van if he were cold and wanted the heat on? Would Sue realize what it meant? She had to know he had successfully tracked her and was planning her rescue.

Hunter shook his head and squeezed his eyes closed. Too much second-guessing. Too much indecision. Act. Move. Now.

He pushed away from the side of the barn and crawled toward the van. He stepped over the dead guy and settled behind the wheel, leaving the driver's door open. The keys in the ignition jiggled as his knee hit them.

He held his phone in front of him and propped it on top of the steering wheel. Dani and Jeffrey had their heads together, their guns at their sides. Sue had Drake in her lap. Good. Keep him safe.

He'd do the rest.

Without another thought clouding his brain or instinct, Hunter dropped the phone and replaced it with his weapon. In one movement, he cranked on the engine and stomped on the accelerator.

The van roared to life and barreled toward the barn

door. As it crashed through and splintered the wood, he got a glimpse of Dani's face, eyes and mouth wide open. Jeffrey had rolled up onto the hood.

Hunter didn't relent, as he kept his foot firmly on the gas pedal. He heard a scream. A thud. A crunch.

He didn't hear any gunshots.

When the van reached the other side of the barn, Hunter bolted from the driver's seat. A twinge of fear brushed across the back of his neck when he didn't see Sue or Drake across the room where they'd been when he started his assault, but he had to neutralize the enemy first.

He kicked aside the debris and wreckage in the barn and stumbled upon Jeffrey, his crumpled body thrown up against some heavy machinery, his head at an odd angle. Hunter felt for a pulse—there was none.

As he turned from Jeffrey's dead body, he almost tripped over Dani's legs protruding from beneath the van's wheels. He crouched down, his gaze meeting her lifeless eyes, still wide-open. He growled, "And that's for my son."

"Hunter? Is it safe?"

Sue's voice calling out to him sent a rush of warm relief through his body, and for the first time that night, his rigid muscles lost a little of their tension.

He lurched to his feet and spotted her across the room, standing on a tractor, Drake clutched to her chest.

"It's safe. They're both dead."

They started toward each other at the same time, and for the first time, Hunter wrapped his arms around his son, safe in his mother's arms.

Epilogue

Ned dangled Sue's badge in front of her. "You're not out of the woods yet, Sue. Hunter took out several of Walid's cell here in DC, but we don't know how many are left and if they're going to be out for revenge."

As Sue hung her badge around her neck, she glanced at Hunter. "And we still don't know who the mole is—but we can all agree there is one."

Ned ran his finger along the seam of his lips. "The intel stays in this room…and with The Falcon's replacement."

"Who is?"

Hunter touched her hand. "I guess you'll never find out. You're off undercover duty."

"Your choice, right, Sue?" Ned raised his brows at her.

"Absolutely. I have a son to raise. Even my father's good with that."

"We've got plenty of analysis duty for you right here at home, but we're extending your leave for a little bit longer." He held up his hands. "For safety reasons only."

"That's fine. I need a break, and I know exactly where I'm going to take it."

Hunter extended his hand to Ned. "Thanks for guiding Sue through the process of coming out from under her undercover assignment."

"Once we got The Falcon's notes, it was easy." Ned crossed his arms. "Do you think you can get Major Denver to come in now?"

"I doubt it. He wants assurances before he surrenders, and the army is not ready to offer him those assurances yet."

"The Falcon made it clear that Denver's investigation was dovetailing with hers."

"Until the mole can be ID'd, I think Denver will remain in hiding."

Sue hitched her bag over her shoulder. "We'd better get going. Our son is with Peter right now and probably has him climbing the walls."

Sue and Hunter collected their son from her coworker and exited the building, with Drake cuddled into Hunter's arms. After Hunter had saved them from the scary barn with the scary people, Drake had been clinging to his father as if he'd known him all his life.

They drove back to her place and Sue hesitated on the threshold. Her space, her life had been violated and the terrorists she'd been tracking for over three years were still out there...and Hunter had another deployment around the corner.

Hunter returned from his brief survey of her condo and nodded. "All clear."

Sue put Drake down and tousled his hair. "I think we should order pizza—one cheese and one with everything on it."

"Sounds good to me." Hunter patted his stomach.

Drake scampered to the packed suitcases in the corner of the room and tackled one. "Mama going?"

Sue's eyes stung and she sniffled through her smile. "You're coming with me this time, cupcake. I already told your aunt and cousins, and maybe they can visit us. We're going to Hunter's home in Colorado. He even has horses."

Drake skipped to Hunter and threw himself at his legs. "Horses."

Hunter scooped him up in his arms and flew him around the room a few times before settling on the sofa with him in his lap. Hunter touched his nose to Drake's. "You'd like a daddy, wouldn't you, Drake?"

Drake nodded and grabbed the buttons on Hunter's shirt. "Daddy."

Sue put a hand over her heart. It was as if he already knew.

"Well, I am your daddy. Is that okay? You can call me Daddy instead of Hunter. All right?"

Drake snuggled farther into Hunter's arms, burrowing against his chest. Still hanging on to the shirt button, he said, "Daddy."

"I guess that's settled." Hunter rested his chin on top of Drake's dark hair, a look of serene satisfaction softening the hard line of his jaw.

"And after Colorado? After your deployment?"

"I'm still gonna be Drake's dad…and your man, if you'll have me."

Sue meandered to the sofa where her two guys, her two heartbeats, cuddled together. She sank down next to Hunter and rested her head on his shoulder.

"If *I'll* have *you*? My concern is the other way around. I abandoned you. Lied to you. Kept your son from you and lied again."

"And I still love you. What does that say about me?" He pressed his lips against Drake's temple.

"That you're loyal and forgiving and a little bit crazy." She rubbed her knuckles against his chin. "You *did* crash headlong into a barn."

Dragging his fingers through her hair, he said, "My life was in that barn. My family. And I'm not gonna give up on my family—not now, not ever."

And just like that, Sue had her job, her man and her son back in her life.

* * * * *

COMING SOON!

We really hope you enjoyed reading this book. If you're looking for more romance, be sure to head to the shops when new books are available on

Thursday 12th December

To see which titles are coming soon, please visit

millsandboon.co.uk/nextmonth

MILLS & BOON
MEDICAL
Pulse-Racing Passion

Set your pulse racing with dedicated, delectable doctors in the high-pressure world of medicine, where emotions run high and passion, comfort and love are the best medicine.

MILLS & BOON

THE HEART OF ROMANCE

A ROMANCE FOR EVERY KIND OF READER

MODERN

Prepare to be swept off your feet by sophisticated, sexy and seductive heroes, in some of the world's most glamourous and romantic locations, where power and passion collide.
8 stories per month.

HISTORICAL

Escape with historical heroes from time gone by. Whether your passion is for wicked Regency Rakes, muscled Vikings or rugged Highlanders, awaken the romance of the past.
6 stories per month.

MEDICAL

Set your pulse racing with dedicated, delectable doctors in the high-pressure world of medicine, where emotions run high and passion, comfort and love are the best medicine.
6 stories per month.

True Love

Celebrate true love with tender stories of heartfelt romance, from the rush of falling in love to the joy a new baby can bring, and focus on the emotional heart of a relationship.
8 stories per month.

Desire

Indulge in secrets and scandal, intense drama and plenty of sizzling hot action with powerful and passionate heroes who have it all: wealth, status, good looks…everything but the right woman.
6 stories per month.

HEROES

Experience all the excitement of a gripping thriller, with an intense romance at its heart. Resourceful, true-to-life women and strong, fearless men face danger and desire - a killer combination!
8 stories per month.

DARE

Sensual love stories featuring smart, sassy heroines you'd want as a best friend, and compelling intense heroes who are worthy of them.
4 stories per month.

To see which titles are coming soon, please visit

millsandboon.co.uk/nextmonth

JOIN US ON SOCIAL MEDIA!

Stay up to date with our latest releases, author
news and gossip, special offers and discounts, and
all the behind-the-scenes action
from Mills & Boon...

 millsandboon

 millsandboonuk

 millsandboon

It might just be true love...

MILLS & BOON
MODERN
Power and Passion

Prepare to be swept off your feet by sophisticated, sexy and seductive heroes, in some of the world's most glamourous and romantic locations, where power and passion collide.